Marching with Caesar
Catualda the Usurper

by
R.W. Peake

Also by R.W Peake

Marching With Caesar® – Birth of the 10th
Marching With Caesar – Conquest of Gaul
Marching With Caesar – Civil War
Marching With Caesar – Antony and Cleopatra, Parts I & II
Marching With Caesar – Rise of Augustus
Marching With Caesar – Last Campaign
Marching With Caesar – Rebellion
Marching With Caesar – A New Era
Marching With Caesar – Pax Romana
Marching With Caesar – Fraternitas
Marching With Caesar – Vengeance
Marching With Caesar – Rise of Germanicus
Marching With Caesar – Revolt of the Legions
Marching With Caesar – Avenging Varus, Part I
Marching With Caesar – Avenging Varus Part II
Marching With Caesar – Hostage to Fortuna
Marching With Caesar – Praetorian
Marching With Caesar – Usurper

Caesar Triumphant Parts One and Two
Caesar Ascending – Invasion of Parthia
Caesar Ascending – Conquest of Parthia
Caesar Ascending – Pandya
Caesar Ascending – The Ganges
Caesar Ascending – The Han

With L.R. Kelly
The Tenth

Critical praise for the Marching with Caesar series:

Marching With Caesar-Antony and Cleopatra: Part I-Antony

"Peake has become a master of depicting Roman military life and action, and in this latest novel he proves adept at evoking the subtleties of his characters, often with an understated humour and surprising pathos. Very highly recommended."

Marching With Caesar-Civil War

"Fans of the author will be delighted that Peake's writing has gone from strength to strength in this, the second volume...Peake manages to portray Pullus and all his fellow soldiers with a marvelous feeling of reality quite apart from the star historical name... There's history here, and character, and action enough for three novels, and all of it can be enjoyed even if readers haven't seen the first volume yet. Very highly recommended."
~The Historical Novel Society

"The hinge of history pivoted on the career of Julius Caesar, as Rome's Republic became an Empire, but the muscle to swing that gateway came from soldiers like Titus Pullus. What an amazing story from a student now become the master of historical fiction at its best."
~Professor Frank Holt, University of Houston

Foreword

"While Germanicus was spending the summer in visits to several provinces, Drusus gained no little glory by sowing discord among the Germans and urging them to complete the destruction of the now broken power of Maroboduus. Among the Gotones was a youth of noble birth, Catualda by name, who had formerly been driven into exile by the might of Maroboduus, and who now, when the king's fortunes were declining, ventured on revenge. He entered the territory of the Marcomanni with a strong force, and, having corruptly won over the nobles to join him, burst into the palace and into an adjacent fortress." -Tacitus *Annals* Book 2.62

I suppose it's not particularly smart for an author to admit that he dreaded writing his latest book, but that's the truth; I've been worried about Volume XIX (although I didn't know it would be XIX) for the last two-plus years. The short explanation is that there just wasn't much going on in the Roman world that would require Gnaeus' involvement, and as readers learned in Volume XVIII, *Praetorian*, I wasn't willing to keep Gnaeus in Rome as a Praetorian, if only because other authors have taken that route with their characters, and have done a better job of it than I would have, if only because I never forget that, in its essence, the *Marching With Caesar* series is a "grunt's-eye view" of their world. And, as I learned during my own time in the Marines, special duties are a requirement for anyone making the military a career, but those special duties are temporary, or at least, they're supposed to be.

So, here I am, with Gnaeus returning to the Legion where he belongs, but with nothing for him to do, and while I don't keep track of such things, I guess that I spent at least a month just poring over the various histories, looking for *something* compelling, and the passage above is what I found, although to be fair, it wasn't just Tacitus who steered me in this direction; Dio mentions Roman connivance in the plot to depose Maroboduus. From this, Volume XIX was born, a story in which I fully employ the other side of the double-edged blade that every author of historical fiction wields, where what *isn't* said is as important as what is. Since neither contemporary author is specific about what form Roman aid took, I made it a Roman Legion, along with a Centurion who's being extorted into helping in Gnaeus, and of course, where Gnaeus goes, Alex will follow. Hopefully, y'all, my faithful readers, will enjoy the story.

Meanwhile, the outside world seems intent on intruding, and while I try to avoid commenting on such things, I think we can agree that it's impossible in certain cases. Specifically, I'm referring to the war in Ukraine and the horrors being perpetrated on innocents, and on a level that Europe hasn't seen since World War II. Let me be clear on one thing; I'm a Cold Warrior, in every sense of the word. I grew up in the era of duck and cover drills, black and yellow fallout shelter signs and the air raid siren on top of City Hall in my hometown of Houston being tested every Friday at noon. All of my training in the Marine Corps was focused on the Soviet Union as our most likely enemy. (Ironically, when the invasion started, I dug up all of my material on what was termed "The Soviet Threat," and I learned that, despite it being more than 30 years old, in terms of the weaponry and tactics, they're pretty much up to date. The same T-72s and T-80s, the same BTRs, and the same BMPs are currently smoking hulks littering the roadways of Ukraine...and that makes me very happy.)

What this all means is that Russia's government has always been, and I suspect always will be my enemy. In turn, that means that I am and always will be Team Ukraine, and I'm in awe of their courage, resilience, and ability to show the world what a paper tiger (or bear) the Russian military is. If that offends any of my readers, I make no apologies, but I suspect that it won't.

Thanks to Beth Lynne, not only for what she always does, but for remembering my characters and their respective fates better than I do. She's kept me from either killing a character a second time, or resurrecting them from the dead several times now, and just for that alone, I owe her. Also, thanks to Laura Prevost for the cover; while, as of my writing this I haven't seen it, she always does a fabulous job of translating what's in my head into a great cover.

Finally, for those of y'all who interact with me on the Marching With Caesar Facebook page, I can't thank any of you enough for your wishes and support of Optio Sadie as she spends her last days on this side of the river with us. Considering that, in November, we were told that if she survived through Christmas it would be a miracle, every day since then has been a gift. She is declining, but it's been much slower than anticipated, and thanks to the Prednisone, she's living her best life thanks to the combination of her voracious appetite and my mom (whose dog Sadie has more fully become when Ducanus Titus arrived) indulging it by showering her with treats. She's had more steak in the last three months than she's had in her previous decade of life. I don't know how much longer she'll be with us, but she'll always be Crazy Sadie, with boundless energy, a nose that means you can't hide anything from her, and who could care less whether I sell one single book...a long as it doesn't impact her supply of treats.

Semper Fidelis
R.W. Peake
April 26, 2022

Historical Notes

As I mentioned in the Foreword, this story is based on just a couple of sentences in Tacitus' *Annals*, but while *Catualda the Usurper* is grounded in the record, there is one thing I want to get out of the way, and that is my decision to skip a year. The events described in Volume XIX, of Catualda deposing Maroboduus, with the aid of Rome, actually occurred in 18 CE, and not a few months after the triumph of Germanicus, which occurred in May of 17 CE. I offer my apologies to the readers for my arbitrary choice of moving that up a year, and I hope it doesn't detract from the story.

Otherwise, as always, I try to rely on primary source material, such as it is. Catualda is a real person, as is the Marcomanni king, but there are several spellings of his name, of which I chose Maroboduus. Gaius Silius has made several appearances, going back to *Marching With Caesar-Revolt of the Legions*, but the *Quaestor* Gaius Visellius Varro makes his first appearance. There is no record that he served as *Quaestor* in Germania...but there's no record that he *didn't*, which suits a certain author of historical fiction. And, given that in the year 21 CE, which is when *Marching With Caesar-Catualda The Usurper* ends he's the *Praetor* of Germania Inferior, while Gaius Silius is still the *Praetor* of Germania Superior, I don't think it's much of a stretch that he had served in Germania prior to his appointment. However, it wasn't until 85 CE that Germania Inferior and Superior became a separate province; before that, Germania was part of Gaul, and I was unable to find exactly when the two halves were deemed important enough to have a *Praetor* for each half.

There are several locations mentioned that are at the very eastern edge of Roman influence, specifically in the lands of the Gotones tribe. I mention a place called Wawelska, but while the name is my invention, it is based on Wawel Hill, which is the first known name of Krakow, Poland. According to the maps and source material I could find, Krakow was at the western edge of the land belonging to the Gotones, and Krakow has a history extending back to the Iron Age; hence, Wawelska.

The location of the Marcomanni capital is a bit less arbitrary. Just outside and south of Prague, in the suburb of Závist, there is an Iron Age hillfort called the Závist Oppidum that is attributed as Casurgis. My description of the terrain is accurate; the hillfort is on the left hill of a pair, with a deep defile separating the two, while the Vltava runs on a north/south axis on the western side of the hillfort hill. It's probably not surprising then why I chose that hillfort to be the site of the citadel; the size of Casurgis, and its occupying of the eastern hill and the flat area in between them, is my own invention. Also, there are accounts, one of them being in Tacitus' *Germania* of a deep natural cavern, upon which the palace of Maroboduus sat, making it a natural repository for the wealth the Marcomanni had accrued from their raids on surrounding tribes, particularly the Suebi. While Tacitus has Marobduus fleeing across the Danube, because my story has a Roman Legion involved, he accompanies them back to Mogontiacum, but ultimately, he ends up in Ravenna.

As is my practice, my description of the terrain over which Gnaeus and the Alaudae must traverse is as accurate as Google Earth can make it, although I also used a series of online topographical maps to get a better idea of what the ground would look like as the army approached Casurgis from the west, and by doing so, it was easy to see why the Marcomanni felt protected from that direction. The Sudeten Mountains curve down from the north, while the line of lower hills that swing up from the south leaves only a relatively flat and narrow passage through the modern town of Cheb. When Gnaeus accompanies Catualda to the village of "Nehurgo", this is also an invented name, but is based on the town of Nehvizdy, Czech Republic, while the village of Nim is Nymburk.

The aqueduct that Gnaeus and the 1st and 20th worked on existed; it is referred to as the Vorgebrige Aqueduct, which as Gnaeus notes, originated in some hills about sixteen miles west of Ubiorum, and it was the predecessor to the more famous Eifel Aqueduct that was constructed in 80 CE.

Finally, I purposely condensed the aftermath of the death of Germanicus, mainly because it's going to be a recurring theme in Gnaeus' story. I've made no secret that I believe Germanicus is, next to the "what if" that created the *Caesar Ascending* series that readers either love or hate, the most intriguing "what if" in Roman history. Given what follows his death; Tiberius' spiraling descent into disconnection and depravity, only to have Germanicus' son turn out to be crazier than a shithouse rat, I believe that someone like Gnaeus who is witnessing events in real time would be haunted by that question.

Table of Contents

Chapter 1

It did not take long for me to realize how valuable it was marching back to Ubiorum from Rome for my first month as the Primus Hastatus Prior, because it gave me a chance to assess the men, as well as my new Optio Quintus Bibaculus, although to be fair, he was not new to his post; I was new to mine. Melander, the chief clerk of the Legion, had been unsparing in his assessment of the Fifth of the First, although he had allowed that while the morale of the Fifth Century was the lowest in the First Cohort, there might have been worse Centuries in the Legion. By the end of my first week, I went to Melander to flatly inform him that he had been too kind in his assessment; the Fifth of the First was definitely the worst in the Legion when it came to morale. I do not want to cast aspersions on my predecessor; while there are certainly men in the First Cohorts of Legions across the Empire who were only there because of patronage, that was something that had not yet occurred to the 1st Legion, thanks mainly to the efforts of Tiberius Sacrovir, our Primus Pilus.

No, by all accounts, Varo had been a good Centurion, but then just before we left Ubiorum the last year of our four-year campaign against Arminius, his wife had died of a fever. While he had been withdrawn, which was understandable, according to Bibaculus, the *Signifer* Tiberius Lentulus, and the *Tesserarius* Numerius Vinicius, he had performed his duties the same as he always had, which is always a little different from one Centurion to the next. No, what had done Varo in was his son's disappearance, in an incident eerily similar to mine that left me more than once thinking about Fortuna and how she chose which of us mortals to reward with her caress, or spurn as she had Varo's son. Like me, Varo had been on one of the ships scattered because of the vicious storms that buffeted those Legions like the 1st, who had been assigned to return to their camp by sea after our defeat of Arminius, as incomplete as it may have been. Unlike me, he and all of the men with him on his ship had vanished, never to be seen again, whereas I, and the men of the First and Second Centuries of the Fourth who had been with me, had returned. That I had also returned with Bronwen, who we learned very quickly during our march back to Ubiorum, had been transformed from the daughter of a prosperous merchant in Prausetaugas into a princess of the Parisii by the men who had been with me, a belief that was supported by her looks and the manner in which she carried herself, was just another example of the gods' favor that has left me with more sleepless watches than I care to admit. In Varo's case, the twin losses proved to be too much, and it was on the march to Rome that it became clear to the Primus Pilus that Hastatus Prior Varo had ceased to be effective, preferring the company of Bacchus to his duty. Sacrovir was well within his rights, both by regulation and custom, to have broken Varo back down to the ranks, and while they were not on campaign, the fact that they were on a march to Rome meant that the Primus Pilus could have had him flogged, and only a few eyebrows would be raised. In fact, I was a bit surprised to learn that not only had Sacrovir not punished Varo in any way, he had given Varo his retirement warrant to take back to Ubiorum so that he could go through the process of leaving the standard and returning to life as a civilian.

It had also thrust Bibaculus into a position, that as I determined within my first week in command, for which he was completely unprepared. I do not say this to cast aspersions on him; indeed, he is still an Optio even now three years later, but not only was he still relatively green at the time, having served less than a year in that post, after being promoted into it after Idistaviso, now that he has served as an Optio for this amount of time, both as my Optio and as the Optio for a third line Cohort where he is now, *if* he ever qualifies to be elevated into the Centurionate, it would not be with a front line Cohort, and certainly not with the First Cohort. There is a saying among Centurions that I suppose has been around ever since Divus Augustus made his reforms after Actium, back when my great-grandfather was one of the first Camp Prefects, and that is that twice the men bring twice the problems. Although the Fifth had not been plumped up yet; the process had been delayed once it was learned that the 1st would be marching in Germanicus' triumph, we were still marching with one hundred twenty-nine effectives, although Bibaculus had assured me that there were eight men who had been left behind in Ubiorum because they were not sufficiently recovered to make any kind of march, even a relatively leisurely one, but who were expected to be ready for duty on our return. Without my normal method of introducing myself to my new command of using the training ground, it meant that I had to do something that did not come naturally to me, and that was to mingle with the men of every section, spending time marching alongside their section during the day.

I confess that there was a time back when I was a newly minted paid man where my reluctance stemmed from my disdain for the men of the lower class, thinking that it was impossible that we would have anything in common. Fortunately, my father knocked that nonsense out of my head, almost literally, but this was when I discovered something else about myself, and that is that I am more comfortable with smaller groups of people in informal settings. I was also acutely aware that, as much as I was observing the men of the Fifth, they were doing the same with me, and while I did my best, it was difficult to avoid wincing when one of my jests fell flat, or I inadvertently touched on a sensitive subject among the men of a certain section, like the time I overheard some of the men of the Eighth Section chattering about a woman back in Ubiorum, one I happened to know quite well from my days before Bronwen came into my life, but I will not shame her by naming her here. Thinking that this would be a good way to form a connection, I boasted of my time with her; while I knew by the awkward silence that I had stepped in it, naturally, none of the men of the section were going to tell me why. That fell to Bibaculus, who I went to find at the next rest stop.

"Ah." He suddenly looked embarrassed, giving me a hint

that I would not like what I was going to hear. "She hasn't worked in almost two years, Centurion. She's Fronto's woman now."

Now, in my defense, this is a very common occurrence, and I am far from the only one who has referred to a woman by her previous occupation, unaware that she has attached herself to a man who is usually but not always under the standard, thereby violating an unwritten rule about bringing up a woman's past; unless, of course, the intention is to start some sort of trouble with the man to whom she is now attached. That, obviously, was not my intent, and I am afraid that I had to work especially hard with Fronto to repair the damage I had done. This was not the only awkward moment, nor the only setback in my attempt to establish my command over the Fifth, which meant that at the end of more days than I would like to admit, I would be in a foul mood for my nightly visit with Bronwen and the baby.

They shared a tent with Algaia and Iras, and since we were in friendly territory, there was no ditch and wall, just the picket stakes outlining the boundaries of the camp, which meant that I could easily see their tent because Alex made sure to set it up on our side. I had warned her beforehand that, while I would come to see her and the baby at the end of the day, I would be spending my nights in camp, circulating the fires, which I had stressed was an important thing to do for a new leader. Now, I believe that sufficient time has passed to admit that this was not the main reason; putting it simply, between Titus' teething and her own ill temper because of it, I elected to remove myself from what I viewed at the time as her incessant complaining about the hardship of traveling with an infant. Titus was certainly fussy, although I found the rivers of slobber that would put a drunken ranker to shame the most off-putting; all in all, as brief as my visits were, they almost inevitably ended in harsh words, and I am ashamed to say that not all of them came from Bronwen. It got so bad that Algaia would simply take Iras outside the tent to play, knowing what was coming, although I swear to the gods that I did try and avoid unpleasantness, but I now know that I could have done a better job of not responding with my own sharp words. There was another factor that did not help my mood, especially that first week, and that was how fatigued I was at the end of the day, a reminder of just how slack duty in the *Praetorians* was compared to the Legions, and how quickly one loses their fitness for marching. My side bothered me some as well, but when Alex took my stitches out, that helped a good deal, although I was still somewhat restricted in twisting movements. Marching on good Roman roads as we were, in the height of summer, meant that our progress was rapid, although Sacrovir had us stop for a day every five, except for the first one, which came at Bononia and was on our sixth day, but that was because we had to cross the mountains between Florentia and Bononia. I did spend that first rest day with Bronwen and the baby, and it was as if the previous week of snapping and snarling at each other had never happened. It also gave me the first opportunity to ride Latobius, who showed how he felt about being neglected by biting me, hard, on the back of my left arm when I turned away to get his saddle, eliciting a yelp from me that the others, especially young Iras, thought was the funniest thing they had ever heard.

"I *was* going to let you ride with me, but not now," I grumbled, although most of my ire was at my horse, who was every bit as unrepentant as my companions.

Otherwise, it was pleasant riding up into the Apennines, certainly more so than sweating up the opposite slope the day before, and we stopped at a small *taverna* that I had noticed on the way, with a magnificent view of Bononia down below. It was not all for the purpose of relaxation I had suggested coming to this spot, and I had forewarned Bronwen about it, and on my signal, she had suggested to Algaia that they wander off with the children to go enjoy the view by following a path that would take them to an overlook a short distance away.

Naturally, Alex immediately saw through this, saying flatly, "You're having trouble finding me a spot."

This was only partially true, and I said as much.

"Actually, three other Cohorts want you, and their Pili Priores told me they'd make space for you somewhere, and two of them said they'd have you as their clerk." I hesitated, then added, "Macer is one of them."

5

"I know," he replied simply, but I noticed that he did not seem all that interested in looking in my direction.

"Did he already offer you a spot?" I asked, more sharply than I intended, and I should have known better than to think the two men I considered my best friends would go behind my back.

"Of course not!" Alex snapped, and I could see the glint of anger in his eyes. "He said that only if nothing else worked out, and that I'd have to accept the junior position, which is fine with me since it would mean replacing Lucco."

It was, I instantly realized, something I should have thought of before I opened my mouth. Lucco was Alex's best friend among the clerks, and it is not in Alex's nature to betray anyone for his own ambition, let alone a friend.

"I suppose I'll just have to sack one of my clerks," I sighed. "Although I don't know what for. According to Bibaculus, they're both competent."

"No, don't do that," Alex countered, although to my ear not as quickly. "That's not right either."

"Well," I allowed, "we still have three weeks to go. Who knows?" I grinned at him. "Maybe one of them will get caught skimming or something."

"Just as long as it's not you who finds them," my friend retorted. Standing up, he said, "Let's go find our women and make sure some pleb isn't slobbering all over them."

"That I'd like to see." I laughed. "Between Bronwen and Algaia, that poor bastard wouldn't have a chance. He'd be better off letting Cerberus chew off his balls."

Somewhat to our disappointment, no such entertainment was taking place, but the view *was* magnificent.

Another thing the time on the road gave me was the ability to get an idea about who the troublemakers, malingerers, and shirkers were among the Fifth Century, and I was dismayed at what I observed. Such was my distress that I actually sought out the Primus Pilus, through Melander, of course, but I was not surprised that I had to wait an extra day; in fact, I expected it, as Sacrovir's way of reminding me that I was back under the standard and that I was just one of fifty-nine Centurions. I also knew that if it had been truly important, I would have been granted an immediate audience. As it was, Sacrovir did not seem surprised to see me, and he confirmed as much when he waved me to sit at the small table in his private quarters.

"I've been wondering when you'd show up," he began the conversation, then gave me a smile that was almost cruel, at least to my eyes. "And I can guess why you're here. You've noticed you have a higher than average number of the liars, lame, and lazy, even for a First Cohort Century, and you're wondering if I've dropped you in the *cac*."

Now, this was exactly what I was wondering, but I was not so foolish as to admit that, so I hurried to assure him, "Not at all, Primus Pilus, at least the last part. I know you wouldn't do anything like that." I hesitated, trying to frame my thoughts, then finally said carefully, "It's just that it *is* unusual for a Century of the First Cohort to have so many men trying to conjure their way onto the sick list, especially on such an easy march. And," I knew I had to tread carefully, "I'll be honest; the punishment list I've had Euphemios submit is...lighter than it should be."

"I would have been more surprised if it wasn't," Sacrovir replied, but while there was no censure in his tone, I saw his lips thin slightly, which I had long before learned was a sign that we were nearing dangerous territory. He regarded me for a heartbeat, then asked, "If you were back leading the Fourth, and one of your Centurions," one corner of his lip twitched slightly, "let's say your Hastatus Prior, came to you in this situation, what would your advice be to him?"

Is this a trap? This was the first thought that came to me, but I could not see an advantage for him, so I thought for a moment before answering, "If the circumstances were the same, I would give him a few weeks to handle it on his own, without any interference from me. Then," I shrugged, "if it wasn't resolved to my satisfaction, I'd have to step in."

"Which is exactly what I'm going to do with you," Sacrovir did not hesitate, but then he lifted a hand, "except with one condition."

While I was happy to hear that he and I seemed to be of a like mind, I did not really care for the idea of a condition, and

I asked warily, "And what is that, Primus Pilus?"

"That you don't thrash any of those bastards badly enough to put them on a wagon. Since," for the first time, he grinned, and when I saw that he was missing a lower tooth, I tried to remember if I had noticed that during our time in Rome, "with half of them, you'd be giving them a free ride, which is what they want."

He was right, and I knew it the moment he said it, but while this was settled, I had to move to more uncomfortable territory. This time, however, I did not think it through, just plunged in headlong.

"How did it happen, Primus Pilus? How did the Fifth go to *cac* so quickly?"

It was only after the words were out that I recalled that Varo and Sacrovir were friends, having been *Tiros* together, and his lips thinned down again, but it was also accompanied by a narrowing of his eyes that I knew from experience presaged a storm.

I was completely unprepared for him to say, although only after he expelled a harsh breath, "That's my fault, Pullus. When his woman Rufina died, I...stopped thinking of Varo as one of my Centurions and thought of him as one of my oldest friends, and I looked the other way when the problems began. Then," he sighed, "Tiberius vanished, and while I knew I should have stepped in then, I didn't have the heart to do it."

Now, since whoever is reading this will be of my blood, which means they will be Roman, I do not have to point out the obvious, that it was entirely possible that the fact that Varo's son's *praenomen* was the same as that of the Primus Pilus was entirely coincidental, given the almost comically short list of *praenomen* available to Roman men, but I did not think that it was. Naturally, I immediately put Alex onto finding out, almost as soon as I left Sacrovir's tent, and it did not take him long to learn that my surmise had been correct, but what was more important to me in the moment was something else.

"What about Bibaculus? What did he do to try and get the men back on their good books?"

Rather than answer directly, Sacrovir echoed, "What

about Bibaculus? You've been with the Fifth for almost two weeks now; you tell me."

I did not have to think long about it, since I had already begun to form an opinion. "He told me that he'd only been Optio about eight months when Varo's woman died. And," I admitted, "it takes at least six months for an Optio to season in with an eighty-man Century, so he was at a real disadvantage."

"It does," Sacrovir agreed. Then he surprised, and irritated, me when he said, "And it takes a Centurion coming from an eighty-man Century about the same amount of time with a First Cohort Century. Fortunately," he stood in a clear signal, "things have been quiet on the Rhenus all year, and there's no sign that it will change." As he walked me to the partition that led to the outer office, he reminded me, "Just make sure that you don't stripe any of those misbegotten bastards to the point where they get a free ride, Pullus. Otherwise, you're free to handle the problem the way you see fit. And," he smiled, but it was the kind of smile that sends a ranker's heart down into his *caligae,* "once we're back in Ubiorum, I don't care if you fill the hospital up. Do whatever it takes to get the Fifth back to a point where they're worthy to be in my Cohort."

I promised him that I would, but I was inwardly seething at his implication that it would take me six months to do it, and that did not bode well for the men at all.

Marching northward, as we got closer to our destination, the next topic of conversation was whether we would be embarking at Augusta Raurica, using the Rhenus route, or continue marching. Naturally, our progress slowed once we reached the Alps, making barely fifteen miles a day north of Augusta Praetoria, but thankfully, it was still summer, and the weather was mild. Now that I was back to being fit to march and had an idea of what I was facing, and more importantly, what I would do about it, the tension between Bronwen and me vanished as if it had never been there, and we began to enjoy each other's company again in every way. The tougher terrain also made it easier on the officers in the sense that the men were too tired to fight with men from one of the other Legions, and the four Primi Pili had agreed before the march started to secure all *gladii* from their men, locking them away in their Century wagons. There had been some debate about the *pugiones* as well, but the fact is that the men use their *pugio* for so many different things other than fighting that it was short-lived. Despite the precautions, it was inevitable there were fights, but I had been fortunate, and in fact, the entire First Cohort had avoided any kind of trouble. Once we cleared the Alps, and got closer to our respective homes, tension began to build, as men bearing a grudge against a ranker from another Legion who was not permanently stationed with them realized their chance for revenge was decreasing with every mile. The 1st and 20th would be back in Ubiorum together, but the 5th was heading for Mogontiacum, while the 14th would be returning to Vetera to rejoin the 2nd, although I was most concerned with the 5th because of my own history with that Legion. I had given orders to Bibaculus and the section Sergeants, of which there are twenty in a First Cohort Century, a fact that I was still getting accustomed to, that if any of their men tangled with men of the 5th that they would be punished as well, something they universally believed was unfair. Their discontent was such that I finally decided to take Bibaculus aside to explain my seemingly unreasonable decision.

I summoned him to my tent, where I began by asking, "Do you recall hearing any talk of a...dispute between me and a Centurion of the Alaudae?"

Bibaculus' initial reaction was to frown, but then I saw a glimmer in his eye, and I was rewarded when he spoke, slowly, "Now that you mention it, I do seem to remember something about you beating the *cac* out of someone, in Mogontiacum, was it?"

"Yes, it was in Mogontiacum. It was Lucius Petronius..."

I did not finish, because I did not have to, as Bibaculus' eyes widened as it came back to him. He exclaimed, "That's right! He was the Quintus Pilus Prior at the time." His expression changed then, telling me he knew the entire story, which was confirmed when he said simply, "I understand, Centurion. I'll make sure the boys behave themselves until we're back home."

Honestly, I do not believe that anything more that I could have said, about how Primus Pilus Nerva still felt raw about Petronius' suicide, supposedly because he could not bear the shame of the beating I inflicted, which was not only savage, but had been premeditated, as part of a strategy to quell the talk that inevitably resulted with my posthumous adoption by my real father, and the revelation that I was his natural son would have kept what would be taking place in a few days from happening. What I will say was that we had no problems with the 5th...until we arrived in Mogontiacum.

Speaking of my mother, I cannot say which of us was more excited about the prospect of seeing her again, Bronwen or myself, although it was for the same reason, and that was to introduce her to her grandson, even if he was teething and was generally a fussy, damp mess. This was why which route we took was more than of passing interest, because it could conceivably give us more time in Mogontiacum if there was not enough shipping available to transport both the 1st and the 20th the final leg of the journey back to Ubiorum. If we took the overland route, while it was possible that we would arrive in Mogontiacum on a scheduled rest day, by our best calculations, it was not likely to happen, and while I did not say this to Bronwen, I also thought that even if it was, Sacrovir would be unlikely to take the day off since it would mean letting the men out into the city, a reluctance that I completely understood. I knew that he was like me, holding his breath with every passing day with no incident, worried that we would be wakened by our clerk, or worse, by our Optio with word that one of our rankers had been unable to keep their temper in check.

When we were told that the 1st would be staying an extra three days in Mogontiacum to wait for the river barges to return after transporting the 20th, it was impossible to tell who was happier, the men of the Fifth of the First or their Centurion. Bronwen was in an absolute state the night before we arrived in Mogontiacum, fretting about all manner of things that it took all of my resolve to pretend was not ridiculous.

"What if your mother thinks he's ugly?" was one of her more memorable worries, and I am afraid I was at such a loss that I ended up throwing up my hands and returning to camp, something I had not done for a couple of weeks.

Still, it was hard to contain my excitement, and my impatience, when we marched through the gates of the permanent camp outside what is now one of the largest cities on the Rhenus, which makes sense, since it is the provincial capital. So much has changed even during my time under the standard, while early in my father's career, it had been nothing but the kind of shantytown full of whores, sharp operators, and intrepid merchants who are willing to risk the danger of living on the frontier in exchange for a chance at riches. Now, there is a stone wall enclosing the original town, but it is surrounded on three sides by neighborhoods, save for the river side, which remains clear of dwellings, the only buildings a few blocks of warehouses servicing the docks lining the river. The Legion camp, which is still a four-Legion camp, is across the river, but the pontoon bridge was replaced several years earlier, with stone pilings but a wooden structure.

I am afraid that I unashamedly dumped the duty of making sure the men were settled on Bibaculus' shoulders, although before I turned over command to my Optio, I stressed the orders that had been in place for weeks about staying out of trouble, then I leapt aboard Latobius, who I had had Alex saddle and one of my men lead from our last rest stop, and moved at the trot out of the camp. Alex was waiting at the wagon just outside the gates, and we clattered back across the bridge, following the now-familiar route to my mother's villa, the only difference being in who greeted us at the gate, which turned out to be nobody because the gate was open, something that I thought was unusual. As large as Mogontiacum has gotten, it is still a military town, yet while my mother was undoubtedly aware that the Legions were returning from Rome, she had no reason to think that her son would returning with them, but when I thought of playing a trick on her by simply sweeping in unannounced, I was stopped by the largest woman I have ever seen. While she was not my height, the top of her head came to just below my eyes, which meant she had to be six feet, but it was her breadth that was truly impressive, making it impossible for me to slip through the doorway past her even if she had been inclined to let me. Which, judging from her expression, she was not, nor did she seem concerned that she was confronting a very large man, especially for a Roman, one holding a *vitus*.

"Who are you, and what do you want?"

Her appearance had led me to believe that she was a German, and her accent confirmed this, but she still gave no sign of stepping aside, then from the *triclinium*, I heard my mother's voice.

"Grimhilt, who is it?"

"Some big Roman," Grimhilt called over her shoulder, and when speaking loudly, her voice matched her build.

I was suddenly reminded of the campfire tales about the shield maidens of the Suebi, and how I had dismissed them as figments of overactive ranker imaginations; suddenly, I was not so sure, but I did not have long to contemplate the idea that I might be facing one at this moment, because my mother appeared in the vestibule, her eyes wide with the surprise I had been hoping to achieve by our unexpected appearance. Unfortunately, while I took in my mother, noticing that there were a few more strands of silver in her raven-black hair, my eyes went immediately to the man behind her, instantly seeing that he was not a slave or a freedman servant.

That is why the first words to my mother were to snarl, as I suddenly shoved Grimhilt aside hard enough that she stumbled into the wall, so that I could point my *vitus*, "*Who the fuck is that?*"

And, of course, I bellowed this, causing Titus to waken from where he had been sleeping, his head on Bronwen's shoulder as she stood just behind me, which was how my mother learned that she was a grandmother, and I discovered that she had taken a lover.

Not surprisingly, it took some time for things to calm down, but I must give young Titus all the credit, as both mother and grandmother temporarily forgot my behavior; the man, I was grimly pleased to see, couldn't seem to take his eyes off me, and quite wisely in my view, chose to be part of the furniture as I introduced my son to his grandmother. My mother did not seem to mind the slobber in the slightest, while Titus gave her a gummy grin and actually reached his arms out to her, which caused Bronwen and me to exchange a glance that conveyed our mutual surprise; to that point, Titus had been extremely shy around strangers, and seeing him actually reach for my mother was not only unusual, I felt my throat closing off as a lump formed.

"I think he knows Avia is going to be a soft touch," I said jokingly; it would be a comment that Bronwen would be reminding me of, and not always with pleasure.

Only then did my mother seem to realize that we were still standing in the entry vestibule, and with an ease that should not have surprised me since she had undoubtedly done the same with me, slung Titus around onto her hip, calling out, "Grimhilt! Please bring refreshments to the *triclinium*." Addressing Bronwen, she asked, "Is Titus hungry, Bronwen?"

"He," my wife laughed, "is always hungry..." She shot me a mischievous look then finished, "...Avia."

This brought my mother up short, and she turned to give us both a mock glare as she demanded, "Do I look like a grandmother to you?" Before we could say anything, she added, "Do not answer that." I happened to see the flash in her eyes that I had learned was a warning that she had some mischief of her own in mind, and I quickly learned what it was when she smiled sweetly as she said, "Lucius certainly doesn't think I look like a grandmother." Turning to Lucius, who looked to me like he was trying to decide if he had the time to dash to the nearest window and dive out, she finished, "Do you, *meum mel*?"

"N-no, of course not!" he stammered, and I decided to take pity on him, after a fashion, crossing over to him while extending my arm.

"Since my mother has forgotten her manners in her old age, I won't bother introducing myself since you obviously know." I was smiling as I said this, but I also made sure to flex my arm slightly, ignoring the sight of Bronwen rolling her eyes just at the corner of my vision. "And you are...?"

"L-Lucius Cornuficius Censorinus," he replied, accepting my arm; as I suspected, his hand was smooth and soft, although I grudgingly acknowledged that he had a firm grip. However, I was distracted, because the name was familiar.

"Wait," I exclaimed, it suddenly coming to me. "Weren't you one of the *duumviri* of Mogontiacum?"

"I still am," he confirmed, but now I looked at my mother, who was disengaging Titus' chubby fist, which had curled around her necklace, a fine piece of work with tiny gold links and an enameled pendant that I didn't recall ever seeing before.

While she looked up at me, I saw the silent plea there, but I am somewhat ashamed to say that I was not in the right frame of mind to heed it.

I was just opening my mouth to say something when Bronwen saved my mother.

"That must be a very challenging posting, *Duumvir* Censorinus! Mogontiacum seems to get bigger every time we are here. Is that not true, my love?"

Whereas my mother had offered a plea through her expression, I heard, and understood, the warning in Bronwen's tone; if the other adults heard it, they wisely pretended not to, but for once, I heeded it.

"Yes, it is," I agreed, and I saw my mother's shoulders slump slightly, making me feel a bit ashamed of myself that I had been about to make what should have been a joyous moment into a potentially unpleasant encounter.

"As of last month, we have averaged a hundred new residents a week," Censorinus said, with all the pride of a man for whom such things are important. "And those are just the ones who come to the *Praetorium* to be legally registered so that they can be put on the rolls."

The idea that there were new inhabitants to Mogontiacum who were not going through the process legally intrigued me, mainly because I had heard talk around the huts in Ubiorum that most of those who did such things had a reason, but the next little bit of time was spent in getting comfortable and settled on the couches, whereupon my mother immediately began bouncing Titus on her knee, causing him to chortle happily. I noticed that Censorinus seemed about to settle himself on the same couch as my mother, as if it was his accustomed spot, but he glanced over at me and chose one of the chairs instead.

This earned me a sharp elbow in the ribs from Bronwen, who hissed, "*Stop it.*"

"Stop what?" I whispered back, using Alex and Algaia's answering my mother's questions about Rome as cover. "I didn't say anything!"

"You know perfectly well what I mean," she shot back. "You're looking at that poor man as if he was a *Tiro* who has displeased you and you are about to thrash."

Now, this was *exactly* what I was doing, but I was not about to admit it, so I just grumbled, "I can't win."

"No," she agreed, "you can't."

"Gnaeus, is that true?"

I confess I came perilously close to panicking at my mother's question just then, realizing that I had not been paying attention to anything Alex had been telling her.

"Which part?" I asked, stalling for time.

"That you're now commanding a Century in the First Cohort, of course!" she snapped.

"Ah, yes." I nodded, hiding my relief that it was not something else. "Yes, the Primus Hastatus Prior decided to take retirement while the Legion was marching to Rome for the triumph." Realizing something, I turned and asked Alex, "What did you tell her about the Praetorians?"

"Just that Germanicus realized his mistake in assigning you to them under that snake Sejanus in the first place," my mother answered for him.

Deciding that this was as good an explanation as any that my time in the Praetorians only lasted about six months, I continued, "Yes, well, when Germanicus transferred me back to the 1st, he made it clear that it was up to the Primus Pilus where to put me, but honestly, I was hoping to go back to the Fourth, but that wouldn't have been fair to Licinius. Still, I wasn't expecting a First Cohort Century."

I decided that this was not the moment to go into the details, how Marcus Macer, who had been offered the posting first by Sacrovir, had removed his name from consideration once I returned to the Legion.

"How is it handling a First Cohort Century?"

I could not hide my surprise, not at the question, but who it came from, although I did not hesitate to reply to Censorinus, using the standard line, "With twice the men, there are twice the problems, I suppose is the best way to put it. But," I allowed, "I think Fortuna was looking out for me with this march, because it's given me a chance to get to know the men without much distraction."

"Although," Alex cut in, "Gnaeus was quite disappointed at first."

"Oh? Why?" my mother asked, and I got a hint of warning by what can only be called the smirk on Alex's face as he answered, "He would prefer just bashing them one at a time like he did with his Praetorians."

"By the gods," I groaned. "Not this again."

Naturally, and as he knew she would be, my mother was interested in having Alex elucidate on his comment, which he was quite happy to do, forcing me to sit there listening, and watching once Alex, with urging by Algaia, Iras, and Bronwen, began acting out what I had learned very quickly was a foolhardy challenge to face each and every man in my Century with a *rudis*, in one day. At first, I was not very happy, but then I sneaked a glance over at Censorinus; suddenly, I felt better and decided to enjoy Alex's performance, and that was exactly what it was. By the time he was finished, panting and with his tongue hanging out, his entire audience was laughing, and I include myself, while Censorinus joined in, but nervously.

"It wasn't that bad," I grumbled once the mirth had died down, then after a beat, I grinned. "Not quite, anyway. But I couldn't raise my arms for a couple of days."

"I just wish that was all that happened," Bronwen sighed, and it was my turn to glare at her as I whispered, "Not now."

"Why? What else happened?"

It was the way her eyes narrowed that warned me that my mother had intuited there was quite a bit of information missing from what we had said about my time in the Praetorians to that point, something she did with a disgusting frequency, but there was no way that I was going to mention

17

anything that remotely smacked of the political situation in Rome in front of an official appointed by the Imperator. However, I could see that my mother had the proverbial bit in her teeth and was not likely to give up on this line of questioning. Fortunately, I was saved, by a quite unlikely hero when, suddenly, Censorinus stood.

"Giulia, I'm afraid that I must bid you and your loved ones a good evening," he announced, trying to look regretful but failing miserably, though I did not fault him for wanting to get out of there given how things had been going.

"Oh, Lucius! No, please stay!" My mother's voice took on a quality that I had never heard before. "I promise that we'll behave ourselves." She turned to me and gave me a challenging, direct look. "Won't we, Gnaeus?"

"I didn't realize I was misbehaving," I replied, immediately remembering my first words concerning Lucius Censorinus, and I mumbled, "at least now, anyway."

"It's not that at all, I assure you," Censorinus lied, but he was also moving towards the exit as he spoke.

Sighing, my mother turned and handed Titus back to Bronwen, murmuring something to my wife as she stood to walk her guest out, while Titus immediately began howling in protest, reaching for my mother, which in turn made me eye Bronwen a bit nervously at what I suppose could have been viewed as my son expressing his preference for who held him at that particular moment. For her part, Bronwen tried not to look hurt, giving me a smile that was not convincing in the slightest. I heard my mother and Censorinus speaking in the vestibule, and while it was impossible to hear what they were saying, there was an intimacy there that I did not care for at all, so I was a bit distracted and probably did not offer Bronwen the support for which she was looking at the moment. I heard my mother's footsteps, and I waited for her to reenter the *triclinium*, and the instant she reappeared, I opened my mouth.

"What aren't you telling me about what happened in Rome?"

"Isn't that your best friend's husband?"

Our questions came out at exactly the same time, while Bronwen, Alex, and Algaia sat there, frozen in whatever posture they were in, and I remember how Alex's cup was hovering in midair, halfway to his lips, while Bronwen stopped trying to distract Titus with the rag doll Legionary she carried everywhere with her, which my son snatched and promptly stuffed into his mouth, leaving my mother and me glaring at each other.

Finally, her shoulders slumped and she said, "I suppose we each have something to tell."

"Yes, Domitilla was married to Lucius," my mother explained, apparently deciding to go first after we had both settled back down, both physically and emotionally. "But they were divorced almost a year ago."

On its face, this was not anything unusual; Romans of my former order, like patricians and high-ranking plebeians, view marriage more strategically, and once a union no longer brings an advantage, almost universally to the man, the spouse is quickly discarded. Indeed, it is not uncommon for a Roman to remarry within a matter of watches of the bill of divorce being delivered, in front of witnesses, provided of course, that the original ceremony was *coemptio* and not *confarreatio*, the former being our ceremony in *jus civis,* while the latter, which is older and is based in our religion, making it almost impossible to obtain a divorce, which is why almost no Roman uses it. No, what my mother was telling me was not troubling...on the surface, but I could not seem to keep my mind from going to places I knew it would not do either of us any good to go. I was not helped when I glanced over at Bronwen, and I saw the shadow of a frown on her face, of the type she got when she was performing some sort of calculation; later, I would learn that was exactly what she was doing. My mother, and being fair, Bronwen as well, often accused me of not really paying attention to what she was telling me, and there was certainly truth to that; however, not paying full attention is not the same thing as not paying attention at all. In the back of my mind was a nagging thought, about how, during my time in Britannia, my mother and this woman Domitilla had some sort of falling out. She had only mentioned it in passing, yet even then, and only partially paying attention, I was certain I heard a forced quality to her tone, as if she was trying to sound casual about an event that was anything but, which was where my mind went as we sat there in her *triclinium*. Could their falling out have something to do with Domitilla's husband? Was my mother the cause of their divorce? Certainly, by this time, I had at least partially accepted that my mother was an attractive woman, and as a widow, she had every right to enjoy the company of a man, in all senses of the word, but I cannot lie and say the idea that she might have begun an affair with Lucius Censorinus before he was legally unattached did not bother me a great deal. In fact, I opened my mouth to demand the truth, but what came out was not what I intended, at all.

"Does he make you happy, Mama?"

Her mouth dropped open, clearly as surprised as I was by my question, but she did not hesitate, long, before answering quietly, "Yes, Gnaeus. He does."

"Do you intend on marrying him?"

"Gods no." She laughed. "Not only has he not asked, why would I give up the freedom I have now as a widow?"

It was the mention of her status that reminded me of something else, something that was only slightly less dangerous and possibly contentious than whether she was having an affair with Censorinus while he was still married, but I decided to get it all out that night.

"Fair enough," I said in a signal that I had no intention of pursuing the topic any further, and she signaled her understanding by the expression of relief that flashed across her features, which made me feel a bit ashamed, but as I usually did, I plunged on by saying, "On our way to Rome, we stopped in Mediolanum."

"Oh?" Her demeanor changed with an impressive swiftness, and she asked lightly, "Did you have an urge to see the places where you made so much mischief?"

I do not believe she knew that she was handing me the perfect opening, but I could not help grinning as I said, "Something like that, but I didn't actually plan on going to Proserpina's Lair; it just happened."

My mother made a small cry, but she turned to look at

Bronwen, and I assured her, "She knows about my history with Proserpina's Mama. And," I added quietly, "she met Nasica."

"*Nasica*?" she gasped, but then her mouth twisted into a grimace of distaste and contempt. "Why on Gaia's earth did you see him?"

"It wasn't by choice," I replied grimly. "Trust me."

Taking a breath, I went on to explain all that had transpired in Mediolanum, leaving nothing out and including the fact that Nasica actually believed he had just cause for a grievance against our family, thanks to Quintus Volusenus, the man I had thought was my father, who Nasica believed had cheated him out of a contract to provide the labor to construct a series of new *insulae*.

I finished by asking bluntly, "Is what Nasica told me true? Did my...did Quintus cheat him out of a contract?"

She did not reply immediately, but then with a slow nod, admitted, "Yes. I confronted him about it once I learned what he was up to." She paused, and I understood why when she asked, "Do you remember when I went to Bononia for the thermal baths? It was right around that time."

I did; in fact, I remember being quite put out that my mother had made the decision seemingly overnight without telling me, and leaving before I woke the next morning. I was also ashamed now that the cause for my pique was that I felt that she had abandoned me with my father, who had very little to say to me under the best of circumstances, and he was even colder than normal, I recalled.

"Your father broke my arm," she continued quietly. "I left so that you didn't have to see it." I suppose that it is a good thing that we cremate our dead, because otherwise, I might have traveled to Mediolanum and dug Quintus Volusenus up out of the ground to hack his bones apart with my real father's *gladius*. I also believe that she saw her own opportunity, because she said, "Now, it's time for you to tell me what you've been trying to avoid about what happened in Rome."

As the gods as my witness, I planned on telling her, but neither will I lie and say that, when the sharp rapping on the outer gate sounded, which I had closed, I did not offer up a brief prayer for the reprieve. My happiness was to be short lived, because when Grimhilt returned, it was with Bibaculus, and my Optio's expression was grim.

"The Primus Pilus requires your presence back at camp, immediately, Centurion." I felt somewhat guilty about my initial feeling of relief that I could postpone telling my mother about Rome and my dealings with Sejanus. That sentiment evaporated when Bibaculus continued, "There's been a killing in town, and the Primus Pilus is requiring every man of the 1st to return to camp, regardless of rank, and we're confined to our Legion area."

I believe it was the way that he glanced over at the women, although I was accustomed to the manner in which men's eyes lingered on Bronwen, that I sensed there was something significant that he was not saying because of them.

What it might be came to me with the force of a punch to the gut, which prompted me to gasp, "Was one of ours involved?"

The instant the words were out of my mouth, I realized that Bibaculus might think I was asking if it was a man of the 1st and not what I meant, in our Century, but he correctly interpreted my meaning, proving it by saying a single word; more accurately, a name.

"Florus."

"Pluto's cock," I groaned, not even bothering to ask whether or not Florus, who was in the Fifteenth Section, was the victim, certain that he was not only the victor, but was in all likelihood the instigator.

"Do I need to ask whether it was with a civilian or even a man from another Cohort of our Legion?" I asked, without much hope, and when he said that it was neither, I braced myself for even worse news about the identity of the other Legion, but he said he did not know.

Turning to my family, I did not even get the words out, my mother offering me a resigned smile.

"Go back to camp, Gnaeus." She smiled at her grandson, who was beginning to nod off, undoubtedly tired from all the excitement. "Bronwen and the baby are staying here, and of course Algaia and Iras are welcome to stay as well."

While I expected as much, I was still relieved and

thankful, and while Alex still did not have a spot, I decided I would take him back to camp with us, but I did not have to ask, seeing him stand up.

"I'll send Alex back as soon as I know what will be happening," I promised.

The three of us left, and once outside the walls of my mother's villa, we all immediately noticed the tension in the streets, receiving nervous glances from the citizens we passed, and we heard shouting a street over that sounded much like the kind of noise that occurs when the provosts are involved. In fact, we were still a few blocks from the city gate when, as we reached an intersection, four provosts suddenly appeared from the gloom where they had been waiting in the pool of darkness between torches, a favorite trick of theirs, and they arrayed themselves across the street directly in our path.

I am certain that they had not seen my *vitus* or Bibaculus' white stripe because of the darkness, but he clearly saw it in my hand, although there was no mistaking the hostility in the provost's voice as he demanded, "What Legion are you with, Centurion?" Pointing at Bibaculus, "And you, Optio."

Despite knowing this was not the time to let my temper get the better of me, I still felt that shifting sensation deep inside me as I replied coldly, "I'm the Primus Hastatus Prior of the 1st Legion, and this is my Optio, Provost."

"You're not authorized to be inside the city walls, Centurion," the provost said. "The duty Tribune has issued orders to detain any man of the 1st Legion and take him to the *Praetorium*."

"There's no need for that," I assured them, indicating Bibaculus. "I was visiting my mother, and my Optio just came to..."

"I don't care, Centurion," the provost cut me off sharply. "I have my orders, that any man of the 1st I find is to be brought to the *Praetorium*. It," he offered me a smile, but there was nothing nice or apologetic about it, "is for your own safety."

Perhaps if I did not catch the glance two of the other provosts exchanged, or notice the manner in which they shifted their grips on the cudgels they carried, letting them slide down so they were grasping the grooved handle, I might have acquiesced, but along with my growing anger, I felt a tingling in my *gladius* hand that I had learned not to ignore.

Without thinking it through, I suddenly took a step closer to the provost who, to this point, had done all of the talking for his party, employing one of the few tricks that I had learned even before those my father taught me, pleased to see how the provost suddenly did not seem quite as certain of himself now that I was within arm's reach, yet I did not raise my voice when I asked, "Do you know who I am, Provost...?"

"Provost First Grade Gnaeus Bibulus, and yes, I know who you are. You murdered a friend of mine."

I confess that, at first, I did not take his meaning, and I protested, "I've never murdered anyone. Unless," I sneered, "you were friends with that Cherusci *cunnus* Arminius before he betrayed Rome, because I've killed a *lot* of Cherusci."

"That's not who I'm talking about!" he snapped. "I'm talking about Lucius Petronius!"

"I didn't murder Petronius!" I shot back.

"You might as well have." Bibulus' voice was getting louder, rising in pitch, and I noticed the other three men began looking nervous, making me wonder if this Bibulus was unpredictable, because unpredictable men are dangerous men. "You baited him into a fight, and the beating you gave him was so savage that he was never the same after that! He could barely remember his own name, and there was no way he could carry out his duties."

Suddenly, I had a flash of what might have been an insight, that Bibulus and Petronius were more than just friends, but the truth was that I did not care.

"He insulted my mother." I was certain he was aware of this, but I thought it might be a good idea to remind him. Bibulus' lips twisted into a sneer, and he opened his mouth, but before he could say anything, I assured him, "If you're as stupid as Petronius was and are thinking of saying something like what earned him the beating, know this much. I won't stop like I did with Petronius."

"You just threatened a man of the provosts!" he gasped, then turned to the others. "You heard him!"

"I heard him say that if you insulted his mother, he'd do

something that any one of us would do, Bibulus." This comment from the comrade to Bibulus' right rear earned him a glare over the shoulder, while I tried to hide my pleased surprise, but the other provost, who I saw was a bit older than Bibulus, was not done. "Besides, don't act like you didn't know that Petronius was a troublemaker. How he got into the Centurionate I'll never know, let alone making Pilus Prior. How many times did we have to go to The Happy Legionary because he'd beaten some poor sod half to death just because Petronius didn't like the look of him?"

"He was a good man, and loyal to Rome!" Bibulus bellowed, temporarily forgetting me, his ire clearly aimed at this other provost.

"So am I," I said. "And I'm going to camp, just like I was ordered to. And," for the first time, I raised my *vitus*, "it doesn't look like your men are all that keen on helping you stop me." I knew it was a reckless thing to do, but I was sufficiently angry to poke him in the chest with my *vitus,* hard enough to send him staggering back a step. "Do you think you can do it on your own, Bibulus?"

For a span of a couple of heartbeats, I thought Bibulus actually was going to try, but then his shoulders slumped, and he stepped aside.

"Don't stop until you're in your camp, Centurion," he muttered.

I thought about saying something, but I decided that this was enough of a victory; besides, I needed to know more about what was going on with Florus.

By the time we arrived outside the Primus Pilus' quarters, I had convinced myself that I was prepared for the news to be as bad as it could possibly be, but I quickly learned I was wrong.

"According to multiple witnesses, your man Florus," Sacrovir said grimly, "headed directly for one of the *tavernae* that's a regular haunt of the Alaudae."

"Alone?" I gasped, but Sacrovir shook his head.

"No, he was with his close comrade, and another pair of men from your Twelfth Section."

Although I knew that Florus, who I had learned very quickly was at the top of the list of troublemakers, was close comrades with Vibius Paterculus and friendly with a man from the Twelfth Section, I had to turn to Bibaculus, who supplied the names of the Twelfth Section men.

"Florus was *Tiros* with Sextus Dentulus in the Twelfth, one of the armorer *Immunes*, and Dentulus' close comrade is Tiberius Serranus."

"That's them." Sacrovir nodded, although he had to refer to the tablet Melander had given to him, and I did not take it amiss that the Primus Pilus addressed Bibaculus. "Florus, I know about. His name has crossed my desk more times than I can count, and now I regret denying Varo's request to have him scourged the last time, but the actual offense didn't merit it. But what's the story with this Dentulus? I don't remember seeing his name on the punishment list, or if he has been, it hasn't been frequently enough that I remember it, or Paterculus for that matter."

"If Dentulus was with Florus," Bibaculus answered, immediately and with a firm tone, "it was to try and keep Florus from doing something stupid."

"He didn't do a very good job of it," Sacrovir said sourly, but while I did not know Dentulus to the level that Bibaculus did, I still felt compelled to say something in his defense. Before I could, the Primus Pilus lifted a hand and added wearily, "That's unfair to Dentulus. Florus was a rock in Varo's *caliga* for a long time, and he's been building up to something like this. And," he added with a sigh, "the same goes for Paterculus. I've seen his name a time or two, but not for anything like what Florus has done."

I decided to treat that as an opening, and I asked, "What exactly *did* happen, Primus Pilus?"

Sacrovir actually looked a bit embarrassed, mumbling something that might have been an apology as he reopened the tablet, which I could see was emblazoned with the symbol used by the *Quaestor*'s office, to whom the provosts reported in Mogontiacum because of its importance as the provincial capital of Germania Superior when the Legate was not present, while *Duumviri* like Censorinus handled all of the civil administration of the city.

Sacrovir briefly read the contents of the tablet before beginning, "According to this, when Florus showed up, he was already drunk."

"Wait," I interrupted. "I thought he went directly to this *taverna* once we were dismissed."

I should have known better, and Sacrovir snapped, "If you had waited a moment, Pullus, you would know the answer already."

"Yes, sir," I mumbled. "I apologize for interrupting."

He glared at me for an extra heartbeat before continuing, "According to his close comrade, Paterculus admitted that they got their hands on a jug of wine at Buconica, and they switched out the water in their canteens." I could not stifle the groan, because it was my responsibility to ensure this kind of thing did not happen, but the truth was that I had taken the opportunity of the last rest stop to go tend to my family and inform Bronwen that we were only ten miles from Mogontiacum, Buconica being the last relay outpost. To my pleased surprise, Sacrovir was almost kind, telling me, "Don't beat yourself up, Pullus. We check in the mornings, and at the noon halt, but you know as well as I do that it's next to impossible to stop these misbegotten bastards if they're determined to get their hands on wine." Without waiting for me to reply, he returned his attention to the tablet as I braced myself for what was to come; I quickly learned it was an impossible task. "That's why they were already drunk when they got to..." he paused and looked up at me as he said, "...The Happy Legionary." This time, I added a curse to my groan, my eyes searching his face for a sign that, for reasons I could not fathom, he was jesting, but his expression instantly dispelled that notion. "I can see that you remember The Happy Legionary, Pullus." I only nodded, and he had to return his attention to the tablet. "Yes, well aside from their choice, Paterculus also swore that Florus didn't tell him what he had in mind, but he, Dentulus, and Serranus all agree that Florus didn't choose a man at random, that as soon as he entered, he paused just long enough to scan the room, then headed straight for a ranker who was seated at a table with three of his friends.

And," Sacrovir paused for a heartbeat, "he had a...companion, sitting on his knee."

This was the moment when a stray bit of gossip dislodged itself in my mind, and I glanced over at Bibaculus, who, to his credit, understood, giving me a nod.

"This was about the woman," I told Sacrovir, but then I indicated that Bibaculus should take the lead, since this had all originated even before the Legions left for Rome to march in the triumph.

"Her name is Minerva, at least that's what she calls herself, although from what I've been told, she's Ubii. When we were on the Campus Martius, *Signifer* Lentulus came and told me about a rumor that this Minerva, who Florus claimed as his woman about six months ago, had been seen with a man from the 5th just before we left."

"Isn't she a whore?" Sacrovir asked, with a fair amount of scorn. "What did Florus expect?"

"She was," Bibaculus seemed to confirm, "but according to Florus, she had given it up so that he could take care of her." Shrugging, he said, "We did a good job of keeping the boys apart on the march down to Rome and back, so this was Florus' first chance to see if it was true with his own eyes."

Truthfully, this is one of the most common causes of disputes among men, not just of different Legions, or of the same Legion but different Cohort or Century, when a ranker, or even an officer thinks he's convinced a woman to give up her way of making a living in exchange for being a wife in everything but name. The most common form of disagreement is when two men have the same designs on the same woman, or more rarely, when one or more men object to the idea that their favorite whore will no longer be available. A woman misleading a man about her intentions is fairly common as well, but while I had not had that much time with Florus, I had seen enough to believe that it was a distinct possibility that Florus had heard what he wanted to hear, not what this woman Minerva had actually said.

"What about the woman?" I asked. "Did he go after her as well?"

"That," Sacrovir acknowledged, "is a good question." He

studied the tablet for a moment, then shook his head. "It's not clear from this report; all it says is that she wasn't injured, but while the dead ranker's close comrade suffered a stab wound to his hand, he'll be fine."

"Where is Florus now? And what about the other three?" I asked.

"The provosts have Florus in a cell in the *Praetorium*," Sacrovir answered, "and the provosts determined that the other three didn't know what Florus intended, but they're restricted to their section huts on my orders until I have a better idea of what's going to happen."

This was the moment something else occurred to me; I blame all the other bits of information floating around in my head, but finally, the identity of the *taverna* connected with my own history, and I asked, with some trepidation, "What Cohort and Century was the ranker from?"

Sacrovir actually looked grimly amused, and I had the feeling that he had been waiting for me to ask.

"First of the Fifth Cohort, Pullus."

"Fuck me," I breathed, wondering how long it would be before Primus Pilus Nerva would make the connection and figured out a way to somehow blame me.

As it turned out, I was about to learn within a matter of heartbeats.

We could hear the banging on the outer door of the Primus Pilus' quarters, performed in a manner that was highly unusual for anyone seeking entrance into the chief Centurion's office, unless it was some sort of emergency. Alex had remained in the outer office with Melander and the other two clerks, and I heard Melander's voice, although I could not make out the words, but I heard the indignation in the clerk's voice. So too did Sacrovir, who came to his feet, and in the kind of habit only another Centurion would understand, snatched up his *vitus*. He had just gotten around his desk when there was the slapping sound of hobnails on the wooden floor, and in an astonishing breach of courtesy, the door to Sacrovir's private quarters was flung open, and not by Melander. Standing there in the doorway was Primus Pilus Nerva, but while he had been looking in the direction of Sacrovir's desk, his eyes immediately moved to me where I was standing, and I will swear on my eagle that I saw a glint of malicious triumph in his eyes. He did not address me, however, although his gaze was still on me as he spoke.

"Primus Pilus Sacrovir, I'm here with these provosts," he jerked his thumb over his shoulder, and that is when I saw Bibulus, who was making no attempt to hide his satisfaction, "to take custody of the three accomplices to your man Florus, and deal with another matter as well."

"Accomplices?" Sacrovir frowned. "That's not what this report says..." He turned back to pick it up off the desk, so he missed the glance that Nerva exchanged with Bibulus, the Centurion giving the provost a nod, who cleared his throat.

"Yes, Primus Pilus Sacrovir, about that. We've received new information from other witnesses who overheard the four of them outside The Happy Legionary just before Centurion Pullus' man Florus attacked and murdered *Gregarius Immunes* Publius Ambustus without provocation that make it clear they were aware of Florus' intentions, and were there to provide support in the event that Florus was stopped before he could commit the murder, and to aid in his escape."

I did not care for the fact that my name was associated with Florus and this whole business, but nor could I argue with Bibulus' words, despite my certainty that this was the provost's own measure of revenge for making him back down not long before. Since it was Sacrovir who Bibulus was addressing, it was the Primus Pilus who was the man to answer, and I held my breath as I hoped that he would ask what I considered the most important question.

I should have had more faith in him, because Sacrovir not only asked what I wanted to know, he ignored Bibulus to demand from Nerva, "These witnesses. Are they men from the Alaudae? From the Fifth Cohort by any chance?"

"What does that matter?" Nerva shot back, his face flushing as he blustered, "Are you implying something, Sacrovir? Are you calling my men liars?"

"I'm saying that it's very...convenient," Sacrovir replied coolly. Then, he apparently decided to at least try to reason with the other Primus Pilus, which if I had been asked, I would have assured him was a waste of time. "Put yourself in my *caligae*, Quintus. If the situation was reversed, and I suddenly appeared in your quarters claiming that I had...found...some men who just *happened* to be from the same Cohort, maybe even the same Century as my murdered man that implicated the men with him that wasn't mentioned in the initial investigation, what would you think?"

As I expected, this had absolutely no impact on the other Primus Pilus, who snorted then said, "I'm not in your *caligae*, Tiberius, because *my* men don't go running around murdering men from other Legions..." this was when he turned to glare up at me, "...even if they don't succeed immediately."

We never spoke of it, but I feel certain that this was the moment when Sacrovir understood something that I had discerned almost immediately, that this was as much about me and what I had done to Lucius Petronius, despite the fact that my beating of him had been more than two years earlier, and his suicide a year after that, as it was about Florus. What neither of us anticipated was the lengths to which Nerva, with the help of the provost Bibulus, was about to go in order to exact vengeance.

"*If* I agree to turn over the other three men, it will only be for tonight," Sacrovir said, then indicated me. "And their Centurion will be present for the questioning, because these men are not only citizens and under the standard, I have serious reservations about this...*information* you say you have."

This was when Nerva struck, affecting a look that I suppose he thought communicated a level of regret, but the three of us were completely unprepared when he turned to Bibulus, who cleared his throat and stepped out from behind the Centurion.

"Yes, about that, Primus Pilus Sacrovir. Along with the new information from the witnesses outside The Happy Legionary, we've learned something else, from *Gregarius* Florus himself." He had to know how much of a risk he was running with the look of malicious happiness he gave me, but I suppose he could not help it. "I just learned on my return to the *Praetorium* that, under questioning, *Gregarius* Florus admitted that his Centurion not only knew what he intended to do to *Gregarius Immunes* Ambustus, but he told *Gregarius* Florus where he could be found."

"Which," Nerva interjected, and he did not really even try to seem anything but happy, "we all know Pullus knew about, since that's where he ambushed Pilus Prior Petronius."

It was not until it was too late that I realized what Nerva was trying to do, and the only thing I can say was that I retained enough of my wits not to touch him, but before I had a conscious thought, I was standing less than six inches away from Nerva, towering over him as I snarled, "*Ambush*? I didn't ambush that *mentula*. He was a fucking bully boy who thought he couldn't be beaten! He insulted my mother's honor...and he learned just how wrong he was." I knew it was a bad idea to continue, but I couldn't stop myself. "And I've had to work a *lot* harder beating other men than I did destroying Petronius. Did you know that at the end, he was begging me to stop beating him? He was crying like a woman, pissing himself because he couldn't take the pain..."

"That's enough, Pullus."

Sacrovir did not yell this, but the words managed to cut through my growing rage and caused me to take a step back from Nerva, and I did not miss the flash of relief that crossed his features.

Turning his attention to Nerva, Sacrovir said flatly, "You're not taking Pullus anywhere, Nerva, not until I've had a chance to check this so-called information out myself."

"Do you really want me to get Varro involved?" Nerva countered.

At the mention of the *Quaestor*'s name, I saw Sacrovir hesitate, and I understood why. Gaius Silius, the *Praetor* of Germania, and the Imperial Legate, had accompanied Germanicus on his embassage, supposedly because of his extensive experience in both the military and diplomatic arenas, but naturally, there were a number of rumors floating around about what was actually going on. Also missing was Aulus Caecina, who had finally retired from public life and remained in Rome as well, which meant that Varro was currently the highest ranking official present in Mogontiacum and was, in effect, running the province. I would come to learn more about Lucius Visellius Varro, and more than once, I have wondered how I would have behaved if I knew at that moment what I know now; the best conclusion I have reached is that in all likelihood, my ignorance probably saved my life. At the time, all I knew about Varro was that he was old to be a *Quaestor*, that his father had been Consul about five years earlier, and that he was well connected, although this was not much of a revelation. If Silius had been here, I was certain that Sacrovir would have been on firmer ground, but Varro was more of an unknown quality; at least, that was my assumption. One piece of information that I recalled in the moment was a passing comment Sacrovir had made on the march back from Rome, that Nerva had boasted about his relationship with Varro, begun when Varro arrived in Mogontiacum in early Februarius to assume his duties.

"Nerva swears that he has the new *Quaestor* ready to sit up and beg if that's what he wants," Sacrovir had commented.

"Primus Pilus," I spoke up in his office. "I'll go with them, if only to keep an eye on the men."

I also wanted a chance to talk to Florus, because at that point, I strongly suspected that Bibulus or Nerva were lying about Florus' supposed statement of my collusion.

"We will be transferring them from the camp *praetorium* into the city, where they will be questioned further," Bibulus announced.

"As long as you keep in mind that they're under the standard and aren't to be treated like common criminals," Sacrovir said firmly. "Which means that you won't be marching them through this camp in chains." We could instantly see by the shared expression of disappointment of both Nerva and Bibulus that this was exactly what they had intended. "Give us a moment in private," Sacrovir addressed Bibulus, making it clear that it was not a request. "Pullus and I have some things to discuss."

When Bibulus opened his mouth to protest, it was actually Nerva who stopped him, and I could just hear him mutter, "He's not going anywhere, Bibulus." To Sacrovir, he said curtly, "I'll be waiting in the outer office."

Once they left, Sacrovir wasted no time, keeping his voice low, but I could clearly hear the urgency. "Pullus, don't do anything stupid and give Nerva and that *cunnus* provost the chance they're looking for." Frankly, I was somewhat miffed that he felt the need to issue this warning, but when I opened my mouth to protest, he cut me off. "I've seen what happens when you lose your temper, Gnaeus. And Nerva has seen the result of it with Petronius, so you can bet a year's pay that they're going to try and make you lose your temper." It was good advice, and I knew it, yet at the same time, I felt that mulish stubbornness that was such a source of exasperation for my mother and still is for Bronwen, although I did manage to refrain from saying that I would like to see them try it. Instead, I assured him that I would do my utmost to maintain my self-control. Moving on, he assured me, "I'm going to speak to Varro first thing in the morning."

"You mean that I'm going to have to spend the night at the *Praetorium*?" I made no attempt to hide my dismay, although in the moment, I was thinking more about Bronwen being angry at my absence, which I would learn very quickly was the least of my concerns.

"Maybe if you manage to guard your tongue and keep your temper in check, Nerva may let you go. But," he finished grimly, "I don't think that's very likely, if I'm being honest."

Primus Pilus Sacrovir was right.

Our walk out of camp and across the bridge into the city and to the *Praetorium* was mostly silent, except for a moment when Bibulus had the temerity to try and seize me by the arm as we left Sacrovir's quarters.

"You know what the punishment for laying hands on a Centurion of Rome is, *provost*?" I snarled.

"My authority comes from the *Praetor*," Bibulus insisted, then thought to amend, "Or in this case, the *Quaestor* since *Praetor* Silius is absent. And I have the right to take anyone into custody..."

"He's not in custody, Bibulus," Nerva snapped. "You don't want to end up like Petronius, do you? I know you and he were...close, but I don't think you want to share his fate."

There was no mistaking the leering quality to Nerva's tone, while the provost looked as if he had been slapped, but all I cared about was that his hand dropped back to his side.

I knew I should thank Nerva for his help; instead, I heard myself saying, "You've been waiting a long time for this, haven't you, Nerva?"

"I don't know what you're talking about, Pullus," Nerva replied stiffly, but I noticed he refused to look in my direction.

"Yes you do," I snorted. There had been something bothering me, and I decided that bringing it up would not make matters any worse. "You could have gotten your revenge in Rome by refusing to participate in what Primus Pilus Sacrovir did to support me and Tribune Asprenas. If it had just been the 1st, Galba probably would have thought it worth the risk to arrest us. And," I reminded him, "at the very least, it would have ruined my career, which is all this is about now."

"That was different," Nerva replied angrily. "And this is about *justice*, nothing more!"

"For who?" I shot back, but then we arrived at the doors to the brick *Praetorium*, and by silent consent, we stopped our bickering, neither of us wanting the pair of rankers standing duty to overhear us.

When we entered, I saw that we were headed for the stairs leading down into the basement level, where there was storage space and a series of cells where I assumed my men would be held. The stench assaulted my nostrils before we were halfway down, as I realized that I had never had occasion to visit this part of the *Praetorium* in Mogontiacum, but it was the sight that greeted me that caused me to whirl about and, without thinking, grab Bibulus by the collar of his leather cuirass then begin shaking him like a dog shakes a rat.

"*What have you done to Gregarius Florus?*" I bellowed, loudly enough that it made even me wince because of the enclosed space. "*You tortured him, you gutless* cunnus! *Why?*"

Bibulus was terrified now, to the point I heard the clatter of his cudgel dropping to the stone floor, and he began babbling, "I didn't touch the *Gregarius*, Centurion!"

"Then who did?" I demanded. "And who authorized it?"

Bibulus betrayed Nerva then, his eyes darting over to the

Primus Pilus, who glared up at me in defiance.

"*Gregarius* Florus was refusing to cooperate," he snapped. "He needed some...persuasion."

With my free hand, I pointed to Florus, who was lying in the nearest cell, and even in the dim light of the pair of oil lamps hanging from the opposite wall, it was clear to see that Florus had been savagely and thoroughly beaten.

"Persuasion?" I sneered. "You call that *persuasion?*" Only then did something else occur to me. "And by what right does a Centurion have to order punishment of a ranker from another Legion without consulting with that man's Centurion?"

In that moment, I was certain I had scored a telling blow, because it is absolutely unthinkable for a Centurion from another Legion to unilaterally decide to punish a ranker from another Legion without consulting with a Centurion from that man's Legion, so I was completely unprepared for Nerva's reaction, which was a grim smile.

"I was given permission by *Quaestor* Varro," he said coolly. "He's as concerned as I am that the men of the 1ˢᵗ have a bad habit of accosting and either injuring or killing my men."

Realizing that, at least in the moment, I was outflanked, I deliberately changed the subject, addressing Bibulus. "Have any of you thought to summon a *medicus?*"

The provost looked uncomfortable, but he mumbled, "Not yet, Centurion. We haven't had time."

"Oh, I know," I shot back scornfully. "You've been too busy dragging me and my men here and trying to make a show of it for the Primus Pilus here." I pointed at Nerva, knowing that he would not like it but not caring. "Now, go fetch a *medicus*. In the meantime, I'm going to do what I can for him."

I did not wait for an acknowledgement, or a protest, turning and walking to the cell, which was nothing more than a stout wooden cage on three sides, with one of the outer walls serving as the back of the cell, while the door was secured by a simple latch, around which was a chain and lock, although while the cell door was closed, it was not secured with the chain. As bad as it was from a distance, when I knelt next to Florus, it was even worse, and I heard myself gasping. This was how I learned Florus was conscious, because he moved his head in the direction of my voice much as a blind man does. His eyes were swollen completely shut, and blood was caked around them, while his nose was similarly swollen and little more than a misshapen lump. He opened his mouth, and I could see the jagged stumps of his teeth, but it was how his lower jaw was misaligned, with the left side of his jaw a bit higher than the right side that told me it had been shattered, making me wonder if he would ever be able to eat solid foods again.

"C...Centurion P-Pullus? Is that you?"

I supposed that because of his teeth, his speech had a sibilant, hissing quality, and I was amazed he could speak at all because of his jaw, but I answered quickly, "Yes, it's me, Florus. Now, save your strength. I've sent for a *medicus*."

I do not know what I was expecting, but it was not what sounded like a laugh, although it quickly ended with a wet cough, and because I was kneeling next to him, I felt the spray of blood spattering my arms.

"I appreciate it, Centurion, but it's too late. That bastard Canus broke me up good. I'm bleeding inside, I can feel it."

"Canus?"

"He's a member of the *Praetor*'s staff," I heard Nerva say behind me, close enough to tell me that he had moved so that he could listen to us.

Turning to look over my shoulder, I saw that he was standing in the open doorway of the cell.

"A 'member of the *Praetor*'s staff'?" I mimicked, and I saw his face darken. "You mean he's a torturer."

"That's one of his duties," Nerva allowed reluctantly.

"Centurion," Florus whispered, and when I turned my attention back to him, I could clearly hear that he was wheezing even more than he had been just a moment before, but then I saw the frothy bubbles on his lips. "I-I want to tell you that I'm sorry. I didn't want to, but that *cunnus* just wouldn't stop..." His voice broke then, and he began sobbing, spraying me again with his blood, but despite the fact that I was certain he could not see me do so, I did not recoil or wipe my face. In that moment, I was struggling with my own sense of guilt and shame at the thoughts I had entertained less than a watch earlier about how Florus being executed would be overall a positive development for the Fifth Century. Seeing his battered body, lying on the cold stone floor of a cell, as he was breathing what I was sure he knew would be his last breaths, suddenly I was not nearly as certain of that as I had been.

Realizing that my time was limited, I leaned closer to Florus and whispered, "Florus, I don't blame you for whatever you told Canus, but I *do* need to know what you said about me. And," I warned him, "please keep your voice down. Nerva is standing nearby."

He did not answer immediately, his breathing having become even more labored, and I was about to repeat myself when he finally responded, thankfully in a wheezy whisper, "Canus told me that he would stop if I just said 'Yes' to the questions he was asking me." Suddenly, one of Florus' hands shot out, fumbling for my arm, but his fingers had been broken, so he couldn't actually grasp it. "Centurion, I swear on our eagle that I held out for as long as I could! But he said the only way it would stop is if I either answered yes...or die."

"I believe you, Florus," I assured him, although I would have said it even if I did not, but the fact was that I did believe him. Because of my distraction, it took him saying something a second time for my mind to register it as significant, but before I pressed him, I glanced over my shoulder again to see Nerva, still standing there, except he was now clearly nervous. Returning my attention to Florus, I bent over even closer to ask, "Florus, are you telling me that Canus basically said everything, and all you had to do was say yes or no?" He nodded, and I continued, "What was it Canus said?"

"Just that you told me where to find that *cunnus* who stole Minerva from me," Florus muttered, and even whispering, I could hear the bitterness in his voice; more than that, the hurt of a man who feels betrayed, making me wonder about this Minerva, and worry that he would forget what the topic was. At first, my fear seemed justified. "I should have known that once a whore, always a whore," he said, but before I could admonish him, he continued, "He also wanted me to say yes to supposedly telling you that I was going to kill..." he cocked his head, "...what was his name, Centurion? The man I...killed, I mean?"

"Ambustus," I told him, a bit louder than necessary, and I was rewarded by the hiss of indrawn breath behind me that confirmed Nerva was still listening. Dropping back to a whisper, I felt it necessary to remind him, "Florus, you know that your fate is sealed, don't you? That there's nothing I can do that will save you from being executed?"

I was relieved to see him nod.

"I know, Centurion," he said simply. Then, he gave that rasping laugh again. "I knew that when I walked into that *cac*hole...what was it called?" I supplied the name. "That's right. The Happy Legionary. But if I can't live with Minerva," he shrugged one shoulder, and I assumed his other one was injured in some way, "I didn't see the point. Centurion Pullus," there was a new note to his tone, a pleading quality, which I quickly understood, "before I cross the river, I do have one favor to ask." I confess I was not eager to agree, which was the cause for my hesitation, and he asked, "Please?"

"If I can," I said cautiously.

"Please forgive me, Centurion. I know that I've been on the Century's bad books more than most men, and you haven't been the Hastatus Prior for that long, but I swear on the black stone that I didn't want to give that bastard what he wanted!" He gave a choked sob. "I just couldn't take the pain anymore! So, please, I beg you!"

What, I thought, do I do? The truth was that I had been prepared to be angry at Florus, and essentially tell him that he was getting what he deserved, but at least for me, when you are looking down at man who has been so savagely and thoroughly beaten that, even if he survived, and was not going to be executed and only flogged, he would never be under the standard again because he would be crippled for life, it is hard to stay angry.

I heard footsteps descending the stairs, and assuming that it was Bibulus returning with a *medicus*, I briefly considered waiting to reply until after the *medicus* did what he could, but quickly discarded it.

Giving him an awkward pat, I said, "I do forgive you, Florus, and I don't blame you. If I had to go through what you've gone through," I said honestly, "I suspect I'd have done the same thing."

Florus replied with another sob, then Nerva announced tonelessly, "The *medicus* is here at your request, Centurion Pullus. Please step aside so that Brennus here can do his work."

Only later did I realize that I should have been warned by Nerva's use of the *medicus'* name, but I was sufficiently distracted, although I did notice that, while he had the bag slung over his shoulder, the man, short and completely bald, seemed uneasy, which I put down to the circumstances.

I suppose Florus heard Brennus approaching, because he used the last of his waning strength to call out, "I want to change my statement! I lied to Canus about what Hastatus Prior Pullus knew! He never told me anything, and I didn't tell him that I was going to kill anyone! He didn't know!"

I could not help shooting Nerva a triumphant look, but he did not look surprised, or all that angry, another warning that I missed. My attention was turned back to Florus because, immediately after his outburst, he began wheezing, and yet Brennus did not seem to be in all that much of a hurry, unslinging his bag as he knelt by my man in an almost leisurely fashion. As I dictate these words to Alex, I now realize I have no excuse for being surprised by what was coming. Florus' wheezing was becoming worse with every heartbeat, and he began arching his back as he struggled to get enough air into his lungs, while the *medicus* leaned over and placed his ear against the ranker's chest.

"A rib must have punctured his lung," Brennus announced after he sat back upright, yet instead of looking at me, he looked to Nerva, saying nothing but shaking his head.

"Pullus," Nerva spoke softly, indicating with his head to follow him out of the cell, where he walked over to the stairway before he addressed me. "Your man is going to die," he said flatly.

"Yes, I gathered as much," I replied, trying to maintain a neutral tone and not sound accusatory.

"While by regulations we should do whatever we can to keep him alive so that he can be tried before he's executed, I don't think that will be possible." I agreed, though I did not see why he would care, and when I said as much, he replied, "I won't pretend that I don't want to see him punished, Pullus. But I'm not a cruel man, no matter what you may think. Brennus," he nodded towards what I thought was the *medicus*, "can send him on his way, just as if he was on the battlefield and couldn't be saved."

I should have known better; I should have asked where the other three of my men were, but since they were not in either of the other cells, I assumed they had not been retrieved yet, but Florus was in obvious agony, and as irritated as I was with him, and with all of the liars, lame, and lazy like Florus, I had no desire to watch him suffer more, so I nodded to Nerva, who signaled Brennus. Who, as I expected, withdrew a bronze razor from his satchel, although it took him some rummaging to find it. Normally, men look away when a comrade's life was being ended in this fashion, but I was his Centurion, so I left Nerva and walked back to Florus, kneeling down beside him and taking one of his hands, yet while I tried to be gentle, he still winced from the pain to his shattered fingers.

"Florus," I said quietly, "we're going to be sending you on your way now, do you understand?"

"W-wait," he gasped, but instead of wanting to postpone his death like I assumed, he managed, "Where's Vibius? He has my will, and I want to say goodbye."

It took a heartbeat for me to recall that Vibius was Paterculus' *praenomen*, which in turn made me think about where the other three men were, so I turned to ask Nerva and Bibulus. Things happened very quickly then, but I turned just in time to see Nerva clearly signal Brennus, and Florus gave a gurgling scream, causing my head to swivel back to Brennus, who was frantically sawing his razor back and forth across Florus' throat.

"*What are you doing?*" I bellowed, never seeing a *medicus* botch a job so thoroughly, and this was the instant where the thought that Brennus was not what Nerva said he was first entered my mind.

Florus was thrashing about, and for the first, and last time, he managed to open his eyes widely enough that I could see them, even with all the swelling; I will take the look in those

41

eyes across the river in Charon's Boat with me, and without thinking, I laid my body across his, snatching the razor from Brennus, and sliced his throat, deep and wide. It was over in less than another three or four heartbeats; then I stood up and turned on Nerva and Bibulus.

"Where are my other men? Why aren't they here yet?"

"They are here," Nerva countered. Then, he pointed to the opposite side of the room from the cells, and that was the first time I noticed the single door, made of solid wood but with a grated grill. "They're in the secure cell."

I was about to demand to know why, but then it came to me; unlike the three open cells, anyone inside the secure cell could not see out, because the cell was built into the wall. Unless, of course, the small wooden door that covered up the gate was open, but I was not surprised to see that, when I strode across the room, it was shut. It also told me that they had already been brought here, or perhaps I had been too distracted dealing with Florus and had not noticed them being escorted past us. This was disturbing in itself, but hearing my men talking in low tones inside the cell drove that question from the forefront of my mind, yet when I tried to open the heavy wooden door, it was locked and I turned to Bibulus and ordered him to come unlock it.

When he looked to Nerva first, I had had enough, and I snapped, "You can either come do it yourself, or I can come and take that fucking key and do it myself, Bibulus. Nerva doesn't command my men; I do."

Bibulus did come then, though not without another glance at Nerva first, fumbling with the key in such a way that it made me think that this was another delaying tactic, or it could have just been I was seeing what I wanted to see at this point. When the door swung open, the interior was so dark that I had to reach over and snatch up one of the oil lamps before entering the cell. My three men were standing there, blinking against the light, and I noticed how they stood side by side, making it impossible for anyone to get around them, but it was how they all had their fists clenched in a signal they were ready to fight that made me proud and concerned in equal measure. Whether it was my size or that my features were illuminated, I saw the expressions of relief on their faces, and as one they came up to me.

"Thank the gods!" Dentulus exclaimed. "Centurion, what's happening?"

"You mean you don't know?" I asked in surprise.

"No, sir," Paterculus, Florus' close comrade answered. "Just that provosts showed up and said we were to come with them to the *Praetorium*." His expression altered slightly, and he glanced at the other two before he continued, "I mean, I know that it has to be about Aulus, but we haven't seen him and had a chance to talk to him either."

"Wait." I was startled. "What do you mean you haven't seen him?" I gestured over my shoulder. "He's out there in one of the cells."

This was clearly news to them, and Dentulus assured me, "He wasn't there when they brought us in and stuck us in here, Centurion."

This answered my question about when they had actually been taken from camp, which meant that at the very least Bibulus had lied to Sacrovir about escorting them here since they had clearly been here for some time, but there was a more pressing issue as far as I was concerned.

"You didn't hear what he just said?" I asked, my heart sinking at their look of confusion.

"We heard voices, but with the door closed and that grill shut, it's impossible for us to make anything out." Serranus spoke for the first time, and he added grimly, "And trust me, Centurion, we tried. Each of us put our ear up against the door once we heard the talking."

I did not want to, but I felt compelled to ask, "And did you hear anything else? I mean, before that?" When it was clear they did not comprehend my meaning, I realized that they were about to see the evidence themselves, but I wanted to prepare them, particularly Paterculus. "So, you didn't hear any...screaming? Or anything that sounded like someone being tortured?" Dentulus and Serranus looked alarmed, while Paterculus suddenly looked ill, but they all shook their heads, and I told them, "A man from the torture detachment worked Florus over. He's in one of the cells out there now, and...he didn't survive."

The other two men immediately looked to Paterculus, Dentulus reaching out to grasp the man's shoulder, and I decided then I would not mention that Florus broke under torture, even though he had recanted just before he died.

"Follow me," I said. "At the very least, you should be out of this *ca*chole sitting in the dark. Although," I warned them, "while I'm going to try to make certain that you can return back to camp with me, Primus Pilus Nerva and that *cunnus* provost Bibulus are doing their best to make life difficult, but you at least won't go blind."

They did not look happy, but I did not blame them, and I led them out into the larger room, where the first thing I saw was Nerva, Bibulus, and Brennus standing huddled together; it was the manner in which they suddenly stopped talking and Brennus looked as if he had been caught stealing a candied fruit that made me stop momentarily. Since they were standing at the far end, next to the stairway, I told the other three to stay put, and I approached the trio.

Nerva cleared his throat, then said, "Under the circumstances, Pullus, I believe that your men can return to the 1st's area. And," he did look, if not ashamed then uncomfortable, "they can take Florus' body with them." Looking past me, he called out, "Which of you is Florus' close comrade?" Paterculus identified himself, albeit in a sullen tone, but Nerva made no issue of it. I understood why when he said, "While I'm allowing you to take your comrade with you, you are not to complete the burial rites yet. Do *not* clean his body in case *Quaestor* Varro wants to examine it himself."

This was when I and the other three men realized that all Nerva cared about was getting rid of a dead body before it started to stink, confirmed by the angry muttering behind me, but while I considered making an issue of it, in the moment, all I thought about was that Nerva was releasing my men, so I confess I spoke more harshly than necessary, snapping, "*Silete.* Do as the Primus Pilus says. Take Florus with us."

Nerva did not say anything, but as I was about to learn, this was on purpose, because he must have sensed that my use of "us" was a ploy. I stepped aside to let the three file past, and

they went into the cell, bending down and, with a tenderness
that would seem odd to anyone who had never witnessed it
before, lifted Florus' body off the stone floor. With some
difficulty, they maneuvered through the cell door, as Nerva and
the other two scrambled out of the way to avoid being spattered
by any of the blood still dripping from Florus' corpse. His head
lolled back with that limpness only the dead possess, which in
turn made the slash across his throat gape open, the blood still
oozing, but even through the gore I could see the cords and
tendons that I had severed, along with the marks made by
Brennus' botched attempt. Once they passed and began
ascending the stairs, I moved to follow them, which was the
moment Nerva sprang his trap. The fact that he was the one
who stepped into my path was no accident, because just as it is
illegal for a provost or anyone of a lesser rank to put their hands
on a Centurion, the same held true among the Centurionate,
especially a Primus Pilus.

"Where do you think you're going, Pullus?" Nerva asked
in what was almost a conversational tone.

Even though I had begun to have a suspicion that there
was something afoot, I still was surprised.

"I'm heading back to the 1st with my men, Primus Pilus.
You heard Florus. He recanted!"

Nerva feigned a look that I suppose was meant to convey
his confusion, shaking his head as he said, "I'm not sure what
you're talking about, Pullus. Florus was unconscious the whole
time. He never said a word."

Unlike Nerva's, my own astonishment was completely
unfeigned, even as a part of me was inwardly groaning for not
seeing this coming, and I did not even bother looking at
Bibulus, who was openly smirking, choosing instead to turn to
Brennus, who, if I was any judge, was seriously considering
dashing up the stairs.

I suppose he realized by my stare that he would have to
speak up, but what came out was a squeak, and it took him two
tries before he got out, "It...it...is as Primus Pilus Nerva says.
The prisoner never regained consciousness, and his injuries
were so severe that I had no choice but to..."

"*You* had no choice?" I sneered, realizing I had taken a

step towards Brennus only by the manner in which he leapt backward, his feet tangling together and sending him staggering backward to land heavily on his ass on the stairs. "You *butchered* Florus, you incompetent *cunnus*! I'm the one who ended his suffering, not you!"

"That's your version," Nerva said, and now I heard the smugness there, of the type when a man is certain that he has outwitted an adversary. "However, both Provost Bibulus and I were here, and we saw that Brennus performed his duty to the best of his ability. And," he reminded me of the salient point, "that *Gregarius* Florus was unconscious the whole time and never made any kind of statement." He turned and addressed Bibulus, "Provost, I think that, given the gravity of the situation, Primus Hastatus Prior Pullus should be kept in the secure cell. *Gregarius Immunes* Ambustus was *very* popular, and if word gets out about Florus' confession that Centurion Pullus knew beforehand what he intended for Ambustus, well," he gave an elaborate shrug, "I'm afraid some of my boys might be tempted to take justice into their own hands. Do you agree?"

"Absolutely, Primus Pilus." Bibulus nodded, and while I had just met the man, I was certain that he was happier than he had ever been in his life. "It's wise to take precautions." Turning to me, he said with an unctuous smile, "It's for your own safety, Centurion."

My mind was racing, and for the span of a heartbeat, I seriously considered forcing the issue and following my men, who had ascended the stairs by this point, but seeing that I was not behind them, I heard Serranus call down, "Centurion Pullus? Are you coming?"

I swallowed the hard, bitter lump down and called back, "No. I'm still being detained by the Primus Pilus. He," I did not need to try and sound scornful, "is terrified that he can't control his own men and says he's doing it for my safety, but that's a lie. Go tell the Primus Pilus they're holding me, and in the cell you were in. He'll know what to do."

That, at least, was my hope. Without another word, and with Nerva glaring at me with a poisonous hatred, I turned and walked to the cell. It was as the door slammed shut that I remembered; something similar to this had happened to my father when he was serving in Pannonia. Maybe, I thought with bitter humor, the gods just want me to feel closer to him.

Chapter 2

One thing I learned very quickly, that when you are in utter darkness, with no way to see the sun, or the moon for that matter, it is very easy to lose track of time. At least, that was the case with me, and once I learned what my men had told me, that even with an ear pressed to the door, as long as whoever was on the other side was not speaking loudly, it was impossible to make out what was being said, I decided to settle down and rest. I found the slop bucket by kicking it, some of the contents sloshing out onto my foot, the feeling and smell making me gag, but after some more groping, I found the hard wooden surface of the cot that was chained to the wall. When I dropped down onto it, it gave a sharp cracking sound that, in turn elicited an alarmed squeak from something in the corner of the cell, followed by the scurrying of little paws as whatever it was went dashing for safety. The truth is that I barely noticed, because right then, I was in a bit of a daze, trying to understand how something that I was barely involved in could have landed me in a totally dark, damp cell with only a rat for company. Hard on that thought was the image of Bronwen and the baby, who were presumably still at my mother's villa, and as much to pass the time as anything, I began thinking through the likely series of events that transpired after I left for the *Praetorium*. Alex had been in the outer office with Melander, but at the moment I could not recall what I told him to do; stay put in Sacrovir's office to wait on developments, or go to my mother's villa to inform them that I would be delayed. I dimly recalled it being the latter, which would likely mean that Alex was in the city and not back in camp, so that when Dentulus and the others returned to the camp with Florus' body and reported to Sacrovir, there would be a further delay in Alex learning of my whereabouts. Immediately on the heels of that,

I realized that it was far more likely that the three men reported to Bibaculus; the idea of three rankers from another Century feeling confident enough to go knocking on Sacrovir's door was very remote. Ultimately, I decided that the best I could hope for was that Sacrovir would appear within a third or at most two-thirds of a watch, reminding myself that, as important as this was to me, Sacrovir had an entire Legion to run. Specifically, arranging for transport the final leg back to Ubiorum was a massive undertaking, no matter how many times it had occurred. This was my last thought before I fell into a light doze.

The noise that brought me awake was far more than conversation, and the quality of it got my heart racing, my first thought being that there was a small riot taking place just on the other side of my door, my second being that perhaps it was my men coming to my rescue. As I would learn, my first idea was not far from the truth, but all I could tell pressing my ear against the door was that it involved far more than just a handful of people, they were all men, and the tone seemed to be split equally between angry protest and bellowed orders, along with sharp cries of pain. Only gradually did the noise die down to a buzzing hum that was similar in nature to when the men were standing in the ranks, waiting for the call to *intente*, and I have no idea how long I stood there before returning to my cot. This time, I was more careful about taking my seat, realizing that I was both hungry and thirsty, but I was certain that Sacrovir, or perhaps Bibaculus, would be showing up virtually any moment. And, not long afterward, I heard the rattling of keys, bringing me to my feet. I did not expect to see Sacrovir, and while it was a provost, it was not Bibulus but one of the men who had shown up with Nerva at Sacrovir's quarters. He did not say anything, just stepped aside in a gesture that I should exit the cell; when I did, I could not suppress a gasp of shock. All three open cells were crammed full of men, but more than that, it was how many of them I recognized, one in particular, that wrenched the gasp from my lips.

"*Lentulus*? What are you doing here?"

My *Signifer*, who had leapt to his feet when he saw me emerge from the secure cell, shook his head. Pointing at the provost who had opened the cell, he said disgustedly, "Ask him, Centurion, because none of us have any idea."

I turned to the provost, a mousy little man with a weak chin who had one slightly crossed eye, which meant I was not sure if he was looking at me when he replied, "Orders from the *Quaestor*. All men of the 1st who were outside the camp were outside without permission. And," he shrugged, "we rounded them up."

"That's not true!" I exclaimed. "Primus Pilus Sacrovir gave the men the liberty of the city! I was there when he did it!"

"Yes," the provost seemingly agreed, "but that was for yesterday only. Once the midnight watch ended, that liberty expired, and the *Quaestor* gave orders to round up these men for violation of orders."

I was too astounded, and alarmed, to argue the point, so I did not try, asking instead, "Am I being released? Why did you come get me?"

"The *Quaestor* wants to question you," he said, then indicated the stairway with his arm. Only then did I see that Bibulus was standing there with a pair of other men, while Bibulus was grinning broadly and tapping his cudgel into one palm.

"Lentulus," I called to my *Signifer*, "I'll get to the bottom of this."

"Thank you, Centurion," he called after me as I headed for the stairs, but while he dropped his voice, I heard him mutter, "but it looks like you've got problems of your own."

Which was certainly the truth, although I took a petty revenge by suddenly speeding up the last couple of paces, as if I was charging at Bibulus, then quickly pivoted to bound up the stairs, while he let out a surprised squawk as he tried to hop out of the path he thought I was going to take right through him. The roars of laughter were my reward, but it was when I reached the top of the stairs that I got another surprise, in the form of the light streaming through the windows.

"What time is it?" I asked the provost who was still by my

side.

For a heartbeat, it seemed as if he was not inclined to answer, then shrugged and said, "About a third of a watch after first call."

I had been summoned to Sacrovir's well before midnight, it having just gotten dark, so clearly, what I thought of as a short doze had been longer, but it also meant that Bronwen and my mother would be beside themselves with worry. There was not much time to dwell on this because the provost reached the door to the office normally occupied by the *Praetor*, while the small desk that effectively blocked the door was similarly occupied by a rather nondescript man who, while not looking over much like a scribe, certainly did not look like the man the provost was about to identify.

"Canus, is *Quaestor* Varro ready for the Centurion?"

Canus, who had thinning hair and a long, lean face that, in a moment of insight, made me think that Canus might be his *cognomen*, barely glanced up from the scroll he was examining. Thanks to my height, I could see that, instead of writing, it contained drawings, of the type that a certain type of man likes to indulge in; that I was of that type before meeting Bronwen should be enough to tell you what they were. I did spot some scrapes on his knuckles, and they seemed to be uniformly distributed between his first and second knuckles, telling me that, while he had had his hands wrapped for beating Florus, he had either improperly applied the *pankration* bandages, or they had slipped.

He must have sensed my gaze because, as he set the scroll down, he looked up at me, offering a slight smile, then stood and said in a bored tone, "I'll go see."

By the time he reached the door, I was yearning for the opportunity to beat him to death, and I offered up a quick prayer to the gods to make it so. Rapping three times in rapid succession, he opened the door and disappeared without being bade to enter, which I took to mean that the pair had a deeper relationship than one might assume. He was not gone long, probably no more than a pair of heartbeats, before reopening the door to beckon to me. I do not know why, but I was surprised when the provost, instead of coming with me, turned and walked off; I was *not* surprised when, after I entered, Canus made no move to leave, closing the door before walking to the opposite side of the room so that he would be behind me as I stood facing Varro seated behind the desk.

I had seen the *Quaestor* once before, though only at a distance, and he had not warranted more than a quick glance on my part, so I took the opportunity to examine him more thoroughly on my short approach, stopping the prescribed pace away. What I took in was a type of man with whom I had become familiar in Rome; in fact, he reminded me of Tribune Galba, although they did not physically resemble each other. Perhaps it was the pomade that I could smell, the rings on every finger, or the fine cut of his tunic with the purple Senatorial stripe. I doubted he was thirty-two, the ancient minimum for a man to be in the Senate, although that was essentially a thing of the past thanks to Divus Augustus, who lowered it to twenty-five; the fact that he was wearing that stripe also marked him as a dangerous man. Overall, before my time in Rome, I would have dismissed Lucius Varro as a threat, simply because he exuded softness, but I had learned a hard lesson that there was more than one battlefield, and just because this Varro would have lasted only a matter of heartbeats against me with a *gladius*, it did not mean he was not a threat. Nevertheless, when I squared myself in front of my desk, I refused to render a salute; in our hierarchy, a *Quaestor* outranks Tribunes, which means they outrank Centurions, but Varro was a civil *Quaestor* and not attached to the Legions in any way.

"You requested to see me, *Quaestor*?" I did try to sound polite but not deferential, although his expression betrayed nothing about how he felt about my small act of defiance.

I suspected that his refusal to answer immediately was both repayment and perhaps a warning, but despite the fact that I was staring at a point above his head, I could see him studying me.

Finally, he gave a sniff, then said in a level, almost bored tone, "I did, Centurion. But," he added with a smile, "you mischaracterized it. It wasn't a request."

Understanding the game, that he was trying to impose his authority, I actually felt more comfortable, which sounds odd,

I know.

Pretending to be puzzled, I replied, "I didn't realize that you held a military command, *Quaestor*. That would be the only way that you have the authority to order me to report. I," I returned his smile with as much sincerity as his was offered, "am simply being courteous."

"In the absence of the *Praetor*," Varro replied tightly, "I am the ranking authority. And," he emphasized, "*Praetor* Silius is also the supreme Legate of the Army of both the Upper and Lower Rhenus, is he not? Therefore," he held his hands out, palms up, in a gesture of helplessness, "it follows that in his absence, my authority extends to both the civil and military administration."

I pretended to consider this before dropping my gaze to look him in the eye while asking, "And I suppose you can point out the regulation that makes that clear?" I indicated the wooden rack that we use to store scrolls against one wall. "Maybe they're over there," I said helpfully.

Varro glared up at me, and I heard a soft scraping sound behind me that indicated that Canus was moving, and I glanced over my shoulder at him, causing him to freeze, although he returned my stare without any trace of fear or concern, telling me that he either thought very highly of himself...or he did not know anything about me.

Returning my attention to Varro, he broke his glare first to answer with a sigh, "Centurion, I don't have the time to rummage through hundreds of scrolls to find something that supports my position." His expression changed, subtly but noticeably, giving me the impression that he had thought of something, which he confirmed by pointing out, "But this matter of the attack of *your Gregarius*..." he glanced down at a tablet laying open on his desk, "Florus, on *Gregarius Immunes* Ambustus occurred out in the city and not in the camp. Is that correct?"

"It is," I replied; I had known that my ploy was not likely to work in the long run, for the very reason he was citing now, but my heart still sank nonetheless.

"That makes it a civil matter, and as such it falls under my jurisdiction, which gives me the authority to summon anyone I deem important to the investigation. And," he tried to sound regretful; or, perhaps he did not, "according to this," he indicated the tablet, and for the first time, I noticed a dark smudge on the wood that was likely blood, "we have the testimony of *Gregarius Ordinarius* Florus that you were aware of his plans to *murder Gregarius Immunes* Ambustus of the First Century, Fifth Cohort of the 5ᵗʰ Alaudae. So," he shrugged again, "I'm confident that *Praetor* Silius will support my actions in this matter."

Deciding at that moment not to pursue this approach any longer, I did point to the tablet, asking bluntly, "That smudge there. Is that blood?"

Varro looked down at the tablet with a frown, then visibly recoiled as he dropped it on his desk, telling me that he had either not noticed it or had thought it was something else.

"It appears so," he replied cautiously, "but I'm not sure why that's relevant."

"It's relevant because it's either the blood of *Gregarius* Florus or the man who tortured him." I turned and looked directly at Canus as I said, "And I don't see any marks anywhere on Canus here that indicates that it's his, although," I pointed to the scrapes on his hand, "I suppose it could have come from those. You *are* the brave one who beat and tortured a bound man, aren't you?" For the first time, Canus' face registered emotion, in the form of a scowl, but he compounded his error by clenching his fists and took a step towards me. "That would be a mistake, *freedman*," I sneered, and held out my hands. "I'm not trussed up like a pig."

My taunt about Canus' status had been a guess; he was not wearing the normal attire of a freedman, but I had learned that the farther one gets from Rome, the laxer the authorities are about whether a freed slave can wear an Equestrian tunic, or even a toga. From the deep flush that darkened his otherwise sallow features, and the manner in which his lips pulled back from his teeth in a snarl, I realized I had guessed correctly. And, I thought, he *does* look like a dog right now.

"Centurion, I would be careful about insulting my...servant," Varro spoke up, but I was certain I heard a nervous edge to his voice. "He represents me in important matters."

"Like torturing a Legionary?" I retorted. "Who is a Roman *citizen*, and not a freedman?"

"*Gregarius* Florus refused to cooperate," Canus spoke for the first time. "I had no choice but to use...other means."

"You mean that he refused to agree to say what you told him to say," I shot back, then before Canus could respond, I addressed Varro. "*Quaestor*, I'm certain you had nothing to do with it, but your servant here beat Florus in order to get him to bear false testimony about my role in what happened at The Happy Legionary."

"Oh?" Varro arched an eyebrow, then leaned over slightly to look past me at Canus. "What is he talking about, Canus?"

"I have no idea, *Quaestor*," Canus replied, but before I could say anything, he added, "but given what *Gregarius* Florus said, I can see why the Centurion is so eager to call it into doubt."

"Yes," Varro agreed quickly. "I agree, which is why you are here now, Centurion. *Gregarius* Florus' confession of your role is a *very* serious matter, wouldn't you agree?"

"I would," I agreed, which clearly surprised him, "but that 'confession'," I pointed at it and made no attempt to hide my contempt, "isn't worth the wax it's inscribed on. Besides," I finished, "he recanted just before he died."

At this point, I was certain that Varro was at least aware of Nerva's enmity towards me, and that it was a strong possibility that he might know something about what Nerva was up to, but what I did not know was the depth of his knowledge, and, judging from the manner in which he reacted, he had not been informed about this; it was yet one more thing I would turn out to be wrong about.

"Oh?" he asked with what seemed like genuine surprise, and once more leaned over to address Canus. "Is that true, Canus?"

"Not according to the witnesses who were there," Canus replied, not even bothering to hide his pleasure.

"Wait," I interjected, and turned to face Canus directly, not wanting to miss something. "How could you know? This just happened, and you weren't down there."

"Yes, Canus, how could you have heard something about an event that just happened?"

I regretted my decision to face Canus, because there was something in the way Varro said this that seemed odd to me, as if he was prompting his torturer.

"I just happened to bump into Primus Pilus' man Brennus," Canus answered, and for the first time, I saw a glimmer of hesitation. "He told me about it."

I wasted no time in pouncing. "Told you about what? If it didn't happen as you say, he'd have no reason to mention it."

"How should I know why he mentioned it?" Canus retorted, but he was clearly rattled now.

I did not even bother with Canus, knowing that, ultimately, it was Varro who mattered, and I turned back to look at him just in time to catch his glare at the other man.

He cleared his throat before he said, "Centurion, you make a point, and I assure you that I will investigate it further. However, as of this moment, I am working off of this." He indicated the tablet. "And this says that *Gregarius* Florus confessed that you were aware of his intentions when he went to the *taverna* with the intent to kill *Gregarius* Ambustus. So," I suppose he at least tried to sound regretful, "I am afraid that we must adjourn this meeting until such time I can determine whether your claim that Florus recanted has any validity."

That was the moment I knew that I had lost, because the chances that Nerva, Bibulus, and Brennus would admit the truth was about as much as me becoming a Priestess of Vesta. Varro gave Canus a signal, and he disappeared from the room, so I decided to roll the dice.

"Why are you doing this for Nerva, *Quaestor*?" I asked Varro, but this time when he affected surprise, it was easy to see that it was not genuine.

"I'm not sure I take your meaning, Centurion," he replied coolly.

"Oh, I think you do." Deciding a change of tactics was in order, I asked challengingly, "Are you really telling me that you don't know anything about my...history with the Alaudae?"

"I...may have heard something about some sort of

disagreement," Varro allowed, then gave a laugh. "Of course, it's probably easier to remember when you soldiers from different Legions *don't* have some sort of disagreement."

"So you don't know about Quintus Pilus Prior Lucius Petronius?"

Varro cocked his head as if he was trying to recall, then admitted, "The name is familiar, but I'm afraid that I can't place it or remember why."

I was about to press him further, but Canus returned, and he was not alone; the provost who had escorted me to Varro's office and another provost I did not recognize were standing there, and I felt my stomach flip.

"What's this?" I demanded.

"These men will escort you back downstairs," Varro answered, and I whirled about, not believing what I was hearing.

"*What*?" I gasped. "Why can't I return to my Legion?"

"Because," Varro replied as if I should have known, "your Legion is packed up and about to leave for Ubiorum. And," he shook his head, "until this matter is resolved, you're staying here in Mogontiacum."

Oh, how I wanted to fight, but fortunately, I kept my wits, understanding very quickly how unwise that would be. It took an effort, but I turned and walked over to the provosts and Canus, who was offering me a triumphant smile.

"Pullus," Varro called to me just as we reached the door, and for the first time, I saw what I would learn was the real Lucius Varro, his face a mask and radiating a coldness that was almost palpable across the room. "Don't make the mistake of believing that I do the bidding of someone like Primus Pilus Nerva. I answer to a *much* higher authority than any Centurion, no matter what his rank."

Then, he turned away and opened one of the shutters to the window behind his desk, in a signal that could not have been clearer.

As we walked back to the stairway, Canus whispered, "I'm going to make a sacrifice to Dis that you end up in my chair, Centurion."

I looked down at him, fighting the urge to snap his neck

right then, choosing instead to give a mocking laugh.

"And who's going to put me in it, Canus? You?"

"As many as it takes, Centurion," Canus replied coolly. "In case you haven't noticed, you're not very popular here. And," he actually stopped at the top of the stairs, calling down to me as we descended back to the cells, "you're not going to have your Legion here to protect you."

With that cheerful thought, I returned to the secure cell to wait.

The cells were still full, but when Lentulus called to me, asking what was happening, all I offered was a shake of my head. It was partially because I did not want to worry him and the other Fifth Century men who were present, although the truth was that my head was still spinning as I tried to fully grasp the severity of my plight. Returning to the secure cell, when the provost I had not seen before closed the cell door, he opened the small door blocking the grill, which at least gave me a bit more light. Within a couple heartbeats, I was not certain that this was a favor, because it gave me enough light to examine the cell, and the first thing I noticed were the series of marks etched into the stone wall. My first thought was that it was from some poor soul clawing at the walls; thankfully, it only took another heartbeat for me to see that they were far too regular, in both the length and spacing between each to be that, meaning that it was someone who was marking the days of their confinement. More to pass the time than anything, I began counting the marks; when I reached two hundred, I stopped, mainly because it suddenly occurred to me that, while my initial assumption was that these were days, they might have been something else, like weeks. With the grill uncovered, I could hear better, so I sat there trying to listen for anything useful as the men talked, but they had been in the cells since sometime after midnight, and it was now midmorning, so what talk there was, was desultory in nature and not very loud. Now that I had a better idea of the time, I tried to keep closer track, so my guess was that it was just before noon when the noise level increased again, but this time, I could hear clearly enough to   recognize voices, specifically that of my Primus Pilus.

Leaping to my feet, I was still a pace short of the door when the light from the grill was obscured by a dark shape.

"Pullus? Are you in there? It's darker than Pluto's bunghole!"

I cannot describe the flood of relief that washed through my body; I would have cause to recall that with some chagrin in the immediate future.

"Yes, it's me, Primus Pilus," I answered. Before he could tell me, I asked, "So is it true? The Legion is leaving for Ubiorum?"

"It is," he answered grimly, but then he took a slight step backward, and I realized that it was so that I could see he was not alone.

Standing next to him on one side was Alex, and in my excitement, I cut Sacrovir off to ask Alex, "Did you go to my mother's villa?"

"Yes," Alex assured me, and I did not try to hide my relief. "I told her everything I knew and that you were going to be delayed."

I expected Sacrovir to be irritated; that he was not worried me, and I quickly learned I was right to be concerned.

"Varro refuses to allow you to leave with us, Pullus," he said. "And last night, there was...trouble."

"I know about that," I told him. "Lentulus told me."

"That was only part of it," Sacrovir shook his head. "Right now, our boys are as angry as I've seen them since the revolt." He lowered his voice. "Paterculus, Dentulus, and Serranus brought Florus' body the long way through our Legion area so that everyone got a good look at what whoever did that to him did, and it almost caused a riot."

While my attitude towards Florus had certainly altered somewhat over the last few watches, I did point out, "Primus Pilus, he *did* murder Ambustus in front of witnesses, so he was a dead man regardless."

"I know that," Sacrovir agreed, perhaps a bit sharply. "But he was also denied his rights under the regulations, and supposedly, that's what angered the men. Although," he allowed, "whoever worked him over did a good job of it. I can't remember seeing someone beaten that thoroughly before."

59

Without thinking, I told him, "I know who did it. His name is Canus."

"Canus?" Sacrovir repeated, cocking his head, which I knew was a sign he was trying to think. "Is he with the *Praetor*'s torture detachment? I'm not familiar with his name, so maybe he's new."

The moment he said it, I realized that I had assumed the same thing, but Sacrovir would have known the men of the torture detachment better than I; besides, in the moment, I also recalled how Varro referred to Canus as "his servant" and I said, "No, I'm almost certain that he's Varro's man and isn't attached to the *Praetor*."

There was a silence then, I suppose so that we could absorb the situation, then I turned to Alex.

"I know that you want to get back to Ubiorum..." I began, but he cut me off.

"I'm not leaving here until you do," he said firmly. With a grin, he added, "Besides, Algaia thinks of Bronwen as a sister, and Iras considers Titus her baby, so they won't budge unless it's with Bronwen, and Bronwen won't budge without you. So," he shrugged, "I'm not going anywhere."

This was a relief, yet I had another worry, but I addressed Sacrovir for this.

"Primus Pilus, I'd like to request that some men from the Fifth be detached and be sent to my mother's villa."

I was initially relieved that Sacrovir clearly was not surprised, nor did he seem disposed to deny my request, but he did hesitate.

"Pullus, I think that might be a good idea," he began, "but...I think that it might be better if I speak to Licinius and tell him to give me some men from the First of the Fourth."

"Why?" I asked, not understanding; when Sacrovir glanced over at Alex, my confusion only deepened, but Alex replied immediately, "Because they know Bronwen, and more importantly, she knows them. She hasn't spent much time with the Fifth boys, and it's a First Cohort Century, so the chances are she won't recognize them."

On its face, this made sense; besides, I could see that Sacrovir was getting impatient, the cells almost empty as the men were filing out, so I turned to him and asked, "Would you speak to Pilus Prior Licinius and ask him if he can spare," I thought briefly, "Cotta, Fimbria, Crassipes, and Cocles, please?"

I saw by Alex's reaction that he understood why I had named these men; each of them had been with us on the *Brizo*, which meant they had been stranded in Britannia with me, although they had been allowed to leave by Cogidubnus while I had been held for ransom. They knew Bronwen, but more importantly, Bronwen knew them, and if my eyes were any judge, each of them was a little bit in love with Bronwen, although that is not hard to do.

"Are any of them Sergeants or *Immunes*?" Sacrovir asked.

"Unless they were promoted while I was gone, no." I shook my head.

This satisfied him, and he said briskly, "Then I'll tell Licinius; I won't ask him. Now," he looked a bit embarrassed, "I'm afraid that I have to leave now, Pullus. I'm sorry that it has to be this way. And," he assured me, "as soon as I get to Ubiorum, I'm going to talk to the Camp Prefect about this and see what can be done." Suddenly, he glanced about, but while I could not see anything to either side, clearly he felt it safe, although he leaned forward and lowered his voice. "I also need to warn you about something I just learned about Varro." I do not know whether it was the way he was behaving, or if in the back of my mind, I had already worked it out for myself; whatever the cause, when he said just above a whisper, "The *Quaestor* is very close to Praetorian Prefect Sejanus," I was not that surprised. "I know I don't have to tell you to watch *everything* out of your mouth with a man with ties to Sejanus. Especially after what happened in Rome."

There was nothing that I could say to that, other than assure him I would in fact be very careful in what I said. If I had known how long it would be before I saw my wife and child again for more than a handful of moments, I like to believe that I would have thought of something more memorable to say. I also wish that Sacrovir had explained that his "suggestion" to use the men of my old First of the Fourth was based in the fact that the men of the Fifth of the First were not just angry at Varro and Canus, but at their Centurion. That, however, is for later.

There is a saying that goes something like, when a man is looking backward, only then is his vision clear, and certainly in my case, this is the truth. My detention was part of a larger plan; that, at least, became clear fairly soon after the 1st departed for Ubiorum. Once I was isolated from my Legion, I was moved from the secure cell to one of the open cells. It meant that I had to endure Bibulus parading past several times a day with a broad grin on his face, although after he came too close once and I made a sudden lunge in the same manner I had when I was ascending the stairs, I took some satisfaction in how he always made sure he could touch the opposite wall, putting him just out of my reach. He also tried to taunt me a couple of times, but I quickly learned that a simple mention of Petronius' name, accompanied by an appropriate leer, along with grabbing my crotch and thrusting my hips, put that to a stop. I was fed, twice a day; not enough, but I was surprised that it was as much as it was, and the quality told me that it was standard army fare, not the slop reserved for the slaves, or even for the clerks and servants. On the second or third day, it struck me that it was as if they wanted to keep my strength up for something; otherwise, though, I was largely ignored. By placing me in the cell nearest the stairs, I could look up the staircase and keep track of time by the light, but I refused to make any marks on the wooden bars like previous occupants had. It also allowed me to catch snatches of talk if someone was close to the head of the stairs, and the day after the 1st's departure, as I sat with my back to the stone wall, I heard what started out as a conversation, but then both the volume and the tone changed, bringing me to my feet to move to the front of the cell, which gave me the best view.

"Gnaeus! Gnaeus! Are you down there? Can you hear me?" It was Alex, and naturally, I immediately answered, "Yes! What's happening?"

"I tried to come see you, but this provost Bibulus is refusing to let me!" I cursed bitterly, but I was not surprised. "Are you all right?" he called down, then I heard him snap,

"There's nothing illegal in asking him that, Provost!"

While I would have liked the company, I was not willing to let it be by Alex sharing my cell, so I hurried to assure him, "I'm fine, Alex. They're just trying to bore me to death, nothing more."

"Are they feeding you? Should I bring you something to eat?"

I was about to reply that, of course I would like more food, but then Bibulus called down, "Anything he brings will be confiscated, Centurion." His voice took on a gloating quality, "After all, we can't have you trying to kill yourself before your trial."

Trial? I thought, my heart suddenly picking up speed. Was that what Varro's plan was?

"They're feeding me enough, Alex. And I don't want you to give that *cunnus* standing there next to you the chance to bugger you...or maybe he wants you to bugger him, if what I've heard is true." Despite the distance, I heard the hiss and muttered curse of anger, and I felt a grin split my face. "Go back to the villa, tell Bronwen I'm fine, and for her to kiss the baby for me. I'll see her soon." I felt a stab of shame then, prompting me to ask, "How is she? How's Titus?"

"She," Alex sounded amused, "is spitting she's so angry. I've had to talk her out of coming here..."

"Make sure she doesn't!" I barked. "That will just make things worse!"

"I know!" he assured me, then I heard him snap, "Get your hands off me, Provost! I'm leaving."

Before I thought about it, I had grabbed the wooden bars, trying to spread them apart, my only thought getting out of the cell to dash up the stairs and fulfill the promise I had made to myself to bash Bibulus' brains out. Ironically, it was the slight cracking sound that snapped me out of my growing rage, realizing that it would only make a bad situation worse, although I cannot deny that the idea of how Bibulus and Varro would react at the sight of the shattered wooden bars was not tempting me to continue.

"I'm leaving, Gnaeus, but I'll be back tomorrow!" Alex promised.

"No!" I called out. "Don't give this *cunnus* the opportunity! I'll be fine, I promise." Now, I had no idea if that was true, but I did not want a rampaging Parisii woman storming the *Praetorium*. It also reminded me of the four men from the First of the Fourth, and I shouted, "If I'm not out in a week, then tell Cotta and the others I'm releasing them! They'll need to get back to the Legion!"

Alex promised that he would do so, and as I knew he would be, was good to his word, not showing back up himself, while I sat in the cell, pondering my fate.

Exactly a week later, I itched from my growing beard and the vermin biting me, and I stank as if I was on campaign, not even getting a scraping. And, as the gods as my witness, I was barely holding on to my sanity from the boredom of sitting in a cell, although the monotony was broken on three occasions, when some drunken rankers were dragged in and thrown into the cells next to mine. On two of them, that bastard Bibulus had the duty, and he snarled at them to keep their mouths shut around me, but the instant he left, they began babbling at me. None of them were in the 5th, which I am certain was a good thing; twice they were men from the 21st, and the other time it was four auxiliaries from the Batavian Cohorts, specifically the cavalry, their accent reminding me of my father's good friend Gaesorix, who I had learned had died while I was in Rome, Macer telling me about it when we saw each other. From the 21st men I learned that, if anything, Sacrovir had been downplaying the tension between the men of the 1st and 5th, although just from the tenor of the comments by the 21st men, their sentiments definitely leaned in the direction of the men of the Alaudae, which made sense since they were stationed here together. I know that it seems odd to outsiders, but while here in Mogontiacum, men of the 5th and 21st hate each other, they will still band together when interlopers, either from Ubiorum with us and the 20th, or Vetera, where the 14th and 2nd are stationed show up in Mogontiacum. Even in neutral territory, the men from twin Legions tend to stick together, so I just kept my mouth shut with the Legionaries, although even without my *vitus*, which had been confiscated as a weapon, I am certain that more than one of them recognized me, but since I just offered a seemingly sympathetic ear, there were no unpleasant questions aimed my way. The Batavians were far more forthcoming, and made it clear very quickly that they knew my identity.

"I rode with Prefect Batavius," one of them told me, who had Romanized his name to Herminius, which is understandable given that another German whose original name was Herman had reverted back to it from Arminius. "I was in Decurion Cassicos' *ala*."

Since I had read my father's account, I was more than happy to let Herminius know that, not only was I familiar with both men, and had learned the story of how, after my father's error in choosing a shorter route back to Siscia during the Batonian Revolt, they had been ambushed by rebel Varciani, and Cassicos, who had only been a trooper then, had been taken prisoner. Gaesorix, my father, and the rest of the Batavian escort, had climbed into the mountains, which my father was familiar with because of his service in Pannonia, finding the rebels in the process of flaying Cassicos. Obviously, he had survived, and my father had paid him the supreme compliment.

"My father," I concluded the story, "said that Cassicos was the toughest man he had ever known, and he counted Prefect Gaesorix as one of his closest friends."

One of the others said something in their tongue, and it caused Herminius to laugh; when I asked him what was so humorous, he said, "Arnfrid says that the first time he saw your father, even though he was dressed as a Roman Centurion, he refused to believe that he was not German."

"Did you serve with Decurion Cassicos?" I asked, gambling that he knew more Latin than he let on; besides, many times, men can understand perfectly well but are not comfortable speaking another tongue.

Arnfrid nodded, saying something to Herminius, which he translated, "He says the first time he saw the Decurion's back, he did not understand how he survived."

We spoke a little more about my father, Gaesorix, and as time passed, we began talking about the last year of the campaign against Arminius. Honestly, I was not certain this was wise; I knew that many men of the German tribes that are friendly with Rome held sympathy towards Arminius to varying degrees, including the Batavians, although they fight for us, but since they brought it up, I felt it safe to talk about. What I learned was that the four of them had narrowly escaped disaster, being part of the force that had been caught by the incoming tide in the Amisia (Ems) River, for which they unanimously blamed the Roman Legate in command, Publius Vitellius. We had heard this was the case, but having it confirmed was sobering, and I decided to lighten the mood by talking about my own ordeal.

Once I finished, they glanced at each other, but I suppose since Herminius had been the one who had done the most speaking, they decided to let him speak for them, and he said carefully, "So, you were swept out to sea, then stranded in Britannia. But you only lost one man because of the storm, and when you returned, you had a woman?"

When put that way, I saw why they were not particularly sympathetic, and I had to laugh at myself, which they happily joined in. Not long after that, we drifted off, then shortly after the *bucina*, which I could now hear, sounded first call, they were released into the custody of their Ducanus, while I settled down to wait for the morning meal. Instead, I was greeted by Bibulus, who looked anything but pleased.

"*Quaestor* Varro requires your presence," he announced, but rather than move to the door of the cell, I took my own revenge by walking over to the bucket to relieve my bladder first.

Looking over my shoulder, I grinned at Bibulus, though not with any friendship.

"Don't peek, Bibulus," I chided. "I don't want you getting any ideas."

Once I finished, I walked to the cell door, and he lifted his cudgel as if he was thinking of using it, but a hard stare from me disabused him of the notion. He was behind me as we ascended the stairs, and I turned my head just enough so that I could see him at the edge of my vision, but he was sufficiently cowed not to try anything. Canus was seated at the desk again, except this time, he got up immediately, barely giving me a glance and did his three raps on the door. Like last time, I did not have to wait long, Canus beckoning to me from the doorway before disappearing into the office, where I found him standing in the same spot as the previous time. Varro was seated behind the desk, and while I squared myself, I refused to salute again, except that Varro got his own form of revenge by wrinkling his nose.

"You smell, Centurion," he said, almost cheerfully. "And you're beginning to look like a German with that beard."

"You wanted to see me, *Quaestor*?"

"Obviously, I did," he replied, though he did not seem upset, which put me even more on guard. "There are important matters to discuss." I thought this was quite the understatement, but I said nothing, and I saw the flash of irritation, making me believe that he wanted some sign from me that might indicate my level of desperation or concern. After a pause, he continued, now trying to look apologetic, "I regret to say, Centurion, that, despite a thorough investigation of the murder of *Gregarius* Ambustus, we were unable to find any witnesses to support your claim that *Gregarius* Florus didn't inform you of his intentions." In the back of my mind, there was a tickling of a memory, from the days when I was Gnaeus Volusenus, a haughty Equestrian youth, whose tutor in rhetoric once gave him a lesson of the impossibility of proving a negative. "Of course," Varro interrupted my thoughts as he held his hands up in a helpless gesture, "it didn't help that *your* Primus Pilus chose to take your Legion back to Ubiorum."

It took a heartbeat for this to register, then I heard a gasp that I know came from me.

"What do you mean he *chose* to? He didn't have any choice in the matter!" Suddenly, I was struck by doubt. "Did he?"

"As I recall," Varro replied coolly, "it was you who reminded me that my authority as *Quaestor* doesn't extend to the Legions, Centurion. So," he asked reasonably, "how could I have ordered him to depart with your Legion?" It was, I thought miserably, true, but before I could respond, Varro continued casually, "Now, perhaps I *did* suggest that, given the overall situation and state of tension between Primus Pilus

Nerva's men and those of your Legion, that what happened last week when we were forced to round up all of the 1ˢᵗ men we found out in the city would be what he could expect as long as they were here." He smiled then, and it was the kind of smug smile that one who is a master at tables offers a neophyte at the game, and I desperately wanted to smash his face in. More importantly, however, it warned me of the likelihood that this was part of Varro's larger design, whatever it was; very quickly, I realized that there was no way I could have been prepared. "Your Primus Pilus made what I think you'll agree was the wise, and the only decision, to remove the 1ˢᵗ back to Ubiorum. However, that absence doesn't help your situation, I'm afraid. Therefore, I'm informing you that, pending approval from Rome, since the *Praetor* is still with Germanicus on his embassy, you will be standing a Tribunal for complicity in the murder of *Gregarius Immunes* Ambustus of the 5ᵗʰ Alaudae."

It was with a sickening feeling I knew what was coming that I asked dully, "When you say approval from 'Rome,' who do you mean, exactly?"

"Why," he sounded surprised, "from the Imperator, of course. Although," he added helpfully, "I suspect that, given his overwhelming responsibilities, such things have been delegated to someone else. In fact, I've heard that Praetorian Prefect Sejanus has taken on a great many responsibilities. And," he smiled then, with a glittering malice that told me that he was aware of at least part of the history between me and Sejanus, "I suspect that when he sees your name, he will take a...personal interest in the matter."

I was too far away from his desk to grab it for support, and the chairs had been moved out of the way, and I felt myself reel a bit before I regained my composure, as the thought shot through my mind that perhaps the other gods had finally decided to remind me of how much I had been favored by Fortuna and even things out.

"W-what happens while I'm waiting?" I managed to get out.

This elicited an arched eyebrow in what I took to be surprise.

"Why, what always happens with prisoners waiting for their trial," he replied. "You'll be returned to your cell. Although," he allowed, "perhaps a trip to the baths before that is in order. Under guard, of course."

Then, in a clear sign of dismissal, he picked up a scroll, unrolled it, and began to read, or pretended to, while I heard Canus' footsteps as he crossed the room, and I prepared myself for his smirk before I turned about. With an overblown courtesy that sent its own scathing message, Canus gestured to the door, and I suppose I was in enough of a daze that I dumbly obeyed.

Just when my hand touched the latch, Varro cleared his throat, but in a manner that I knew was meant to get my attention, and said, "However..." I turned back to see that he was still examining the scroll, but he continued, "...there *may* be a way where we can both help each other, Centurion." He looked up then, and asked with a smile, "Are you interested in hearing about what I have in mind?"

Every fiber of my being screamed that this was some sort of trap, that I should twist the latch, open the door and walk out, returning to my cell, refusing even the offer of a bath. Instead, I turned and walked back to his desk; I am still unsure whether I made the correct decision.

"Are you familiar with a Gotones nobleman named Catualda?" Varro asked, after deigning to allow me to sit, and actually having Canus pour some wine, which Varro's man clearly did not care for, making a show of my odiferous state by holding his breath as he poured.

I ignored him as I considered the question, both to recall what I remembered, and try to determine what danger there might be in answering.

"I've heard his name," I replied slowly. "But I'm not familiar with the Gotones."

"That's not surprising," Varro replied. "Their lands are well to the east, beyond the Marcomanni, along a river named the," he had to look at a tablet, "Vistula River."

"I've never even heard of the Vistula," I admitted.

"There's no reason you should have. Anyway, the

Imperator sent his son..." he amended, "...his natural son Drusus to meet with Catualda."

I could not suppress a small gasp of surprise.

"Tiberius was willing to risk sending Drusus all that way, through territory where Arminius still has influence?"

"No." Varro shook his head. "Catualda was a guest of Maroboduus at the time, but he managed to slip away and come meet with Drusus here."

"What was the purpose of this meeting?"

"Whether or not he's of the proper metal to suit the Imperator's purpose," Varro answered, then took a sip from his cup, giving me the impression he was deciding something. Setting it down, he continued, "There's a feeling in Rome that Maroboduus hasn't been sufficiently...energetic in finishing Arminius off. Drusus was sent to determine whether or not Catualda would be a better choice for sitting on the Marcomanni throne."

"But you said he was a Gotones," I objected.

"His mother was Marcomanni," Varro explained. "And she was kin to Maroboduus, although I don't know how."

Growing impatient, I said, "This is all fascinating, but what does it have to do with me?"

"I just received orders from Rome." Varro indicated a scroll, and I saw the dark red seal on it used by the Imperial message system. "The Imperator has heard Drusus' report, and has decided to offer Catualda our support. You," he smiled, "are going to deliver that message."

I sat there, unable to speak, staring at him, then I realized my throat had suddenly gone dry. Reaching for the cup, I saw my hand was shaking, yet I could not seem to help it, but I had far more pressing concerns, one of which I asked then.

"Why me?"

He did not reply immediately, and when he did, I was unprepared for him to ask, "Are you aware that your name is known among the German tribes?"

"No." I shook my head. "Not *my* name. My father's name."

"That's true," he granted. "But from what I've been told by those who knew your father, you more than favor him in your size and strength, that there's a strong resemblance in your features." I certainly had heard this, particularly after the truth came out, and I had to endure comments from both friends and acquaintances about how they could have missed it. Varro went on, "Also, I understand that your father was awarded for bravery by Drusus the Elder, the Imperator's brother, after slaying..." He looked down at the tablet, but I supplied the name, "Vergorix, of the Chatti."

"Yes," he nodded, "that's it." Looking at me, he asked, "Do you have that torq?"

"Of course," I frowned, still trying to grasp what was happening, "but why?"

"Because I think it will be in the best interests of Rome when a representative of the Imperator presents himself to this barbarian, that he be wearing his full uniform, along with all his decorations, especially one that is known by them."

Since it was inconceivable that, if Varro wanted me in uniform wearing my decorations that I would do so in my present state, I would definitely need a bath and a shave.

"I'd like to get cleaned up before I go to my mother's villa to retrieve my uniform and the torq," I said, then despite not particularly wanting to be jocular with this man, I did offer a smile. "My wife is likely to have a stronger reaction about my...state than you did if I show up like this. Then I'll go speak to this Catualda. You said he's here. I assume you know where he's staying."

Now, when Varro looked down at his cup, I did not detect any artifice, and he seemed truly, if not regretful, then embarrassed.

"Er, yes, about that," he began. "He *was* in Mogontiacum to meet with Drusus, but that was weeks ago. Because I had no idea what the answer from Rome would be, when he requested to return to his own people, I had no reason to refuse."

A lead ball suddenly materialized in my stomach, but it was only going to get worse.

"You said he was a guest of Maroboduus, so is it wise to assume that's where he is now?"

"No." Varro shook his head. "We decided that, in order to avoid the possibility of word somehow reaching Maroboduus that we are courting his replacement, it would be better if he wasn't in Maroboduus' reach."

"Which he wouldn't have been if he stayed here," I countered, but Varro again shook his head.

"Centurion, surely you know that Maroboduus has eyes and ears here in Mogontiacum," he chided. "For that matter, so does Arminius, as does every other tribal chieftain on both sides of the Rhenus." This was true, certainly, but Varro was not through, and it was only later, when I learned more, that he inadvertently gave me a crucial piece of information. "And it's not just here. Maroboduus has friends in Rome, powerful friends, who have loaned him vast sums and would be most unhappy if he was no longer in a position where he could pay them back."

If only I had asked about the identity of these men, perhaps Varro might have slipped up, but I was laboring under an assumption at the time.

Almost certain I knew the answer, I sighed and asked, "So, you're expecting me to travel across Germania, a Roman officer, all alone, and pass through Marcomanni territory to find this Catualda?"

"You won't be going alone," Varro assured me. "You'll have a guide, a Gotones sworn to Catualda who accompanied him here to Mogontiacum and stayed behind to await word from Rome." He hesitated, and I understood why when he added, "Also, Canus will be traveling with you."

This brought me to my feet, and I spun about to stare at the man, but while he returned my gaze, his customary sneer was nowhere to be seen, and it was clear to see that he was no happier about this than I was.

Turning back to Varro, I said flatly, "No. He's not going. Not only do I not trust him, I have no idea whether he can handle himself in a fight."

"Oh, you don't need to worry about that, Pullus," Canus snarled. "I've killed better men than you!"

"Were they facing you?" I shot back, my contempt matching his, which I showed by keeping my gaze on Varro. "And not tied to a chair?"

"Any time you want to..." Canus began, but Varro lifted a

hand, and I was impressed how quickly his man obeyed him.

"Stop this quarreling," Varro sounded weary. "Pullus, this is not negotiable."

"Then you can find someone else," I replied immediately, gambling that he needed me more than he was letting on.

"Very well." He shrugged, then in an almost bored tone, he said, "Canus will take you back to your cell."

"And who's going to take your message to Catualda?" I asked, jerking my thumb over my shoulder. "Him?" I knew I was taking a risk, but I was struggling to control my temper now that I knew Canus would be involved, which was why I challenged Varro by pointing at him next and laughing, "You?"

I confess I was disappointed that this did not seem to anger Varro, who replied, "Surely you don't think that you were my only alternative, Centurion. I have others. Canus," he leaned to look past me, "please take Centurion Pullus back to his cell."

I was defeated, and I knew it; even worse, so did Varro.

"I'd still like to take a bath before we leave," I said in a tacit signal of my submission.

"Of course," Varro nodded. "Although, if I may make a suggestion? Don't shave. The more you look like a German, the better for you."

My state of mind as I approached my mother's villa, under escort, of course, though thankfully not by Bibulus but by the only provost who had proven to be a decent sort named Lucius Niger, was a mixture of anticipation and dread in almost equal measure. When we reached the gate, I hit the knocker, and almost immediately, the small door in the grill was opened, and I recognized the eye peering out, though it took a heartbeat to recall her name. Fortunately, Grimhilt was already opening the gate, stepping out of the way with a grunt that could have meant anything, but I saw her wrinkle her nose. I thought briefly about making a jest about smelling like a German, quickly dismissing it because I was certain that she packed quite a punch and I did not want to risk the ignominy of being knocked off my feet by a woman, especially in front of Niger.

Who, for his part, looked embarrassed as he said,

"Centurion, I'm sorry, but the *Quaestor* gave me orders that I have to accompany you wherever you go."

Fortunately for both of us, I had assumed as much, and I was just thankful that it was not Bibulus; still, I could only issue a curt nod as I followed Grimhilt, who had turned and headed towards the front door without a word.

"Dominus Gnaeus is here..." she called out, but even before she finished, I heard more than one feminine cry, then running footsteps.

Bronwen came rushing out of the *triclinium*, while I held my hands out, not to sweep her into my arms but to warn her, "My love, I need to warn you. I haven't had a bath and I smell..."

"I don't care!" she cried even as she was launching herself into my arms, and for a brief span of heartbeats, neither of us spoke, both of us almost consumed with the joy of being together again.

As I kissed my wife, I saw my mother emerge, followed immediately by Censorinus, and while my mother was smiling, and her eyes gleaming, I saw there was a sad quality to it, although it was Censorinus' grim expression that told me they both either suspected or knew that my visit would be brief; what I did not know was to what detail, specifically, my destination and mission.

Finally, Bronwen was satisfied she had kissed me enough to stop, and as she stepped away from me, she said ruefully, "You *do* smell, my love."

I got my answer about how much my wife knew when she said briskly, "But that can be remedied quite easily." She began turning to Grimhilt to order for water to be heated for the tub, but I caught her sleeve, and she stopped. Looking up at me, she must have seen in my expression the truth, because her chin began quivering and her eyes shining.

I was about to inform her when, from behind me, Niger cleared his throat, and I whirled about, ready to snarl something at him, but before I could, he said, "Centurion, if you don't mind, my throat is parched. I was wondering if I could impose upon your servant here to lead me to the kitchen where I can quench my thirst?"

Immediately understanding, I nodded my thanks, knowing that it would not be wise to utter anything that might cause Niger difficulties on his return to the *Praetorium*. Yes, my mother trusted Grimhilt, but I did not know her, so we waited for her to lead Niger away.

Once I was certain they were out of earshot, I turned back to Bronwen. "There's much to tell you, and not much time to do it, *meum mel*. Let's go into the *triclinium*." As we headed down the short passageway, I asked, "Where's Alex? And," I became more concerned, and chagrined that I had forgotten, "where are the men?"

"Alex allowed them to leave yesterday, which was a week, just like you told him to," she reminded me. "And now he and Algaia took Iras and the baby to the market," Bronwen answered, and my heart sank, but I tried to sound unconcerned when I asked, "Any idea when they'll be back?"

Bronwen shook her head, but since she was walking ahead of me, I did not see her expression, though I heard the choked sob as she replied, "They just left. You just missed them."

It was with some difficulty that I shoved this into the back of my mind, but when we entered the *triclinium* and I saw my mother and Censorinus sitting together on the couch, I could not restrain myself, snarling, "I'm sorry to interrupt this happy domestic scene, Mother, but I'm afraid I won't be staying long, so you're going to have to stop being wooed for a moment."

I do not think if I had slapped her physically she would have had a stronger reaction, her face going pale as her mouth dropped open, and I felt Bronwen glaring up at me, but it was Censorinus who reacted most strongly, leaping to his feet to cross the room to stand in front of me. Despite my scant acquaintance with the man, it was easy to see that he was scared as well as angry, but his fists were clenched, so he was clearly more angry than frightened.

"Your mother," he said with a barely controlled fury, "hasn't slept more than a watch or eaten more than a bird has for a *week*, Centurion! She's been worried sick about what's happening with you and knowing that there's nothing she can do to help, so I will *not* stand for you treating her in such a manner, when all she's done is care about your fate!"

Despite myself, I was impressed; I was also acutely aware that, in sentiment, I was decisively outnumbered, and I was certain that, had Alex and Algaia been there, their expressions would have been identical to that worn by Bronwen.

"That," I said softly, "is what I needed to know, that you truly care about her." I looked at my mother, saying, "I apologize, Mama. I was being unduly harsh, and unfair. But," I went on, deciding that a timely lie was in order, "I needed to know that the *Duumvir* here can be counted on for what's coming."

I do not know whether my mother believed me, or she chose to pretend to, because she sounded almost normal when she replied, "I agree, my son. So, tell me what's happening."

By the time I was through, Bronwen looked as if she was about to faint and had dropped onto one of the other couches, while my mother appeared to have aged ten years, but it was Censorinus who, looking more thoughtful, piqued my interest.

"You don't look surprised, *Duumvir*," I said pointedly. "Did you know about what Varro had planned?"

Censorinus shook his head. "No, at least not that you were involved in his plans."

"But you knew what he had planned?" I pressed, and this time, although he shook his head, it was not quite as convincing.

"How long will this take, Gnaeus?"

"I don't know, Mama," I confessed. "Our guide is sworn to this Catualda, but I haven't met him yet. But while Varro doesn't know exactly where he is, I'm sure that this man does." Not wanting to let Censorinus off the hook, which I suspected was what was behind the timing of my mother's question, I pressed him, "What I heard you say was that you didn't know of my role...but you're aware of *something* going on, is that correct?"

This time, before he replied, Censorinus actually strode over to the doorway and peered out into the passageway, then returned to where he had been standing in front of me, speaking just above a whisper.

"Just like with anyone of his status, Centurion, there are more rumors about Varro than I can list right here, but there are some that are...consistently whispered about both his ambitions, and his connections."

"I've heard some of them," I said, a bit impatiently. "Namely that he's not working for Tiberius, he's working for Sejanus, at least behind the scenes."

Censorinus nodded, but then said, "That's the rumor, but it's not the only one. This business with Catualda; what exactly is the message that you're supposed to give him?"

I stiffened, suddenly alert. Quite deliberately, I hadn't mentioned the purpose of this mission, only that I was to pass a message to Catualda, and now here was Censorinus probing to learn. He quickly realized how his question sounded, and he held up a hand.

"Forgive me, Centurion, I can see why that would make you suspicious." He paused for a moment, I assumed to think of a different way to put it. "How about this? I'll tell you what the rumor is about this purpose, and I'll leave it up to you to decide whether or not to respond at all. Is that fair?" I considered for a beat, then nodded. "What I've heard is that Drusus' visit here, which was done while you and the other Legions were in Rome for your triumph, wasn't the inspection tour of the defenses that it was said to be, but that he was meeting with Catualda to determine whether he would be acceptable to Rome as a replacement for Maroboduus." He paused, but while he was absolutely correct, I did not say anything; to his credit, he did not seem disappointed at my silence, and he went on, "Now, *if* that was why Drusus was here, this would be about the time a message arrived from Rome once Drusus returned to give his report to his father. And, if Drusus' report to the Imperator was that he didn't think this Catualda character was a suitable candidate to supplant Maroboduus for whatever reason, I doubt that Tiberius would send orders to Varro to send a party across the breadth of Germania to the opposite side of Marcomanni territory to tell the man that Rome wasn't interested in supporting him. More likely, he would just be left to stew in his own juices back in his lands until he figured out that Rome wasn't interested."

This was, I realized, very logical, and I, grudgingly, silently acknowledged that Censorinus was no fool, although given my mother's interest in him and her lack of tolerance for such, especially men, it should not have been a surprise.

Realizing that I should provide some sort of answer, I said slowly, "That does make sense."

"Yes, I thought so as well," Censorinus replied tartly. "But, consider this." He actually lowered his voice even more, and I saw Bronwen leaning forward to listen, but my mother sat there, hands folded in her lap, giving me the strong sense that she had heard this before, or perhaps had drawn the same conclusion. "What if the message from Rome actually said that the Imperator was *not* going to work with Catualda?" This startled me, but he was not through. "In fact, what if there *wasn't* a message from Rome? At least not from Drusus or his father?"

"But why would Varro send us if what you say might be true actually is? What does he stand to gain by it?"

Censorinus did not answer directly, instead asking, "What do you know about Drusus and his relationship with Prefect Sejanus?"

It did not take more than a heartbeat for it to hit me, in the form of a memory of reading my father's account, specifically about the revolt. While I had my own experiences, they were exclusively with the Rhenus Legions, while my father, because of his relationship with Germanicus, was in the unique position of witnessing both the revolt by the Pannonia Legions and the Rhenus Legions. What I recalled specifically was that Tiberius, who had been Imperator for only a matter of days since it had been the death of Divus Augustus that had triggered the whole affair, had Germanicus summoned from Gaul by my father and Tribune Asprenas to deal with the Rhenus Legions, and had sent Drusus to deal with the Pannonian Legions...and accompanying Drusus had been the then-Praetorian Tribune Sejanus, while my father was sent to Pannonia by Germanicus because of his familiarity with the Pannonian Legions, specifically the 8th, and Titus Domitius, one of the leaders of the revolt. There had been an incident between my father and Sejanus, but what was germane to this conversation was remembering my father describing the tension between Drusus and Sejanus. Now that I had my own firsthand experience with

Sejanus, I had insight into the kind of visceral hatred Sejanus holds for anyone who threatens his authority, or makes him look less than what he sees himself to be, which was my father's offense as far as the Prefect was concerned.

Aloud, I answered, "Yes, I see what you're saying. If the rumor about Varro working for Sejanus is true, then this is a gods-given opportunity for Sejanus to damage Drusus. Although," I added thoughtfully, "that would be a really dangerous game for Varro to be playing."

"Not necessarily."

I looked in surprise over at my mother, who had been the one to speak.

"Why do you say that?"

My mother did not reply to me at first, addressing Bronwen instead.

"Daughter, I'm going to say something that you'll find upsetting, but I know that you're strong enough to hear it."

Bronwen's face had gone very pale, but I also saw the tightening of her jawline, and recognized it for what it was, so I was not surprised when she answered, "You are going to tell Gnaeus that this Varro is not taking that much of a risk because he is certain that Gnaeus will not survive the trip across Germania to find this man."

My mother was not surprised either; if anything, she looked proud as she nodded.

"Exactly right, Daughter."

Bronwen flushed with pleasure, and it did my heart good to see how quickly the two most important women in my life had grown so close that my mother was calling Bronwen "daughter"; while it did not entirely assuage my worries about things in my absence, it certainly helped. Otherwise, my mother's clear-eyed assessment, which I had missed, clearly resonated with Censorinus as well, because he was nodding his head. And, I thought bitterly, they don't even know about Canus coming along either, although now, it made even more sense that he would be doing so.

"I think Bronwen and your mother are right, Centurion," Censorinus said quietly. "And it certainly fits with what I've been hearing about Varro. Is there any way to avoid making this trip?"

"Not if I want to avoid a Tribunal," I replied bitterly. Shaking my head, I said, "No, that *cunnus* did me neatly, I have to hand it to him."

"I'm going to have Alex send word to Primus Pilus Sacrovir," Bronwen promised.

"I appreciate it, but it won't make any difference," I told her.

"It will make the *Quaestor* nervous knowing that your Legion knows what he is up to!" she declared, and I realized that she was saying this as much for herself as for me, so I tried to sound sincere as I pretended to consider it before saying, "You're right, of course, *meum mel*. Of all the things Varro wants, it's not Primus Pilus Sacrovir poking around." I gave her a grin, "Especially when he's worried about someone as famous as I am."

"I know you're making a joke," my mother said, "but it's also true."

"If it is," I countered, "it's not because of me, it's because of my father."

"That," she seemingly agreed, "is true..." then she surprised me, "but not to the extent that you seem to believe. *Your* name is known, Gnaeus. No," she admitted, "not to the extent that your father is known...but you're also younger and haven't been under the standard as long."

Whether she was being honest or trying to make me feel better, I do not know nor did I ask, but it did make me feel slightly better. Before our conversation could continue, we heard the sound of footsteps approaching from the direction of the kitchen, and Niger appeared, followed by Grimhilt, who was glaring at his back.

"I'm sorry, Centurion," Niger said awkwardly, and I felt badly for the man, because he was the recipient of the same kind of hostile stare from his front as he was to his rear. "But if we don't return soon, the *Quaestor* won't be happy."

"Who gives a rotten fig if *Quaestor* Varro is happy?" my mother sniffed, but before Niger could say anything, I spoke up.

"I do, for one, Mama," I said, not missing the relief on

Niger's face. "Besides, Provost Niger is just doing his duty, and I'm sure that the *Quaestor* was probably quite explicit about how he was supposed to never let me out of his sight." I turned to Niger, "Isn't that right?"

To my relief, Niger immediately understood, and he nodded vigorously.

"Yes, Centurion. You're quite correct. He said that if I let you out of my sight, that I could expect to be put on latrine detail for the next month!"

"I'll go get my gear," I announced, and promised Niger, "I won't be long, Provost."

Naturally, Bronwen followed me, and we had a whispered conversation, but despite the temptation, while I did not think that Varro would do something excessive to Niger, I was not sufficiently certain to try and steal a few more moments of passion. She helped me pack, though there was not much to do since I had essentially dropped my pack in the bedroom a bit more than a week before. On an impulse, I packed Scrofa's *gladius*, though I did not know why, and made sure that Vergorix's torq was still in the bottom, carefully wrapped in soft leather which was secured with leather thongs. When I returned to the *triclinium*, I discovered my mother had begun crying, and she hugged my neck so tightly, I was beginning to see stars by the time I extricated myself. Once I did so, when Censorinus thrust out his arm, I took it without hesitation.

"Watch over them, *Duumvir*," I said, hoping that my tone conveyed the level of warning that I wanted it to.

"I will," he answered solemnly. "You have my oath that I'll do everything in my power to make sure that they're not disturbed in any way."

I gave Bronwen one last kiss, then gestured to Niger to lead the way out of the room.

"I need to saddle my horse," I told him, but while he looked unhappy about it, he did not argue; after all, I would have to be mounted, and this he could at least justify to the *Quaestor*.

Very quickly, I realized that I had forgotten to pick up a piece of fruit or bread; I was reminded by Latobius when he stretched his neck out, took a sniff around my waist...then grabbed what I am certain was an equal amount of tunic and my flesh with his big yellow teeth, wrenching a yelp of pain from me. It did not help that I saw Niger grinning broadly out of the corner of my eye, though I did not comment on it, at least to him.

"I owe you for that," I grumbled as I began the process of saddling him, hoping that Alex had exercised him that morning and knowing that if he had not, it was my horse's habit to try and throw me, just as a reminder that he was allowing me to ride him and not doing it because I compelled him.

"You're out of practice, Centurion," Niger commented in a neutral tone, but I knew that he was not fooled that I was stalling; what I was stalling for I also was certain he did not know.

It turned out to be a close thing, and I did not get everything that I wanted, but just as we exited the gate, I saw Alex round the corner...alone.

"Where are the others?" I asked first.

"Iras heard someone in the market talking about a litter of puppies, so she dragged Algaia to see them. And," he laughed, "if you think I was going to pry the baby loose from Iras..."

Despite what was happening, I had to laugh, even as I was struck with a twinge of melancholy that I was missing this minor piece of family life that would still be a momentous event to Iras, although Titus was too young to have any memory of it.

"Why do I think that you're getting a puppy?" I teased, and his expression at this confirmed it, and I hated myself even more for what I was about to do.

Once I was finished explaining, to his eternal credit, Alexandros Pullus' first and only question was, "When are you leaving, and where should I meet you?"

I left my mother's villa wondering if I would see it and the occupants again, and if I did, how long it would be, but almost as strong was the guilt I felt at the turmoil I was causing with my friends and family.

Chapter 3

"Your guide's name is Otmar," Varro told me as he handed me a leather pouch. I opened it to look inside, and saw three scrolls, but when I reached to extract one to examine the seal, he said sharply, "There is no need for that, Centurion. Besides, time is pressing." I thought for a moment about forcing the issue; I wanted to see the seal on the scrolls to determine who they came from, but decided there would be ample opportunity to do it later. It was just after the beginning of the third day watch, shortly after noon, and Canus was not present. When I asked Varro, he explained, "He's in the process of getting mounts and supplies. He'll come and inform us once he's done."

"I don't need a mount," I assured Varro, who seemed surprised. "I have my own horse, and he's saddled and ready outside."

"I ordered him to requisition a spare mount for each of you, so now you'll have one more spare." He shrugged.

I almost caused myself more headaches then, but I managed to avoid mentioning Alex would be accompanying us, realizing that the horse meant for me would act as his spare.

"Where is this Otmar?"

"He'll be waiting for you at the one-mile marker east of camp," Varro answered shortly. He looked up at me then, his lips a bloodless line. "Pullus, do I need to tell you how important this is? The future of not just Rome, but Germania rests on this mission. Maroboduus has been largely unsuccessful in bringing Arminius to ground, and I don't believe I have to tell you that as long as that savage draws breath, he's a threat to Rome."

I did not take his meaning at first, but he was regarding me intently, and it slowly dawned on me that he was aware of the circumstances of my father's death.

"No." I heard the coldness in my voice. "I assure you, *Quaestor*, you don't have to remind me of how dangerous Arminius is, or the threat that he still poses." Deciding it was in order, I added, "Arminius has cost me more personally than anyone who's been sitting back in Rome the last few years, *Quaestor*." Knowing it was dangerous, and stupid, I still could not resist, pretending that I was asking sincerely, "Were you serving here on the frontier then, *Quaestor*? I don't remember seeing you, but," I laughed, "I confess we weren't this close to the Rhenus very often."

"No," he answered tersely. "This is my first posting to Germania, Centurion."

We were both rescued then by a knock, and Canus stuck his head in the door.

"Everything is ready, sir."

"Good." Varro nodded. "Pullus, you're dismissed. I need a word with Canus before you leave."

Again, I did not salute, and I saw the flicker of irritation there, then passed Canus without glancing at him, thinking, He's probably going to remind Canus that he needs to cut my throat as soon as I'm of no more use.

"Centurion." I turned to see that it was Niger, while Bibulus was standing a couple paces away, once again tapping the cudgel against his palm as he glared, not at me but at Niger's back. "May the gods be with you on whatever you're setting out to do, Centurion," he said this quietly, but loudly enough that Bibulus clearly heard him.

"Your mouth is going to get you in trouble, Niger," he called out. "I don't think the *Quaestor* will be happy to know that you're running your mouth about Imperial business."

Since Niger was facing me, I saw him blanch, but his tone was even as he replied, "I'm not the one who just said it was something the *Quaestor*'s involved in, Bibulus." He pointed past me to the open doorway, where Latobius and the other animals were visible. "Since I escorted the Centurion here, I know that's his horse. And now, there are other horses with it, and two of them are packhorses, so only an idiot wouldn't know that the Centurion is about to go somewhere. Are you saying you're an idiot, Bibulus?"

Bibulus couldn't see Niger's broad grin, but he could see mine, and I laughed as I offered my arm.

Lowering my voice, I warned, "Bibulus may be an idiot, Niger, but watch your back around him."

"I will, Centurion."

Then, I went outside and leapt aboard Latobius, who had been waiting for this and arched his back in his signal that he wanted to have some fun, and if it ended up with me on the ground, so much the better.

"Not now," I warned him, curbing his reins in the signal he had learned that I meant business. "I don't want Canus the *Cunnus* to see me pitched on my ass."

In response to my wit, Latobius snorted and twitched his ears, and I was still grinning when Canus emerged from the *Praetorium*.

"What's so amusing, Pullus?" he demanded suspiciously, but I waited to answer, watching him clamber aboard his own mount, a roan gelding that looked like a pony next to Latobius, who is one of the largest horses I have seen even now, and I could see that he was not an experienced horseman, which in turn made me wonder if that would be a problem given where we were headed.

In reply, I told Canus coldly, "First, that's 'Centurion,' or if you prefer, Primus Hastatus Prior. And second...it's none of your business."

Without waiting, I turned Latobius' head, although I did take up the leads of one of the spares and the packhorse carrying my armor and other gear. As soon as we left the city, I intended to don my *baltea*, while I noticed that Canus was wearing a dagger that was longer than our *pugio*, but it was hidden by his cloak, although the weather did not call for it, and he wore it strapped to his back so that it was almost horizontal. It came to me suddenly; he wears it like that so it's hard to see, and when he draws it, it will be coming from an unexpected direction since most men wore a dagger on their left side, and consequently would swing the blade from left to right, while the way Canus was wearing it, an attack would come from the opposite side. At the time, it was interesting, but that was all; only later would I learn how important an observation it was. Going to a trot, I headed for the eastern gate, which was technically the *Porta Praetoria* since, by centuries' old custom, the main gate of a Roman army camp is always oriented towards the enemy, but nobody in Mogontiacum referred to it as such. It was the *Porta Decumana* in everything but name, although another difference was that the shantytown around the eastern side of the camp was much smaller than even that outside the rear gate of Ubiorum, although Ubiorum is just a bit more than half the size of Mogontiacum. This, I assume, is due to the fact that, unlike at Ubiorum, the civilians, almost exclusively the families of Legionaries and auxiliaries do not have the protection of the Rhenus, a consequence of building the army camp on the eastern bank of the river. Frankly, it was something I did not understand; the first time I saw Mogontiacum, I asked my father, who had been part of what would turn out to be Drusus the Elder's last campaign, when Mogontiacum was less than a year old, but he did not know why this choice had been made.

The gates were closed, but they had either been warned ahead of time, or they were lax in their duties, because we were only delayed by the opening of one gate without any demand to see our orders, which was a good thing since we had none, another fact that I overlooked at the time. I had been concerned that it might be 5th men standing post, but while we merited examination, it was curious in nature, without any hostility, and I could only imagine what they were thinking. I had changed into a clean tunic at the villa, not a Legion tunic but one that I had worn before I joined that my mother had kept, which meant it was quite tight through the chest and shoulders, and had not even had a scraping, while my face itched from a week's worth of whiskers. My hair, both on my head and my face grow rapidly; Bronwen once attempted to convince me to shave twice a day, complaining about my stubble by the time the sun was down, but I knew there was no way I could pass for a German for at least the first few days of this journey. Deciding to wait on strapping on my *baltea*, we rode in silence, the sounds created by the Legions in the camp and the citizens of the shantytown fading behind us. I do not mean to give the impression that the countryside was deserted; there were farms on either side of the road, which was now paved for a distance of ten miles, where there is an outpost manned by a Cohort of Gallic auxiliaries, so the distance in between Mogontiacum and the outpost was settled, looking much like the western side of the river in terms of its peaceful and prosperous air. The mile marker was plain to see next to the road, a stone obelisk with the numeral "I" carved on it, and even easier to see were two men, one dismounted and the other mounted but on the opposite side of the road. As we drew closer, I actually recognized Lightning before I recognized Alex, he being the one still in the saddle, while the other man was bearded and wearing the long tunic and *bracae* favored by the German tribes.

Canus muttered, "That must be our guide..." His face screwed up as he tried to think of the name, and I finally supplied it as I looked over at him in surprise.

"His name is Otmar, but you don't know what he looks like?"

"I've never seen him before," he replied irritably. "Why would I know what he looks like?"

When put like that, I realized there was no reason; yes, Catualda had been in Mogontiacum, but nothing Varro had said gave any indication that he had laid eyes on him or on this Gotones nobleman, yet I found this troubling. Before I could pursue this, Canus noticed Alex, which caused him to jerk on his mount's rein, and for a moment, I thought he would be thrown as his horse rebelled by rearing a couple feet off the road.

"Who's this *cunnus* sitting there like he's waiting for something?" he muttered suspiciously once he got his animal under control.

"Because he is," I replied. "He's waiting for me."

"For you?" It was Canus' turn to look startled.

"Yes," I said nothing else, prompting him to demand, "Does *Quaestor* Varro know about this?"

"I didn't mention it." I shrugged.

We had not stopped our progress, and we were now about thirty paces away, and I called out, not to Alex but to the

German, in a challenging manner, which was by design, "*Salve*. Who are you?"

Rather than being offended, the man, about my age and whose tunic was a muted brown but with green swathes arranged in a pattern that I had never seen before, seemed amused.

"Who is asking, Roman? I," he replied in heavily accented but understandable Latin, and made an elaborate shrug, "am particular about who I identify myself to in these troubled times." He smiled. "I have seen how many of you Romans still harbor a grudge over what Herman did to Varus and his Legions."

Understanding that he was doing the same thing I was, I returned the smile, but Canus, growing impatient, hissed, "Pluto's cock! We don't have time for this!" Thrusting his finger at the German, he snapped, "Are you Otmar? You serve Catualda? Yes or no, barbarian!"

"I am," Otmar replied calmly, but I thought I heard anger there.

"You're taking us to him, so he," Canus jerked a thumb at me, "can deliver a very important message to your master."

"I serve Lord Catualda," Otmar seemingly agreed, but now he let his anger show, "but I am not his slave." He took a breath. "But yes, that is why I am here, waiting at the agreed upon point. And," he glanced up at the sun, "it is late to be starting a long journey like this."

Canus turned to Alex, and said, "The Centurion says you're with him. What's your association with him?"

Before I could answer for him, Alex said, "I serve Centurion Pullus."

"So, what? You're his body slave?" Canus sneered, then made a barking kind of noise that I would learn was his version of a laugh. "You won't be needed where we're going." Looking over at me, Canus gave me a leering smile. "I'm afraid that you'll have to do without your comforts, Centurion."

"First, he's not a slave," I replied, nudging Latobius closer to Canus, watching as his hand moved slightly from where it had been resting on the front of his saddle to his thigh. "And second, he's actually killed Germans in battle. Have you?"

Canus glared up at me, then gave his answer in an abrupt shake of his head. "Then he's coming. Now," I said casually, "if you want to waste more time by scurrying back to *your* master and ask for instructions, I suppose you can do that. We," I shrugged, "will be a few miles east by then."

Without waiting for an answer, I pulled the packhorse closer, untied the straps, and extracted first my *baltea*, which I strapped on, then the *baltea* that the spare *gladius* hung from, which I tossed over to Alex. Before Canus could do anything about it, we were both armed, and without another word, I nudged Latobius back into motion, heading east. Also without saying anything, Otmar fell in beside me, while Canus hesitated for a moment before kicking his own mount, bouncing in the saddle as it broke into a trot. Alex, with a small smile on his face, also fell in, but for the next couple of miles, he rode behind Canus, in a silent signal that he was now outnumbered...and watched.

By the time we stopped the first day, a few miles beyond the last outpost, I decided that I liked Otmar, while Canus clearly had the opposite feeling about our guide. He had a ready wit, and a keen eye for small details, both in general and in our surroundings, which I took as a good thing as we got closer to Marcomanni territory.

However, most of my time was spent with Alex, not surprisingly, whose first comment was, "I didn't want to say anything when we saw each other in Mogontiacum, but Gnaeus....you smell *bad*. And," he made a show of doing so, "I'm already itching just riding next to you."

"Oh, go piss on your boots," I grumbled. Then, "Please tell me you brought at least a flask of oil and a strigil."

"Of course I did," he assured me. Raising his voice, he grinned as he added, "What kind of luxury body slave would I be if I didn't, Master?"

We burst out laughing, as did Otmar; Canus did not find it amusing, and fairly quickly, he removed himself from our conversation by dropping back a few paces behind us. Which, I confess, made me nervous, and I suspect that was by design, his repayment for Alex doing the same thing.

"What route are we taking?" I asked, and I could not help sounding plaintive when I asked, "And are we really going all the way through Marcomanni territory?"

"Our route is yet to be fully determined, Centurion," Otmar answered. "It depends on whether the fall rains start early; our witches say they will this year." Even as he said this, he glanced up at the sky, and I followed his example, although to me, the clouds looked like normal clouds. It was now two days past the Kalends of September, and it is certainly the case that autumn brings rain, and mud, so Otmar's answer made sense. "As far as how far we have to travel," he continued, looking at the sky as he said vaguely, "our lands are east of the Marcomanni, and have been for generations beyond counting."

That was not an answer, not really, and I glanced at Alex, who I saw was of a like mind, but then Canus came trotting up to demand to know when we were stopping.

"There has to be a roadside inn somewhere ahead," he said, and while I do not know what he was expecting, judging from his reaction, it was not the three of us bursting out in laughter.

"An *inn*?" I did not try to hide my scorn. "On this side of the Rhenus?" Suddenly, I realized something, but I asked to make sure, "Have you or the *Quaestor* ever been on the eastern side of the Rhenus?"

Canus did not answer immediately, but when he finally did, it was with a sullen shake of his head. I opened my mouth to rub it in a bit more, then decided against it; what mattered was that this reinforced my growing certainty that, once my role was done, my mother's warning was one I must heed, that Canus' own task was to ensure that I did not return. This also made his reaction to Alex's inclusion in our party even more of a telltale about his intentions; I believe this was when my own plan began to form. We chose a stopping point where we could camp in a copse of trees a short distance from the road, which was no longer paved, but it was well-traveled, with two deep grooves from wagons. Entering the grove, we immediately saw signs of other travelers using this spot, which as at least three of us knew from experience meant that we would have to either use part of our small supply of charcoal or range farther for anything to burn.

"Canus," I said, "go find some firewood."

"I don't take orders from you!" he snarled, which did not surprise me, and I had been prepared for this. "Fine." I shrugged, then turned to Alex, who simply nodded, taking both my and Otmar's net forage bag that we all carry strapped to our saddles. Once Alex rode away, heading north to the ridge that paralleled the road and whose slope was covered with trees, I returned my attention to Canus, pointing to the small iron pot that had been packed away. "Since you're not foraging for wood, you have the choice of cooking or cleaning up afterward."

"I'm nobody's slave!" Canus shot back, but there was an edge to his voice there, something that told me that this was more than just a free Roman's reaction to the inference he was not.

"Then," I replied calmly, but under the guise of walking over to my own pack, I moved closer, "you better have something to eat packed away for yourself."

He shifted, and I saw the look of dismay flash across his features, but as the rest of us would learn, while Canus had a streak of cunning, altogether, he was not very bright.

"I have some bread and cheese," he muttered. "But only for tonight." In a more plaintive tone, he said, "I thought that there would be inns and *tavernae* along the way. Not," he added hastily, "all the way, but at least for the next few days."

"Sooner or later, you're going to have to pull your weight," I told him. "If you don't start tonight, you'll be doing it tomorrow."

"And I suppose *you* 'pull your weight' like the rest of us?" he challenged.

I could have simply said yes, but I was honest and replied, "When we're marching under the standard, and I'm commanding a Century of one hundred sixty men, give or take? No, I don't have time. But out here," I indicated our surroundings, "with just four of us? Yes, I do and I will. In fact," I grinned, and now I was lying, "I'm going to do the cooking tonight, and I can do wonderful things with soldier's porridge. Too bad you'll miss it."

Pointedly turning away in the signal I was done, I walked over to where Otmar was just finished rubbing down his own horse and was moving to one of the packhorses. Because he was a stallion, I had Latobius picketed at the opposite end from Otmar's mount, also a stallion, so I took Latobius' brush and walked over to the other packhorse next to Otmar.

"Exactly how far is it to your lands? And how deeply do we have to go to reach wherever Catualda is?" I asked bluntly.

"Your *Quaestor* did not tell you?" Otmar asked, clearly surprised, then before I could say anything, he said more to himself, "Although I can see why he would not." He took a breath, and I quickly understood why. "Using Roman miles, it is more than five hundred of them to our western border with the Marcomanni, and it is another hundred to Wawelska, which is the largest town belonging to us Gotones."

I was fortunate that I was clutching the bridle of the packhorse with one hand as I was brushing, because I would have staggered backward.

"*Five hundred miles*?" I gasped this.

"What did he just say? Did that savage just say we have five hundred miles to go?"

While I shared Canus' dismay, I also felt it necessary to point out, "You know that he speaks and understands Latin, don't you, Canus?" Something more important than Otmar's feelings occurred to me, and I turned my full attention on the other man. "So, you didn't know about this?"

"No!" Canus shook his head adamantly, but I suppose he saw the doubt there; I also think he was sufficiently shaken that, rather than blustering, he said, "The *Quaestor* didn't tell me, Centurion, I swear it!" Almost to himself, he muttered, "Because if he had, I don't know if I would have agreed to go."

Given what I had seen so far, it did not seem to me that Canus had that kind of relationship with the *Quaestor*, but this was not the time to probe that; besides, something else had occurred to me.

"You sounded as if the *Quaestor* knew," I said to Otmar. "Are you sure that he did? Or are you just assuming so?"

"No, Centurion," he assured me. "My master was very specific in his message to the *Quaestor*. I...saw him write it himself, in Latin."

Once again, this would prove to be a piece of information that would come back to me later, not what Otmar said, but in the almost imperceptible hesitation in his words.

"Do you even know how to read Latin?" Canus challenged, but while I could see this angered Otmar, his tone was even as he replied, "Yes, Canus, I can...can you?"

Any further exchange was cut off by the sound of hoofbeats approaching at a trot, and there was just enough light left for us to see that it was Alex returning, with three full forage bags of kindling and wood.

"I had to go almost halfway up the base of that ridge," he called out. "It's pretty much been picked clean by other travelers." By the time his feet touched the ground, he took in the three of us, sensing the tension, which prompted him to ask me, "What did I miss?"

Not seeing any point, I did not prolong his suspense, telling him what we had just learned, and Alex's first reaction was to turn and ask Canus in surprise, "You didn't know?"

"No!" Canus snapped, then subsided a bit as he rubbed the back of his neck. "I'm just as surprised as the Centurion is." He dropped his voice to just above a whisper, but we could still hear him mutter, "That bastard."

I made the decision then.

"There's nothing we can do about it now," I announced. "Let's get the fire started so that I can start on my famous soldier's porridge."

Alex looked startled, but when he opened his mouth, I gave him a shake of my head, along with a wink, although in the moment, I did decide to include a few of my small supply of peppercorns, counting on Otmar to notice and comment, reminding Canus of what he was missing.

The next day was spent mostly in silence; I believe the enormity of the task was sinking in, and Otmar was sensible enough not to aggravate Canus by saying anything at which Varro's man could take offense. Our third day, we were not quite back to normal, I suppose, but it was better than the second, as I pressed Otmar for information about the Gotones since I knew so little about them.

"We are a small tribe," Otmar explained. "With the Marcomanni to our southwest, the Vandalii to our south, the Gepitae to our north, the Venedi to the east, and the Suebi to our west. All of them," he said bitterly, "are more powerful than we are. Although," he smiled but it seemed to me mixed of equal parts a wolfish satisfaction and bitterness, "the Suebi are now vassals to the Marcomanni...just like we are."

"Varro said something about Catualda being related to Maroboduus through marriage?" I had to think for a moment. "Maroboduus is married to a relative of Catualda?"

Otmar looked amused, which he explained, "Yes, you could say that, but that relative is Catualda's aunt, his father's sister."

"Wait! You mean this Catualda is that bastard's *nephew*?" Canus burst out from behind us.

"I cannot speak for Rome," Otmar replied with a straight face, but I was beginning to learn that he had a sly sense of humor, "but yes, that is how it works with our tribes. The sister, or brother, of one of our parents is considered our aunt or uncle, as is whoever they marry." He looked over his shoulder in mock surprise. "Why? Is it not the same with Romans?"

"It's the same!" Canus sounded indignant, and Otmar winked at me.

"Then yes, Maroboduus is Catualda's uncle."

"What kind of relationship do they have?"

It was Otmar's turn to be caught out at Alex's question, but that was because to this point my friend had not said much. I happened to be looking at Otmar, and I saw what in the moment I put down to surprise that the question came from my servant, although he would learn very quickly not to underestimate my "little Greek"...an appellation he hates, which is why I use it.

"I would say that it is...complicated," Otmar said slowly. "When he was a child, he would spend summers as part of the king's household. His aunt was Maroboduus' first wife..."

"You mean your aunt died?" Canus interjected, which irritated Otmar, though I quickly learned that it was not about being interrupted, or by who was doing it.

"No," he answered tersely. "She did not die." He fell silent, but I suppose he realized we were waiting for more, and with a sigh, he said with a shrug, "She got old, and Maroboduus became bored with her."

"So he divorced her?" I asked, which was met with a look of confusion. "I mean, he set her aside?"

"No, he did not banish her from his hall," Otmar admitted. "Just from his bed."

Now, I was the one who was confused.

"I didn't realize that the tribes in Germania allowed men to have multiple wives," I said.

"It is not common," Otmar replied, then shrugged again. "But the rules for a king are not the same rules for the rest of his tribe."

"Ah," I understood now. I was unsure how to phrase it, so I simply plunged ahead, "Is that when Catualda fell out with Maroboduus?"

"Fell out?" Otmar frowned.

"Began to see Maroboduus in a different light," Alex offered.

"Ah, yes." Otmar nodded. "It was about that time. He had looked up to Maroboduus before that, but then he saw the king for what he was. Still, they saw each other several times after that."

My thought at the time was that Otmar seemed to take his master's own grievances to heart, because just a glance told me that the subject made him angry.

"How well do you know King Maroboduus?" I asked. "Were you ever with Catualda when he visited Maroboduus?"

"Oh yes." Otmar nodded. "I was with Lord Catualda every time." He paused as he thought, then repeated, "What is Maroboduus like? He was a great king once. But now," he shook his head, "he's grown old and cautious."

"He was right about Arminius," I pointed out, as much a test as an observation.

"He was," Otmar acknowledged, but while I thought there was hesitation there, I also was not certain; it was what he said next that I would have cause to remember. Turning to give me a direct look, Otmar added, "And Arminius will not forget that when he called on the Marcomanni, Maroboduus did not answer."

As it would turn out, we were a matter of a couple days from finding out just how true that was.

On our fifth day, we were not nearly as far as I would have hoped, but Otmar, counseling caution, was leading us along the Moenus (Main) as it meandered eastward, and whenever we spotted a party of travelers our size or larger, we sought cover. I bridled at this, but Alex convinced me that it was in our best interests to trust Otmar.

"If we're caught by someone loyal to Arminius," he had argued, "it's going to go even worse for Otmar than it does for us. Although," he had laughed, "you look more and more like a German every day."

"At least I don't smell as bad as I did," I replied, but he just looked at me without agreeing, so I gave him a shove.

The result was, that while it was with barely concealed impatience, I allowed Otmar to set the pace; I had already accepted that he would know the best route. Canus was becoming more sullen and withdrawn, which I had not thought possible, but once more, it was my friend who identified the cause.

"He's never been in enemy territory," Alex explained. "At least, not like this. Although," he lowered his voice, "I have learned that he was with a *collegia* in Rome. That's where Varro found him."

I was surprised, but then I thought about it and recalled seeing the two talking over the course of the previous days, while I already knew that Alex has a knack for putting people at ease.

"So Varro hired a bully boy," I mused.

"No." Alex shook his head. "It runs more deeply than that. He wouldn't talk about it, but if I had to guess, Varro saved him from some sort of trouble with the Urban Cohorts. Whatever it was, I think he's more loyal to Varro than just because he's paid."

That afternoon, it began to rain, picking up in intensity until we had to break out our *sagum*, though it was not cold enough for my fur-lined one for colder weather, which I had packed, thinking that at the rate I believed we would be traveling, we would be reaching this Wawelska place by the middle of September and returning by the first week of October, which would mean that I would only need the fur-lined one the last two or three days. While I had initially hoped we could make at least forty miles a day, between our meandering route and our frequent stops to allow parties to pass, a good day was thirty, and now that the rain was coming down, on this day, I thought twenty-five would be more likely. It also wrought havoc on the visibility, which was how, as we rounded a bend in the track that we were following, we almost literally ran into a party of more than a dozen men, all of them armed. I believe what saved us from going immediately at each other was that they were clearly as surprised as we were, drawing up as well, and while hands dropped to hilts, no weapons were drawn; I also knew it would not take much for that to change.

"Let me do the talking," Otmar whispered, though there was no need since I certainly could not pass for a German if I spoke, though I had learned enough to curse someone's mother in several dialects, and I understood them better than I spoke it.

Holding a hand up in the universal gesture of peaceful intention, Otmar nudged his horse a few paces forward, while one of the men of the other party did the same. It was pouring now, which made it hard to be heard, and Otmar cleverly raised his voice a bit louder than necessary so that we could hear as well without raising suspicion. Their leader was blonde, not unusual, his beard twisted into several plaits in which bones were tied, supposedly the knuckle bones of his slain enemies. I was more interested in catching a glimpse of the color and pattern of his tunic, though this was difficult because of his cloak, which was brown but without any kind of adornment other than a silver clasp, while at the same time, I tried to determine in whose territory we were, barely a hundred miles east of the Rhenus. Were we in Chatti country? I wondered. Or Hermunduri? It would be better if it were Hermunduri; they had remained loyal to Rome when Arminius had rallied so many tribes to his cause, but I did not think we were far enough south to be in their lands...which meant that we were likely in Chatti lands. Yes, we had vanquished the Chatti along with Arminius, and we had made widows of the gods only knew how many warriors, but I knew it would be foolish to think that, if these were Chatti warriors, and they discovered that three of this small party were not only Romans but two of them were with the Legions, they would remember they had surrendered and thrown themselves on Rome's mercy and would be punished for slaying us. I did not have to check and see if Alex was aware of this, but Canus was beginning to worry me, because as Otmar and the other man talked, calmly enough from what I could tell, he was beginning to grow visibly more nervous by the moment. Just when I thought that I would have to do something to calm him down, Otmar called out the customary farewell, then turned his horse and came trotting back to us, and as he returned to us, I watched the German do the same, although his gaze lingered on us as he slowly turned his horse around.

"We can continue," Otmar said, but when he said nothing else, Canus demanded, "And? What's happening?" He pointed a finger at the Gotones, and I was close enough to see it shaking. "What did you do? Did you make some sort of deal to betray us in exchange for your own skin?"

"Shut your mouth," I snarled. "And keep it shut and keep your eyes to yourself as we pass by, or I swear if it's my last act, I'll gut you before any of those *cunni* can!"

For an instant, I thought he would argue, but to my surprise, his mouth snapped shut and he gave a curt nod.

"I will explain once we are safe," Otmar promised. "And the Centurion is right. We are not completely out of danger yet, so please keep that in mind as we pass each other. And," he reminded us, something that I should have thought about, "it is likely that one or more of them will say something in an attempt to get a reaction, Centurion. Not all of his men are happy with Gundoc's decision."

In order to make room, we dropped into single file, but the Germans, in what was undoubtedly an attempt to instigate something, remained riding three abreast, forcing us to the edge of the track. I had one advantage that, because of my size, they couldn't glare down at me as they filed past, but it was more difficult than I thought.

"I think that one was dropped on his head, Gundoc! He looks like an oaf. A big, stupid oaf."

It was said in Latin, by a black-haired warrior wearing a helmet with crow's wings, his speech sibilant because of his missing upper and lower front teeth, uttered just as he was passing by me on Latobius, surprising me just how hard it was to keep my eyes averted and my right hand sitting on my thigh and not reaching for my great-grandfather's *gladius*. Somehow, Canus retained his composure, probably because he was ignored, and both of our parties passed by, quickly vanishing from each others' sight in the downpour. That did not stop me from dropping back behind Canus to watch our trail before I realized in order for them to catch us, we would hear them coming. I moved back up at a trot as Otmar guided us off the track and into the relative shelter of a thick stand of trees, noting with approval that he picked a slight bump of ground that, while not very high, had steep sides that we had to scramble up.

"They," he said without preamble, "are Chatti." This confirmed my guess that we were too far north to be in Hermunduri lands, but then he did not say anything else, prompting me to demand, "And? Why is an armed band of warriors out in the countryside in violation of the treaty?"

For that was one of the terms of Chatti capitulation; they agreed that if they were in a group, it would be only for the purposes of hunting, and no more than ten men in size.

Otmar clearly did not want to answer; I understood why when he said, "They are Chatti, but they are rebels who have joined Arminius. They volunteered to ride west to intercept any Marcomanni who are trying to reach Mogontiacum."

Alex and I exchanged a glance, and he was clearly as alarmed as I was, but Canus beat us to it.

"Why would they do that?"

"Because," Otmar replied grimly, "Arminius has finally done it. He has attacked Maroboduus."

"Pluto's *cock*!" I barely recognized my own voice. This

was staggering news, but then I thought of something, and I did not like the blooming of suspicion I felt because of it. "Wait. Why did they let us pass? We're coming from the west. If I were their commander, I'd at least want to know what we were about, but they just let us pass? That," I shook my head, "doesn't make sense."

"I told them the truth," Otmar answered, then amended, "At least, I told them part of the truth. I showed him this." He held out his hand, and for the first time, I noticed the large golden ring, making me think that he had just slipped it on. "I told him that I was loyal to Lord Catualda, and that Catualda is rallying the Gotones to rise up against Maroboduus. And," he shrugged, "I *might* have led him to believe that I was doing so because Arminius had sent a message to Lord Catualda requesting his assistance." I suppose he saw my skepticism, and he added, "It is no secret that Catualda and Maroboduus had become estranged, and there have been rumors for the last year that a reckoning was coming."

"And he believed you?" Alex asked quietly.

"He let us go, did he not?" Otmar countered. "If he did not, do you think we would be free right now?"

That, I concluded, was true. With that, we resumed our journey, leaving me to ponder what exactly this did to the agreement Catualda made with Rome.

They did *not* believe us, which we learned sometime after midnight. The reason that Alex and I are alive to recount what happened is due to the fact that we made preparations for an attack, beginning with moving our camp after we had prepared and consumed our meal at a spot not as far from the track as we normally did. Although the rain had stopped, there was not enough dry wood, so we sacrificed a large portion of our supply of charcoal, making sure that the glow from it could be seen from the track, then removed ourselves a couple hundred paces deeper into the woods to the north, higher up the steep slope and just below the crest, making it difficult for anyone to approach us from the north. I certainly did not believe that it would completely fool Gundoc and his band should he choose to come for us; what I did hope was that it would give us sufficient warning so that we could escape. To that end, we did not unsaddle our mounts, although I did take Latobius' off to give him a rubdown while he munched on his oats in his feedbag. I had not used the spare mount once, a black gelding, although Otmar had switched from his regular mount, predictably named Tyr, which is the favored name for Germans' mounts, a couple of times. Once I was done, I resaddled him, but instead of picketing him as normal, I wrapped the lead around my left wrist, then found a tree to lean against. We had drawn lots for watches, with Otmar drawing the first, Alex the second, Canus the third, with me going last, and I recall debating with myself about switching out with Canus, not particularly wanting to rely on someone who was so out of his element standing the watch after midnight. While the rain had stopped shortly before sunset, the leaves were dripping, and I wrapped my *sagum* around me while trying to get as comfortable as possible in a sitting position, dropping off to the whispered conversation Alex was having with Otmar about something.

"*What was that?*"

While I had certainly improved in my ability to go from a state of sleep to wakefulness, it still took a couple heartbeats for me to become completely alert, and it almost cost my life. I was just coming to my feet when Latobius, with a bellow of what I recognized as rage, swung his head around as he launched a mighty kick with both rear legs, and in the process jerked me by my left wrist, sending me staggering in that direction. Because of the total darkness, what sense I could make came from my ears, and the sound of what sounded like an ax striking the tree I had been leaning against was accompanied by a deeper, thudding sound, mingled with a whooshing noise that had to be the air rushing from the lungs of Latobius' target. Since I had had my eyes closed, I did at least have the advantage that my vision was as sharp as it could be in the darkness, so I saw the shadowy form of the Chatti who had swung the ax just as he jerked it free from the tree where my head had been leaning, preparing for another attack. I have no memory of drawing it, but thankfully, my *gladius* was already in my hand, fingers wrapped over thumb, ready to launch my own thrust from the first position, when Latobius, with another bellow, swung back around to face another threat...with his lead still wrapped around my wrist. This time, I did not keep my feet, landing flat on my back, the impact driving the air from my lungs and causing a thousand stars to explode in my vision. Because my sight was obscured in this way, I have no idea how I knew to roll to my left in the eyeblink before the Chatti's ax came down again, this time to bury itself in the ground where I had just been, but I did feel the blade slice through Latobius' lead from the tension suddenly releasing.

Since I had rolled to my left, my *gladius* was in position for a countermove, which I am somewhat ashamed to say was nothing more than a wild swing, but the gods were with me, because I felt the edge slice into the meat of the Chatti's calf a few inches below the knee, stopping when it struck one of the bones. His scream of pain was the loudest noise to that point, and he pitched forward to land right next to me, the agony he was feeling delaying his reactions so that, before he could even bring his hands up to protect himself, I lashed out again, this time with the pommel of my *gladius*. It was only through Fortuna that I struck exactly where I had envisioned, right in the man's open mouth, his screaming cut off and taking on a choked quality from the blood and shattered teeth, but I was already rolling away to leap to my feet, although as soon as they were under me, I did remember to perform a hard downward thrust into the Chatti's back.

"Gnaeus!"

I turned in the direction of Alex's voice, just as another shadowy figure came hurtling in my direction, my friend's warning giving me just enough time to do nothing more than bring my *gladius* up, my attacker essentially killing himself by running his body onto my blade. I was blasted by the by-now familiar stench of rotting teeth and onions of his last breath, but I still twisted the blade, then used his body as its own weapon by shoving him in the direction of another man who appeared to be heading in my direction.

There was a shout of surprise as my victim's corpse collided with the second man, but I was unprepared to hear that it was Canus, who began shouting, "Pluto's cock! Someone get him off me!"

With quite a bit of chagrin, I hurried over to grab the slumped figure off of Varro's man, then helped him up with a muttered apology.

"Where's Otmar?" I asked, though I did not really expect an answer.

"Gnaeus! There's too many of them! We need to get away!"

"We have to find Otmar!" I shouted back, just as there was the sound of metal clashing that turned out to be Alex parrying a Chatti *gladius*.

"I am here, Centurion! By the horses!"

"Let's go!" I grabbed Canus, but he moved well enough, though with a slight limp.

There was another exchange between Alex and his foe, and I turned to help him, but before I took a step, I could just make out Alex executing a second position thrust that caught the Chatti in the throat, dropping him to his knees. Then he was with us, and we rushed the dozen paces over to where we saw Otmar leaping into Tyr's saddle while, in the same motion, swinging his *gladius*, the longer blade favored by the German tribes, although his did have a needle point and was partly sharpened on its upper edge. A tree obscured my view of what he was aiming at, but then a Chatti came staggering backward in our general direction with both hands to his face, screaming from the pain of having half of it sliced off, while Alex finished him as he rushed over to Lightning. For a heart-stopping moment, I did not see my horse, and I had to try twice before my lips were wet enough to use the whistle I had trained him to respond to, but thank the gods he came immediately, barely slowing down as he swept by, while I grabbed the saddle with my left hand and, allowing his momentum to help me, swung up into the saddle. A Chatti, this one on horseback, came rushing out of the darkness, but seeing that I was already mounted and I had my *gladius* ready, he veered away, shouting a curse at me. Canus had gone rushing at his horse, spooking it; I do not know whether he was trying to imitate what I had done, but when he leapt, there was no horse there and he landed flat on his face, although he did manage to scramble to his feet immediately. Using my knees, I turned Latobius slightly, gripped my horse with my thighs and dropped the reins to snatch Canus up by the back of his cloak and tunic, lifting his feet off the ground.

"Canus! It's me!" I shouted when I saw his hand reach down for the long dagger. "I'm getting you out of here!"

Thankfully for my left arm, I saw his mount, which had slowed slightly as it tried to decide what to do, and using all of my strength, I raised my arm and dropped Varro's man onto his saddle.

Without waiting for any kind of response, I spun Latobius in a circle as I tried to get an idea of the best avenue for escape, which was when I saw that Alex still had not mounted Lightning, but when I shouted at him, he called back, "Wait. I have an idea!"

What the idea was took a moment to become clear, hearing a loud smack that was instantly drowned out by a whinny of alarm and pain, followed by a series of shapes that were our spare mounts who, in unison, broke into a gallop, heading downslope towards the track to the south.

"Now! Let's go!"

While I watched our spare horses vanish into the night, with alarmed shouts in the Chatti tongue competing with the receding hoofbeats, Alex appeared, aboard Lightning, and without another word, rode up and over the crest of the hill as the Chatti pursued our spare mounts in the opposite direction.

We rode hard for what was probably at least a third of a watch, heading north, weaving through the trees in the darkness as quickly as we could safely go before, finally, by unspoken consent, we drew up.

"Is anyone hurt?" Alex asked, but aside from some bumps and bruises, the most serious wound was a gash down Otmar's arm that had sliced through the sleeve of his tunic, which Alex inspected and hastily bandaged up, telling Otmar that he would examine it more closely when it got light.

Alex had managed to snatch up the lead of one of our packhorses, and he went to it now and discovered that it was the one carrying his and my baggage, which meant that, although my animal carried some of the rations, the bulk of our food had been left behind, along with the rest of the charcoal.

"Why did you grab that horse?" Canus fumed. "We need food more than Pullus needs his comforts!"

I had donned my *hamata* when we stopped for the meal, and of course I was wearing my harness and *gladius*, but everything else, including what, if Varro was correct, was an important piece in Vergorix's torq was still in my pack. Fortunately, my personal tinderbox and scraps of kindling were in my pack as well, but we quickly decided to wait to light a fire. We did not hear any sounds of pursuit, but we also did not want to take any unnecessary risks, and now that we knew there were no serious injuries, that could wait. Sooner or later, our collective attention would have turned on Canus, but he had hastened it by opening his mouth to complain.

"How did the Chatti get so close to us, Canus?" Otmar asked him quietly as Alex bound his arm. "It was your watch."

"How should I know?" Canus replied, and there was a quality to his voice that caught my attention; a quick glance at Otmar told me that it was not my imagination.

"Were you asleep?" I asked him, matching Otmar's tone. "Is that how?"

"No!" Canus shook his head, but even in the dark, I was certain that I saw him blanch. "Of course not!"

"It happens." I shrugged. "You had the worst watch to stay awake." I paused then before I went on, "Although, if you were under the standard, at the very least, you'd be flogged with the scourge. At worst, you would be beaten to death by your own comrades."

"Nobody's going to flog me!" he snarled, and his hand moved; so did mine, except that mine was balled into a fist, and even in the gloom I did not miss, striking him on the point of his chin and dropping him like a stone.

Even so, I noticed that his dagger was halfway out of its sheath, reinforcing my belief that, when he chose to, Canus could move swiftly. I had not applied all of my strength, so he was not unconscious, but before he could think to do anything rasher than he already had, I reached down and pulled the dagger the rest of the way out from under his body and tossed it out of his reach. Then, I extended my hand to help him up as he came to one elbow, holding his jaw with that hand as he glared up at me before finally taking my hand with his free one and I hauled him to his feet.

"Don't fall asleep again, Canus," I told him, then in a sign that it was over as far as I was concerned, I turned to Otmar.

"What now, Otmar?"

"I was hoping you would have a suggestion, Centurion," he said lightly, then went on, "but I do not think we can stay here much longer." He peered up at the sky, but I had already done so, and like me, he saw that while it was still no longer raining, the clouds obscured the stars and the quarter moon. "I would guess that we are about five of your miles north of the Moenus. Would you agree?" I thought for a moment then nodded. "At some point, we need to resume heading east. How many of those Chatti did you kill, Centurion?"

"Two I'm sure about, and one more may not have been killed, but Latobius put him out of action for a good amount of time if I had to wager."

Turning to Alex, Otmar asked him the same question, and Alex replied, "I know one for sure, and another one might bleed to death."

"I killed two," Otmar said confidently, and I confess I felt a prickling of irritation, seeing it as his way of claiming equality with me as a warrior, but he had already turned to Canus.

"I...I don't know," Canus admitted. "Maybe one, but I don't think I got my blade in deep enough."

"That leaves five men," I said, "maybe six." Thinking of something, I asked Otmar, "Were either of the men you killed Gundoc? None of mine were." Otmar shook his head, while Alex shrugged and said, "It was too dark to tell, and I only saw Gundoc mounted, but I don't think my man was as tall as Gundoc." I did not bother asking Canus. "That makes the odds too close to even for Gundoc to continue chasing us, so I think we're safe."

"Oh, I agree that I do not believe Gundoc is pursuing us," Otmar agreed, then hesitated for a moment, as if he was waiting for me to work it out. When I did not, he asked in an almost gentle tone, "Centurion, do you really believe that Gundoc only had a dozen men with him? What would you do if the situation was reversed and you spotted the other party first?"

I had actually thought about this, so I was ready with a reply, "Oh, I would have had men off the track hiding in the woods. But," I reminded him, "you were there. The Chatti were just as surprised to see us as we were to see them."

"It certainly seemed that way," Otmar agreed. "What if he was not? But," he hurried on, "I agree with you, he was surprised. So, what would he do once his attempt to capture us failed?"

"Capture us?" Canus interjected. "They tried to kill us!"

"No, they didn't." I was almost as surprised that it was my voice I heard, because honestly, I had made that assumption early on as well, but Otmar had planted a seed in my mind. "They were trying to capture us," I spoke slowly, allowing my mind to work out where I thought Otmar was going. "And, when they didn't, he wouldn't try and run us down." This was when it hit me, and I almost groaned aloud. "He's heading back east, looking for help to cut us off."

"That is what I believe he is doing," Otmar agreed. "So if we resume our eastward journey, I also believe it is likely that we will run into more trouble of this nature."

"But we *have* to get to this Catualda *cunnus*," Canus insisted, and there was an edge to his voice that sounded close to panic. "We *can't* fail the *Quaestor*!" When none of us said anything, he almost shouted, "You don't understand what's at stake here!" He began looking at each of us, one to the other, all sign of the hard man who coldly beat one of my men to death gone. "The *Quaestor* can't fail! We *must* find a way to get to your master!" he implored Otmar. Then, he said a word that chilled my blood; actually, it was a name. "If he fails Sejanus..."

He stopped then, his head dropping to his chest, leaving me to stare at Otmar in shock, and I immediately saw that he did not look surprised. Very quickly, my state of confusion of an eyeblink before seemed as if it was the height of enlightenment.

"My lord thought this might happen, and he made...other plans," Otmar said calmly. Turning to look at me, he continued, "But you are not going to like them very much, Centurion."

"Why?"

Honestly, it was the only thing I could think to ask.

"Because we are going to be meeting a force large enough that we will not have to worry about being intercepted. And," he smiled then, but it was one I had not seen before in my short association with him, "we are heading in the right direction already. Which is why I propose that we continue heading north."

"Into the heart of Chatti country?" I shook my head. "You would have to have a few thousand men to be safe from the Chatti falling on us, but even then, they might because they'd have cause if there's so many Gotones in their territory, especially given how far away your lands are from theirs."

Otmar shook his head. "They are not Gotones." He took a breath and I understood why when he said, "It is one of your Legions." I was, understandably I believe, too shocked to speak, and he clearly came to a decision because he said, "There is something else you should know. My name is not Otmar. It is..."

"Catualda."

Alex sounded calm when he uttered the name, and since he is writing this, I will let him explain.

I began to suspect that "Otmar" was not who he said he was a couple days earlier, although I did not immediately think he was Catualda. There were a couple of moments during our conversations where he seemed to have such a deep insight into Catualda that my first inclination was that he was a brother, but as I thought about it, I could not think of a reason why Catualda would hide his identity from us, because it would make what would be a dangerous trip through hostile territory unnecessary. Nevertheless, it was not until our meeting with Gundoc that the idea that Otmar could be Catualda occurred to me, but since I did not have a chance to talk about it with Gnaeus, I kept my thoughts to myself. Then, they attacked us, and it was during our flight that I began to put more pieces together.

The now-identified Catualda looked over at Alex with, if I was any judge, an equal mixture of surprise and respect, and he nodded his head in acknowledgement.

"Yes, Alex, and I want to offer an apology, but I believed it was...necessary to achieve our aim."

"And," Alex continued, and while those who did not know him would have said his tone remained the same, I heard the anger there, which I was about to share, "you never had any intention of traveling all the way to Gotones territory. Since," my friend's mouth twisted into a sardonic smile, "we were on our way to meet with *you* in the first place."

Catualda shifted in his saddle, and I saw him glance over at me as if gauging the distance between us, but honestly, I was still too shocked to be angry, although that would be coming shortly.

"Yes, and I apologize for that as well. It was also necessary, both to fool those who might want to stop us..."

"Like Gundoc?" I interrupted, but he shook his head. "No. At least," he grimaced, "I did not think he wanted to stop us." His expression changed then, and he seemed to speaking to himself, "Unless he was lying about being allied with Arminius against Maroboduus. But," he shook his head, "I do not think so, or he would have attacked us then."

"Only if he knew who you were," I pointed out, and there was no mistaking the expression of guilt that flashed across his features.

"I did tell him, but only after he said that he was with Arminius."

"Maybe he changed his mind," I suggested, but Alex, as is his habit, kept his mind on the more important matter.

"Who are we meeting north of here?"

"One of your Legions," Catualda repeated calmly, as if it was the most natural thing in the world. "But I do not know which one your *Quaestor* will be sending."

As one, we all spun to face Canus, who I believe would have slinked off if we were not in the middle of hostile territory and surrounded by men who had just tried to kill us.

"You need to start talking, *and*," I snarled, "telling the

fucking truth."

My *gladius* was out by the time I had finished speaking, while I nudged Latobius so that he was crowding Canus' mount, but from the left, placing his dagger hand on the opposite side and my *gladius* in perfect position to strike.

"I don't know anything!" Canus burst out, but even as flustered as he clearly was, he realized how absurd this was, and he added quickly, "I mean, I don't know anything other than what the *Quaestor* told me!"

"And what was that?" Alex asked, which irritated me at first, until he indicated me. "I think you'd rather answer me honestly than let the Centurion have a chance to...ask, wouldn't you?"

By the time Canus was through, there was one thing that I was certain of; my belief that removing myself from Rome would remove me from the danger posed by the machinations and ambitions of Prefect Sejanus was folly. Even worse, it was clear that aiding Catualda in his usurpation of Maroboduus would be the best, and perhaps the only way of assuring that Alex and I lived through the coming winter.

"The *Quaestor* is taking advantage of *Praetor* Silius' absence with Germanicus," Canus had explained. "When Drusus returned to Rome, he reported to the Imperator. And," he shrugged as if it was to be expected, and knowing what I did, he was right, "naturally, Prefect Sejanus was with Tiberius when Drusus gave his report." He glanced at Catualda, and while I would not say it was a nervous one, I understood why when he continued, "Supposedly, Drusus said that Catualda wasn't ready to challenge Maroboduus yet, and in Drusus' opinion, wouldn't be for another two or three years after gathering more support from both his own people, and some Marcomanni nobles who were ready for a change."

Naturally, I looked over at the Gotones, and despite the gloom, I imagined I saw him flush, although his expression remained neutral.

"What are Sejanus' instructions to your master?" Alex asked, eliciting a scowl, though that was all that Canus did.

"What he told you," Canus answered. "We were to escort

this *cunnus* to meet," he gave a bitter laugh, "with himself."

I had deduced that Canus was as surprised to learn the Gotones' true identity as I was, but a thought occurred to me, although I was opening my mouth to ask when Catualda spoke.

"The *Quaestor* knew my real identity," he said. Then, with a ghost of a smile, he added, "He should, since we had a meeting."

"When was this?" Canus demanded.

"A few weeks ago, at Confluentes," Catualda replied.

I looked over at Canus, thinking that he not only looked upset, he looked hurt.

"I was with him on that trip," he muttered. "But then he sent me on to Ubiorum to *investigate* something that turned out to be nothing but a rumor." When he shook his head, there was no missing the bitterness. "He lied to me, which means he doesn't trust me."

I do not know why, but I actually felt a stab of sympathy for Canus; perhaps it was seeing that, for whatever reason, he was devoted to the *Quaestor*, although in my view, he was a fool for thinking that that devotion would run in both directions.

"That," I agreed, "is a possibility. But it's also a possibility that he was told by Sejanus to keep you in the dark."

An almost pathetic look of hope bloomed on Canus' narrow face, and he nodded vigorously.

"That's it, I'm sure of it! He didn't tell me because Sejanus warned him not to; that's the only reason he wouldn't."

None of this really mattered, and now that I felt confident that Canus had been as uninformed as we were, I returned my attention to Catualda.

"What did Varro tell you specifically about why he's doing this?"

"Practically nothing," Catualda replied, but seeing that I was unconvinced, he added, "I swear it, Centurion." Pausing, he went on, "But while he did not specify his reasons, he did say things that give me an idea about his motives." I nodded to him to continue. "While I cannot be certain, I believe that what Varro is doing, while he is clearly involved with your Praetorian Prefect, he is doing because he thinks that is what

Tiberius wants. And," I did not miss the flash of bitterness there, "while I clearly did not impress his son as much as I believed I had, I do not think Varro believes that Tiberius wants to wait to replace Maroboduus as his son advised."

As I considered this, I glanced at Alex.

"It makes sense," he replied to my unasked question, then pointed out, "and it would have an added bonus to Sejanus. If Catualda is successful now, it casts doubt on Drusus' judgment that he wasn't ready. And," he finished with a shrug, "I tend to agree that Tiberius wants to deal with Maroboduus sooner rather than later."

Something else occurred to me, and I voiced my thought aloud.

"All of this depends on *Praetor* Silius not returning, because even if he agrees in principle with what Varro is doing, he's not going to stand for his *Quaestor* taking this kind of action on his own."

This elicited a snort from Canus who, when we all turned our attention on him, clearly realized he had some explaining to do.

"I wouldn't worry about the *Praetor* returning anytime soon," he assured us with a smile that glittered with malice. "First, he has to make the journey back from Asia and wherever the fuck Germanicus is now. Even then he's going to come to Rome to report to the Imperator first, and when he does, Prefect Sejanus and the *Quaestor* have...plans for the *Praetor*, and he's going to have his hands full for some time to come."

"What about?" I demanded. "And why?"

"I don't know any details," he replied; seeing our skepticism, he cried, "I swear it! That was another thing the *Quaestor* didn't share with me. As far as the why?" His mouth twisted into a sneer. "Because Silius is a high-handed *cunnus* who thinks his *cac* doesn't stink, and he made sure the *Quaestor* knew that Varro's bloodline didn't match the *Praetor*'s, that's why!"

That did not sound anything like Silius; if he had been speaking of Caecina, I would have immediately believed him, but Gaius Silius was a highly competent general, and while he was a strict disciplinarian, and could be harsh when needed, he was almost as respected as Germanicus. Not adored, certainly, but between my own experiences with the grandson of Divus Augustus and reading my father's account, I do not believe that we will ever see someone with his combination of valor, charisma, and honor, at least in my lifetime. Sitting there in the dark, I also realized that none of this mattered in the moment; if Silius returned to Mogontiacum from his time with Germanicus in Asia, it would be Varro who had to answer for what was happening.

"You said there was a Legion," I waved a hand in a northerly direction, "somewhere north of us waiting, but you don't know which one?"

"No," Catualda shook his head, "I do not know."

"It's almost certainly going to be one from Mogontiacum," Alex offered, but while this made sense in one way, I pointed out, "If we have to ride north, that's going to put us closer to Ubiorum."

"That's true," Alex agreed, "but do you see Primus Pilus Sacrovir being willing to bring our Legion over to this side of the Rhenus on the orders of a *Quaestor*?"

He was not finished before I knew he was right, but I still was not willing to completely capitulate, admitting, "No, I don't. But Neratius might." My friend did not reply, just regarded me steadily until I grumbled, "Fine. It's not going to be from Ubiorum, and it certainly won't be from Vetera, so that rules out the 2nd and 14th. Which means," I finished bitterly, "it's going to come down to either the 21st or those Alaudae bastards."

"Centurion, I have a suggestion to make," Catualda spoke up. "Now that you know my identity, and that we will have one of your Legions, it is even more crucial that we evade detection as we move north." Before I could point something out, he held up a hand to forestall me. "Yes, I believe that, for whatever reason, Gundoc has decided to side with Maroboduus, or at least earn a sizable bounty for bringing me to him before he returns to Arminius' fold, but I also am certain that he is not pursuing us north, because it would be foolhardy for us to do so since it puts us in the heart of his tribe's lands. He is hurrying east, counting on us turning back in that direction now that he knows who I am." He paused, I supposed to wait for me to absorb this, and I indicated my agreement that his logic was sound so he continued, "But it *is* dangerous, even without Gundoc pursuing us, so my suggestion is that we travel only by night from this point."

"We'd be blessed by Fortuna if we made fifteen miles in a night!" I exclaimed. "Besides, what do you expect us to do? Fumble about hoping that we just somehow stumble across the Legion?" A thought occurred to me. "And when was this Legion supposed to cross the Rhenus?"

"Six days after we departed," he answered.

"That's today!" Canus gasped.

"They were to go to Confluentes," Catualda, ignoring Canus, continued. "Then once across the river, they are to head northeast following the Laugonas (Lahn) River to its headwaters, then they will cross a low ridge, where they will find the Visurgis, which they will follow downstream to a village in Marsi territory, on the edge of Chatti lands. That is where we will meet them."

"One Legion?" I shook my head. "One fucking Legion is supposed to march across most of Germania, just south of wherever Arminius and what's left of his bunch is holed up?"

"The *Quaestor* assured me that the situation is so unsettled with the tribes that they could not get organized quickly enough to stop your Legion," Catualda said somewhat stiffly, making me wonder how much of this plan was Catualda's doing. "Also, what you and your Legions did last year is still fresh in the memories of all Germans, and they know what would happen if they violated the treaty. It *does* give Rome the right to cross the Rhenus at any time and for any reason, does it not?"

That was true, certainly, but what was real on a scroll and what was real here, in a dripping forest on the wrong side of the Rhenus, was something else entirely.

"Gnaeus," Alex intruded into my thoughts, "let's talk." Without waiting, he turned Lightning and walked him several paces away, turning the horse so his back was to Catualda and Canus. When I drew alongside, he wasted no time. "Gnaeus, we don't have any choice but to go along." He would have been shocked to know that I had already reached that conclusion, but I wanted to know why he thought so, and I pretended to be doubtful, rubbing my chin. There was no missing the impatience as he whispered, "Think about it. If we return to Mogontiacum without helping Catualda, do you have any doubt that Varro will go through with his threat? Especially if Catualda and whatever Legion is with him is successful? The *Quaestor* is gambling everything on succeeding, and he's counting on Tiberius being so happy that Maroboduus has been removed that he will forgive Varro for anything he might have done outside the regulations. Sejanus is in the same position, and he'll do everything he can to protect Varro, as long as it's not a complete catastrophe. Varro can't afford to leave a loose end, and we are both loose ends now, no matter what the outcome, but the only way we get out of this is do what we can to make sure Catualda succeeds."

"And then," I said grimly, "we need to make sure we take care of Canus before he can do anything to us."

Alex hesitated, then gave a nod.

"Yes, we do."

Before we returned to the other two, I whispered, "It's just this is so fucking complicated."

"Yes, it is," he agreed.

In the immediate aftermath, I wondered if, had we been aware of what was taking place at that moment with Maroboduus, whether we would have been better off just going back to Mogontiacum and taking our chances.

The first immediate problem to confront us was that none of us were familiar enough with the ground we were covering to choose the best route for avoiding attention. More than once, we were forced to detour when the ridge or hill we were ascending became too steep even for the horses, and we would have to turn to traverse the face first in one direction then the other, which meant that we probably did not cover three more miles before we agreed we needed to stop for the day. Fortunately, finding a spot to hide was not difficult, and once it was light we risked a small fire to prepare what rations we had left from my packhorse. Once again we stood watch, but I insisted that Canus take the first watch, not wanting him drowsy later in the day, while the rest of us fell immediately to sleep. I had stripped off my *hamata*, though I still slept with my *gladius* close to hand, and while the clouds were threatening, it did not rain. I had drawn the middle watch, relieving Canus, who did know to whisper as he reported to me that he had heard the bawling of cattle.

"From which direction?"

"I can't be sure, but I think that it's that way." He pointed, and I stifled a curse when he pointed north.

"All right," I decided. "Catualda has the watch before it gets dark; I'm going to have him scout ahead to make sure there's not a farm or settlement up ahead."

Varro's man gave me a sidelong glance at this.

"You trust him not to betray us?"

It was a superficially sensible question, but I was confident when I shook my head.

"If he did, then what do you think happens to him and his chance to overthrow Maroboduus?" He still seemed unconvinced, and I pointed out, "And when he shows up to whatever Legion we're meeting without us, what do you think is going to happen then?"

"I suppose," he muttered, yet he did not seem convinced, but I had spent all of the time I was willing to waste convincing someone I was probably going to have to kill at some point in the future.

"Lie down and get some sleep. If tonight is anything like last night was, you're going to need it."

When it was time to rouse Catualda, I noticed how, like a warrior should, he came immediately awake, whereupon I explained what Canus had heard.

"I will go now," he got to his feet, and walked to Tyr, then added, "and perhaps you should go with me."

"There's still too much light." I shook my head.

"We will be cautious," he promised. "Besides, if we get there while it is still light enough to see, then it will be easier to tell if it is something we can slip past once it is dark, or we need to make a..." He fumbled for the word, which I provided,

"Detour." "Yes." He nodded. Seeing I was still hesitant, Catualda grinned. "Unless you consider yourself too clumsy being so large for a Roman. Then I will go myself."

"Oh, go piss on your boots," I growled, irritated as much at myself for responding to the Gotones' naked ploy.

I got Latobius saddled, and he and Tyr were of like mind, not appreciating being disturbed from their doze, but without discussing it, we did not mount, choosing to walk our horses. I roused Alex and whispered what we were doing, then we climbed up and out of the bowl that had recommended itself as a hiding place, being deeper than it appeared so that our mounts had not been visible from any direction. The ground was relatively level, but then we reached a small stream, so we stopped, both to let our mounts drink and to slake our own thirst.

"We need to bring the other horses here once it gets dark," I whispered, and Catualda agreed.

Pressing forward, we saw a lighter area ahead that signaled a clearing, but it was the sudden lowing of a cow that alerted us that, in this at least, Canus had been correct.

"Let's tie the horses here," I whispered, and again Catualda agreed.

Dropping into a crouch, we spread out so that he was about twenty paces to my right, and we approached cautiously, but Catualda moved more quickly than I was willing to go, so he was about ten paces ahead of me yet still twenty paces to my right when, suddenly, I heard a voice. Instantly dropping to the ground behind a fallen log, I had to move a bit so that I could see Catualda, who was still standing there, and it took an extra heartbeat for me to make out that he was not alone, with a shorter figure standing in front of him. Even if I could have comprehended the words, I was too far away, so I was forced to go by the tone of what I realized now was a boy, probably one of the sons of whoever's cattle these were, and despite the tension, I had to admire how cool Catualda sounded. He actually said something that made the boy laugh, then I saw that he was gesticulating behind his back, but I could not see what it was, so I slowly raised myself up so the log did not obscure my vision of his lower body, seeing that he was patting the air behind his back in a gesture that I took meant he wanted me to stay put. Then, adding to my distress, the boy turned about and began walking off, with Catualda following him out into the pasture. I was not about to stay where I was because I could not see out into the pasture beyond the first fifty paces or so, but I chose to crawl on all fours, climbing over the log and moving slowly until I had reached a vantage point that allowed me to see, about two hundred fifty paces to the north, a couple of low buildings, made of wattle and with turf roofs that I knew from experience made them blend in to the surroundings.

I was slightly relieved to see that it was neither a village nor a farm where more than one family worked, but that feeling was washed away when I saw a figure emerge from the building that was slightly larger than the other that, judging from the heap of manure against the side, was the barn. It was a man; I assumed the boy's father, but then another figure emerged, and this one, also male, was almost the size of the adult, and I judged that this was a lad in his young teens. The boy gestured to Catualda, and I saw the father shifting the implement in his hand, a pitchfork, holding it in a way that would transform it into a weapon. What am I supposed to do? I thought with a fair amount of dismay. While the farmer was clearly cautious, he did not appear to be alarmed...yet, while Catualda pointed in my general direction, then in the opposite direction, north. Surely he's not telling the farmer the truth! I could not stop a soft groan from escaping my lips, and I was about to get to my feet when, suddenly, the farmer turned and strode towards the farmhouse, with Catualda and the man's sons walking behind him. Neither youth seemed alarmed, and I guessed that the young boy was chattering excitedly to Catualda, because I saw the Gotones throw his head back and laugh, and despite myself, I began to relax slightly. They disappeared inside, and I settled down to wait, the time dragging by until I began to worry about whether Catualda was expecting me to come to his aid. He had not given me any kind of signal...had he? I wondered, trying to recall what Catualda had done on his short walk from barn to farmhouse. Had his laughing at whatever the boy said been it? I was about to stand up and run back to get Latobius, and Tyr, when I heard the snapping of a branch behind me, though some distance away, and I twisted my head, hand on my *gladius* to see that it was Alex and Canus.

Despite myself, I was relieved to see them, though I certainly did not show it, demanding of Alex, "What are you doing here? I didn't tell you to come here!"

He was totally unfazed, saying only, "You've been gone too long. And," he looked around, "where's Catualda?"

I was just pointing when, from inside the farmhouse, we heard a shrill scream, along with a deeper shout of alarm. Without saying a word, I leapt to my feet and began sprinting for it, followed closely by Alex, and not quite as closely by Canus, although he had drawn his dagger, while Alex had Scrofa's blade in his hand. Before we got within fifty paces, however, Catualda emerged, his own *gladius* in one hand while using a piece of cloth to clean his blade with the other. His expression was grim, but we quickly learned that it was not because he had just slaughtered four people, only one of whom could have been described as a warrior, though of the type that fills the native levies and not a professional warrior that Romans love to kill.

"I had no choice," he said by way of greeting. "But there is something you need to know." He took a breath, then said, "Arminius has launched an attack on Maroboduus. They are at war."

"I had no choice, Centurion, You do know that, do you not?"

I did not reply immediately, but then with a sigh, I agreed, "I do. But," I felt it necessary to add, "I just hope that they're not missed immediately. Yes," I held up a hand, "we did as good a job of getting rid of the bodies as we could and cleaned the blood up, but that manure pile isn't going to hide them from wild animals very long."

That was something he could not deny, and he did not try, riding on in silence for a bit longer. I never asked him, but I suspect that his mood was similar to mine; in fact, I was strongly considering turning west and trying to get back across the river, a part of me thinking that not even Varro could hold us responsible for events beyond our control. As proof that Alex truly knows my mind, he chose this moment to speak up.

"Are you thinking of giving up, Gnaeus?" I was startled, though I realized I should not have been, and I nodded. "That's what I thought, but we can't."

"Why not?" I tried not to sound annoyed, which is my usual response when someone disagrees with me; that Alex knew my thoughts without asking compounded it.

"Because Varro will have his back to the wall now, and he'll be desperate." He hesitated, "And now he'll need a scapegoat to sacrifice. And," he finished quietly, "given everything that's happened, you would do nicely. A Centurion who is already in trouble, one who's known for being...rash," I did not care for that characterization, but neither could I dispute it, "tries to salvage his reputation by conducting this mission to have Catualda replace Maroboduus...on his own."

My stomach clenched, a sign that at least part of me accepted this, but I was not yet convinced, so I argued, "But how would I know about anything concerning Catualda and Maroboduus?" I laughed, but it was forced. "You were with me. I was in Rome for the last..."

I stopped then, because this was the instant I fully realized that Alex was right. Because of my time in Rome, and in the Praetorian Guard, Varro would make the assumption that I was like so many other Praetorians in the Centurionate, that I was politically attuned to the nuances and undercurrents that were a daily part of life, and would be avidly listening for any bit of choice gossip that could advance my own aims. The fact that I did not recognize the existence of those undercurrents before I arrived in Rome, and once I did, I floundered in them so much it almost got me killed, would not be something about which Varro was aware, unless Sejanus had sent ahead a detailed account of our clash. And, as much hubris as I may possess, I was close to certain that I was not important enough to warrant Sejanus spending the kind of time and effort necessary. No, I realized, Varro would believe that I had put everything together even if I had not...and because of that, I would be, as Alex said, a loose end that needed to be tied up no matter what. Returning to Mogontiacum would guarantee my death, and in some ways even worse, Alex's death, because this was even less his doing.

Stifling a curse, I said, "All right. We keep going. But," I moved to the other problem, "in the event that the Primus Pilus of whatever Legion is waiting for us doesn't know, we *must* tell him that Arminius has gone to war with Maroboduus."

"If we do that, what do you think that Primus Pilus will do?" Catualda asked, and it was easy to see that he was worried, as he should have been. "You know each of them, at least somewhat, do you not, Pullus?"

"It doesn't matter which one it is," I said flatly, ignoring the Gotones' sudden lack of formality. "No Primus Pilus is going to risk his entire Legion on something like this."

Alex coughed, and I had to stifle a groan, knowing what that meant, and I prepared myself for him to bring up something I had not thought about.

Which he did, very quickly, "I'd agree about Sacrovir, Neratius, and especially Turtullus," he began, naming the new Primus Pilus of the 21st last, "who's only been Primus Pilus for a few months. But Nerva?" He shook his head. "From what you've told me, it sounds like he's tied himself to Varro in order to get to you by using what Florus did."

Not surprisingly, three sets of eyes turned on Canus, and at first, he did not seem to be interested in speaking, but I supposed that he thought through his situation and realized something. Yes, crossing Varro was dangerous, but he was with three men, one of whom already had reason to harm him, more than a hundred miles from where Varro was sitting in Mogontiacum. Before he worried about Varro, he needed to survive to get to that point, and if I did not loathe him, I might have had some sympathy for his plight.

"It's as your freedman says, Pullus," he said reluctantly, and I opened my mouth to snap at him about using that term with my friend, but Alex shook his head. "Nerva actually approached the *Quaestor* with the idea once your man Florus killed his in The Happy Legionary. And," he shrugged, "this was Varro's price."

"Pluto's cock," I muttered. "I didn't realize that Nerva hated me that much."

"Oh," Canus interjected. "Nerva didn't know that this would be what Varro would want from him when he made the agreement." The smile he gave then once again reminded me from where his *cognomen* probably came. "But he found out soon enough. And now," he shrugged, "he's fucked because unless he's an utter fool, he knows that the *Quaestor* has set everything up quite nicely to destroy Nerva if he doesn't go along."

"So, what?" Alex asked. "Nerva thought that what Varro would want is for Nerva and his Alaudae to look the other way if they had duty on the docks so that Varro could dip his beak?"

Canus looked impressed, although he sounded cautious. "Yes, it was something like that." I suppose he decided it did not really matter, because he added with a shrug, "The *Quaestor* has...business interests with some tribes on this side of the river."

"What kind of interests?" I asked sharply, but this was all Canus would say about it, and after a few more attempts, I let it drop.

After all, I had even more to think about.

For the next three days, we essentially crept northward, still moving only at night, avoiding all settlements and farms, not wanting a repetition of what had taken place at the first farmhouse, not because we cared about the occupants, but because leaving a trail of bodies behind us would help any pursuer determine our course. We knew that we had to be getting close, which meant that we had to stop traveling by night if we wanted any chance of intercepting whichever Legion was wandering about, although now that I knew that Varro had leverage over him, I was certain that it would be Nerva. Which, as Alex and I discussed, would create a whole other set of problems, and dangers to the both of us.

"If it is Nerva, don't be surprised if he blames you for his predicament," Alex had advised.

Although my first instinct had been to argue this by pointing out that I had not held a *gladius* to his throat to make him try to exact revenge on me and put himself in a position where he was controlled by Varro, I did not bother, understanding that it would be pointless because I knew he was right.

"Just remember," I told him, in both irritation and amusement in equal measure, "that this whole mess was your idea to begin with when you advised me to go after Petronius."

I had expected him to argue the point, but instead, he said simply, "I know." I glanced over at him in surprise, and he admitted, "I think about that a lot, actually. If I hadn't told you to beat Petronius, none of this would have happened."

"Nobody expected him to kill himself, Alex," I replied firmly, not wanting him to carry this burden. "And," I added jokingly, "if it hadn't been Petronius, I would have gotten myself in this kind of trouble some other way."

As I hoped, this made him laugh.

"That's true," he agreed. "And who knows, it might have been worse?"

This was typical of the conversations we had as we moved through the forests, heading north and now slightly east, with the intention of running into the Visurgis (Weser), although none of us were certain we would know it. Although I was familiar with this territory, it was only in a general sense, and ironically, Catualda was even less so; his expertise would show itself once we crossed the Visurgis, and he assured us that by the time we reached the Albis (Elbe), he would be able to guide us to Casurgis (Prague), Maroboduus' capital.

"That's even if the bastard's there," I commented sourly. "If he's north of those mountains..."

"You Romans call them the Sudetes," Catualda supplied.

"Yes, those, then what?"

"That is a possibility," Catualda admitted. "But I do not think it is a strong one."

"Why not?"

"Because it would mean that he has pushed Herman back north, and," he shrugged, "I do not believe that Maroboduus has the ability to defeat him in battle, even outnumbering him as he does now that Arminius is only leading the Cherusci."

"Not just the Cherusci," I countered. "Remember Gundoc?"

"So he has a handful of rebels from some of the other

tribes," Catualda replied dismissively.

"If it was just a handful of Chatti, that would be one thing," Alex said. "But how many 'handfuls' are there?" Catualda did not seem to comprehend his meaning, so he elaborated, "How many tribes besides the Chatti might provide some rebels?"

"Ah, I see." He thought for a moment, then allowed, "I can think of three or four more, but that would mean a few hundred men at most."

"And how many Marcomanni spears can Maroboduus muster to march against Arminius?" I asked, deliberately using his Romanized name, and hiding my grin at the Gotones' scowl; this had been my habit since I met him, taking what I am certain Bronwen would call a childish satisfaction at his displeasure.

"Perhaps six thousand." He did not sound certain, and after I stared at him for a few heartbeats, he explained, "That is the latest information that I have, Centurion, and it depends on how many spears he is willing to call from other strategic locations throughout their lands. Those six thousand men are all within a day's walk to Casurgis, and include his royal bodyguard of two thousand hand-picked warriors."

I thought for a moment before I said, "So if he does strip his capital of his bodyguard, it wouldn't take an entire Legion to take it. The Primus Pilus could send a Cohort to do that and still have enough men to deal with Maroboduus."

"That is my thought as well," Catualda agreed.

"But first, we have to find that fucking Legion," I grumbled, and we lapsed back into silence, while I digested this last bit of information, trying to suppress one thought that kept coming back to nag me.

What if Maroboduus, once he understood that the sudden appearance of a Roman Legion was a threat not to Arminius, who had never submitted to us, but to him, would he throw himself at Arminius' feet and beg our mortal enemy for help? It was a remote possibility, yet it was one that I could not shake, and with every mile closer to our meeting point, it seemed to loom ever larger.

Despite our resolution to avoid any contact with the tribespeople, first with the Chatti, then the Marsi, whose southern lands we thought we were in, it became obvious that, while we were not lost, exactly, we needed a more precise sense of our location. To that end, we decided to continue moving once it became light, after giving the animals a short rest. Also, despite cutting down to half rations, we had run out of food the day before, nine days after we left Mogontiacum. When possible, we used what passed for roads and tracks since we were traveling at night, then always moved well away from them shortly before the sun came up, but on this day, we stayed on the path we had been using that was heading in a northeasterly direction. It was more than a cattle path, but not by much, there only being a very shallow pair of grooves, narrower than those left by a wagon, and it was this we were following, with me leading the way, when Latobius' head suddenly came up, his ears pricked forward while taking in a breath through his huge nostrils that warned me that he was about to whinny.

"Latobius! No!" Even as I whispered this, I was leaning down to pinch off his nostrils, the sign to him that I did not want him making any noise, but I was too late.

His neigh was instantly answered, both by one of his own kind and by a shout from one of my kind, but while I could not understand the words, there was no mistaking that it was not overtly hostile, and from the underbrush on the left side of the track, a German who I assumed had issued the challenge came walking his mount into view less than a hundred paces away. He had a spear, but he was holding it vertically, and he repeated the query again, although this time, it was with a bit more urgency.

"He thinks you're German!" Alex hissed from behind me.

My beard had grown in, although it was not nearly as long as many Germans', but I was also still wearing my civilian tunic and my *bracae* because it had gotten cooler. My *caligae* would have been a dead giveaway, but Latobius' muscular shoulders and the distance between us meant that he could not see them clearly. I was wearing my *sagum,* but there were many Germans who wore one, albeit as a trophy of war, signaling that they had slain a man of the Legions. And, of course, there was my size; all of these factors added up to this German not immediately placing me as a Roman. Understanding Alex was right, I called out to him in a greeting that I knew was used between Germans from different tribes, but in doing so, I exhausted almost half of my vocabulary. Initially, I was encouraged because he returned it, but then he said something, and all I could think to do was repeat myself. The change in his demeanor was instantaneous, the smile vanishing and replaced with a suspicious scowl, whereupon he repeated himself, but in a more menacing tone. I was only vaguely aware of hearing one of my party closing on me from behind, yet before I could say anything else, although I had no idea what I would say, I heard Catualda's voice. When he finished, just as he drew alongside Latobius, the German's demeanor transformed yet again, and just as quickly as he had become suspicious, he began roaring with laughter.

While he was thus occupied, Catualda whispered, "I told him that you are simple, Centurion, and that is all you know how to say. Now, let me do the talking."

I was torn between relief and anger; hearing Alex snickering behind me did not help, but I naturally did exactly as Catualda said, and once again, I witnessed how, when he chose to, Catualda could charm others, because very quickly, the German was obviously no longer suspicious or on guard. They talked for some moments, and I heard Catualda mention his own name, but it was when he mentioned Maroboduus that the other man, who turned out to be Marsi, leaned over and made a show of spitting on the ground.

"What's he saying?" Canus at least whispered from where he was sitting next to Alex, directly behind me.

"Shut up," I whispered back. "We'll find out soon enough."

"Yes," Catualda muttered while the Marsi was speaking. "Please be quiet. This man is being very informative."

The exchange went on for a few more moments, but despite the amicable tone, I began growing restive. Then, my eye caught some movement off in the trees, just on the other side of the Marsi, and I stared into the underbrush until my eyes began to water, it taking a couple dozen heartbeats for me to recognize that this Marsi was not alone. Although I could not be sure, I thought I counted at least a half-dozen other riders, thanks to a horse twitching an ear, or stomping, or a man reaching up to scratch his face. Otherwise, they were motionless, but as alarming as it was, I chided myself; he's just being cautious, that's all. You'd do the same thing in his position, keeping some men nearby in case there was trouble. I did not dare look over my shoulder to warn Alex, because I could not trust Canus not to react again; this would prove to be a bad decision.

Finally, Catualda murmured, "We are not far from a branch of the Visurgis, and if we follow it north, it joins the main river. The village where the Legion is supposed to be waiting is no more than five miles from there. I will explain the rest once we are past them."

He kicked his horse into motion, while I fell in behind him, saying nothing since I was supposed to be simple, and I tried to perfect looking like an idiot, briefly considering drooling before deciding against it. The Marsi was grinning broadly, resting the butt of his spear on his thigh, and he said something to me, which I answered with a puzzled stare that made him roar with laughter. He barely glanced at Alex, and I was already past him when it happened.

"There are men in the woods! It's a fucking trap!"

I turned in my saddle just in time to see that, when he chose to, Canus could move with blinding speed, drawing his long dagger and, though he was forced to lean over, thrust it into the throat of the Marsi, killing the man before he could even begin to bring his spear into position.

"*Run!*"

I knew it was my voice, but I did not remember shouting; I do recall kicking Latobius, hard, in the ribs, and as I expected, he behaved as if he had been loosed from a *ballista*. Catualda understandably did not react quite as quickly, first twisting about to see me and my horse barreling up the track towards him, and while I would never trade Latobius for any horse, I could not fault how quickly Tyr went to the gallop, but we still came perilously close to colliding.

"Alex!" I shouted, and was relieved to hear him shout back that he was right behind me, but then he called out, "Wait! What about Canus?"

"Fuck him!" I snarled, and that was the last we spoke for some time.

Catualda was leading the way, and I wondered what lay ahead, but then, without any warning, he suddenly veered to the left, and a heartbeat later I saw that the track we were on intersected with another, narrower one, making me wonder if the Gotones was randomly taking this one. Turning as we did, it gave me an instant where I could look to my left, and I saw that Lightning was doing well, keeping within a few lengths of my horse, but to my disappointment, I saw that Canus was close behind, holding on to his saddle with both hands, the bloody blade of his dagger clenched in his teeth. In the bare instant of time I had left, I looked beyond Canus, but to my shock, I saw the pursuers drawing on their reins in a spray of dirt just before spinning their mounts about. Are they giving up? I wondered, yet despite not seeing how they would be so quick to abandon the chase, I knew what my eyes saw, but then I had to pay attention because not only was this track narrower, it was more sinuous, winding around clumps of trees and undergrowth, all of which Catualda navigated with ease. Despite what was happening, a part of me was detached enough to admire the Gotones' horsemanship, reminding me that, while it was not all German tribes, many of them are superb riders, their only handicap in the quality of their horses, which Divus Julius had noticed and remedied, mounting his bodyguards on the superior horses of Italia and Hispania.

After about a mile, while we continued moving at less than a full gallop but more than a canter, I was beginning to relax, thinking that, perhaps, the Marsi *had* given up the chase. Shortly after that thought, we reached a fork, and again without hesitation, Catualda nudged Tyr's left flank, making a shallow curving turn onto the right fork. We had been in a thick forest, but had been going gradually downhill, then we emerged out into the open, and just ahead of Catualda, I saw the silvery glint of water, quickly identifying that it was a river, and that it had to be the tributary to the Visurgis that Catualda mentioned. It was not that wide or that swift, but Catualda made no attempt to cross, turning instead to parallel, and deciding to trust him, I followed along, glancing over to see that, while Lightning was laboring more than Latobius, Alex had kept him just a half-dozen lengths behind me. Canus was farther behind, and his mount was clearly struggling to keep up, and I was tempted to leave him and let him fend for himself, but then I realized how unlikely I thought it would be for him to withstand the kind of questioning he liked to inflict, betraying us in the process.

"Catualda! We need to slow down or we're going to leave Canus behind!"

The Gotones showed we were of a like mind because he did not immediately slow Tyr, but just as I was about to shout at him again, his horse dropped to a quick trot, and I urged Latobius to pull next to Catualda.

"We can't leave him behind, as much as I'd like to," I commented, and he nodded.

"Yes, I know," he sighed. I was looking straight ahead, but I saw him look up at me. "You know that he is going to try and kill you, I assume? And Alex?"

"I do," I agreed, then I smiled down at him. "I know that he's going to *try*."

"I will watch him, as I am sure will Alex," he said solemnly, and I thanked him. Indicating a line of low tree-covered hills that ran from our left to right at an angle, he explained, "The Marsi that Canus killed told me that, just beyond those hills, this river runs into the Visurgis, and the village will be another two miles north."

This was good news in a relative sense, but I was skeptical about something.

"I don't see whoever's coming will actually take a Legion into that village, because he's going to have to choose between killing everyone in it or putting a heavy guard to keep anyone from escaping."

"I thought that as well," Catualda replied. "So where do you think they would be?"

"Someplace defensible where they can build one of our camps," I answered. "Either in an open area where there is no cover surrounding it, or without a forest like that," I indicated the thickly covered slopes ahead of us but still more than a mile away, "where they can cut down a few trees and clear away the underbrush. Ideally, they would find a bare hill by itself, but," I could not help hissing in frustration, "without knowing the ground, we don't even know where to begin looking."

We fell silent then, slowing to a walk after checking behind us again to ensure that the Marsi were not pursuing. When I thought about it later, I suppose I noticed that, rather than being one long ridgeline that was oriented on a straight north/south axis, instead, it ran at an angle that meant that, while it paralleled the river we were following, terminating perhaps a hundred paces from the western bank, giving us a narrow passage between the ridge and the river, it was actually a ridge then one small hill that was closest to the river, which meant there was a narrow draw to our left and about three hundred paces from the riverbank. Consequently, we learned that the Marsi had not broken off their pursuit when, without any warning, they burst out from the small trees and undergrowth that choked this narrow passageway, neatly cutting us off from the gap. I do not recall any of us shouting an alarm or giving the order to go to the gallop, but only because it was not needed, although I did give a quick glance over my shoulder to see that Alex and Canus had closed with us and were just a length behind. There was nothing else we could have done but charge for the gap, although I suppose we could have turned about, but the Marsi, who I guessed were already twenty in number although more riders were emerging from the cut, were already at full speed, and would undoubtedly have run us down from behind. Within a couple of heartbeats, Latobius was at the gallop, as was Tyr, but Alex was hampered by the packhorse, which was not as sound as our mounts, despite carrying a much lighter load.

"Cut the packhorse loose!" I shouted over the wind roaring in my ears, despite the fact that it contained valuable items to me, both professionally and personally.

However, as painful as it would be to lose the torq awarded to my father in his first campaign by the Imperator's brother, it was not worth Alex's life, and despite all that was happening, I remember having the conscious thought of how I would never be able to live with the shame that my closest and most faithful friend had fallen because of it. Not that it would matter; it was almost instantly obvious that there was no way that we would avoid being cut off from the north and any possibility that the Legion would be nearby and in position to save us. I had never drawn my *gladius* with Latobius at the gallop, yet I somehow managed, then risked a glance at Catualda, who was to my right and even with me, seeing that he had done the same thing, and I envied him his longer blade. I could not have looked away from our front for more than a heartbeat, but when I returned my attention to what was a line of horsemen who were far enough ahead of us to begin to form a single line facing our direction, what met my eyes was extremely confusing. Why were some of their horses rearing? More strangely, why did two Marsi suddenly fall from their saddles?

When we talked later, none of the four of us saw any of the javelins that came streaking out from the underbrush, hurled by a Century of Legionaries of the Cohort that had been sent out by their Primus Pilus searching for Catualda. From our perspective, some men just began falling out of their saddles, while others yanked frantically on the reins of their mounts, only a couple of them bothering to hurl one of their short throwing spears into the undergrowth at the base of the slope before whipping their mounts and racing back to the cut from where they had sprung their ambush. Three or four men did try to rescue one of their fallen comrades; experience told us that it was likely a blood relative, but after one of them was struck by two javelins, joining his fellow Marsi in the dirt, the others abandoned their attempt, leaving nine fallen comrades behind. For our part, we slowed before coming to a stop, watching as what I recognized was a section of Legionaries materialized from the undergrowth, moving cautiously with their *gladii* drawn, but it was their helmets that elicited a curse from me, although I was not that surprised, because they each had a pair of feathers jutting up above the crown.

"Fucking Alaudae," I muttered. "I fucking *knew* it."

I had done it without conscious thought, but when I pulled Latobius to a halt, I made sure it was well out of javelin range, and one man from the section watched us warily as his comrades moved among the fallen, dispatching those who were still breathing, ignoring the hoarse pleas from two of them. An Optio appeared then, striding past his men, but I noticed he stopped just a half-dozen paces away from them to address us, and I got another surprise.

"Are you Catualda of the Gotones?" Since that Gotones was next to me, it was possible that he was addressing him, but he was pointing directly at me.

It's the beard, I realized, followed by a happier thought; *he doesn't recognize me!*

Nevertheless, knowing that I could not have maintained the ruse for more than a couple heartbeats, I shook my head.

"No," I pointed to Catualda, who looked amused, "this is Catualda."

"You're Roman?" The Optio was clearly surprised. Then, his expression altered, his voice going flat, telling me that he knew my identity now. "You're Centurion Pullus."

"Yes," I replied, and I knew that I should not make an issue of it, but I snapped, "And since you clearly know who I am, I believe the regulations are the same for the Alaudae as they are with the 1st, aren't they?"

"They are," he replied warily.

"Then why aren't you at a position of *intente* when addressing a superior, Optio? And," I added, "what's your name, Cohort, and Century, and who is your commanding Centurion?"

It was easy to see this angered him, but he obeyed, snapping to the position as he answered.

"Optio Lucius Considius, Fourth of the Tenth, Centurion, and my..."

"Decimus Princeps Posterior Tiberius Falco," a new voice interrupted, and I shifted my gaze from Considius to the Centurion, who I had not seen emerging from the underbrush.

If anything, his tone was colder than Considius', but while I could have demanded it by virtue of my superior rank, if not my grade by virtue of being a Centurion of a First Cohort, I did not require Falco to salute.

Instead, I asked bluntly, "Is it safe to assume that all of the Alaudae are here on this side of the Rhenus?"

For this had been another topic of debate between us, whether or not Nerva would have sought a way out by offering up only part of his Legion, which I thought was a possibility, while Alex was certain he would not dare run that kind of risk of losing part of his Legion. Better for Nerva, he had argued, to lose his entire Legion, which would mean his death as well, than have to explain to the Imperator how he had sacrificed part of it, and for what.

"It is," he answered, proving Alex right in the process, and I did not have to look over my shoulder to see his grin. "The rest of the Legion is in a camp about two miles west of here." He hesitated then, but I understood why when he said, "Whoever found you was to immediately escort you to our camp, but we weren't expecting any trouble. So far, every barbarian we've seen has turned and run like rabbits."

"I imagine this bunch would have done the same," I said, then sensing an opportunity to ease some of the tension now that I knew they were aware of my identity, I added sincerely, "You and your men did an excellent job with his ambush, Centurion. They clearly had no idea you were there. And," I smiled, "frankly, neither did we."

"No, we just saw men falling from their horses," Catualda spoke up. "It was very well done, Centurion."

"Yes, please extend our compliments and our thanks to your men." I was slightly irritated that Catualda had spoken up. "We were well and truly fucked."

It was clear to see that Falco was pleased at this praise, as he should have been, and as I would have been in his position, but then his expression altered, giving me the impression that he remembered how he was supposed to view me.

"Yes, well, it looks like my men have finished taking care of these bastards." He had turned to see the section standing together, comparing their respective take from the bodies, and Falco bellowed, "*Oy!* You bastards better not be sneaking anything into your purses before Considius looks at them!" Turning back, I saw his eyes go to a spot beyond us. "It looks

like your man has retrieved at least one of your packhorses."
Glancing over my shoulder, I was surprised to see that it was
not Alex but Canus who had gone off to retrieve the packhorse,
aided by the fact that the animal had been following us at a trot.
"Did you have any other pack animals? If they're not too far
away, we can go look for them."

"We did," I replied. "One pack animal and a spare mount
for each of us, but we lost them..." I actually had to think, but
Catualda supplied, "It was five days ago, I believe."

"Yes," I remembered. "And we haven't had anything to
eat since yesterday. But this is the only animal we have."

"Well," Falco turned away, beckoning to us to follow, "I
suspect we can round up a couple loaves from my boys to hold
you over until we get to camp. But," he warned, "it will be
standard soldier's fare."

"That," I assured him, "is perfectly fine with us." Canus
had just caught up with us, and I looked at him over my
shoulder as I added, "I can't speak for Canus here. He might
be accustomed to lark tongues and fresh oysters."

As I hoped, Canus did not appreciate this, scowling at me,
but I was unprepared for Falco's reaction.

"You're Canus?" he asked in obvious surprise, then
indicated Alex. "I thought he was Varro's man."

"Why would you think that?" Alex asked, and one did not
need to know him to hear the indignation.

"I don't know, really." Falco shrugged. "I just assumed
you were. But," he addressed Canus, "the Primus Pilus told us
that if we found you, we're to take you to him immediately."

This was not only a surprise, it was alarming, and a glance
at Catualda told me he was of a like mind, but there was no
chance to discuss it; I suppose Falco's insistence that we ride
in the middle of their column, with five sections in front and
five behind was simply for our protection given what had taken
place...but I did not think so.

Chapter 4

Nerva, as one would expect of an experienced Primus Pilus, had chosen the site for his camp well, taking advantage of a large natural clearing, and while it was nestled in a small valley surrounded by hills of the same height and steepness as the ridge, the slopes were far enough away that, even if the Marsi had artillery, which they did not, there was no threat to the camp. We could see the walls more than a mile away, which just happened to correspond with my mouth going so dry that I drained the rest of my canteen before we reached the gate. Our progress had been delayed as the Fourth met with the Third of the Tenth, while the Fifth and Sixth Centuries had been on the other side of the river feeding the Visurgis, so they arrived later.

My heart was thudding against my ribs, but once more, I was thankful for my beard, because it helped mask my features and made it difficult for others to see my nerves, or so I hoped. The Decimus Princeps Prior called out the watchword, and we were allowed entry, but my hope that I would not be recognized by the men standing on the ramparts would be a forlorn one, although I should not have been surprised that one of their comrades entering with us had warned them that the hated Centurion Pullus was the big, bearded bastard. What did surprise me slightly was that, while there were certainly some men regarding me with open hostility, they were in the minority, with the rest seemingly split evenly between curiosity and, if not approval, then at the very least no censure, reminding me that Petronius had not been loved by men outside of his Cohort, and indeed, not every man in his Cohort had cared for him. The men of the Tenth split off, while Falco led us to the forum and the Primus Pilus' tent, which, in a single Legion camp without a Legate, also serves as the *praetorium*. We were immediately allowed in, but then Nerva's clerk, obviously alerted to our arrival, was waiting in the outer office.

"Centurion Pullus, Lord Catualda, Primus Pilus Nerva has instructed me that you are to wait here." He turned to Canus. "The Primus Pilus will see you first. I understand that you have orders for him?"

Canus nodded, then his eyes darted over to me, and while I found it hard to believe, he looked apologetic, though he did not say anything as he followed the clerk, who rapped on the wooden piece hanging next to the partition. He was answered immediately, and I recognized Nerva's gravelly voice, the pair disappearing, pushing the leather flap aside and replacing it so quickly, I did not even catch a glimpse of Nerva.

"That," Alex whispered, "can't be good."

"Did you know that *cunnus* had special orders?" I demanded of Catualda.

"No, Centurion." He shook his head. "I did not. But," he sighed, "I can imagine what they might be."

The problem was, so could I. Since the reason for my presence had been a fabrication, and I now knew that I was simply a piece in Varro's game of tables, and one of convenience, now that Catualda had united with the Legion who would aid him in his attempt to overthrow Maroboduus, I was not only expendable, I was inconvenient. I was in the process of ruminating on this when, without any warning, the flap was thrust aside, and Nerva's clerk appeared, looking, if not panicked, at the very least quite flustered.

"The Primus Pilus wants you," he addressed Catualda, and then looked at me, "and you immediately." Before I moved, I turned to Alex, indicating that he should come with us, but the clerk said, "He didn't say anything about whoever this is."

"Either he comes with me, or I don't come."

It was an extraordinarily reckless thing to do given my situation, but the clerk did not even try to argue, saying only, "Fine," before reentering Nerva's private office, Catualda just behind him.

"Why are you dragging me into this?" Alex whispered, but I just grinned and replied, "Why not?"

Nerva was behind his desk, but he was standing, and looking agitated, which I understood when, without requiring any kind of military courtesy, demanded of me, "Is what Canus says true? That Arminius attacked Maroboduus?"

"That's our information." I nodded, but he clearly did not care for what I suppose he viewed as my prevarication, but then Catualda added, "The Marsi that I spoke to earlier today confirmed it. A call for aid has gone out, both by Arminius and by Maroboduus as well." This was news to me, but when I glared down at the Gotones, he just shrugged. "I did not have the chance, Centurion. As you will recall, we did not have much time to talk."

This was true, so I did not press the matter later, while in the moment, Nerva began pacing back and forth, his battered features creased by a thoughtful frown, and I felt quite certain he was calculating what was most dangerous for him, and for his Legion. And, I wondered, what will matter most to him? His own career, or the lives of his men? We were still several hundred miles away from our goal, but honestly, I did not believe that we would meet resistance strong enough to slow us down, let alone stop us, and as we had learned over the previous years campaigning against the German tribes, they had to significantly outnumber us to have a chance to defeat us. Between the losses to their ranks over the previous four years, the low morale from the defeats they had incurred at Idistaviso and the Angravarian Wall, then the internecine struggle between factions within each tribe, from my perspective, the biggest threat facing the Alaudae would be if Maroboduus and Arminius could set aside their personal enmity to make common cause against us. If they did that, Nerva and his Legion would be stranded deep in Marcomanni territory, five hundred miles from the Rhenus.

"Pullus!" Nerva shouted, making me jump, and realize my attention had been elsewhere so certain was I that he would ignore me.

"Yes, Primus Pilus?"

"I asked you what you thought."

"Thought?" Now I was completely mystified. "Thought about what?"

"Whether or not I should leave the third line Cohorts behind here in this camp," he snapped. "If the Gotones here is right, that Maroboduus only can muster about six thousand spears, it won't take a full Legion to take care of them. If," Nerva turned to fix Catualda with a hard stare and unleashed another surprise in the process, "he's telling the truth about having at least two thousand of those Marcomanni loyal to him."

"What?" I stared at Catualda, not missing the fact that he was avoiding meeting my eyes. "Why am I just being told this?"

"It was not important," Catualda answered evasively. "Not to our task."

"Our *task* was never necessary in the first place because I thought I was being taken to Catualda by Otmar," I shot back. "I didn't know I was already *with* Catualda!"

"What?" Nerva was clearly more confused now, but before Catualda or I could say anything else, he roared, "I want everyone out of my quarters except for Pullus!"

Naturally, he was obeyed, and it was no more than a handful of heartbeats before it was just the two of us, glaring at each other.

Nerva broke the silence by saying, "I think it's time we set our differences aside, at least for the moment."

"Why?" I asked, my anger catching me by surprise. "The only reason I'm here right now is because you saw an opportunity to even the score about Petronius!"

He stared at me, but I was completely unprepared for him to ask in apparent bewilderment, "What are you talking about, Pullus?"

"Please don't try and deny it. The *Quaestor* told me part of it, Canus told me another part of it, and I figured out the rest on my own."

"Then tell me what you think you've figured out," he said evenly, and I did.

He listened, his face betraying nothing as I talked; once I was done, he shook his head with what appeared to be sadness.

"Pullus, I know what you think of me," he began, but I cut him off, "And I know what you think of me as well, Primus Pilus."

I expected him to explode, but instead, he heaved a sigh

and said, "No, I don't think you do. Not," he held up a hand, "what I think now." He fell silent for a heartbeat, then continued, "I knew Petronius was a troublemaker, and I knew that he insulted your mother. But," he held his hands out from his sides, palms up in a helpless gesture, "he was a man of the Alaudae, and there was...pressure on me from some of the other Pili Priores. Remember what was going on, Pullus. This was not that long after the mutiny, and I don't have to tell you that not everyone, both in the ranks and the Centurionate, was happy with the settlement with the Imperator." This was certainly true, and I gave a nod in acknowledgement. "Your...handling of Petronius didn't become a major problem until he," he swallowed, and I guessed he did not want to say the word, "did what he did. That provost Bibulus began spreading it about that it was because you had addled his wits and made him unable to carry out his duties." This was the first time I had heard anything that specific; when Nerva had confronted me about it, he had simply said that Petronius could not live with the shame of my beating. "Over time, that became what most of my Centurions believed, or chose to believe, and they came to me saying that I should bring charges against you with the *Praetor* for crippling a fellow Centurion from another Legion."

As I am certain he knew, I was aware that this was a serious charge, but I sensed a hesitancy in Nerva that prompted me to ask, "He was a Pilus Prior. Did he seem addled to you?"

At first, I did not believe that Nerva would answer, but, while it was with obvious reluctance, he shook his head, admitting, "No, he didn't. Not," he hurried on, "that he wasn't changed, because he was. But no, it wasn't his wits that were scrambled. Once a man like Petronius is beaten like he was, it...breaks something in him; call it his *animus,* or maybe it's his *dignitas* that's destroyed." I will never forget how he looked at me then, not in a challenging manner, but more thoughtful in nature. "I can only imagine what it must be like to be bigger and stronger most of your life, then you run into someone who's bigger and stronger. Now that I think about it like that," he shook his head, "I should have seen it coming with Petronius."

I have no idea why I felt the need, but I said, "It's not just a matter of size and strength, Primus Pilus. I have a..." I searched for the right word, then decided to use the one that Alex, Bronwen, and others have ascribed to it, "...a gift of sorts."

Nerva's expression altered, suddenly giving me a shrewd look.

"Would it be the same *gift* your father had?"

"You know about that?" I gasped.

"Tiberius told me about it," he replied, then I suppose he thought he needed to clarify. "I don't mean the Imperator, I mean your Primus Pilus." He clearly saw my surprise, and he said, somewhat defensively to my ears, "Sacrovir and I haven't always been at odds, Pullus. We have shared more than one cup together, and I remember him coming to talk to me after your Legion returned from saving Segestes and came back with Arminius' bitch." I do not believe he was feigning his sadness at the memory of that time after the death of my father, a period that is still mostly a blur to me. "He told me what he'd seen your father do before, and how it was like watching Mars come to earth. I'd never seen him cry before that night." Clearing his throat, he looked at me. "Is that what you're talking about?"

"Yes," I said simply, then decided to be fully forthcoming since he seemed to be doing so. "And I knew that Petronius would say something that would cause the...whatever it is, to come out. Honestly," it was my turn to shrug, "he didn't have a chance, Primus Pilus."

We fell silent then, which he broke by saying, "What Varro told me," he continued, "is that you had escaped from your cell, although Varro claimed that he had no intention of bringing you up on charges. But, since you ran, he instructed me to take you into custody when you showed up with the Gotones. Which," he held a hand up, "I have no intention of doing, Pullus. I swear on my eagle that this business with Petronius is done and finished. I'm sick of it."

This was, naturally, good to hear, yet it did not take me more than a heartbeat to realize that, if anything, it made me even more of a loose end with Varro.

"What does Varro have over you?" I decided to ask, since there was apparently no *quid pro quo* with me, although I was aware that Nerva could have been lying, but I did not believe so. "How was he able to get you to do...this?"

"That," he replied stiffly, "is none of your business, Pullus." He did relent slightly. "Let's just say that I put myself in a vulnerable position, and Varro is squeezing. That *cunnus*," he jerked his thumb towards the outer office, "isn't here to watch just you." As far as I was concerned, Canus was here to do more than watch me, which made me wonder if Varro would be so mad to order Canus to try and kill a Primus Pilus when surrounded by the men of his Legion, and if he was, whether Canus was so loyal to the *Quaestor* that he would essentially commit suicide. Nerva intruded on my thoughts by saying, "I have a proposition for you, Pullus."

I believed I could be forgiven for being wary, and I asked cautiously, "What's that?"

"Stay with the Legion and see this business between the Gotones and Maroboduus through to the finish," he said. "Then, when we return to Mogontiacum, I will do everything I can to get Varro to drop his business with you."

"In what role?" I asked, although I had already made up my mind that I would; frankly, I did not see I had any choice.

The irony, however, was not lost on me that I would be relying on Nerva, and I wondered what Sacrovir would think.

He thought a moment, then replied, "You and your party are mounted, and Varro wouldn't give me even a *turma* of cavalry. The best he would do is a section from the Batavians. I would have preferred Gauls, but," he shrugged, "I can't be choosy. You can help them scouting ahead, although I suppose we're going to have to rely on the Gotones to pick the best route." I stared down at him, which he noticed. "What? Why are you looking at me like that?"

"Primus Pilus, did the *Quaestor* tell you that Catualda knew some route?"

"He said that Catualda knew Marcomanni territory well." He sounded cautious, which I understood when he groaned, "Pluto's cock! I just assumed that meant he would know the best way to *reach* Marcomanni territory."

"We're still about two hundred miles from the western edge," I told him. "And we still have to negotiate Semnones and Suebi territory."

"Well," he sighed. "We might as well get started planning this." Raising his voice, he called out for the others to rejoin us. As they were filing in, Nerva said, "And, Pullus, as soon as we're done, shave that fucking beard off. I won't have a Centurion of Rome looking like a German." He wrinkled his nose and added, "I'd tell you to take a bath too, but we're on campaign, so a scraping will have to do."

To my utter surprise and happiness, it turned out that the section of Batavians was the one that my former cellmates belonged to, meaning that I was reunited with Herminius and Arnfrid, who barely acknowledged me because they were admiring Latobius.

"I remember your father riding him," Herminius patted his neck, but while Latobius was generally leery of strangers patting him, he must have sensed that Herminius, like most Batavians, was a horseman, because he immediately stretched his neck out, then began snuffling around the other man's waist.

"Careful," I warned, "he's looking for an apple or chunk of bread, and he has a habit of biting if he doesn't find anything."

"He would not do that to me, would you, eh?" Herminius asked, and while he got a sudden blast of air through Latobius' nostrils, he did not get a chunk of flesh taken out of him, which miffed me slightly.

"Why don't you do that with me?" I grumbled.

"I understand we will be riding together?"

"Yes." I nodded, then added grimly, "Although we're going to be riding blind." Herminius looked at me in a way that told me that he was unaware, and I explained, "Catualda doesn't know the ground this far west. Once we get to the western edge of Marcomanni lands, he can guide us the rest of the way."

"We have been farther east," Herminius said, but he looked glum, and I understood why when he explained, "but farther north than here, close to the coast."

We were sitting our mounts, waiting for the command to begin the day's march, but I was not clean-shaven, because after telling Alex what we were going to be doing, he immediately pointed out that, since we were going to be ranging ahead of the column, it was better that I remain bearded.

He was right, and I immediately returned to the Primus Pilus' tent, but while he did not appear pleased, he grunted, "If you want to look like a hairy German, I suppose I can't stop you since you're not from my Legion."

Naturally, by the time the sun rose the next day, my disguise was useless with the men of the Alaudae, all of them knowing my identity, and I endured the glares from the Legionaries as they fell into their spot in the column. Nerva had decided the night before, after a fairly long discussion that I was allowed to attend with the Pili Priores, that we would be marching in column, and the kind of looks I was getting now I had experienced the night before. There had been some debate, which Nerva allowed, surprising me somewhat, about whether it was better to be cautious by marching in *agmentum quadratum*. While he did not dismiss the idea out of hand, he finally held up his hand for quiet.

"According to our best information, if we march in column, we will reach the edge of Marcomanni territory in about a week. Marching in *quadratum* doubles that time, and I don't have to tell you that we left Mogontiacum with exactly one month's supply of food, planning on replenishing at," he had to look down at the tablet, "Casurgis, and after we have helped Lord Catualda," he inclined his head to the Gotones, while I thought, at least he finally learned his name, "usurp Maroboduus and installed him as King." Snapping the tablet shut, he finished with, "Nothing that we've seen indicates that either the Semnones or Suebi will pose a threat, especially since we're at the southern edge of their lands, and they will almost undoubtedly have their attention turned farther north, watching Arminius and the Cherusci, waiting to see who prevails between them and the Marcomanni. Who knows?" He offered a grim smile. "If Fortuna smiles on us, Arminius and

Maroboduus will inflict so much damage on each other that we can walk right into Casurgis and take it."

That ended the discussion, and to my surprise, I was impressed with the deft touch Nerva had displayed here, thinking it was more along the lines of my own Primus Pilus. Now, in the chilly early dawn, the *bucina* sounded the preparatory call, the men hefting their *furcae*, while the Alaudae *Aquilifer* hoisted the eagle, the sun peeking over the eastern hills reflecting off the golden wings, and as always, the sight stirred my heart. Even if most of these men hate me, I thought, there's still nowhere else I would rather be than with a Legion on the march, even more so because there was a prospect of some form of action. It had been more than a year since the Angrivarian Wall, and while it was, and is something I would never admit to Bronwen, I missed battle, something that I would learn she knew all along. With the Legion in motion, our scouting party, which was now ten men strong, began moving at a trot, heading east, where we would cross the Visurgis at a ford that Herminius and his Batavians had discovered the day before. The truth was that we should only have had nine men—the six Batavians, Catualda, Alex, and myself—but Nerva had flatly refused to allow Canus to stay with the main column.

"I don't trust that *cunnus,* and I don't want him skulking about my boys causing the gods know what kind of trouble," he had growled. "As far as I'm concerned, you brought him with you, he's your problem."

For a heartbeat, I considered arguing that I had certainly not wanted to bring him, quickly realizing that it was pointless; besides, I reasoned, once I informed Herminius and Arnfrid about Canus and my suspicions about his instructions from Varro, he would be significantly outnumbered, with eyes on him almost every moment. To be fair, Canus clearly was as unhappy being included in our party as I was to have him, and we set the kind of pace that had him bouncing in his saddle, gripping it with his free hand as we moved away from the Legion column.

While I outranked Herminius, who was the acting Ducanus, I deferred to him, and he had announced that he wanted us to be five miles ahead of the Alaudae, but immediately, there was a problem when he said, "We will split into three groups, two of them with three men, and one with four. One group of three will be..." he paused as he thought, "...two miles north of our line of march, the other group of three will be the same distance but to the south, while the group of four will ride along the line of march. I will be in that group," he turned to me, "as will the Centurion and Lord Catualda."

"That means Alex is going to have to be with Canus," I muttered, unhappy about this.

"So will Arnfrid," Herminius replied, his face giving nothing away, "and I have spoken to him about your fellow Roman Canus."

This was somewhat reassuring, although it still was not ideal, but I just nodded and gave him thanks, albeit somewhat curtly. We stayed together until we went splashing across the Visurgis, pausing only long enough to make sure that the stakes that the Batavians had set out marking the ford were still in place, although judging from the muddy banks on either side, this spot was used quite often.

"Watch him," I said softly to Alex, who gave a grim nod.

"I will as well," Arnfrid muttered as he rode past.

"I *knew* you could speak our tongue, you sly dog!" I exclaimed, and he offered an insolent grin.

"It hurts my ears to do it," he countered. "You sound like dogs barking."

I had to laugh, knowing that he was deliberately repeating the complaint Latin speakers use about, well, every other tongue, with the exception of Greek. Reassured, I watched as they trotted away to the north, then we resumed our own progress. Beyond the Visurgis, the ground was gently rolling, with tracts of forest but interspersed enough that we could avoid passing through them, and we knew that Nerva and the Alaudae would essentially do the same, even if it did add a mile or two to take a more sinuous route. Nevertheless, every mile, we would pause, and the other Batavian in our group, Barvistus, would dismount and stack rocks in a pile in the signal to the Legion they were heading in the right direction. We came across four villages before noon, but as is the German habit, they were located a short distance from one of the tracts of forest, and it was not lost on any of us that the villagers, which Herminius confirmed were Semnones and who chose to stand and stare at us as we rode by were exclusively women, old people, and children.

We stopped at each one, with Catualda asking them questions, but to nobody's surprise, they were singularly unhelpful, answering in monosyllables or grunts, though it was impossible to miss the hostility.

"They're watching us from the trees," I murmured as we left the first village, but instead of ready agreement, I saw how Catualda and Herminius exchanged a glance. Irritated and worried in equal measure, I demanded, "You obviously have other thoughts."

Neither answered immediately, but then Catualda replied, "You are probably right, Centurion. But there *is* another possibility, and it is one we should not discount."

I understood instantly, and experienced a stab of chagrin for not thinking of it myself.

"Their men might have gone to join Arminius," I said, but if I thought I had plumbed the depth of the potential problem, I was quickly proven wrong.

"That," Catualda responded, "would not be a bad thing, Centurion. Not only would it help us cross through their lands without worrying about them trying to stop us, every Marcomanni they kill for Arminius makes our own task easier. No," he shook his head, "my concern is if the Semnones have joined with Maroboduus."

I could not contain a gasp; this was the first Catualda had ever mentioned this as even a possibility, and we had spent whole watches discussing every possible development we could think of...so why now?

"Why did you never mention this before?" I asked angrily, which turned immediately to worry. "And how likely is something like that to happen?"

"I did not mention it before," he said, unconvincingly to my ears, "because I did not believe it merited being mentioned. But now that I have talked to their women," he continued worriedly, "there is...something in their manner that worries me."

"What is it?"

"I do not know!" he cried out, and I could see that he was truly agitated. "They are just very..." His hands flapped about as he vainly searched for a word in Latin.

"Smug?"

Catualda looked puzzled.

"What does this word mean?"

I actually had to think for a moment before I came up with, "As if they know something you don't, and it's something they know you won't like."

"Yes!" He nodded enthusiastically. "That is the word! Smug," he repeated it again, "smug. I," he grinned, "like this word." The levity vanished instantly, "But yes."

"Why would they do that, though? I thought the other tribes who joined Arminius hate Maroboduus because he refused to join him, and they think his spears would have tipped the balance." I did not add that it would not have mattered in the overall outcome, although it would have been a more costly victory.

"Gold," Catualda answered simply. "Even with his setbacks, Maroboduus is a *very* wealthy man, and the Marcomanni are one of the richest tribes in all of Germania. Only the Venedi to the east on the other side of the river you call the Vistula might be wealthier."

"Venedi?" I frowned, trying to recall from where I had heard the name, and it took a heartbeat to come to me, from the account of Prefect Pullus. "They're a tribe from Gaul."

"That is a branch of the original tribe," Catualda replied, then offered me a grin. "We Germans like to travel." Returning to the original topic, he shrugged again. "I am not saying that it is a certainty, or even a strong possibility, but it *is* something we need to consider."

"Well," I decided, "I'll let you tell Primus Pilus Nerva about that possibility when we make camp tonight."

We continued on, occasionally seeing one or at most two mounted Germans, always heading away from us, with the same treatment at the other villages, although I did not see anything in their collective demeanor that made me think they knew something. I wanted desperately to speak with Alex, because with every mile we moved eastward, I began wondering if I had imagined what I had seen in Catualda's face as he talked about the possibility of Marcomanni gold going into the purses of Semnones. Naturally, it was a disturbing thing to ponder, but I could not shake the feeling that what I saw in Catualda's features was the disappointment of a man who had expected that gold to be his, and not because of the conceivably tougher struggle it would take to vanquish Maroboduus. Over and over, the question kept coming back to me; was Catualda more concerned with getting rich than he was leading the Marcomanni?

"We're getting close, but we're still marching blind, and I don't like it!"

It was now the end of the fourth day, and the terrain had started becoming more undulating, but more troublingly, we had left behind the wide swathes of open ground, meaning that we would be marching in heavily forested territory. More importantly, for Nerva's current mood, was that we were now in Suebi territory, and I recalled reading about them in the Prefect's account; more recently, they had held aloof from Arminius, the belief at the time being that they feared that Maroboduus would invade their homeland on the pretext that he was demonstrating his fidelity to Rome by attacking them. To my way of thinking, that made it less likely that the Suebi would enter into an agreement with the Marcomanni, knowing how long and deeply held the tribes of Germania hold grudges. Regardless, I also shared Nerva's dislike of how little we knew, both with the Suebi and the larger situation between Arminius and Maroboduus; that was about to change, and in a way, that impacted me. Nerva was reading from the tablet containing the compiled notes from our three scouting parties, which Alex was responsible for collecting when we returned to camp. He was the scribe for his party, not trusting Canus, while the men of the other party, all Batavians, were illiterate, but like all such people, their memory for detail was astonishing, and Alex wrote down their report for the day. It was from them that my prospect of a restful night was shattered.

"It says that there's a sizable village about four miles south of here, and that unlike the others we passed, the scouts spotted a fair number of men of warrior age." He looked up at me. "Was that your party, Pullus? Or one of the others?"

"One of the others, Primus Pilus," I answered, and only then did he turn to Herminius, asking bluntly, "Are they any good, Herminius? Can they be trusted?"

I heard the Batavian's hiss of indrawn breath, but his tone was level as he answered, "Yes, Primus Pilus. Ellanher is very experienced, and if he says that he saw something, he did."

"Well." Nerva slapped his portable desk. "I'm not willing to stay blind like this. So," he returned his attention to me, "you and your scouts are going to that village tonight, and I want you to snatch two prisoners. Although," he added, sounding as if he was thinking of ordering one more dormouse pie from a *taverna*, "three would be better."

Frankly, I thought he was joking, even if for the life of me I could not see the humor, so I gave a forced chuckle, while he sat there, staring at me.

"Do I look like I'm jesting, Pullus?"

"N-no sir," I managed, but I still was in a state of disbelief. Thinking I had misunderstood at least partially, I asked, "Who else will be coming with my group?"

"Nobody," he said flatly. "I wouldn't send more than ten men for a job like that anyway, Pullus. And," he pointed out, "you're going to be mounted." Returning his attention to Herminius, he asked, "You still have spare mounts?"

"Yes, Primus Pilus," Herminius confirmed, but he sounded more resigned than angry.

"Then you'll take two," Nerva said crisply, then sounding as if he was conferring a great benefit, he finished, "I've decided that two will have to do."

With that, he turned his attention to the other business, while I sat there with Herminius, ignoring the smirks on the face of the four Pili Priores who had proven to be intractable in their hostility towards me, although Petronius' replacement as Quintus Pilus Prior was not one of them, which I found interesting. He dismissed us, and we all got to our feet, while Nerva waited until I was almost at the partition when he called my name. Stepping aside, I whispered to Herminius to go to our tent that we were sharing and alert Alex and his Batavians, while I planned on informing Nerva that Canus was staying behind, no matter what Nerva said. I was completely unprepared for him to step out from behind the desk and walk over to the small table where he took his meals, extending a hand to the stool.

"Have a seat, Pullus. I need to talk to you about something."

I did as he bade, warily, my suspicion deepening when he poured a cup of wine for both of us, though he added water to both of them.

"I want to tell you why I won't let you have more men to snatch prisoners," he began. Naturally, I was interested in hearing it, but he seemed more concerned with staring into his cup, but finally, he continued, "I need someone I can trust leading this effort. And," he grimaced, "the truth is that I don't have anyone, let alone a Centurion, who I think has the skills to accomplish what I'm asking. And, Pullus, we *need* more information about what we're likely to be facing." He hesitated, then asked suddenly, "What do you think about Catualda?"

This startled me, which was probably his goal.

"I'm not sure what you mean," I said carefully, though I was beginning to have an idea.

"How far do you think he can be trusted?"

Since I had been thinking about this a bit, I did feel somewhat confident in saying, "As far as whether he might somehow betray us?" I shook my head. "I don't think you have cause for worry, Primus Pilus. Not only would that make achieving his own ambitions more difficult, if not impossible, he knows that Rome doesn't forget, and it doesn't forgive. You know that as well as I do."

"I do." Nerva nodded. "But, still..." he shook his head, "there's something about him that makes the hair on the back of my neck stand up, and I've learned never to ignore that."

Perhaps if he had said something else, I might not have felt compelled to express my own misgivings.

"I do know what you mean, Primus Pilus," I said. "But

like you, there's nothing I can put my finger on. Although," I recalled the conversation from the first village, "he did seem upset about the Semnones coming over to the Marcomanni to help Maroboduus fight Arminius. Which," I hurried on, "is understandable, but it's just that I couldn't shake the feeling that it was the idea of Maroboduus spending gold that was more important to Catualda than what it was for."

He pursed his lips as he considered this, then shrugged.

"I suppose that we will find out soon enough. But," he stood, signaling the end of the audience, "first I need those prisoners, Pullus. I'm counting on you."

"You can count on us, Primus Pilus," I assured him, and I did not think it even worth mentioning; later, I regretted that I did. "We're going to leave Canus behind here in camp."

"No," he replied immediately, and firmly. "He needs to go with you."

"Why?" I could not fathom what possible reason Nerva would have, but he proved me wrong.

"Because I don't have anyone skilled in torture, and you may not have time to get the prisoners back if you're being pursued," he said. "Varro told me that Canus is...skilled, not just at getting answers, but at getting them quickly."

Frankly, I immediately saw the sense in this, so I did not try to argue. I suppose it sounds odd, but as I was leaving his quarters, the truth was that I was more disturbed with this new amity that Nerva was showing me than the prospect of sneaking into a Suebi camp in the dead of night.

Alex and the others were in the process of getting ready when I entered the tent, which was a Tribune's tent, making it a bit larger and roomier, and Alex had partitioned off a section for our personal use, sharing it with Catualda. The Gotones had laid a knee-length chainmail vest and a leather cuirass on his cot, selecting the cuirass, which I understood. He was of average height for a German, about three inches shorter than me, but had a lithe build that lent itself to the kind of stealth that would be needed, making the cuirass a good choice. Alex actually had a *segmentata* that I had given to him back during the Arminius campaign, but that was the worst type of protection for what we were doing. I had actually anticipated this, and planned on using it as the pretext for assigning him the task of waiting with the horses; I was informed that he had foreseen this himself by the smug look he gave me as he dropped the leather vest with iron rings sewn on over his head.

"Where did you get that?" I asked sourly.

"Barvistus lent it to me." He grinned, making no attempt to hide his satisfaction at knowing my mind and thwarting my plan. "And look!" He twisted about. "It fits perfectly!"

"Oh, go piss on your boots," I grumbled, but even as I did, I was withdrawing my *hamata* from my pack.

"Centurion," Catualda spoke hesitantly as I mimicked them, dropping the armor down onto my shoulders. "Your mail is likely to..."

He did not finish because he saw me withdraw another tunic and don it so that it covered the *hamata*, then I removed the hanging strips from my *baltea* before putting it on.

"What about strapping it to your back?" Alex suggested, and I immediately recalled reading that both the Prefect and my father had done that.

With his help, we attached it so that the hilt extended over my left shoulder, and after a few tries, I felt comfortable that I would be able to get it out, refusing to think about what it would mean if I had to do so. I performed an impromptu inspection; the Batavians were either wearing leather armor, or like me, had an extra tunic they wore over their mail, but when I got to Canus, he was standing there, with his cloak as his only protection.

"I offered him something," Herminius told me, but when I asked Varro's man why he turned it down, he shrugged and looked anywhere but at me.

"I've never worn anything like that because I don't need it."

"And you've never gone up against a Suebi warrior either," I snapped. "They're not like another bully boy on the Aventine or some merchant who owes your master money!"

That got his eyes on me, and he glared up at me, snarling, "You don't need to worry about Canus, soldier boy! I can more than handle myself!"

"Yes," I shot back, not trying to hide my sarcasm, "I saw an example of that when that Chatti bastard attacked us."

He flushed, but he was not quite as defiant.

"I swear, Centurion, you won't have to worry about me."

Knowing that it would not change anything and that he was coming with us anyway, I gave him a disgusted wave. While I was doing my inspection, Alex had gotten busy, first rubbing all exposed skin with oil, then taking some charcoal and rubbing it in so that, by the time he was done, we looked like the Nubians we had seen during our time in Alexandria. Our mounts, along with the spares, had already been saddled and were waiting, and I led the way to the *Porta Praetoria* where, to my surprise, Nerva was standing.

"If you're not back by dawn, we're going to come get you," he said, speaking loudly so everyone could hear. "And gods help us if we end up starting a war with the Suebi, so let's not let that happen, eh?"

"We won't, sir," I promised, thinking as I did that this almost could have been Sacrovir and I instead of the Centurion who I had been certain hated me with an abiding passion.

We let Ellanher lead the way, since it was his group who had found the village in the first place, and not for the first time did I marvel at the Batavians' ability to navigate no matter what the conditions. While we talked, we kept our voices down, going over what we planned on doing.

"I don't like the idea that we're going to have to fumble around a village we've never been in trying to figure out which hut has a Suebi warrior," I muttered.

"We won't have to fumble around, Centurion. I know how to find them."

I twisted in the saddle to stare at Canus, recognizing his voice, quickly realizing I could not pick him out in the gloom since we all were as black as the night.

"How?" I demanded, refusing to believe that he would have some arcane skill that none of the rest of us possessed.

"The snoring," Canus replied. "If you listen, you can tell the difference between a man snoring and a woman."

While I was a bit chagrined, neither was I willing to believe that it was that simple; I also understood we had no other choice but to rely on Canus.

"Can you tell how many occupants are in a hut?" Alex asked, deepening my embarrassment for not asking the obvious.

"Not exactly," Canus admitted. "But you can tell if there's a man and a woman, or even children."

"We're not going to kill anyone unless it's absolutely necessary!" I interjected, hardening my voice. "If a woman or a child tries to raise the alarm, threaten them, and if we absolutely have to, we knock them out, and that's all!"

I was not particularly happy with the muttered response, but I knew it was the best I could expect, and before we had gone a mile, we were silent, until Ellanher whispered something to Herminius, who translated, "The village is on the other side of those hills, but he says that the better approach is on the opposite side."

"But that will mean if we have to leave quickly, we're going to have to circle back around the village," I objected.

"Yes, it does," Herminius agreed. "But Ellanher says that the animal enclosure is on this side, while on the other side, the distance between the slope of the hill is only about a hundred paces."

As soon as he was through, I understood we had no choice. The chances of a group of strange men approaching through the horses of the Suebi, or even the draft animals like oxen for that matter, without them reacting to our scent was practically nonexistent. Using the hills that surrounded the village on our side as a screen, we rode around them until we were essentially facing back in the direction of the camp, but with the wooded hill and the village in between us. We conducted a whispered debate about whether we should dismount there, but it was quickly decided that we would ride our mounts through the woods upslope, then leave them under guard just on our side of the crest, most of us being experienced horsemen who knew that if we took them to the summit, they would be able to scent the Suebi horses, and no matter how well trained a horse may be, there is no predicting how they will react when they pick up the scent of strange horses. Another reason for staying mounted for the ascent of the hill was that, with only a quarter moon that was occasionally obscured by clouds, horses are far superior to men when moving at night, avoiding deadfalls and other obstacles underfoot as long as they are allowed to move at their own pace. Not surprisingly, Latobius and Tyr led the way, there having developed something of a rivalry between Catualda's mount and my own, although to this point, they had behaved themselves around each other, probably because both of their riders were acutely aware of what could happen. It was cold, but my undertunic was already soaked with sweat, which I pretended was due to my *hamata* and not what was coming, but through the trees up ahead, we saw the night sky, telling us we were near the top, whereupon we dismounted. We had not discussed it, but when I turned to Alex with the intention of ordering him to remain behind with the animals, although he whispered, I heard the anger there.

"Don't even think about it."

Before I could say anything, he moved towards the summit, where Herminius, Catualda, and some of the other Batavians were already gathered. I briefly considered Canus, but some instinct told me that we might need his skills that night, so it ended up being Arnfrid who was left behind.

Knowing that he understood me, I whispered, "You need to be ready to come down with the horses if we need to get out of here fast."

He nodded his acceptance, going with me the twenty paces to the top, where there was a bit of clearing that allowed us to look down at the village, and I saw the stumps that indicated this clearing had been manmade, telling me that this was a sentry post used by these villagers during times of trouble between tribes because it offered a good view to the east, beyond the village and towards Marcomanni territory. I made a quick tally, counting thirty-one dwellings, although there were probably twice as many structures, most of those of much smaller size than the huts. More importantly, there were no lights visible, reminding me that these people still did not use things like oil lamps, relying on the light provided by the firepits in the middle of their dwelling, and there was just enough moonlight to see curls of smoke rising through the thatch. In many ways, it was a peaceful scene, and while I hoped that we would be able to get in and out without disturbing it, I also knew how unlikely it was; it was this thought that got me moving.

"We're wasting time," I muttered. "Let's break into our groups." Pointing, I told Herminius, who was leading his Batavians minus Arnfrid, "You take the huts to the right of the headman's hall, we take the ones to the left. We meet back at the base of the hill. Remember, one prisoner apiece."

With that, we split up, Herminius leading his men as he moved at an angle off to the right, while I began moving straight downward since the spot on the summit was already directly above the huts to the left of the common, the headman's hall sitting in the middle of it, which we would avoid at all costs since it is customary for a headman to have men personally sworn to him as bodyguards who live in the hall. It is a mark of prestige, even if it is only one warrior, which, judging by the size of the village, was my guess in this case, or perhaps he had two men. Fortunately, the footing was much better on this side, because all deadfalls had been cleared away for firewood; indeed, I was surprised that the other side of this hill was still so overgrown, though when I thought about it later, I realized this was probably intentional, making it more difficult for an enemy to move with any stealth and surprise whoever was posted on the hill in that lookout spot. There was a wall, not for defense but to keep the animals in, although I supposed that it was better than nothing in the event there was an attack. As Ellanher had reported, it was about a hundred paces away from the trees at the bottom of the hill, and I did not pause long, more to listen than to try and spot any movement. I did spot something, off to our right, but when I squinted into the darkness, while it was impossible to see clearly, I could see enough to know that it was Herminius, if only because the movement that I had caught was towards the village. Not wanting to be outdone, I began moving, not bothering to look behind me, hearing the footfalls of my party, with Catualda just behind me, Canus behind him, Alex watching Canus, and Barvistus, the one Batavian, bringing up the rear.

As I expected, the wall came up to a spot midway between

my waist and the bottom of my ribcage, but I had to stifle a curse when I was close enough to see that, while not defensive, the points had been sharpened. And, of course, I thought sourly, we didn't bring a cloak with us to lay over the top. I was able to vault over, wedging one hand between the points, but Catualda only shook his head, and he was the second tallest man of our party. For a brief instant, I thought about using my *gladius* to slice the points off to blunt them, yet as sharp as it was—I had undergone the ritual of taking it to the armorer *immunes* to sharpen, giving him a *sestertius* in exchange, something that I began doing after reading my father's account—I did not want to risk making noise. Understanding that there was nothing else for it, I stripped off my outer tunic, exposing my *hamata*, and my wince as Catualda clambered over was due as much to the way my armor now gleamed in the moonlight as the ripping noise as holes were punched into my tunic. By the time Barvistus climbed over, there were large rents in the tunic, but I still put it back on, and during this pause, Canus began moving towards the nearest hut. This was not what we had planned; at least, I thought with real chagrin, that was not the plan as I had conceived it in my head, except that I had not articulated it aloud. Consequently, I was left to hurry to catch up with him, doing so just as he dropped to a crouch at the corner of the hut. Looking over his shoulder, he put a finger to his lips; I thought of stabbing him myself right then, but I just gave a curt nod. I did notice that he opened his mouth, which for some reason makes your hearing better, then on all fours began creeping towards the large opening that serves as a window, but I was not surprised when I got close enough to see that the shutters were closed because, although it had not gotten below freezing yet, it was the time of year when a sudden frost can strike. While this was not ideal, I also knew that the standards of construction with Germanic tribes are downright shoddy compared to Romans, meaning that these shutters, while they did muffle sound, did not make it impossible to hear, and it did not take long to hear that there were easily five or six people in that hut.

Canus listened for a moment, then shook his head, and held up two, then three fingers, then pointed to my *gladius*, the sign that he heard men, and if not warriors, then at least of warrior age. I twisted about and shook my head to Catualda, then Canus resumed moving, to the end of this hut, where he paused. Just as I was crawling past the window, one of the occupants unleashed a thunderous fart, and despite the havoc it might have unleashed, I came perilously close to bursting out in laughter. Somehow, however, I managed and joined Canus, seeing the gleam of his teeth as he grinned in the sign he had heard it as well. Waiting just long enough for the five us to come together, Canus pointed across a strip of muddy ground that served as a street, where there were two huts, identical in the thatch and wattle construction of this first one, but to the smaller one slightly to our right. Naturally, nothing was said, but I instantly understood his logic; the smaller the hut, the less number of people in it, and I nodded for him to lead the way, although I waited until he was across the muddy strip before I moved, as did Catualda, then Alex and Barvistus. We were nearer to the doorway, which was naturally closed, but Canus dropped back onto all fours, then crawled down the side to the window. Instead of crouching under it, he suddenly stood up, and I had to bite my tongue to keep from making a sound, the thought leaping into my mind that Varro's man was about to betray us, a silly thought I know, but then he beckoned to me. Perhaps not surprisingly, I approached slowly, although I was crouching and not crawling, and when I reached his side, I saw why he had behaved in this manner; the shutters were open. That did not mean the way into the hut was clear, because as is the custom, there was a sheet of leather hanging down to keep bugs out.

Canus had drawn his long dagger, and he used this to push the flap away so we had a better view inside. The first thing I saw was the sullenly glowing coals from the banked fire in the center of the single room directly across from this window, then I spied two dark shapes huddled together and covered with blankets at the end of the hut farthest from the door, which was to our right. Nobody was snoring, but one of the figures moved suddenly, causing my hand to reach down instead of up for my *gladius*, but by the time I corrected myself, the figure had turned over and settled back down. More importantly, we clearly heard a masculine voice murmuring something, and I surmised that the man was dreaming, and hard on the heels of that came an odd thought; I wonder what he's dreaming about? Whatever it is, I thought grimly, it's going to be better than his reality. I nodded to Canus, but when he reached up with his dagger, clearly intending to slice the leather flap away, I put a hand on his arm and shook my head.

Leaning forward, I exhaled all of my breath before putting my lips to his ear to whisper, "Too small."

I straightened and I saw his mouth open, but then he gave an abrupt nod and followed me back to the front where the other three were waiting. Holding up a single finger, I pointed up at my *gladius* hilt, as much as a reminder to myself where to reach for it the next time, but then I was flummoxed for a moment, then held up another finger and mimicked breasts. Because of the darkness, I could not tell who snickered, but I glared at all of them, then turned to the door, whereupon once more, Canus moved more quickly, shaking his head and pointing to himself. Which, I admitted, once again made sense; there was no doubt that Canus had more experience getting into dwellings, although I did wonder if there was any similarity between the doors of the *insulae* in the Subura and a hut in Germania. Certainly there would be no lock, I reasoned, and that turned out to be true. Kneeling down, Canus used his hands to feel around the area where there would be a latch, then using his dagger, which was still drawn, he slid the point into the gap between the doorjamb and the door. In the darkness, it was impossible to see exactly what he was doing, but it was the way his upper body was moving that hinted at it, and I understood that the door was secured with a locking bar. He was driving the point of the dagger into the wood of the locking bar deeply enough that he could then lift the bar up and above the bracket, while he leaned against the door, which opened a few inches. This was the moment he stopped and looked over his shoulder, which in turn made me realize something else; there was no way for Canus to free his dagger from the bar without it clattering to the dirt floor. Certainly it would not make as much noise as if it was falling onto a tiled or even a wooden floor, but that was not a risk to take, so I held up a hand for him to hold.

Taking a breath, I positioned myself at the left edge of the door, then nodded to Canus, who pushed the door open just enough for me to reach through, then he pulled his dagger free and the bar fell into my hand, everything going so smoothly that it was as if we had practiced it. Thanks to leather hinges, the door did not make any noise as it opened further, while I stepped into the hut, staring at the pair of figures on the opposite side of the banked fire. The first thing I did was look around for any children, but I saw no small shapes, and I set the bar on the dirt floor before I walked as quietly as I could deeper into the single room. There was a table and two benches on the right side of the fire, so I naturally chose the more direct path to the sleeping figures. Reaching the fire, roughly the middle of the room, I glanced over my shoulder, and in the dim, orange light I saw that Alex was holding a set of the leather thongs and gag. Canus was now behind Alex and Catualda, but his attention was on a wooden chest tucked in one corner, and I stifled my impulse to remind him that we were not here to steal anything. I attribute my distraction to not noticing something that would very shortly become extremely important, although when I thought about it later, I supposed that it registered in some part of my brain that the other figure I assumed to be our target's woman was larger than normal. Then, I thought of my mother's maid Grimhilt, who was almost as tall and as broad as I was, so it was no more than a passing thought. Besides, I had another thing on my mind, a memory actually, not of something that I had experienced but I had read, from the Prefect's account, where he recounted the story of his last campaign with the *Praetor* Marcus Primus, whose name was still known through the Empire for all the wrong reasons; indeed, he was executed by Divus Augustus for his actions during this campaign that, as my great-grandfather learned, was nothing more than a treasure hunt. Primus had sent the Prefect, along with a group of *Evocati*, who were disbanded not long afterward by Divus Augustus, to snatch some prisoners.

What came to my mind in that Suebi's hut was a comment by the Prefect about how hitting a man hard enough to render him unconscious but not kill him was not as simple as it might seem. Straightening up, I made my decision, beckoning to Canus, my reasoning being that, of the five of us, he was the man most likely to have needed to learn how much force to apply to achieve the desired result. And, I will say, that when I pointed to the figure we had identified as the man, then mimed knocking him out, Canus did not hesitate, although at first I thought he was refusing because he turned around and crept towards the door, but it was to pick up the discarded locking bar, which he hefted, then made a practice swing before returning. Positioning himself just above the sleeping Suebi, who was on his side with his face turned towards Canus, he signaled his readiness, and I beckoned to Alex, pointing to the sleeping woman, then the thongs in his hand. Nodding his understanding, he knelt down, all eyes going to me while I looked at Canus, both hands around the bar, and I signaled him in kind, whereupon he instantly brought the wood down, making the loudest noise to that point. The sound was akin to that of a stave striking a gourd, and despite myself, I winced, thinking there was no way the Suebi would be of any use, but it was what happened in the next instant that none of us were prepared for, because his sleeping partner suddenly sat upright, blinking in surprise. This was not what shocked us into stillness; it was the beard the "woman" was wearing, but thankfully, he was as surprised and disoriented as we were, except then we saw his mouth open, causing Alex to throw himself onto the man, clamping his hand over the second Suebi's mouth as he began thrashing wildly, inadvertently kicking his partner next to him, who did not react in the slightest. I was moving an eyeblink later, though not in time because I heard someone hiss in agony, only understanding an instant later that it was Alex, and because he had been bitten, yet he refused to let go.

Since they were so entwined, I was not about to use my *gladius*, so I dropped to my knees, then trying to time it right, aimed a punch at the struggling Suebi's head. Fortuna was smiling on us, because more by luck than skill, my punch caught him on the side of the head, stunning him enough that his mouth opened slackly, allowing Alex to free his hand, which was pouring blood that gleamed in the orange light. As he tended to his hand, I grabbed the thongs lying on the floor, rapidly trussing the dazed man, and since Alex was using the rag meant as a gag as a bandage, I gestured to Catualda, who tossed me his, which I promptly stuffed into the man's mouth. With the momentary crisis averted, I thought it safe enough to whisper, and I leaned back on my haunches as I issued my orders.

"Check to see if his skull is broken." I indicated the first Suebi, who had not moved a muscle.

"It's not," Canus whispered back, but he made no attempt to check the man.

"You don't know that!" I hissed.

"Actually, Centurion," he shrugged, "I do. I assure you that he's just out cold. He'll talk when he comes round."

Deciding not to argue more about it, I shifted to kneel by Alex, and I could see even in the dull light the sweat beading his forehead.

"Hurt bad?"

"What do you think?" he managed between clenched teeth. "But I'll be fine. And," he held the wrapped hand up, "at least it's my left hand. I can still hold a *gladius*."

"Hopefully, we won't need it," I whispered as I helped him to his feet. Turning to the others, I was about to ask their opinion on whether to take both Suebi when, before I could, the rest of the Prefect's story came to mind, about how one of the captured men had been dead, and how the other group of Evocati had taken an extra prisoner.

"We're taking both of these men," I ordered, which surprised the others, but it was Catualda who asked why. "In case he," I pointed at the man Canus had struck, "doesn't wake up, and Herminius can't find someone."

I did not wait for any response, walking towards the doorway, where Barvistus had been standing lookout.

"I have not seen any movement, Centurion," he reported, "but I heard a pair of dogs barking from the other side of the village."

"We need to get moving," I decided, not willing to wait for the rest of the village dogs to join the chorus, wondering if it was a portent of disaster.

By size, I should have been carrying one of our prisoners, but I was unwilling to do that, certain that my *gladius* would be better than my strength at carrying heavy loads. With Alex partially out of action, and Canus too slight to haul a burden the size of either Suebi, it left Catualda to carry one man, and Barvistus to carry the other, but very quickly, it became apparent that they would need help. Alex grabbed Catualda's man, the one we had thought was a woman, by the ankles, and I heard my friend's low groan of pain, though he did not drop his load, while Canus did the same with the man he had struck; it was also this moment where I was struck by the odd thought: Well, that explains why these two locked their door. What it meant in a practical sense was that I was their only protection, but I had drawn my *gladius* and was ready. Nodding to them, I pulled the door open, took a glance in each direction, then beckoned to the others to follow me. Stepping out into the muddy street, I could hear that, in fact, more dogs had joined the original pair, but from the sound, they were still on the other side of the headman's hall. Whatever the cause, I knew it could not be long before a tribesman roused himself to deal with it, even if it was just to shout at them to shut up, so I quickened my pace. It was this moment that I suppose Fortuna decided she was bored and needed some amusement; looking down, she saw me, and what she sent to have some fun was a Suebi who needed to take a piss.

For just a moment, one that seemed much longer than I am certain it was, I had the absurd thought that as long as I did not move from my spot dead in the middle of the muddy street, the Suebi who had obviously been in the hut that we had checked first and who was now standing with his cock in his hand, about to piss into the middle of the street not a dozen paces away from me, would not notice. And, honestly, he actually had begun pissing before he looked in my direction, moving his head in a manner that even in the darkness communicated he was half-asleep. I knew that I should be moving; my *gladius* was already drawn, and I am not boasting when I say that for a large man I move with surprising speed, having been told this more times than I can easily count, yet my feet seemed glued to the muddy street, although I do remember thinking that now I understood why it was so foul-smelling if these savages relieved themselves in the middle of it. Consequently, we only stared at each other for what was probably at least two or perhaps even three full heartbeats, but then I sensed as much as saw him open his mouth, and that got me moving...too late to stop him from yelling in alarm, though I reached him before he could pull his *bracae* back up, my cause aided by them dropping down around his knees as he tried to dash back to his hut. I cut him off in mid-shout with a thrust to his side as he was half-turned away from me, his life ending with a gurgling moan and a brutal shove off my blade where he landed, quite poetically in my view, facedown in his own puddle of piss. Any hope that I cut off his alarm before it roused the inhabitants was extinguished by the muffled cries I heard, first from inside the hut from which he had emerged, then the ones on either side.

"Hurry up!" I hissed, though I wondered if there was any need to keep my voice down, waving my blade in a beckoning gesture, and the other four men, with their cargo, materialized from the gloom as they crossed the street.

In the heartbeat of time I took to check on the others, some of the Suebi villagers began to emerge from their huts, and a pair of them, both of them holding spears, were hurrying from one of the huts down the street, both of them shouting the alert to their fellow tribesmen. The sudden change from relative quiet to the clamor as what seemed to be at least a dozen different and distinct voices, all yelling in Suebi, and from seemingly every direction, was disconcerting, but the pair of men who rushed out into the street were directly in the path we needed to take to get to the horses. I suppose that is why, before I had any thought of doing so, I burst into a run, my *gladius* out and away from my body so that I could pick up speed. That, I am ashamed to say, was the extent of my initial plan, just charging at them in the hope that the sight of me would be enough to send them scurrying out of our path; it did not work. I did get the answer about whether they were actually warriors, as without any hesitation, they spread apart, placing themselves on either side of me, the standard tactic when two men face a single foe. However, I did not hesitate either, changing course so that I was headed for the spearman to my right, though not to face him directly, but aiming farther to his left and by doing so blocking his comrade with his own body, if only for the span of a heartbeat or two. It is a tactic that I learned from my father, and I have used it more times than I can readily count; obviously, it has always been successful, and it would have been successful this time...if my sudden change of direction had not caused my feet to slip out from under me. I slammed into the filthy mud, which did soften the blow, though it still knocked some of the wind out of me, but because I landed on my right side, the most important thing was that my blade was trapped under my body, and the pair of warriors once more did not hesitate, rushing for me while raising their spears.

Thank the gods, neither did Alex, though it took me an eyeblink to recognize that it was him, his *gladius* drawn as he rushed past me to interpose himself between me and the two Suebi, while I was consigned to being a very unwilling and uncomfortable spectator, but before I could shout an order to the others to come to Alex's aid, another figure came into my view from the area of my feet, and it took even longer for it to register that it was not Catualda, or Barvistus, but Canus, while my initial thought was that he was a fool for trying to face a spear-wielding warrior who, judging by their behavior was experienced, with only a dagger. However, I saw that Canus' left hand was full, but until I saw him using it, I could not imagine what utility his cloak would have; I quickly learned, and even now it is difficult to describe. I was not completely unfamiliar with the idea of using a cloak, or the heavier *sagum*; in fact, Legionaries do it quite often when they are out in town and someone has drawn their *pugio*, but it is always used defensively, both to protect the left arm somewhat, and to hopefully trap the blade in the folds.

Canus did not use his own cloak, which, being more like a *paenula,* was not as cumbersome, in this manner; instead, he held it by one end and, using it like a whip, snapped it at the Suebi spearman's face while Varro's man was still outside the reach of the warrior's spear. Then, in what seemed to be the same motion and with nothing more than a flick of his wrist, the end of his cloak wrapped around the shaft of the Suebi's spear as if by some sort of magic, whereupon Canus gave a viciously hard pull. It was not enough to yank the spear from the warrior's grasp, but it was enough to make the warrior stumble forward, and what came next happened too quickly for my eye to follow in the darkness, though I saw the result. In that instant, what I saw was Canus moving, first getting inside of the point of the Suebi spear which was now off to his left, while his right hand and arm were hidden from my view by his body for an eyeblink before bringing it across in a backhanded movement that ended with his right arm out from his body to the right, the long dagger in his hand and, most importantly, showing black with blood in the pale moonlight for almost its entire length. He stepped to the side with his back partially turned towards his foe, as if he was ignoring the Suebi, which I thought was an extraordinarily foolhardy thing to do, until I saw the dark, gleaming mass in between the warrior's feet, realizing that they were his intestines just as the man collapsed on top of them. This all happened so quickly that I was not all the way to my feet, and I was not down very long, even if it seemed so, while Alex was just finishing off his opponent with a first position thrust after stepping inside his opponent's own attack with his spear.

"*Arnfrid! Horses!*" I bellowed this with all the power my lungs could provide, and while I was not in the same class as my father, and I knew that he was too far away at the top of the hill to understand the words, I felt confident he would understand what I was ordering.

The way to the end of the village where we had entered was open, and Alex and Canus wasted no time hurrying back to the prisoners, while I looked in the direction of the headman's village to see if I could spot Herminius, hoping to see him already heading our direction, but instead what I saw was a number of shapes that were too numerous to be Herminius and his party; worse, they were the ones heading in our direction, not Herminius and the others.

Glancing back over and seeing that the others were ready

to move, I ordered, "Keep going! Get to the horses!"

"Gnaeus, what are you going to do?" Alex demanded, though what mattered most was that they had begun moving.

"See if I can make them think twice about coming after us," I replied, though I had absolutely no idea how I would accomplish that.

"Don't do anything stupid! Come with us! Herminius can't get to us now, not with those bastards in the way, so they're going to circle back in our direction using the hill!"

It was a sensible thing to do, and I knew that Alex was almost undoubtedly right; of course, I did not move, and I heard him roundly cursing me, but what mattered was that his voice was receding as they hurried away. I had counted nine men approaching up the muddy street, but they got about thirty paces away before I recognized that one of the men was wearing his helmet, though he was still clad only in his tunic. They could have rushed me, but the headman, for that was who I took him to be, both because of the helmet and the fact that he carried a long *gladius* and, most importantly, the others were all looking at him, was clearly confused. I realized why when he spoke in a guttural voice, of which I picked out a couple of words; both names, actually: "Arminius" and "Maroboduus." It was then I remembered my beard, having gotten accustomed to it, realizing that, before he killed me, he at least wanted to know what faction I was part of, and it was out of an impish urge that I pointed to myself and said only one word.

"Roman."

"Roman?" he repeated, then shook his head vigorously enough that I heard the tiny knuckle bones tied in clacking together, followed by a flurry of words that was delivered so rapidly that I did not pick out any of them.

One of his men spoke then, indicating me with his spear, and it was easy to tell that he was urging the headman to stop wasting time, and I dropped into a crouch, still uncertain whether I was going to fight, or turn about and flee. Afterward, and actually up until this very moment, I insisted to Alex that I had seen Herminius and his men hurrying towards us, while not one Suebi looked over their shoulders in their direction.

Even outnumbered almost two to one, one cannot underestimate the value of surprise, Herminius and his Batavians catching the Suebi completely unprepared, and from behind. The truth is that I was watching the headman to the exclusion of everything else, gambling that, as a matter of pride, he would claim me for himself, only allowing his men to intervene if he was in danger of being bested, so I was as surprised as the other Suebi when the air was shattered by the roar of Herminius and his men...and Alex is now glaring up at me now that my secret is out. I was suddenly ignored, as every Suebi, including the headman, spun about in shock, but since I was as surprised as they were, I did not take advantage of the headman's lapse and sprint across the gap to end him. To his credit, he instantly understood that the fight was lost, because with a shouted order, he turned and dashed between a pair of huts on the left side of the street, his men instantly following, leaving Herminius and the others to come running to me, Ellanher bringing up the rear because he had a body slung over his shoulder. There were a pair of bodies lying in the mud that Herminius' men had managed to strike down before they fled, and I decided to add one more.

"We have two," I told Herminius, "so leave your man behind."

"But would three not be better?" He asked, and I understood why.

"We only have two spare horses," I reminded him, and with a curt order to Ellanher, the unconscious man was unceremoniously dumped to join his dead or dying comrades.

Unencumbered, we began running, and my best estimate is that perhaps a total of fifty heartbeats had elapsed since I sent Alex and the others on their way. Behind us, I recognized the headman bellowing what I assumed were orders, and now there were far more than ten or twelve voices shouting, including women, one of whom was now kneeling next to the man I had slain. She looked up as we came rushing past, and our eyes met, yet while I expected to see nothing but hatred in her expression, something that I had found quite disturbing the first few times that now barely registered, I was rocked by the look of unimaginable sadness in them. Without any bidding, I thought of Bronwen, wondering if this would be how she looked at the man who had slain me, and despite myself, I felt my stride falter. Then, I heard hoofbeats, followed a heartbeat later by Alex leading the way on Lightning appearing from the last huts in the village, leading Latobius. Arnfrid was leading the other horses, and we wasted no time in mounting up, rejoining Catualda and Canus who were already on the other side of the wall, both of them busy lashing the prisoners onto the saddles of the spares, and I wondered how Canus had managed to stay aboard his mount when they jumped it. One of them had begun moaning, and just as we rode up, he tried weakly to pull his arm free as Canus tied them to the saddle, which earned him a blow to the head, and he slumped forward onto the horse's neck while Canus finished up tying lengths of rope around each man's ankles underneath the animal's bellies, effectively stopping them from the possibility of leaping off in the event they somehow loosened the bindings that attached them firmly to the saddle; it also informed me that, despite his own inexperience as a horseman, he had at least done this before.

"Ready," he announced, and without being told, a pair of Batavians snatched up the reins of the prisoners' horses then moved into place beside them, answering my unasked question of how we would keep these two unconscious men in their saddles.

We moved at the trot to the base of the hill, slowing to a walk as we ascended it in a retracing of our steps down to the village, and I paused for a moment to peer through the trees, but while I could see movement, it was impossible to make out any details, though we could still hear the shouting. It was the shrill, undulating sound of the horn piercing the night that worried me, wondering what it might mean given that we had already penetrated the village and gotten away. We would find out fairly soon.

Not until we traversed the hill and were on the opposite side did anyone speak, and then it seemed as if everyone had something to say, but this is a normal event after a battle or any kind of sharp action.

I took the opportunity to draw alongside Canus, and it took me two tries to get the words out. "I wanted to thank you for saving my bacon back there."

He did not reply immediately, giving me a sidelong glance before finally shrugging.

"He was blocking our way out of the village, Centurion. I didn't see where I had much choice."

I stifled the stab of anger, as much as I could anyway, but I heard the stiffness in my tone.

"Yes, well, thank you anyway." I hesitated, then added, "I've never seen someone use a cloak like that before. It was...impressive. Where did you learn it?"

My sense was that Canus did not want to be flattered, but he was nonetheless.

"The Subura," he answered, then grinned at me, yet not in a taunting or unfriendly manner. "Just as you suspected, Centurion. I was born and raised there."

"Well, it certainly is effective, at least for that kind of fight."

"No, Centurion." Canus sounded amused. "I can assure you that I wouldn't show up to fight these barbarians with just my cloak in the kind of battles you lot fight."

"And the dagger?" I asked, interested almost despite myself, but that has been the way for me since I was a child when it comes to matters of arms. "When did you start using a longer one?"

He did not answer immediately, but it was because he was trying to think, finally replying, "That's a good question, actually. But about four years ago, I think."

"Why not a *gladius*?"

Neither of us had noticed Alex riding up on Canus' opposite side, but Canus had a better relationship with my friend, and his question made Varro's man laugh.

"Where would I hide a *gladius*? We're about the same size, Alex. Where would *you* carry one where it couldn't be seen easily?"

Alex replied with a laugh of his own, and I chuckled, but then he turned serious.

"I came up here to suggest that maybe we can hold this

conversation another time. Those Suebi might be coming after us."

Stung, mainly because I knew he was right, I snapped, "Why do you think I have Barvistus riding rearguard?"

Alex had long since stopped being cowed when I got irritated, and he did not hesitate to counter, "Why do you think they'd only come up behind us?"

"Oh, go piss on your boots," I muttered...then kicked Latobius to where Herminius was riding at the head of our column, where I ordered, "Send Ellanher ahead, no more than a furlong. We won't be able to see him, but we can hear him shouting if they manage to get ahead of us."

This was done immediately, and once Ellanher went at the canter, since we were still moving at a trot, Herminius asked, "Are you just being cautious, Centurion? Or did one of your *numeni* whisper to you?"

At first, I thought he was jesting, then I remembered that, as a people, the Batavians, while loyal to Rome, were still Germans, and they are notoriously superstitious, which for a Roman to say is quite a statement.

"No," I assured him, trying to avoid replying in a teasing tone. "Nothing like that." I was inspired then to remind him, "Remember what happened with the Marsi. They used a different route and got ahead of us." I shrugged. "We just need to be prepared for that possibility." This made me think of something. "If we do have to start running, Herminius, will Baldovin and Wigmar be able to keep the prisoners in their saddles?"

Even if I had not seen it in his expression because of the gloom, I would have heard the indignation in the trooper's voice.

"Of course, Centurion! They are Batavians! They could do this if they were children! We are born to the saddle, and I am surprised that someone who has been in the company of Prefect Batavius would..."

"I know! I know!" I held a hand up. "I apologize! I knew that it was silly to ask as soon as I said it." Thankfully, this sufficed, and we rode in silence for a bit, then Herminius broke it, sounding hesitant. "Centurion, I was thinking. While yes,

171

Baldovin and Wigmar will be able to keep the prisoners in the saddle, if you are right, and the Suebi in the village do as those Marsi did, we will have to go to the gallop. Then," he held out one hand, palm down and rocked it back and forth, "it becomes much more of a chancy thing keeping the prisoners on their horses. Perhaps we should stop and let your man Canus interrogate them now?"

I had thought about this, but thinking about it again, I shook my head.

"No, we need to get them back to camp," I replied.

It turned out to be a good decision.

What happened with our Suebi pursuers was almost identical to what occurred with the Marsi, as the village headman, obviously having been made aware of the presence of a large Roman force in their area and their general location, knew that we would have to take the longer route back around the hills and led his force of about forty warriors on a shorter course to intercept us. And, if it had been daylight, they would have cut us off about two miles from the camp, but their presence was betrayed by a freshening breeze that often stirs in the watch before dawn. From our perspective, one moment we were moving at a slow trot, then off to our left, a horse whinnied, and without a word being said, either by Herminius, or myself, our entire party went to the gallop. The Suebi materialized out of the night, dark shapes coming from our left, but between our quick reaction and their leader misjudging either the length or the distance between our columns, it gave us the opportunity to get a jump on our pursuers. Later, I realized that what the headman might have been doing was trying to cut off Baldovin and Wigmar because he somehow saw that our prisoners were with them, but if so, it was the wrong thing to do.

Whatever the truth, the result was a wild chase in almost complete darkness, with our prisoners gripped with one hand by their guard, both of whom had regained consciousness, and Canus' precaution of tying a length of rope around each prisoner's ankle underneath the horse's belly not only guaranteed that if they attempted to throw themselves from the saddle, they would die a horrible death but kept them firmly in the saddle. Proving that they preferred an uncertain future to a sure death, neither of them made any attempt, and with their hands lashed to the saddle, they were mere passengers in our flight. I had slowed Latobius so that I was with Barvistus, and at one point when I glanced back, I swore that we were within a spear's length of our nearest pursuer, and despite it being only a quick glance over the shoulder, I saw the outline of a helmet, though honestly, I was never worried. Latobius was not galloping at full speed, and in truth, I was more exhilarated than afraid; nevertheless, when we topped a low rise and saw the torches that I knew Nerva had ordered lit for us, I experienced a thrill knowing that we had achieved our mission, while at the same time, I knew I was practically daring the gods to strike me down. Nevertheless, once we topped the rise, I had just begun the descent, with the others ahead of me, and I risked another glance over my shoulder to see that it was in fact the headman, sawing on the reins of his mount to come sliding to a stop, where he was quickly joined by his warriors.

Even over the shrieking of the wind, I heard him shout, "Roman! Wait!"

Despite my better judgment, I slowed to a stop, spinning Latobius about, although I made sure there was enough distance between us that we had to shout at each other.

"What is it?" I shouted.

"Why are you here, Roman?" Even across the distance, I heard the urgency and the worry. "What is your purpose in Suebi lands?"

I realized that, not only was it a natural question, I could not see the harm in answering, "You have nothing to fear, Suebi. We're not here for the Suebi."

The instant the words were out, I knew I should not have added the last part, and he did not hesitate to demand, "Then why are you here? And," he challenged, "how do I know you are speaking the truth? Romans," he sneered, "lie."

"And Suebi don't?" I shot back, then before this could deteriorate, I hurried on, "But you have my word as a Roman officer, that we are not here to do any harm to the Suebi."

"Very well, Roman," he replied. "But when a Suebi gives

his word, he is not afraid to give his name and his lineage. So," I did not miss that when he pointed at me, it was with his long *gladius*, "what is *your* name?"

Again, I could not see the harm, especially since I was certain that my name would mean nothing.

"My name is Gnaeus Volusenianus Pullus," I informed him, then out of force of habit, I almost complicated matters. "I am the Primus...a Centurion of Rome," I corrected, not wanting to betray that I was a Centurion of the 1st Legion.

"Pullus?" He cocked his head, then repeated, "Pullus?" Then, he shook his head and said, "I do not know why, but this name is not unknown to me."

"Centurion! What are you doing?"

Hearing Barvistus shouting at me broke the spell, and I turned and kicked Latobius back to a lazy gallop, but as I did, I shouted over my shoulder, "Ask your elders about the Roman who slew Vergorix of the Chatti in single combat! I am his son!"

I did not say anything more, arriving just in time to attach myself to the rear of our party as it entered the gates.

Since we had been scheduled to take a rest day, it worked out that we stayed in place while we allowed Canus to do his work. Naturally, we were all exhausted, and I felt a pang of sympathy for Varro's man, but as we quickly learned when we retired to our tent to get some rest, because we were close enough to the tent that served as the *quaestorium*, there was no way we could not hear the screams, which made sleep impossible for me. It did not seem to bother Catualda, who was snoring softly, nor most of the Batavians, making me wonder if I was actually as soft as I had been accused of being early in my career when I was Gnaeus Volusenus. Thankfully, by the end of the first daylight watch, a runner came to alert us that Canus was through and confident that he had extracted the information that Nerva demanded, so I roused Catualda, and we hurried to his tent. The Pili Priores were present already, as was Canus, who was slumped over on his stool, his face gray with exhaustion, and while I had learned from his beating of Florus that he used *pankration* wrappings, I saw that his hands were still swollen and there were the same small scrapes where the edge of the bandages fell on his fingers. Nerva acknowledged our arrival with a grunt, pointing to the pair of stools that had become ours for the duration, and began immediately.

"Arminius delivered a defeat to Maroboduus, north of the Sudetes," he said flatly. "The prisoners both independently claimed this happened more than a week ago, and their last information is that Maroboduus has withdrawn all the way back to Casurgis." Given the lack of reaction by the Pili Priores, it was clear that they had already been told at least this much. He continued, "They also say that while Arminius pursued Maroboduus, he stopped his army on the southern slopes of the Sudetes, and he seems content to wait there. Why that is," he sighed, "they say they don't know."

"What does the torturer there think?" the Secundus Pilus Prior asked, and even as tired as he was, I could see this angered Canus.

"The torturer," he retorted, "says that he's certain that they've told him everything they know. Now," he finished with a tired shrug, "whether Ardilis," clearly realizing he needed to explain, "that's the name of their village's headman, knows more, they didn't know."

"Arminius is probably waiting on reinforcements from the other tribes besides his own Cherusci," the Secundus Pilus Prior said, and I thought I heard a note of real concern. Apparently not seeing enough support among his fellow Pili Priores, he went on by insisting, "You know how these savages are. They're like wolves! If they sense that Maroboduus is fatally weakened, they'll rush to join Arminius so they can be there for the kill and a share of the loot." Shaking his head, he finished flatly, "It's too dangerous to proceed, Primus Pilus." Turning to Catualda, I suppose he tried to sound both regretful and sympathetic; he failed miserably at both, "I am sorry, Lord Catualda, but I'm sure that the Princeps, while he clearly wants to see someone on the Marcomanni throne who's more of a friend to Rome than Maroboduus, won't be willing to sacrifice one of his Legions to do it." He smiled. "I'm sure you understand."

I am not naming the Secundus Pilus Prior, and that is for a reason; it is also a sign of the times in which we live, but I do not believe that I am running a risk in saying that, of all the Pili Priores, he could be counted on to offer resistance to Nerva's commands more than the others combined. He was also a paid man like myself, and the rumor, which I have not seen anything to dispel, was that he was also politically connected to someone powerful back in Rome. Most importantly, he had made little secret that he saw himself as the natural successor to Nerva when the Primus Pilus decided to retire; that he was the only one among his peers who thought so did not seem to matter to him.

I took it as a sign that Nerva was aware of all of this, because rather than explode, he said mildly, "Your opinion is welcomed, as always, Pilus Prior. But," his voice hardened, not much but noticeably enough that it caused the Pilus Prior to sit up more stiffly, "I am in command of the Alaudae, and it's my decision to make, not yours." He held the Pilus Prior in his gaze, not long but long enough that anyone with even a modicum of experience knew sent a final message of its own, then turned to Canus. "You obviously believe them, or you would still be...questioning them." When Canus nodded, Nerva surprised me by turning to me and asking, "What do you think, Pullus? You've faced Arminius like we all have, but you were also part of the mission to get Segestes as well, and there are some similarities there." This surprised me because I did not see them, and my expression must have communicated that, because he explained, "He was very close to getting not only both his wife and unborn child but his father-in-law as well, but he turned back. Now," he spread his hands out, "he has Maroboduus on his knees, and one last blow could finish him. Do you think he will take it?"

"No," I answered immediately, and without thinking.

"*Gerrae*," the Secundus Pilus Prior scoffed. "There's no way you could possibly know that, Pullus."

"No, there's not," I agreed. "But the Primus Pilus asked me what I thought." In a deliberate insult, I turned and asked Nerva, "Would you like me to explain, Primus Pilus?"

"I wouldn't have asked you if I didn't," he replied, but I

saw the glimmer of a smile, and I remember thinking to myself that, when I chose to, I could play the game of flattery.

"As much as Arminius may want to finish Maroboduus off," I began, "I'm as certain as I can be that he doesn't feel as strongly about that than he did about having his wife and unborn child being taken by us." Unbidden, the memory of Germanicus' triumph popped into my mind; specifically the image of Thusnelda, Arminius' wife, standing on the bed of a cart, her son who by that time was almost three years old, standing in front of her, both of her hands on his shoulders while her own were pulled back, with head erect, her expression showing her disdain for her clamoring captors. Like most who saw it, I was impressed despite myself, and I had more reason to hate the woman than almost anyone else crammed into the Circus Maximus that day, since my father had been slain before my eyes during our mission of rescuing her father. Pushing the sudden rush of emotions away, I continued, "But he broke off the attempt to rescue her because it would have damaged his army too much. And," I reminded them, "he was *much* stronger then than he is now that he's down to just his Cherusci and a handful of rebels from the other tribes. No," I shook my head, "I don't think he's going to be willing to risk what little army he has left, especially if Maroboduus is back at Casurgis and protected by its walls. Remember," I reminded them, "while Arminius adopted a lot of our tactics, he was never able to convince his tribe to embrace the use of artillery, which from what Lord Catualda has told me about Casurgis, he would need."

Indicating I was finished, there was a silence of perhaps a heartbeat as we waited for Nerva, and he broke it with a nod, saying as he did, "I agree with Pullus. And," he added, "I would also point out the unlikelihood of old Maroboduus suddenly asking Arminius for a truce. Nor do I see his warriors letting him." He slapped the desk, which I had learned was his way of signaling that a particular subject was closed, which he confirmed by continuing, "Now that we know as much of the larger situation as we're likely to, we need to talk about our next move to Casurgis." He turned his attention to Catualda. "Lord Catualda, do you have a better idea where we are in relation to Marcomanni territory?"

"Yes, Primus Pilus," Catualda replied, standing as he did so, and walked over to the map hanging on the canvas wall behind Nerva's desk that was maddeningly incomplete, although in typical Roman fashion, Nerva had seen to it that it was filled in as much as possible at the end of each day. Pointing to a spot just to the left and below the series of hatch marks that were essentially inverted "V's" that curved in a shallow semicircle with the open end facing down and which represented the Sudetes Mountains, he said, "If we are not here, we are very close to it. This map does not show it, but there is a range of hills south of Casurgis." His finger traced a line that was essentially another semicircle, giving me the impression that the Marcomanni capital was in something of a large bowl of lower ground. "When we reach this point, from a distance, it will appear as if the Sudetes is one solid line of mountains and hills, but it is not. There are actually two passages that will take us into the interior of the Marcomanni lands, one here," he pointed to a spot next to the two bottommost hatch marks, "where we will have to travel about ten miles south before we turn back east. Or," his finger moved to the blank spot below them, "if we turn slightly south now, there is a passage through the southern ring of hills. Both," he finished, "will put us about the same distance from Casurgis once we reach either of these points."

"And how long will it take us to get to these points?" Nerva asked peevishly.

"At the pace we have been marching," Catualda replied calmly, "we should be at the spot where we can choose which route to take by the end of the day tomorrow."

"What's the difference between these two routes?" the Secundus Pilus Prior asked.

"None as far as distance..." Catualda began before he was cut off.

"Then why are you wasting our time?" The Centurion sniffed. "If the distances are equal and we're closer to the northern approach right now, then we need to use that!"

By this time, I had learned that Catualda was very precise in his speech, and if he brought this up, there was a reason.

Fortunately, Nerva either understood this or more likely saw an opportunity to take the Secundus Pilus Prior down a notch.

"I suspect that you didn't raise this for no reason, Lord," he said to the Gotones.

"No, Primus Pilus, I did not." Pointing at the northern approach, he explained, "It does not show on this map, but this passage is not flat ground; it is just that the hills are not as high, but some of them are very steep. And there is a stretch of about two of your miles where the road winds between these lower hills, and the passage is much narrower."

"Perfect country for an ambush," Nerva mused, and Catualda nodded.

"Exactly, Primus Pilus. Here," his finger moved to the southern passage, "while it is not completely flat or open, there is no stretch as dangerous as the northern passage. So," he concluded, "yes, it will take us part of the day after tomorrow to get to the southern route, but we will be safer."

Once more, Nerva slapped the desk, but this time, he stood in another of his signals that the meeting was over. When he dismissed us, I half-expected him to call my name to stay behind again, but he did not, and I was relieved, thinking only of the opportunity to get some sleep, despite the fact that it was fully daylight. Walking to the tent, the one thing I did not allow myself to dwell on was the part of what we had learned that Nerva had not mentioned, and that was that we had no idea how much army Maroboduus had left, but we did know that what he had was behind the walls of Casurgis. There would be time enough for that on tomorrow's march...along with something else.

"I think," I began with Catualda, "that it's time you tell us about these two thousand men you have tucked away somewhere who are supposed to help us with Maroboduus."

I had broached the subject without warning, and while his face betrayed nothing, I thought I detected him shifting slightly in his saddle; Alex, as I had asked, was riding on the opposite side of the Gotones so that he could observe him undetected while I peppered Catualda with questions.

"What about them?" he asked, to my ear with an evasive

tone.

"Don't you think that they were important to mention?"

I was determined to maintain my own composure, knowing it would not do our cause any good if I got angry.

"I did mention them," Catualda protested, then after a heartbeat, admitted, "to *Quaestor* Varro."

The truth was obvious; he had used these two thousand warriors as a sign of his importance, in a signal to Varro that he brought something else to the table besides his nobility and familial connection to Maroboduus. Since I had learned about these warriors from Nerva, I had assumed that Catualda had informed him; at least, I did until that moment.

"So, you told Nerva about them, since I heard it from him," I began; I got the answer by the manner in which he suddenly stared off into the distance, and my incredulity was only partially feigned when I gasped, "What? You're not the one who told him? Varro did?"

"I assume so," he replied, and this time, there was no question he was being evasive, and I had the feeling that if he thought he could get away with it, he would have kicked Tyr and galloped away.

"Well, where are these men now?" I demanded. "And how do they know when and where to meet with us?"

"It is...complicated." Catualda shook his head. "And I do not believe that I can explain it adequately."

"Try," I said, but now I did not try and hide my anger, and I nudged Latobius until our thighs were touching so that I could tower over him.

So, he did, and by the time he was finished, I was not certain whether to laugh, cry, or simply turn around.

However, even after he was finished, I was sufficiently confused to try and relay it back to him. "So, you *think* that there are a thousand Gotones who have entered Marcomanni territory and are waiting in a village fifty miles east of Casurgis, because you told them they needed to be in place by the end of our month?" He nodded at this, and frankly, this was not the part that worried me as much. "But they're going to somehow make sure that their presence isn't detected by Maroboduus or any of his subchiefs." Another nod, though he was looking less happy, and I moved on to the part that concerned me the most. "Meanwhile, you have another thousand Marcomanni, but they're scattered throughout the bands of Maroboduus' subchiefs, who have sworn to rise up the moment that we're spotted, yes?" Yet one more nod, but his reticence was rubbing me raw, and my resolve to not give in to my temper was rapidly weakening. "What does that mean, exactly? You didn't mention that. Are they going to turn on their fellow tribesmen? Or are they going to gather? And if they're going to gather...where?"

"It depends on many things," Catualda replied, still sounding vague. Clearly sensing that I was not going to be satisfied, he continued, "If the information that Canus extracted from those two Suebi is correct, and I think that it is," he held up a hand to cut off my objection, though none was coming, "it means that most, if not all of the men who have offered me their fealty are inside the walls of Casurgis since they said that Maroboduus has withdrawn all of his forces throughout Marcomanni lands to the capital. In that event, when we, I mean, when *your* 5th Legion begins the assault on the city, they will rush the Marcomanni defending the main gate, and open it for us."

This was certainly a wonderful thing, if it happened, yet I still was not convinced, and I asked skeptically, "You're saying that these men will be willing to turn on their comrades? And their own kin?"

"If they are men of honor," Catualda replied stiffly, "they will uphold the vow they made to me!"

Now I was almost certain that this aspect had not even occurred to Catualda, and in this moment, I realized that while my misgivings about him had been steadily growing, they had now reached a point where I almost felt compelled to go to Nerva and warn him against counting on Catualda to deliver on his promises, whatever they might have been. I liked Catualda well enough; he was quite pleasant, and I had seen him in action enough to know that he was an experienced warrior, but the doubts were piling up. Deciding there was nothing more to be gained talking about his Marcomanni allies, I returned our conversation to the other group of men.

"Those Gotones who are waiting in that village," I returned to the original group, "once they're gathered there, then what?"

"They come to Casurgis," Catualda said. "And they will join your Legion in doing what is necessary. In fact," he added almost as an afterthought, "if the Primus Pilus wishes it, I can order them to rush the gate themselves so that he does not need to risk his Legionaries unnecessarily."

This elicited a cough from Alex, which I knew was a warning, but there was no need, since my mind went immediately in the same direction.

"Do your Marcomanni men know about your own tribesmen?"

"Of course not," Catualda replied, sounding indignant. "I would not be so foolish to let either group know about the other. Truly, Pullus," he grinned at me, "I am not a fool."

"But if you offer Nerva the use of your Gotones to assault the gate, which you say will be held by your Marcomanni who are loyal to you, they won't know that they're fighting friends."

Immediately afterward, I realized that I had hoped that this was something Catualda had not considered, but when he did nothing more than shrug, it sent a chill through me.

"Yes," he sighed, "but that cannot be helped." I suppose it was seeing my mouth drop open that compelled him to say, "I have already decided that the families of any of these men who might fall will be taken care of for as long as they shall need it, Centurion." He chuckled. "There will be more than enough gold to do so."

Not knowing what else to say, I mumbled an excuse about needing to piss, peeling off so that I could get away from Catualda. Meanwhile, the column marched on, the line of mountains of the Sudetes looming ever larger off to our left, while the southern ring of hills was just barely visible on the horizon. Barring anything unforeseen, we would be outside Casurgis the next day, and now that I had a deeper understanding of Catualda, I began the process of bracing myself for what I would be seeing, certain that like with everything else, Catualda had not been exactly forthcoming in describing its defenses.

Chapter 5

Catualda had at least correctly described the terrain through the southern passage, and while we were certainly observed by what we all assumed were Marcomanni scouts, the track we were following was up a wide valley where there was no real possibility for any kind of ambush. The sighting of Marcomanni, our first, was the signal that shield covers came off and helmets went on; the Alaudae had been marching in armor since crossing the Rhenus, but more importantly, the chattering in the ranks, while not ceasing, certainly decreased as Centurions and Optios began calling men out for talking too much, the sign that a ranker is distracted. Even our horses, Latobius included, became more alert, with ears forward, nostrils blowing in and out despite moving at a walk as they tried to catch a scent of trouble. The day passed slowly, the line of hills that essentially lay athwart our path showing over the treetops, until so gradually that it caught me by surprise, the straight outlines that mark manmade structures became apparent.

"That's Casurgis," I commented, and Catualda nodded. "And you say that we have to go how far to the ford?"

For that was one of the natural defensive advantages of Casurgis, the presence of a river the German tribes called the Wilt-Ahwa (Vltava) that ran on a north/south axis, along the eastern side of the Marcomanni capital. Even if the river had been fordable, an assault from that direction was impossible according to the Gotones noble, and we would soon see for ourselves that he was right in this, because the riverbank was barely fifty paces wide before the start of the slope, which was so steep that there was not even a gate anywhere on the eastern side. Consequently, when we reached another river, which Catualda said was named the Mies (Berounka) that was barely fifty paces across and shallow, with a rocky bottom, we splashed across it, then turned north to follow it for about two miles to where it fed into the Wilt-Ahwa, which itself was not much wider than the Berounka. This was the best fording spot, according to Catualda, and just before we crossed the Berounka, Nerva summoned us to where he was marching with the First Cohort. To my relief, and the others, Nerva had decided that, given the high likelihood now that we were this close to Casurgis, and knowing that Maroboduus had been made aware of our impending arrival at least the day before, that any Marcomanni party we ran into would heavily outnumber us, he had ordered our scouting party to stay with the marching column. Until, at least, this moment, although I could not really fault him.

"Pullus, I want your party to follow this river up to where it reaches the Wilt-Ahwa." He stumbled over the awkward-sounding word, at least to Roman ears. "Scout that second ford, and tell me what kind of defenses that bastard Maroboduus has in place to protect it."

This seemed to offend Catualda, who said stiffly, "Please believe me, Primus Pilus, I was very thorough in my description of what is waiting for us there."

Nerva gave him a sour smile.

"And you think that now that he knows we're coming, he hasn't added to those defenses you told us about?" he countered, and I saw by the flush rising above the Gotones' beard that Nerva had scored.

I will say that he had the grace to acknowledge, "You are undoubtedly correct, Primus Pilus."

Befitting my post, I saluted on behalf of the others, and as I turned Latobius to carry out our orders, Nerva called out, "And, Pullus, I don't have to tell you that at the first sign of trouble, you need to run back here, do I? Even if it means that we're blind at that ford."

Assuring him that we would do that very thing, we moved at a quick trot, and once we had splashed across the ford, out of the corner of my eye, I saw the others reaching for their *gladius* to pull it partially out of the scabbard, a habit we all pick up to make sure that the blade does not stick, while

Arnfrid and Wigmar, who each carried two sheaths, one on either side of their saddle that were full of short throwing javelins, rattled the shafts about to make sure they were not tangled together. I did the same as the others, though I kept my eyes moving, not particularly happy with the terrain, which was open pastureland, with only a few stands of scrubby trees for cover. Granted, that it meant that we would not be surprised, but that worked both ways, meaning that we were easy to spot, so we continually scanned the countryside, looking for movement. The reality was that this area was barren of life, aside from birds flitting about, yet this was not surprising; like most German tribes, much of the Marcomanni's wealth came from cattle, which was both a food source and currency, so it made sense that even if we had not been in the area, Maroboduus would have moved them to keep them safe from Arminius. Speaking of the Cherusci, I know I was not alone in spending at least part of my attention on scanning the northern horizon, looking for the kind of dust column that would signal that, contrary to what the Suebi prisoners, who we had actually released a bit battered but otherwise unharmed, had told us that Arminius was staying aloof in the Sudetes, he was in fact on the march in our direction. We did not see any movement for the first mile, then ahead of us, a thin trail of dust rose in the air, though not large enough to be from a force that outnumbered us. I called a halt to discuss what we should do, deferring to Herminius as the expert.

"We should stay in double column for now," he counseled. "Let them make the first move."

I suppose that it is not surprising that I did not altogether care for this idea of being in a reactive position, but I did not argue, just reaching down, this time to the *spatha* that Herminius had loaned me that was tied to my saddle, checking to make sure it slid easily from its scabbard as well. We did not alter our pace, just resumed moving, and very quickly the cause of the dust cloud materialized into what were only a half-dozen mounted men, but while it was impossible to tell, the manner in which they suddenly drew up and came to a halt indicated to me that they had believed us to be allies, or at the very least not a threat. This seemed to be confirmed when, suddenly and without any kind of overt sign, they spun around and went galloping off, in the exact direction in which we were headed.

"That must be where the ford is," Alex commented, and we kept moving.

Not helping our cause was the presence of a line of trees that blocked the view of where the two rivers converged; we had gotten close enough to see the silvery glint of water across our right front quarter before it disappeared behind the outer edge of the trees ahead of us, while we kept the Berounka to our left, as the ground we were traversing narrowed to a point. Drawing up about three hundred paces from the obscuring trees, I reassumed command.

"Catualda, Herminius and I are going to get closer so that we can get a look at what's ahead," I announced to the others, ignoring Alex's glare at being left behind.

We slowed to a walk once we were within about fifty paces of the trees, but the small forest was not dense, nor was the underbrush thick enough to completely obscure the view of the Wilt-Ahwa's opposite bank. More by the shape than any detail could I tell that there was a fortification of some sort, but we were too far away to tell whether it was new construction or had been there.

"We better dismount," I decided, though I phrased it in a way that I hoped that if Herminius disagreed, he would speak up, but he did not.

Leading our horses, I kept Latobius' reins in my left hand, while my right was on the hilt of my *gladius*, and we walked slowly into the trees. Suddenly, there was a flurry of movement, but it was not an attack; I saw sprays of water as the Marcomanni horsemen entered the river, emerging onto the opposite bank very quickly, telling us that the horses had not been forced to swim, and were able to touch the bottom.

"Well," I laughed, "at least they told us that it's shallow." Thinking of something, I turned to Catualda. "Do they have any kind of artillery at this outpost?"

"No." He shook his head, then hesitated. "At least, they did not the last time I was here."

This was *not* a satisfactory answer, and I almost forced

him to walk out onto the other side to expose himself to find out, but I refrained. Instead, we approached cautiously, stopping just within the edge of the treeline on the river side. It took just a heartbeat or two to determine that there were in fact two fortifications, and that they were not new. Placed so that they straddled the beaten, muddy strip of track that passed for a road, they were nothing more than two large mounds of dirt with a wooden palisade and a wooden structure atop each one that served as a shelter for what I counted to be a dozen men in each. And, not surprisingly, they were all at least looking in our direction, though we were screened enough to avoid being spotted at first, until one warrior, with a beard that hung to his waist and was split in two, suddenly shouted and pointed his spear at us.

"So they know we're here now," I commented.

We stood there, watching for a bit as what appeared to be a debate began between the mounted men, who were now in the middle of the road between the two fortifications as one of them engaged in a conversation with one of the men up in the fortification on the right. I say conversation; it might have begun that way, but very quickly, the gestures became more emphatic, with a lot of pointing in our direction, and it became clear that the warrior in the fortification was either urging or ordering the mounted men to come back across the river after us.

"I wonder if they're telling that stupid bastard they're not going to commit suicide," I muttered.

"I recognize the dismounted man doing the talking," Catualda said quietly. "His name is Chariovalda. And," he turned his head to look up at me, "he is one of the men sworn to me."

Naturally, my first impulse was to tell him to signal his man somehow to let him know that they were not to oppose our crossing, but thankfully, I smothered that before it could leave my mouth. Still, I thought there must be a way to use this to our advantage, and it came to me almost immediately.

"Step out into the open," I told him, but if I thought he would immediately understand why, the look of horror he gave me disabused me of that.

"Why?" he asked incredulously. "Why would I do that?"

"So," I tried to be patient, "he knows that the time is at hand, that you've come, and that you haven't come alone."

"Then you should come out with me," he retorted. "So he knows that Rome is backing me."

"Do I look like a Roman right now, Catualda?" I asked gently, pointing to my beard. "And even in armor, he's likely to think I'm a German."

"That," he replied, grudgingly, "is true. But it still is too dangerous." He pointed to the two groups, all of whom aside from Chariovalda were paying at least partial attention to us, although it was clear that what was obviously an argument was proving at least as diverting as strangers across the river. "There are at least eight archers that I can see out of those two groups, and the range is not that far."

That was true, but I still felt strongly that it needed to be done.

"I'll do it."

I whirled about, startled at the sound of Alex's voice but also angry, both that he had violated my express orders and that he had managed to do so without me hearing him coming.

"What are you doing?" I demanded. "I told you to stay with the others."

"I was bored," he replied, then before I could remind him that as far as I was concerned he was under orders, he said, "I heard what you two were talking about. And," he addressed Catualda, "Gnaeus is right. He doesn't look Roman. But," he pointed to himself, and more importantly, to the *segmentata* he was wearing, "I do. Your man will recognize the armor at the very least."

"Which you could have looted from a dead Roman," Catualda protested, but instead of replying, Alex just regarded him with the kind of gaze that I have received from him more times than I can count, the one that says he recognizes when the subject of his scrutiny is being deliberately obtuse. Knowing better than to say anything, I stood there watching the silent battle of wills, and finally, Catualda's shoulders slumped in what was clearly a sign of defeat, and he muttered, "Very well." Turning towards the ford, I was surprised that he did not hesitate, although he did say, "I hope neither of us regrets this, Alex."

"So do I," Alex answered cheerfully, but as he strode past me, he added, "because if I got skewered, Gnaeus will be joining me soon, but only after Algaia flays him alive."

With that happy thought, the pair emerged out onto the riverbank, and I found myself second-guessing my insistence at this, knowing that Alex was only partially in jest about what Algaia would do to me. Now that Chariovalda had been identified, I watched him the most closely, although we were far enough away that they were all within my field of vision, but to a man, the Marcomanni seemed frozen in surprise. Then there was a shout that I supposed was of recognition, but it was a warrior in the other fortification who had shouted, and began pointing at the pair as they stood there, and while it would have been impossible for me to make out what the warrior was shouting even if it had been in Latin, it was obvious that he recognized Catualda.

This prompted me to call out, "Is that one of your men, Catualda?"

He did not turn his head, nor did Alex, answering, "I do not recognize him, Centurion." I was about to snap at him, but he answered my question, "I did not personally receive the oaths of all thousand Marcomanni, Centurion. This man *might* belong to one of the lords who swore allegiance to me, but I do not know."

It is impossible for me to say who was more shocked at what happened next, me or Catualda, but while it was Chariovalda who shouted something, what it was became instantly clear when five men in each fortification suddenly raised bows, their draw arms moving backward towards their faces in the same movement as they aimed their arrows at a slight angle in a sign that they were well within range.

"*Run!*"

I recognized my voice, but there was no need, because both Alex and Catualda were already moving, although Alex had the presence of my mind to backpedal, which, while it was slower, still gave him the advantage to track the flight of the missiles, and he did not have long to wait, ten of them streaking across the river on a flatter trajectory than normal. However, while he said later that he was disappointed that the Marcomanni did not consider him important enough to bring down, with every arrow aimed at Catualda instead, although he was the only one. Catualda was hit by one missile, but it was a glancing blow that skipped off his shoulder before embedding itself in a tree a couple paces beyond, although it was enough to wrench a shout of pain and caused him to stagger. I grabbed his arm and we quickly retreated more deeply into the woods, the Marcomanni sending only one more volley our way, all of them falling short. Remounting, we headed back towards the Legion, and as we rode, Barvistus checked Catualda's shoulder, but all he had to show was a bruise and some broken links on his mail shirt.

"At least your man knows we're here," I said, as much to distract the German, who was wincing as he moved his shoulder.

"Yes, he does," he agreed, but tersely and making a point not to look in my direction.

"What do you think he'll do now?" I asked, but all I got was another shrug.

Recognizing that I was not going to be satisfied with that, he said, "He will likely wait until it is safe to tell the other noblemen sworn to my cause."

"How many men is that, exactly? Because," I said pointedly, "you've never really been forthcoming about any of this."

"I took the oaths of thirty-three noblemen, and altogether and as I said, they can muster about a thousand men."

I do not have the head for figures that Alex does, but I knew that worked out to about thirty spears that each of these noblemen had in their service, although I also knew it was not an equal distribution, where one of these noblemen might have a hundred warriors in his service, and another only ten. Nevertheless, it seemed to strain credulity to believe that every single man sworn to one of these lords would keep their mouths shut and not betray him, and by extension, expose Catualda as being involved in this sudden appearance of a Roman Legion. Hard on that thought was the realization that, given that more than one of the warriors at the ford recognized him, that secret was already out. I spotted the eagle by the sun glinting off its wings, and took that as a sign that I was now at a point where worrying about this was not going to help or change anything, but I did pull Catualda aside and extracted a promise from him that he would inform Nerva about Chariovalda and these thousand Marcomanni at the first opportunity, which he swore he would do.

He did not, but I did not get an opportunity to broach this lapse with Nerva, who was understandably more interested in hearing our report on what was waiting at the ford. Once he heard us out, he decided that sending the First Cohort along with a pair of scorpions and one *ballista* would suffice to force the Marcomanni to abandon the fortifications. However, by the time they marched to the ford, the position was abandoned, and, assuming that this was Chariovalda's doing, I decided not to bring it up with Nerva at that moment, giving Catualda an opportunity to make good on his promise. Although we were the first across, we were accompanied by Nerva and the First of the First, and we noticed a pile of logs and rubble that had been hidden from view by one of the fortifications.

"They must have planned on using that to block the road," Nerva's *Aquilifer* commented.

"As if that would have stopped us for more than a few dozen heartbeats," Nerva scoffed. Rubbing his chin in thought, he signaled to Catualda, who nudged Tyr over to him. "Pullus, you and Herminius too," the Primus Pilus ordered. "Now what?" he asked Catualda. "You said that the best approach to the town is from the east." Pointing to the muddy track, which immediately curved south, where the walls of Casurgis were visible running about four hundred paces below the crest of a hill, though far enough away that there was no way to see if they were lined with men, he asked, "If we follow this road, does it curve around the base of this ridge? Will it take us where we need to go?"

"It will," Catualda seemingly agreed, "but the road is within range of the walls."

"I thought you said they didn't have artillery," Nerva

interjected, and Catualda shook his head.

"They do not, but they do not need it. The slope is very steep, and they have piles of stones, all rounded and of different sizes, and they can just roll them down the slope."

Somewhat surprisingly, Nerva did not argue, saying instead, "That would do it. All right," he continued in a signal that we would not be using that route. "How can we get to the eastern side from here?"

"There is a path," Catualda pointed down the road in the direction of Casurgis, "about a half-mile down the road. It is not very wide, but it uses that forest," his finger moved to some treetops off to our left, "as cover so that the defenders cannot easily see our movement."

"They won't need to," Nerva grunted. "They're going to know where we're heading. They know better than we do where the weak part of their defenses are." Turning to me, he ordered, "Same as earlier, Pullus. I want you ahead of the column, but where you can be seen." Glancing up at the sky, he worried, "I don't want to be making camp in the dark, and the sooner we find a spot, the better. I'd rather be behind ditch and wall with some daylight left even if it means we have a couple of miles to go yet."

Besides the trees, it had rained earlier in the day, not enough to turn the track into a quagmire once a couple thousand feet stomped on it, but enough that there was no dust cloud, forcing the Marcomanni to guess about our progress. From my perspective, this would have been the moment that I actually ordered the Legion to march at a quicker pace, thinking that there was an advantage to be gained by showing up more quickly than they expected. However, Nerva clearly did not see it the same way, ordering the same pace we had been setting, but when we reached the track, I could not stifle a curse. I was about to chastise Catualda, but realized it would do no good; being a German meant that what was passable for wagons to him and what it was to us was two different things, and I did not envy the drag Cohort, certain that by the time the baggage train reached this stretch, even without more rain, it would be a bog. Less than a mile onto it, we were forced to ride side by side with barely a hand's width between our thighs, and we were riding in a double column.

"There's no way that even a five-file column will fit," Alex murmured. "They're going to have to start chopping down these trees for the wagons."

He was right, and very quickly, the *bucina* sounded the call for Pili Priores. Since my presence had been required every time, I turned Latobius and trotted the bare furlong to the eagle, seeing that the Secundus Pilus Prior was already there, the Tertius Pilus Prior trotting up to join. Since Nerva had decreed we march in Cohort order, it meant that the Decimus Pilus Prior was the last to arrive, and while he was huffing and puffing from the quick trot, Nerva still snapped at him for his tardiness.

"Have the pioneers from your Cohorts come up here to the front," Nerva ordered them. "We're going to do this as quickly as possible, with my Cohort's men going with Pullus." Frowning in thought, he tried to calculate how far ahead his men, totaling two men from each Century who were skilled in the use of axes, saws, and the long iron bars that, when required, are used to leverage stumps out, should be so that the Tenth Cohort men were even with where we were standing. This is a basic calculation that every Pilus Prior knows, yet to my surprise, the Secundus Pilus Prior did not seem interested in taking this opportunity to demonstrate his superior knowledge, and I was about to open my mouth when Nerva finally said, "Four furlongs, six men on each side. Pullus, you and your men will spread out on either side, far enough apart to cover our flanks."

Personally, I thought he had misjudged, having performed the calculations of number of men and the number of feet each man could reasonably be expected to clear without help and coming up with five furlongs, which Alex later confirmed, but I said nothing. The First Cohort men trailed behind me as I moved Latobius at a slow trot for him, which meant a quick trot for the men, ignoring their muttered curses at our speed. Reaching the others, I relayed the orders, and within a sixth part of a watch from our halt, the sound of axes was ringing out in a line on either side of the track for a distance of four furlongs, while I sat Latobius, looking in the general direction of Casurgis, though even with its height above us, it was not visible because of the trees. This forest was more like the rest of Germania, with deadfalls, low undergrowth, and small rivulets cutting the ground, but it was also dotted with small but steep hills, which of course the track navigated in between, in a winding path, making it good ambush terrain.

The pioneers worked quickly, both because they were experienced, and Nerva had ordered that only the trees and undergrowth that would impede the wagons be chopped away and not a few paces outward on each side as is our normal practice. If the tree was large enough, men paired up, making for quick work, and they aimed the trees so they fell away from the track. Naturally, we were not moving as quickly as if we were unimpeded, but I knew from experience that any Marcomanni who were watching us would be dismayed by the speed with which we made our way down the track, while the Legion waited for several sections ahead of it to be cleared before moving, then grounded their packs and shields, facing back outward. It was already past midday when we began, but it did not take long before there was a shout, on my side of the track, not from Alex who was the nearest man to me on the right, but to Ellanher, who was on the other side of Alex. Given that we were about fifteen paces away from the track and in the underbrush, it meant that I had to rely on Alex because I could not see Ellanher, and I watched as Alex looked in the opposite direction for a moment, then turned to face me.

"He saw two mounted men, on the slope of that hill," he called out, pointing to the hill off to my right front, but I could not immediately see any movement.

Trusting Ellanher, I kept my eyes on the hill, then saw something that took a moment to resolve itself, recognizing that it was a mounted man, wearing a green tunic that made him blend in, but while he was moving about, it was impossible to tell what he was doing.

"Probably picking his nose," I said to Latobius, who tossed his head in what I took to be agreement.

Watching for another long moment, the Marcomanni stopped moving, and I knew that if I looked away, when I returned my attention to him, I would not be able to find him, so I trusted Alex and Ellanher to keep an eye on him as I resumed my own scan of the forest around us. This was the first, but it was not the last sighting, although it was only on my side, which made sense; Maroboduus was going to keep his men between us and Casurgis, and would not be willing to risk us picking off men because they got cut off from the town. We finally emerged from the forest two parts of a watch later, and after curving around to the south so that when we did, we could see Casurgis clearly, just as the Marcomanni could see us. For my part, since I was leading the way, it meant that I was the first Roman to lay eyes on what we had collectively risked so much for, and I had to sit there for some time to collect myself, not sure if I should laugh at the absurdity of the idea that a single Legion could take what I was seeing, or to cry at what was likely to be an utter disaster.

We had referred to Casurgis as a town, and I quickly realized that referring to the Marcomanni capital in this manner had shaped my perception of what would be facing us. I learned I was not alone when Alex rode up alongside me, and when Nerva and the rest of the Legion arrived, I had already braced myself for what was sure to be something to remember. In fact, for a span of a few heartbeats, I worried that Nerva would strike Catualda down as he raged at the Gotones for what he viewed as the perfidy typical of a barbarian.

"You called that a '*town*'!" he bellowed, using his *vitus* to indicate Casurgis. "That's almost the size of Mogontiacum!"

That was an exaggeration, but not by much; it was more along the size of Ubiorum, which at that point had almost seven thousand inhabitants, not counting the Legions. However, more than the size, it was the configuration of the Marcomanni capital that made Catualda's plan for inside aid not just important, but a requirement for success.

"I told the *Quaestor* about..." Catualda began, but Nerva cut him off with a slash of his *vitus*, violently enough I could hear the swishing sound a couple paces away.

"Don't try to sell me that wagonload of *cac, Lord*," Nerva sneered. "You've been with the Alaudae for two weeks, and you didn't mention a *word* about *that*!"

He thrust the *vitus* out and pointed to the twin hills, both of which were covered in dwellings, though arranged in the haphazard fashion typical of barbarians. In a way, from this direction, east of Casurgis and looking west, the two hills resembled a pair of breasts, with a deep cleft in between the two. If the entirety of the capital had been those two hills, with the main gate positioned in between them, this would have been challenging enough, but what was clear was that Casurgis had grown, so the eastern wall was now perhaps five or six hundred paces from the base of the two hills on flatter ground. We could not see this part of the town since it was hidden by the wooden wall that I estimated to be about fifteen feet tall, but there was no missing the large fortress on the left hand hill, situated on the top, which was flat, this being our first view of it since the right hand hill had blocked our view. The citadel was further protected by a wall of its own, extending north to the edge of that hill, which fell steeply away, down to the narrow gorge that separated the two. There were no structures of any kind on either slope above the gorge, understandable given its steepness, while on the right hand hill, if not in style then in relative size, it reminded me of the Palatine, with the structures on it being larger, some of them also enclosed within a wall, the sign that this was where the wealthy and powerful Marcomanni nobility lived.

We were about a mile away from the eastern wall and gate, and as we stood there gaping, we saw small groups of horsemen who had used the main road that hugged the base of the hill around from the river, returning to Casurgis. If there was anything positive in what we were faced with, it was that the ground was flat, with a brook close enough that a channel could be dug for both fresh water and for sanitation, although I certainly did not want to be here that long. The forest that we had used for cover was close, so we had access to firewood and the materials necessary not only to make camp, but to construct siege fortifications. Those, as far as any of us could see, were the positives; while Catualda had not been as forthcoming as he might have been, he had warned us that Casurgis was well-watered, there being several springs, and Maroboduus had ordered wells dug throughout the city years earlier when tensions had first flared between his people and the Cherusci of Arminius. Additionally, we had to assume that, when Maroboduus retreated here after his repulse by Arminius, he had also stocked up on provisions. For the first, but would not be the last time, the thought flashed through my mind that maybe it was us that should be approaching Arminius for a temporary alliance; fortunately, when I broached this with Alex, he was so ruthless in his destruction of this idea, I never mentioned it to anyone until just this moment.

"Let's get camp started," Nerva ordered, and I know I was not alone in hearing the morose note in his voice, and I could not stifle the pang of sympathy I felt for the man, which was surprising in itself.

If someone had told me that I would view Nerva with anything other than hostility, and from my viewpoint, with excellent reason, I would have called them mad, but I could not help wondering what he had gotten himself into that Varro could use to take what would inevitably be the largest risk with his career, his life, and most importantly to anyone wearing the white crest, his reputation, and whether or not I would ever learn what it was. Since we had no role in constructing the camp, I approached Nerva to ask if he wanted me to conduct a more thorough scouting mission.

He thought for a moment, then shook his head and said, "No, it can wait until the morning. They know we're here, and we know that this isn't going to be an easy nut to crack." Giving me a tired smile, he added, "We'll see how tough tomorrow." I rendered my salute as I acknowledged his order, then took his nod as a dismissal, and began to walk away when he called out, "And, Pullus?" When I turned back to face him, while he was not smiling, I heard a hint of humor in his tone as he said gruffly, "Now it's time to shave that fucking beard off and start looking like a Centurion of Rome again."

This was an order I was only too happy to obey.

Once I was clean-shaven, and Alex gave me a good scraping, under the guise of visiting Latobius and Lightning, Alex and I escaped the tent to be able to talk freely.

"What do you think Nerva is going to do?" he asked me,

but all I could do was shake my head, though not because I did not have an idea; I actually did.

"There's no way we can stay here longer than another week," I said glumly, then amended, "at least, not if he's willing to put us on half-rations now in order to squeeze out another week."

"I've been hearing things." Alex lowered his voice even more than necessary, given that we were walking across the forum, which was deserted. "The Secundus Pilus Prior has been putting it about that the orders that sent us on this task didn't come from Tiberius, but from Sejanus."

Now, this was exactly what we both thought to be the case, but we were also of a like mind that this was an extraordinarily dangerous thing to get out into circulation around the fires.

"We need to put a stop to it," I said, without much thought, I confess.

"We do," he agreed, "but how?"

If I had stopped to think about it, I would have never done what I was about to do, but it also happened that we had crossed the forum and were now walking down the street leading to the stable area that took us past the Fifth Cohort on one side, and the Sixth on the other. And, I suppose the gods might have had a hand in arranging it so that it was the First of the Fifth who occupied the street running perpendicular to the one we were walking on.

Without a word, I suddenly turned and walked directly towards the fire of the first tent next to the intersection on the right, which I knew would make it the First Section of the First of the Fifth, and I heard Alex half-gasp, half-whisper, "Gnaeus! What are you doing? Are you *mad*?"

I think that, now that I was freshly shaved, and since I was usually riding, they had gotten accustomed to me looking like a German, because at first, when one of the men happened to glance up to see a Centurion carrying a *vitus*, despite the fact that he was strange, he muttered to the others, who immediately got to their feet, but that was his only reaction. Only when I got within a few paces did I hear the sudden intake of breath that signaled I was recognized, but it was the transformation of the expression of the man who had spotted me first that meant he was the one I was staring at as I spoke.

"How many of you think that I'm responsible for your Pilus Prior taking his own life?"

The ranker I was looking at flushed deeply, but he did not break his gaze, and he raised his hand; he was followed by three others, but the rest seemed content to stand there looking at the fire, hands at their sides.

"Go ahead and sit back down," I said first, using the tone they knew meant that it was an order, but I was not surprised when the first man did not, though the rest did.

"What's your name, *Gregarius*?" I asked him.

"Sergeant *Immunes* Lucius Kaeso," he muttered.

"Well, Kaeso," I said. "I want to hear you say it. Don't just raise your fucking hand."

"So, what?" His lips twisted into a sneer. "You can write me up and have me striped for disrespecting a Centurion?" He gave a harsh laugh, "No thank you, Centurion. Mama Kaeso didn't raise a fool."

"First, I don't have a posting in the Alaudae," I pointed out. "But if that's not enough, I give you my word, in front of witnesses here, that nothing you say will be held against you." I looked at the others. "Is this acceptable?"

"So you say," he snorted, which was what I had anticipated.

"If you're too much of a coward," I said coldly, "then just say that instead. Besides," I turned and handed my *vitus* to Alex, who was looking at me as if he had never seen me before, "if you think I need that or anything else...well," I shrugged, "if he were here, Petronius could tell you differently."

For a moment, I thought I had gone too far, because even those men who did not seem overtly hostile muttered angrily, while only Kaeso still glared at me.

"Fine," he said abruptly. "I think that what you did to Petronius was as close to fucking murder as you can get, because I think you're responsible for robbing him of his *dignitas* to the point he couldn't live with himself." I could see that he was getting angrier as he spoke, and he finished by shouting, "And for what?"

I sensed the movement from the opposite side of the street,

as men who were absorbed in their own nightly routines heard Kaeso shouting.

"Gnaeus," Alex called out, "let's go."

I did not turn, nor answer, just shaking my head.

"Well, Kaeso," I said, and I knew that he was not prepared for me to say, "you're right. I'm responsible for what Petronius did, at least partly." As I expected, this had the effect of eliciting gasps of surprise and shock, which I ignored as I continued, "Now, do you want to know why?"

"It doesn't matter why!" He shook his head vigorously. "It doesn't matter what he said!"

That told me something, but before I responded, I glanced at the others who were already seated, then turned to watch as the men from what would be the Second Section, sitting across the street, drifted over. Looking past Kaeso, I saw the Third Section men approaching, but they were still several paces away, so I raised my voice as I asked, "What would you do if he called your mother a whore?"

This sent a ripple of comments, and some gasps of surprise that told me what I suspected was true, and I was certain I heard a note of something like alarm in Kaeso's tone as he protested, "That's not true! He didn't say that!"

I was opening my mouth to challenge Kaeso, but before I could, one of the men of the Second Section, a grizzled veteran with a knot of scar tissue where one ear should have been spoke up.

"Yes, he did, Kaeso." To my ears, the older man sounded tired. "I heard him say it because I was there at The Happy Legionary when the Centurion here came in." He looked up at me, and I heard the challenge. "But you came there looking for trouble, Centurion. And if you're truly a man of honor, you'll admit it."

"I was," I acknowledged, yet I still felt compelled to add, "because I had heard what Petronius was saying about my mother after my father died." I addressed the men, now numbering almost thirty, and I could see others drifting in this direction, "You all know who my father was, yes?" I was not surprised to see everyone either nod or murmur their acknowledgement that my father was well known under the standard, and beyond just the 1st, or his original Legion of the 8th. Taking a breath, I continued, "And I know there were...rumors about my birth. Those rumors are true." I was not surprised at the sudden rustling of whispers and gasps, and in as simple terms as I could, I explained the circumstances of my birth, my own belief that I was born the son of Quintus Volusenus, a man of the Equestrian Order, and my learning of my paternity only after my father's death, although I did not mention that by that time, I had already begun to suspect the truth.

When I finished, there was a silence, but I was not surprised that it was Kaeso who broke it, nor what he said, "Then that means that the Pilus Prior was..." I was staring at him, and the word "right" died in his throat.

"My mother," I spoke quietly, "was a young girl who fell in love with a man of the Legions." Suddenly turning my attention to the others, I demanded, "How many of you sitting here have a woman? And children?" Several either raised their hands or mumbled something. "And how many of you are married to your woman?" Naturally, every hand dropped, if only because none of them was willing to risk acknowledging that they had been married, secretly, which was expressly forbidden by the army. "What would *you* do if someone called your woman a whore for the *crime* of loving you?"

As I expected, there was muttered acknowledgement that it would go very badly for any man who uttered that kind of slur; more importantly, I could sense the mood shifting away from Kaeso.

"So, yes, I beat Pilus Prior Petronius, and I beat him badly," I admitted. "And yes," I nodded in Kaeso's direction, "I went to The Happy Legionary specifically to confront your Centurion, because I had already heard what he was saying in Mogontiacum. And my mother had moved there not long before, so I didn't want her to be confronted with those kinds of slurs on her character. But that said," I paused before finishing with a partial truth, "I didn't intend to kill him myself, nor did I have any way of knowing that my beating of him would lead to his suicide."

There was a long silence, then my gamble paid off when,

from the outer fringe of the small crowd, a man asked, "Is it true that you were in the Praetorian Guard?"

Out of the corner of my eye, I saw Alex's expression suddenly change, as he realized what I was doing.

"Yes," I replied, then waited for the next inevitable question; I did not get past a count of three.

"Is the duty as good as they say it is?"

In the space of a couple heartbeats, Lucius Petronius was forgotten, even by Kaeso, as I spent the next few moments describing the aspects of life in the Praetorians that I knew these men cared about, not mentioning the politics, and the almost constant fear of saying the wrong thing, or running afoul of a politically connected superior. Instead, I talked only of the easy duty, the extra pay, the nights spent debauching in the greatest city in the world, where the women are as varied as the Empire itself.

"If it's so good, why are you back here?"

"Because, Kaeso, being a ranker in the Praetorians is a far cry from being a Centurion, for one thing. For another, it was always meant to be temporary duty, as long as Germanicus was in Rome. Once Tiberius sent him on his mission to the East, I returned back to where I belonged." This was another partial truth, but I decided this was as good a time as any to achieve my goal, and before he could say anything else, I went on, "In fact, I was with Germanicus when the Princeps was talking to him about Catualda and wanting him to replace Maroboduus. Which," I reminded them, "is why we're here."

"What did you say, Centurion?"

"I was just reminding all of you that we're all here for the same thing," I replied to a man from the Second Section standing next to his one-eared comrade.

I had to hide my smile when he shook his head, saying impatiently, "No, not that. About hearing Germanicus and the Princeps."

"Ah, yes. Some of you might remember that I was honored by Tiberius, who gave me permission to march with the 1st in Germanicus' triumph." Enough heads nodded that I continued, "Remember when we were formed up around the Temple of Jupiter?" Another chorus of assent, "Well, I was summoned to a private audience with the Princeps because he noticed that I was wearing the torq his brother awarded my father during my father's first campaign, and Drusus the Elder's last, where he broke his leg and died of a fever." Shrugging as if it were unimportant, I said, "Well, as I was waiting for the Princeps to speak to me, I heard him tell Germanicus that Drusus the Younger had returned from meeting with Lord Catualda in Mogontiacum, and that he had decided to replace Maroboduus."

I saw some of the men exchange glances, and it was left to the Second Section man to say doubtfully, "Really? That's not what we heard."

"I don't know what you heard," I snapped. "But I know what *I* heard. Is anyone here going say that I'm lying?" As soon as I said it, I recognized I had erred; I had worked hard to lessen the hostility, but my pride had gotten in the way, so I held up a hand as I said, "Aside from that, consider this. If what you...heard was that there was someone else making that decision and not the Princeps, that means that whoever is putting that about is saying that Tiberius, as Imperator, isn't the most powerful man in Rome. Now, does anyone *really* believe that?" I made sure to move my gaze from one man to another, and while I could not meet the eyes of all of them, I could see that enough of them had received my message, though I still added, "And what do you think would happen to the man, or men, who were caught spreading that kind of tale about? That there was...someone else in Rome who was pulling Tiberius' strings? What," I finished quietly, "do you think would happen to your Primus Pilus in that case?"

"We'll make sure that nothing like that happens...Pilus Prior."

I nodded my thanks to Kaeso, and while I thought briefly about correcting him from referring to me by my former rank, decided against it.

"Well," I said, "I've got to go feed my horse. I'll leave you to your evening."

None of them saluted, but I did not expect them to, and I strode off into the darkness, Alex walking beside me in silence for a bit, before finally saying, "That was nicely done,

Gnaeus."

I thanked him, then sighed, "I just hope it's enough."

The next morning, with Nerva riding one of the spares, and looking every bit as uncomfortable as one would expect of a Primus Pilus on horseback, along with his senior *Immunes*, we rode out of the *Porta Praetoria*. We were all tense, understandably so; nine mounted men as a bodyguard was not a number that would scare anyone, and we knew that we had to conduct our examination at more of a distance than was ideal. Our main goal was to get a look at the gate and gateway, which was the obvious choice as a target for our *ballistae*, even without the prospect of help from Catualda's Marcomanni. We also needed to get close enough for the artillery *Immunes* riding with us, naturally a veteran named Gaius Titius, with weathered features that made him look a decade older than his forty years, to get a look at the log wall. If Fortuna was with us, it would be a single layer wall, which was a possibility for the simple reason that the tribes of Germania disdained artillery. The worst case, I knew without being told, was the kind of wall made of a layer of vertical logs with about a third of their length buried in the ground, with a layer of dirt in between, then another layer of logs. Alternately, the second layer could be logs instead of dirt, but arranged horizontally; unfortunately, Fortuna decided to squat and piss on us, because even after moving along the length of the flat part of the eastern wall, Titius could not tell anything other than one thing.

"It's not a single layer wall," he told us glumly. "So there's no chance of a breach with the *ballistae*."

Personally, I had viewed this as unlikely from the beginning, but judging by Nerva's reaction, which was to almost fall off his mount so that he could stomp around in a rage, cursing the Marcomanni, the gods, an unnamed *Quaestor* sitting on his pampered ass back in Mogontiacum, and a further unnamed nobleman of the Gotones, he apparently had held out hope this was a viable possibility. Catualda seemed content to sit on Tyr, wisely choosing to ignore Nerva's thinly veiled vitriol aimed at him, focusing most of his attention on the walls, which was also understandable since they were lined with men, and some women, clearly townspeople who had come to see the invaders. With just a Legion, however, I did not think that the onlookers were suitably awestruck or quaking in fear; another two thousand men, especially when some of those men might be standing next to them on the rampart at that very moment would have made for a different story.

"So we use the *ballista* on the gate," Nerva decided. "And the scorpions will keep their heads down as we send in the ladders." I waited for him to give the number of ladders he intended to use, but when he said nothing, I asked, but I was not expecting him to admit, "I haven't decided yet. What do you think, Pullus?"

If it had been Sacrovir, I would not have thought anything of it, but Nerva was not my Primus Pilus, and it was a sign to me that he was beset by doubts, which was absolutely understandable...and could not happen.

Nevertheless, I did not answer him immediately, turning to ask Catualda, "What about the southern side? Is it as bad as the western and northern?"

"No." The Gotones shook his head. "While the southern wall is about halfway down the hill, it is not as steep. There is a gate, but it is not used often, and when it is, it is usually for driving the livestock out to graze in those pastures." He indicated the open area south of the city. "They have cleared the lower slope of trees, though, so there is no cover."

"There's no cover here either," I countered, but I understood his point; with the focus of our assault on the eastern wall, it meant that all of the artillery would be needed here, and not having some scorpions to force the defenders to keep their heads down and loose their own arrows blindly. Deciding to abandon the idea of suggesting an assault on the southern side, even if it was a diversion, I returned my attention to the eastern wall. By our estimate, the eastern wall was almost a mile long, but the corners were higher because of the manner in which both hills jutted out farther east slightly, creating something of a pocket of flat ground that was about a stadia deep, and about a half-mile across. "I think three Cohorts on a three Century front, two ladders per Century?" I ventured finally.

Nerva responded with a grunt, which was not informative, then nodded, though he did not say anything. He was turning his horse, clumsily, to head back to camp when Catualda cleared his throat.

"Primus Pilus, may I make a suggestion?"

"You can make it," Nerva answered, then added sourly, "but that doesn't mean I'll do it."

"Perhaps a ram would be in order?" Catualda suggested. "Rather than using your artillery?"

"Why by Pluto's thorny cock would I do that?" Nerva sounded more astonished than angry, and I confess I was as puzzled as he was.

"For two reasons," Catualda replied. "The first is that you will probably need to use those pieces for the citadel. I have seen the walls protecting it, and they are almost as thick as the walls your man says you cannot penetrate. You only have a certain amount of ammunition, yes? And," he went on before Nerva could respond, "I know that while you can reuse many of the stones, most of them will be damaged in some way?"

"Yes," Nerva agreed reluctantly. "But," he insisted, "it will take time to construct a ram. And," he lowered his voice, though I have no idea why, unless he was worried about his *Immunes*, "we are about out of rations, so every day matters, Lord Catualda."

"I understand that," Catualda assured him, "but how long would it take?"

"A day," Titius spoke up, proving that he had been listening, "and not even an entire day if we use the frame of one of the wagons." He looked at Nerva, saying apologetically, "I know that you don't like doing it that way, Primus Pilus, since the ram is almost always damaged." He glanced up at the sun, then said, "In fact, if we go back to camp now, we can have one knocked together and ready to use at dawn."

Now, Catualda looked uncomfortable.

"Actually, Primus Pilus, I would need a full day. I am asking that the assault begin day after tomorrow, not tomorrow."

"Then you better fucking explain why," Nerva snapped.

By the time he was through, I had to admit that the Gotones nobleman was right, but it was still up to Nerva, and he sat there, on his horse, glaring at Catualda for several heartbeats before, finally muttering, "Very well. But," he pointed a stubby finger at the Gotones, "you better be good for your word, Catualda, or I swear on the black stone, I'll make you fucking regret the day you popped out of your mother's *cunnus*!"

I thought that, in this at least, Nerva was right as well. The reason Catualda wanted to use a ram, which was only partially due to his concern about needing the artillery ammunition for Maroboduus' citadel, made sense when he explained it.

"If we bombard the gate and gateway, where Chariovalda and the other men who are sworn to me are waiting, not only will many of them be hurt or killed, it will appear as if I had betrayed them by changing my mind. And no oath is strong enough to keep men from wanting vengeance if they have to watch their friends and comrades killed by your artillery. By using a ram, we avoid that, and I told Chariovalda that the moment the ram touches the gate, that is their signal to open it." That, I remember thinking, makes sense, more sense than bombarding the gate, and when I glanced at Nerva, I saw that he was of a like mind. However, Catualda was not through. "It will also give me the time I need to ride to Nim to bring my own men back here." He glanced up at the sun. "If I leave within a watch, I will be there by sundown. While most of my men are mounted, about two hundred of them are on foot, which is another reason I am asking for another day."

Nerva did not answer immediately, so I put in, "We can definitely use another thousand men, Primus Pilus."

"We can." He nodded. "But I'm not about to let Lord Catualda go by himself. I'd hate to have him run into an ambush." On its face, that was sensible, yet I also felt confident that this was not Nerva's biggest concern, and a surreptitious glance at Catualda told me he was aware of this. "Pullus," Nerva turned to me, "you're going to go with Catualda to this Nim and get those men. Take the Batavians, and," he thought for a moment, "I'll scrape up another four men who have some experience riding, and they'll use the spares."

It was not much, but it was better than nothing, and I reminded myself to talk to Nerva to leave Canus behind and give his mount to a fifth man from the Alaudae. While I still did not trust him, that was not my motivation; we would be riding hard, and if Maroboduus had patrols out, we would have to run. With our scouting done, we returned to the camp, beginning our preparations to leave immediately, and I asked Canus to leave the tent with me so that I could give him the news that he would be staying behind.

"We're going to be riding hard and fast," I began, but the look of relief that flooded his sallow features was all I needed to see.

"I'd just slow you down, Centurion," he said, which was true enough. He grinned then, but it was not tinged with malice, or sly, and for a brief moment, he could have been a ranker who is happy to escape onerous duty. "I'll just stay here where it's safe if you don't mind."

He is going to try and kill you at some point, Gnaeus, I reminded myself, yet despite this admonition, I returned his grin.

"You're beginning to think like a ranker, Canus. Nothing makes them happier than the idea of getting out of bad duty."

"I'll remember that," he laughed, "in case I find myself under the standard because the *Quaestor* is tired of me."

It was, I thought later, an odd comment to make, but in the moment, it seemed innocuous.

We left the camp out of the *Porta Decumana* on the opposite side from Casurgis, although I knew it would not fool the Marcomanni. Since it was facing in the right direction, we did not have to worry about getting close to the walls, and best of all, the ground was open and gently rolling, enabling us to make good time. The rankers that Nerva had selected were not expert horsemen, but they had clearly ridden a fair amount, and they rode at the rear of our double column, keeping up without any visible strain. About a third of a watch after we left, Catualda turned his horse more to the north, and while I was not unduly troubled, it did make me curious.

"I thought you said this village was due east."

"It is," Catualda replied, "but I told the man leading my warriors that, if he had not received orders from me yet, he was to relocate to a closer spot on the night after the full moon."

"But that's tonight!" I exclaimed. "Doesn't that mean that he's still going to be in that village you mentioned?"

"Normally, yes," he acknowledged, "but this man is...impatient, and if I know him as well as I think I do, I believe that he already moved, either today or even yesterday."

"It can be dangerous to have a man like that taking orders from you," I commented.

"I agree," he nodded, "but he is my cousin, and there are...considerations I had to make in naming my subordinates."

That was not surprising, and I did not press any further, asking instead, "How much closer is this village?"

"Almost twenty," he answered, then thought for a moment before amending, "Although we are going about five miles north to the river."

"The river?" I frowned, trying to think of what river he was talking about. I was aware that the Wilt-Ahwa changed from its north/south orientation a few miles south of Casurgis to turn east, but that would be to the south, but it was the only one I could think of. "Are you talking about the Wilt-Ahwa?"

"No." Catualda shook his head. "I am speaking of the river you call the Albis."

"Wait." I drew on Latobius' reins, slowing to a walk, ignoring the shout of surprise from Alex behind me. "Are you sure that it's the Albis?"

"Yes." He sounded as startled as I was. "Why does this seem to surprise you?"

Frankly, when I thought about it, I could not actually explain why, other than to say, "I thought it was farther north."

"It is," he laughed, "but it is a long river."

My father had reached the banks of the Albis during his first campaign with Drusus the Elder, and the knowledge that I would at least see that river ignited an odd feeling in me, or perhaps it was just that it caught me unexpectedly. Resuming our journey, while there were no signs of enemy activity, the handful of villages in our path we bypassed, but they were still occupied, the smoke trails signaling that there were eyes on us as we rode past. This part of Germania was different than the thick forests of the lands along the Rhenus farther north, with gently rolling terrain, and while there were forests, they were more interspersed. It did make for good progress, and we had just crested a low hill when Catualda, who was riding next to me, held up his hand.

Pointing to a smear on the horizon, he said, "That is Nehurgo. Now we will see if my men are there."

"If they're not, how much time did we lose?" I asked. He had evaded answering this question to this point, but now he replied reluctantly, "Two of your watches is my guess, Centurion. One going there and one because it is farther east."

"You better be right, then," was all I said.

Since I had no idea what size Nehurgo was, there was no way to tell if the smoke hovering above the village was the normal size, or was created by the extra fires necessary for a thousand warriors. The village disappeared from sight as we descended the hill, our view blocked by another one, but instead of ascending this second one, we rode around it, giving us our first view of the Albis. And, I must say, I was quite disappointed at what I saw before us.

"It's barely fifty paces across," I grumbled to Catualda, who laughed and reminded me, "It is a *very* long river, Centurion. And we are far, far away from where it empties into the sea."

I knew this was true, yet I could not shake my disappointment, even as I realized that it was from reading my father's account of his campaign with Drusus that led me to expect that the Albis would be like the Rhenus, but for its entire length. The village was now about a mile away, off to our right, but there was a stand of trees that blocked our view, yet Catualda did not hesitate, putting Tyr into a rapid trot as we approached. Weaving through the trees, I thought about cautioning the Gotones about plunging headlong out into the open, but I did not, and we burst into the sunlight. My first thought was that, if the warriors who were lounging about the remnants of the dozens of fires on the outskirts of the village were Marcomanni and not Gotones, we were all drawing our last breaths, because to a man, they leapt to their feet, all of them looking in our direction. Some of them went running for their horses then, which were saddled and tied to a long line strung between two trees, and while we were still a couple hundred paces away, we could hear the alarmed shouting. I confess that I was getting nervous, yet when I glanced over at Catualda, he was sitting on Tyr, watching calmly and giving no indication that he intended to move, either towards the village or away from it.

"What are you doing?" Alex asked him, but Catualda did not answer, watching as the warriors got into a semblance of organization.

One of them was clearly in command, and once he was satisfied there were enough men mounted, he leapt into the saddle of his own horse, then with easily fifty men following him, he came towards us at a trot.

"I think it would be wise to lift our arms out from our sides," Catualda said calmly, "although it is not really necessary."

"If it's not necessary, then why do it?" I muttered, yet I did so, then glanced over my shoulder, nodding my head to Alex and the others, who followed suit.

It was when they were about a hundred paces away when their leader, who was close enough that I could see that he had black hair that hung loosely around his shoulders, though not with a full beard but long, flowing mustaches, and he appeared to be about my and Catualda's age, but it was the broad smile on his face that made me relax my hands, as Catualda kicked Tyr and trotted to meet him. Since they were speaking in their tongue, which is similar to the tongue of the other tribes but with enough differences that it made it impossible for me to understand them, I waited as they leaned over and embraced each other, then Catualda turned about and returned to us, and it took them just long enough for me to figure something out.

Therefore, I was ready when Catualda began, "Centurion Pullus, I would like to introduce..."

"Yes, I know," I interrupted. "This is Otmar."

We were on the march about a third of a watch after we arrived at Nehurgo, with about a full watch of daylight left, but not before, completely on impulse, I spurred Latobius into a canter to go splashing into the Albis, swimming across it in a few heartbeats, although Latobius' hooves only briefly lost contact with the river bottom, then turned right back around and came back, grinning, Alex said, like an idiot.

After a brief conversation between Catualda and his cousin, the nobleman assured me, "They have been resting all day, Centurion, so we can march well into the night."

Since we were retracing our steps, there was a part of me that rebelled at this; it is an axiom that, when in enemy territory, a wise commander never takes the same route back that they took going wherever they are going, yet at the same time, not only was there no sign of any Marcomanni forces, it would be dark, but what convinced me it would be safe enough was the practical impossibility for Maroboduus to send any of his warriors out from Casurgis.

"Very well," I agreed. "We'll stop at midnight, rest for a watch, then keep going."

I was not surprised that the men from the Alaudae were unhappy at this, while the Batavians were indifferent, knowing that we had not pushed our mounts on the ride to Nehurgo. And, I admitted to myself, it was good that Catualda knew Otmar well enough that he correctly guessed his cousin would become impatient, because even with the rest, we would arrive back at Casurgis earlier than planned. I had been concerned that Nerva would want to immediately throw us into action on our arrival, but Otmar had unwittingly saved us significant time. There was one source of irritation, and that was that Catualda had informed us that seven hundred of his warriors would be mounted, although they were not pure cavalry, using their horses to get to the fight then dismounting to fight as infantry, while three hundred were on foot and not the two hundred he had originally claimed. Very quickly, it was clear that he had switched the proportions, which meant that it was out of the question to push ahead with the mounted men, another reason that their relocation to Nehurgo was so crucial. Even so, while the warriors on foot moved quickly, at near the kind of pace a Roman Legion could set when they needed to, I chafed at the speed, but thanks to the full moon and the lack of clouds, it meant that we did not need to slow much, if at all. The clear skies also meant that it was cold, to the point that our breath was visible, creating a small fog that hovered about the heads of the men who were marching in what I suppose could be called a column, yet despite it offending my Roman sense of order, it did not hamper their ability to move quickly. Finally, with the moon telling us the time with the same precision as the sun during the day, we called a halt at the same stream that we had stopped to water.

"We'll rest here until dawn," I announced. "We should arrive back in Casurgis by the beginning of second watch."

"Do you think that's a good idea, Gnaeus?" Alex asked, surprising me considerably. When I asked why, he said with a shrug, "Because I have a feeling that if we show up that early, Nerva isn't going to want to wait to start the assault. You know that it won't take long for Titius to build the ram, so I'd wager that it will be ready and waiting."

He was right, I knew it as soon as he said it, yet I still was about to insist that we stick to the original plan when, from the recesses of my mind, my father's voice asked a question.

"Is this for you, or because it's the best thing to do for the plan?"

Understanding the deeper meaning, that this was a moment where my pride wanted to arrive earlier than expected, which I had learned from my father, that promising less and delivering more was one of the secrets to a Centurion's success with his superiors, I altered the orders. I did forbid fires, which was met with grumbling, not just from Catualda and his men, but from my own small command, but on this I refused to relent, and we curled up in our cloaks, while I smugly congratulated myself on remembering to bring my fur-lined *sagum*. It turned out to be a wise choice, because when we woke up the next morning, a hard frost had covered us in a thin sheet of ice, and I thanked the gods that I had thrown my regulation *sagum* over Latobius, who showed his appreciation by nipping me on the back of my leg, giving me a limp for part of the day.

Casurgis loomed ahead of us, unchanged and still

imposing, but the Alaudae had been busy, creating a series of dirt mounds with flat tops that would serve as artillery positions, and when we arrived, about half of them already had their pieces emplaced. They were unprotected, an advantage brought about by the lack of Marcomanni artillery, and in fact, they were placed a bit closer to the walls than normal so that the missiles could reach deeper into the city, but still well out of arrow range. Even so, they would have to be moved inside the city walls to reach the citadel, which meant that we would have to clear every dwelling, the kind of fighting that every soldier loathes, especially those who are assaulting a strange town, and a barbarian town at that. Before I entered Rome for the first time, I had believed that it would be much like Alexandria, with the grid of streets that ran straight and true, but that is not Rome, and in that sense, it resembles the kind of town like I assumed Casurgis would be, where streets seemed to end for no reason, often because a structure had been constructed in its path, curving this way and that, and riddled with dead ends and blind alleys.

First things came first, however, and I was happy to see that someone had surveyed out a spot a for Catualda's men to have their own encampment, although I also saw that Nerva had not bothered ordering a sanitation trench dug...but he had also put their spot downstream from our camp. Even now, decades after their first contact with Rome, the tribes of Germania have proven extremely resistant to adopting any of our ways, particularly with sanitation, despite the difference in the frequency of diseases and plagues that we have determined are caused by improper hygiene. Catualda put Otmar in charge of getting the men settled in, and as we trotted on to the *Porta Praetoria*, where the walls were lining up with Alaudae men watching their new allies arriving. I was prepared for the watchword; Nerva had given it to me beforehand, but we were waved on through, where we found Nerva standing in the forum inspecting the battering ram. The bronze ram's head that each Legion possesses and carries in one of their wagons was being hammered into place onto the end of the log, then the iron nails were placed in the predrilled holes around the flange to attach it firmly to the log, which was much larger round than my thigh and suspended by ropes to the upper half of the frame.

"It does not look very big." Catualda sounded doubtful, but while I actually shared his viewpoint, I did feel it right to point out, "Well, we're not going to actually need to use it, are we?"

He surprised me by saying, "I was not thinking of the main gate."

"Wait. What are you saying?" I felt my stomach clench. "I know you said the walls of that citadel are about the same thickness as the main wall, but what are you saying about the citadel gates?"

"That they are almost the same size," he replied calmly, "and that we will not have anyone inside to help."

"A fortified gate?" I groaned. "Did you tell the Primus Pilus about this?"

I was almost certain I knew the answer, yet I still cursed when he shook his head.

We were almost to him by then, and we dismounted, then as soon as we exchanged salutes and Catualda informed Nerva that he now had a thousand Gotones warriors at his command, I waited for a heartbeat for him to inform Nerva, but when he did not, I said abruptly, "We're either going to need a bigger ram or another one."

Naturally, he looked surprised, but as Catualda explained why, reluctantly, his expression changed, his face turning dark, and he began swatting his leg with his *vitus*, making me wonder if he might actually lash out at the Gotones nobleman. While I could not blame him for feeling this way—it was as if we had to pry every bit of information, important pieces like this, out of Catualda—I also knew that it would be a disaster, and in fact, would probably be as catastrophic to the Primus Pilus as outright failure if he actually did what I was sure he wanted to do.

When Catualda stopped talking, Nerva asked tersely, "Is that all?" Catualda seemed puzzled, and he snapped, "Are there any other things you've forgotten to mention that might get more of my boys killed?"

"No, Primus Pilus Nerva," Catualda replied stiffly. "That is all."

"Are you sure?"

Nerva's tone was dripping with so much disdain that I suddenly began to worry that it might be the Gotones nobleman who struck the Primus Pilus, and I tensed, waiting to intervene and stop him.

Fortunately, he took a deep breath before replying, "Yes, Primus Pilus, that is all as far as the strength of the citadel. Now, how many men Maroboduus will be willing to use to hold the outer wall and how many to hold the citadel? That," he held his hands out, "I cannot tell you."

I did not ask, but I suspect that Nerva realized he might have gone too far, because he said, "I wouldn't expect you to, Lord Catualda. That's something where there is only one way to find out." He turned and looked at the ram, then called Titius over, asking the *Immunes*, "Which would be faster? Making this ram bigger and better protected? Or putting together another ram?"

Titius started, but then rubbed his chin in thought as he looked back at the ram.

"It would be easier to make another ram this size," he said slowly. "Because to make this one bigger would require us to not only disassemble another wagon, we'd have to do some cutting of the frame, and while we can cobble it back together, it won't be able to carry as big a load for the trip back home."

"What about green wood?" Nerva asked, and Titius grimaced at the suggestion.

"Green wood for the ram is one thing, but the whole thing?" He shook his head. "It would be full of sap, and if it *did* catch on fire, and the sap starts boiling..."

He did not need to finish, and Nerva did not need any more information; something like that would turn the wood into an explosive weapon, with hundreds or thousands of splinters of wood going in every direction at speeds faster than the eye could track.

"Make a second ram the same size," he ordered, but now I was the one who had a question.

"What about green hides? Do you have enough for two?"

Truly, I do not know why they are called such, because they're red and bloody, and smell horrible, but they are a necessity because they are hard to set on fire, even when some pernicious substance like pitch or boiling oil is used, especially because they are kept soaking in barrels of water until the last possible moment before they are applied to the roof of the ram, which is more steeply pitched than the roof of a house.

"Fortuna actually was kind to us," Nerva informed us. "Our foraging party found a herd of a hundred cattle hidden away a couple miles from here. That means your men will be able to feast, Lord Catualda," he said with a smile. "But tomorrow night. And," the smile vanished, "I don't want your men drunk on mead, or wine for that matter, tonight. Is that understood?"

"Will the second ram be ready in time for an assault tomorrow?" I asked, only after Catualda acknowledged Nerva's orders, though he looked unhappy about it.

"It will." Nerva spoke up for Titius, and when he smiled at his *Immune*, it was the kind that I have used as well, telling him that there was only one answer Nerva would accept. "Right, Titius?"

"Absolutely, Primus Pilus," Titius sighed. "But it won't be ready until after dark."

"That's fine. We'll set that one aside for the citadel." With this settled, he returned his attention back to Catualda. "What do your men need from us, Lord?"

"Nothing at the moment," Catualda assured him, also the right answer. "We have enough food for tonight, and the men are setting up their tents."

"Good." Nerva nodded. "Then we will have our final meeting at first night watch."

With that, we were left to our own devices, and Catualda naturally went to his camp, while I returned Latobius to the stable, rubbing him down and giving him his feed, then went to the tent, where Alex and the others were resting.

I was not in the least surprised when he said, within a heartbeat after I entered the tent, "I'm with you tomorrow."

A part of me knew I should argue, if only because I knew what I would be facing when Algaia learned the truth, but the fact was that I was nervous, even more so than normal when facing battle. I already knew that I would be with Catualda, although I would not be under the awning of the ram but following behind, so the idea of a familiar face, and one that I knew I could trust with my life, was stronger than my fear of our wives.

"I know," was all I said. "But," I added in a tone I knew he would recognize, "you're carrying a shield, and you're a *Gregarius* tomorrow, is that understood?"

"Yes, Centurion." He drew to *intente* and rendered a mocking salute, but the important thing was that I knew he was serious about obeying me.

Yes, Alex was blooded, and had been in more than one fight, but he had never been in a real battle, nor the taking of a town, although he had been present with my father during his time with the Legio Germanicus when they had taken Raetinium, one of the most horrific fights of the Batonian Revolt.

"Do you want to eat before or after Nerva's meeting?"

I thought, then said, "After is fine."

"Then I'm going to catch up on some sleep," he said, which I thought was a good idea as well, and we moved behind our partition and dropped on our cots.

He fell asleep quickly, but I found my mind was too busy, so instead I lay back and, since my mind had gone to the assault of Raetinium, I tried to recall what my father had written about it.

When the *bucina* sounded the call for the change of watch, I almost jumped out of my skin, leaping to my feet and snatching up my *vitus* as I snapped at Alex, "Why didn't you wake me up?"

"Because I was asleep myself!" he protested, but I was already out of the tent and hurrying across the forum, spotting a couple of the Pili Priores just entering the Primus Pilus' tent, and I broke into a sprint, so that by the time they reached the partition to Nerva's private quarters, I was just behind them, closely enough that it would appear as if I was with them; at least, this was my hope. It is an old trick, but it all depends on whether the party you are trying to join is late themselves or have just managed to slip in without raising the ire of your superior.

"It's nice of you to join us," Nerva said sourly, giving me the answer, but fortunately, that's all the time he devoted to our tardiness.

Catualda was already there, and he waved to the stool next to his that had become mine, and only then did I realize that one of the tardy Pili Priores was the Secundus, who glowered at me, and I suppose he was blaming me for drawing attention to him, while I did the same thing towards him, and I am certain that in one thing we were of a like mind, both sure we were right to blame the other.

"Because of some late information," Nerva began, "we will need two rams, because the citadel has a fortified gate equal to the outer gate, and we will attack the citadel gate with artillery before we send the ram in to take it." Turning to Catualda, he surprised the Pili Priores by announcing, "Lord Catualda and his men who have just arrived are going to lead the assault on the gate...then on the citadel."

This unleashed a dull uproar, serving as a reminder to me that, even paid men who have been in the Centurionate for long enough begin to think like rankers, and the Pili Priores were united in their indignation that the Alaudae would be deprived of the "honor" of assaulting the citadel. What they meant, however, was they were upset that the richest slice of the pie represented by the Marcomanni capital was being reserved for the Gotones.

This was when Catualda stood, bringing a hush as the hard-bitten Centurions of the 5th Legion watched him in stony silence, but he did not hesitate to say, "I can assure you that there will be more than enough wealth that Maroboduus has stuffed away that I intend to share with you and your men in recognition of our contribution, because I know that what we are trying to do would not be possible without your men. But," he added reasonably, "it is only right that it is I and my men who face Maroboduus, who will be cowering inside that citadel."

This mollified the Centurions, although I thought about pulling Catualda aside and warning him that what *he* thought would appease them and their men, and really would appease them were likely to be vastly different, but then I forgot.

Continuing, Nerva said, "The First Cohort will be putting their ladders up against the wall nearest to the southern corner, the Second Cohort in the same spot near the northern corner, the Third will be to our right, and the Fourth to the Second's left. The second line Cohorts will be following Lord Catualda's men in behind them through the gate, but their task will be to secure the flat part of the town."

Before he had finished this first part, I understood what he was doing, and I gave Catualda a sidelong glance in an attempt to see if he divined Nerva's purpose, but his expression was impassive. However, by placing his First Cohort nearest to the southern wall, it put him and his Cohort closer to the southern hill where the citadel was located, which I took as a sign that he intended to be in a position to assault the citadel with the largest Cohort if the opportunity presented itself. Or, I thought with a sinking heart, he might intend to beat Catualda and his Gotones up the hill and begin the assault before Catualda can get there. Of course, there was no way that I would raise that during this meeting, and I also realized it was something that we would have to wait and see, then address it if it happened, despite having no idea what I could do about it.

"Once we have secured the wall, and the flat area of the town, we'll regroup and take stock. If Lord Catualda's men haven't suffered too many casualties, then they will lead the way up the hill to..."

"Primus Pilus," Catualda interrupted. "It does not matter how many men I lose taking the gate. We will lead the way to the citadel. That was the agreement I made with *Quaestor* Varro..."

"Who's not here!" Nerva shot back, repaying the Gotones in kind for the interruption. "But I am, and I'm saying that we will reassess the situation once we have secured the eastern wall!"

I expected Catualda to continue arguing, but instead he shrugged as he said indifferently, "It is a minor point, since I know that we will not incur many casualties taking the gate."

This was when I realized something; Nerva still did not know about Chariovalda, or more specifically, the men he supposedly commanded who were secretly aligned with

Catualda, and I opened my mouth to inform Nerva, while shooting the Gotones a look designed to convey my anger that he had not done as I demanded. However, nothing came out, and Nerva was too absorbed in perusing his wax tablet of notes to notice that I clearly intended on speaking, nor did he catch the pleading look from Catualda that caused me to snap my mouth shut with an audible click as my teeth met. The rest of the meeting did not take long, and we were dismissed, the Pili Priores returning to their quarters to meet with their Centurions, Catualda to spend the night with his Gotones, and me to our tent, seething with anger, though it was aimed mostly at myself. Catualda did try to thank me, but I snapped at him to be quiet before I stalked off to the tent, where I smelled the bread baking, filling my mouth with saliva despite my mood. Alex took one look at my face and knew this was not the time to say anything, handing me a bowl full of lentils and chickpeas, then disappeared outside to retrieve the bread. This was when Canus chose his moment to approach me, standing in the gap between the tent wall and the partition, but with an awkward demeanor that I had never seen on him before.

"Centurion, I was hoping you might do me a favor," he began, and while this was surprising in itself, I was completely unprepared for him to ask meekly, "Is there a way that you can get me a *segmentata* and helmet? Oh, and a shield?"

"Why would you want that?"

He flushed, I suppose at my tone of astonishment, but he answered, "Because I feel like I should be with you and Lord Catualda for...this."

"Did the *Quaestor* order you to do this?"

We both turned our attention to Alex, who was standing there just behind Canus, and despite the tension, my eyes went to the loaf, the steam rising and the aroma making my mouth water even more, while Alex just stared at Canus coldly.

"No," Canus shook his head, but then he hesitated, and allowed, "not really anyway. He *did* say that he wanted me to keep an eye on Lord Catualda, because he's crucial to the *Quaestor*'s plans and he doesn't want anything happen to him. But," he insisted, "even if he hadn't, I'd want to be part of this."

Alex snorted, but I held up a hand, asking Canus bluntly,

"Why? Why is this so important?"

Canus opened his mouth, then closed it, then reopened it to stammer, "I...I don't know, really, Centurion. I just know that it is." His long, lean face took on a troubled expression as he admitted, "I've never really had anything like this happen to me before, so I don't know how to explain it. I suppose it's just that I've been part of this from the beginning, and I want to see it through."

He fell silent then, but I do not know who was more surprised, Canus or Alex when I said, "As soon as I'm finished eating, I'll take you to the *quaestorium* and get you kitted up."

For a heartbeat, Canus and Alex bore identical expressions, mouths open in shock, but it did not last long, because while Canus was clearly pleased as he moved to let Alex pass to hand me my bread, my friend was glaring at both of us. From where I was sitting, it was clear that Canus broke his eye contact with Alex, who continued glaring at him as he entered the larger part of the tent, blocked from my view by the partition, leaving Alex to walk over to me and drop the hot bread in my lap, eliciting a yelp of pain as it burned my thighs, which I knew was his goal.

"Are you *mad*?" He whispered this, but I was certain that Canus could hear, though I did not hear anything from the other side of the partition.

Putting my finger to my lips, I asked in a conversational tone, "Have you eaten?"

"Yes," he replied tersely. "I ate while you were in the meeting."

I consumed the rest of my meal in silence, ignoring Alex as he sat there glaring at me, unwilling to explain why I was doing this, mainly because, just like Canus, I could not readily articulate why I was accommodating his request. When I got to my feet, Alex did as well, but before I could move out past the partition, he blocked my way, then using the method we employ of exhaling before he whispered, he stood on his tiptoes to admonish me, "Don't let him fool you, Gnaeus. Remember what he is, and what he's supposed to do to us at some point." He had to take another breath to finish, "And tomorrow would be a perfect time to do it."

I had actually thought about that, but I also did not think that was what Canus had planned. That did not mean I would not keep it in mind, and I patted him on the shoulder as I moved past him.

"I understand," was all I whispered to him, then stepped out to see that Canus was standing there, waiting.

The Batavians had vanished, and I guessed that they were at the Gotones camp; as familiar as they were with Rome, and as long as they had served us, I knew that they would be more comfortable around men who, even with different dialects, they had more in common with than us. Reaching the *quaestorium*, my first action was to pick up both my *gladius* and Scrofa's blade that Alex was using, which I had dropped off to be sharpened after we returned to camp, paying a full *denarius* for the pair. However, I then ran into some resistance from the supply *Immunes*, but my threat to go find the Primus Pilus so that he could personally assure the man that I was authorized to requisition gear from their stores was sufficient. The shield was set on the collapsible table boss side down so that the armorer could drop the *segmentata*, helmet, and greaves in it, but when he asked if Canus needed a *gladius*, I glanced over at him and was not surprised when he shook his head. Then I told the armorer I needed another shield, this one for Alex since he already had his *segmentata*, helmet, and greaves, the armorer complying while muttering about thoughtless Centurions who made hard-working rankers trudge back and forth the dozen paces to where the shields were stacked. When he returned with one, I took it, then waited for Canus to pick his bundle up, but he did not.

"What about you, Centurion? Aren't you going to get a shield?" When I shook my head, he said, "But I heard Alex talking about how anyone not under the ram is going to need one."

Stifling a curse at myself, I turned, but the *Immune* was already moving, muttering sourly, "I heard him, Centurion."

Once we were finally loaded up, we returned to the tent, whereupon Canus asked hesitantly, "Centurion, can you show me how to put this on and make sure that it's adjusted right?"

It was a simple, and reasonable request...and it was one

that I was supremely unqualified to fulfill, for the simple reason that I had never worn a *segmentata* in my life, yet another reminder that I had not worked my way up through the ranks.

From behind the partition, I heard a sigh, then Alex emerged and said tartly, "I'll do it. Gnaeus has no idea how."

"That's not true!"

It was an automatic and unthinking response, prompting a scornful look from Alex as he made an exaggerated gesture to where Canus was standing.

"Forgive me then, Centurion. I am so sorry! By all means, please..."

"Oh," I grumbled as I walked to my cot, "go piss on your boots."

Dropping down onto it, I lay back, listening as Alex quietly helped Canus adjust the straps and buckles, murmuring why he was pulling this one tight and loosening that one. After a few moments, Alex instructed him to move about, emphasizing twisting at the waist, followed by more adjustments, and I realized I should have at least watched so that I would have some idea how to do it, but my pride had been stung. Instead, I inspected my *gladius*, and while I knew it was not needed, applied another coat of oil so that when the moment came to draw it, I would not have to worry about it sliding smoothly from the scabbard. Alex finished, returning to our spot, and I know that we treasured the relative privacy since both Herminius and Catualda were absent, although we still kept our voices low because Canus was in a similar state, with even more room in his part of the tent.

As he dropped onto his cot, he said loudly enough that I knew Canus could hear, "His armor is adjusted, and I helped him rig up his *baltea* so that he can still carry his dagger like he's used to." In a whisper, he repeated, "I hope you know what you're doing."

"I do," I assured him, although my initial impulse had been to say "So do I," but I knew that it would be hard enough to sleep as it was.

My last thought, that I remember anyway, was that tomorrow would be an interesting day.

We woke before dawn, without prompting, and when Alex lit the lamp, I saw that four of the Batavians had returned to the tent and were snoring softly, but I did not wake them. While they would be mounted and ready, they had no real role in the assault, while outside the tent, we could hear the shouting of those Centurions who wanted their men to get a jump on the day, which on a day like this meant just about every one of them. In an odd way, I found these sounds comforting, and I wondered how much longer it would be before I at least recognized the voices of the other Centurions and Optios. I know that I have not mentioned anything much about Bronwen or baby Titus as I tell this, but that is because, on the several times a day my mind began to wander in that direction, I ruthlessly shoved them back into a corner of my brain. This was neither the time nor the situation to indulge a wandering mind; while I *thought* I had a better idea of everything that was going on, especially as it pertained to Varro's machinations, I also felt certain I was missing something, and my only hope was that it would not be something major.

Once again following in the footsteps of the Pullus men who had gone before me, I prepared myself in the exact same way since I had learned about this family ritual. Deciding it was cold enough, I donned a pair of *bracae,* but this pair was made of fine kid leather, making them sturdier than the wool pair, providing a modicum more protection from a slash to the legs; putting my left *caliga* on first, and lacing the thongs so the left side is over the right side, then the right, doing the same with the thongs, double knotting both then putting on my greaves. I put on the padded undertunic, then slid my *hamata* over my head, shrugging my shoulders a couple of times to settle it before strapping on my harness, finishing this by bunching the mail up above the *baltea* so it did not ride as heavily on my shoulders. At the last moment, I had decided not to wear my decorations, mainly because they reminded me that Varro's flattery had been nothing but a ploy, although I was still uncertain as to why. Picking up my helmet, I stepped around the partition to see Alex, whispering something to Canus as he made another check on Canus' *segmentata,* tugging at it from one side then another before, in a show of comradeship that surprised Canus as much as me, Alex struck him twice, one on each shoulder, the plates absorbing the shock.

"You're ready," he said, then he stood there as I did the same for him, winking at Canus as I repeated Alex's actions, but naturally, I struck him harder, though I was a bit disappointed that his knees did not buckle.

"So is he." I grinned at Canus, turning to exit the tent, and in doing so, I gave Alex a chance for revenge.

"Hey, *Tiro*," he called out, and when I turned around, he pointed to the shield I had drawn, "aren't you forgetting something?" When I returned to snatch it up, he smirked at Canus and rolled his eyes. "You have to watch these *Tiros* every moment, or they'd leave their ass behind."

"We'll see who's laughing later," I growled, but I was pleased to see Alex was in high spirits.

"Let's go; we're meeting Catualda and his men outside the *Porta Praetoria*."

We left the tent, and I noticed Canus actually glanced back over his shoulder at it, and I understood that it was not that the tent held any kind of sentimental value, but he was having the same thought that every fighting man experiences: Will I be returning to this place alive? As always, I had waited to put on my helmet until we were outside, although with a black crest, it was not quite as important as it had been with a Pilus Prior's red crest, tying the chin thong loosely for the moment. Just before matters began in earnest, I would tighten it, and I reminded myself to make sure that both Alex and Canus did the same thing, this being one of the most common things men overlook. By now, the camp was alive with activity, the *bucina* call announcing the official beginning of the day unnecessary, but it still sounded because, after all, that is what a Legion of Rome does. The ram was being pushed by some Alaudae men out of the camp, and we fell in behind them, leaving the camp and giving us our first view of Casurgis this morning. I was not surprised to see that the entire wall was illuminated with torches, the sign that the Marcomanni were making their own preparations. The artillery positions had naturally been guarded the entire night, and it was just light enough to see movement as the artillerymen hurried about.

"Where are those fucking Gotones?"

I recognized Nerva's voice, but when I turned to look towards their camp, I saw absolutely no kind of movement that would suggest a large group of men was heading in our direction, or even getting ready. Guided by his voice, I walked over to where he was standing, along with his first line Pili Priores.

Nerva glanced at me, then gave a grunt, but it was the Secundus Pilus Prior who sneered, "I won't be surprised if those *cunni* sneaked off in the night."

I waited for Nerva to say something, thinking that if that happened, it meant that it would fall on his shoulders to decide what to do about it, although I did not see that he had any choice. We were now more than five hundred miles from the Rhenus, and anything short of a total victory would spell his doom; at the same time, I had come to understand Nerva better, and that he was not all that different from my own Primus Pilus, which meant that he would never return to Mogontiacum if his Legion was not successful. Now, what he would do if the Secundus was right and Catualda had vanished, though I did not think that likely, was a good question. Fortunately, just as the sun began peeking over the eastern horizon, although we were well within the shadow of the two hills the Gotones camp was not, and we saw a stirring of movement which materialized into a mass of armed warriors, the spearpoints bristling above helmeted heads, and by the time they were within a couple hundred paces, I could see that it was Catualda, though he was on Tyr, leading them.

"They took their time," the Secundus sniffed, and this proved to be too much for Nerva, who snarled, "If you spent as much time worrying about your Cohort as you do on these Gotones, I would have no cause for complaint!"

I did not think if Nerva had slapped the man he would have reacted more strongly, but whatever his feelings, or his ambitions, he knew there was only one response, and I did not miss the avid expressions of the Tertius and Quartus Pili Priores, making it clear where their sentiments lay, and they were not with their counterpart. Stiffening to *intente*, the Secundus rendered a salute, saying that he was going to attend to his Cohort, and Nerva responded with nothing more than a disgusted wave of dismissal. Catualda had spurred Tyr to a trot, reaching the five of us and sliding off his horse, and while he did not salute Nerva, he did offer him a small bow.

"My men are ready, Primus Pilus Nerva," he announced. With a smile, he added, "I do not need to ask if your Alaudae are, I know. Where do you want us formed up?"

Nerva pointed at the ram, now about a hundred paces from the *Porta Praetoria*, using his *vitus* to indicate the space between the ram and the ditch.

"There behind the ram, and once you're in position, my first line Cohorts will form up on either side. We'll sound the call to advance, and we'll move," he moved his *vitus* to point to a spot just behind the artillery positions, "just behind the artillery. Each *ballista* will launch ten two-pound stones, and I will be sounding the advance while they're still loosing. It's about five hundred paces to the wall, and you need to make sure that the men pushing the ram match our pace. That's very important."

"May I ask why?" Catualda's tone was polite, but I thought I heard a note of doubt there, and I worried that Nerva did as well and would interpret it as questioning his orders.

If he did, he managed to restrain himself, but while he smiled at the nobleman, it was a grim one, which was understandable, "Because if your ram moves too quickly, and one of those stones is short, we might be out a ram and the gods know how many of your men pushing it. My artillerymen are good," he gave a shrug, "but there's always a short stone or two because a rope stretches out, or it snaps."

"We will make sure that we stay even with you," Catualda assured him.

"Once we're within fifty paces of arrow range of the wall," Nerva continued, "that's when our scorpions will take over. They will only launch a bolt when they have a target, and while that will make those bastards over there more cautious, it's not going to stop arrows from coming your way. Normally, they'll leave the rampart and loose blindly from behind the wall, but they'll still be dangerous." A look of what might have been embarrassment flashed across his face, which I understood when Nerva asked, "Have the men pushing the ram doused their tunics?"

"Yes," Catualda replied, which was a relief, because I had forgotten to mention this myself. "That is why we were late, Primus Pilus. I also had another twenty men do the same in case any of the original men fall."

"Good." Nerva nodded, then there were no more instructions to be issued. Clearing his throat, he said, "Yes, well then." He signaled to his *Cornicen*, whose horn commands we would be following from this moment forward. "Sound assembly, battle formation."

The notes were played, and I was turning away when Nerva called my name.

Thrusting out his arm, he said, "May Mars and Bellona favor us, Pullus."

Taking it, I repeated the words fully instead of using the abbreviated form we use in the 1st, then I followed Catualda, who handed Tyr's reins to Herminius, the Batavians now gathered outside the camp as well, though they were all dismounted. The pair exchanged a few words, though I did not hear them, more intent on finding Alex in the mass of Gotones, but he was actually easy to pick out, his curved, rectangular Roman shield and helmet standing out among the flat oval shields and high helmets of the Germans. Canus was standing next to him, looking nervous but trying not to, more resembling just another *Tiro* facing their first battle than a hardened killer born and raised in the Subura. I was happy to see that Alex had not tried to push his way to the front of what could not even charitably be called a formation, choosing a spot roughly ten rows deep, but on the outside file to the left, and I joined him there. Briefly, I considered calling to Catualda and urging him to put his men into at least a semblance of a formation, but quickly dismissed it as probably creating more issues than it would solve.

Because the First Cohort was actually at the southern end of the line, it had taken Nerva and his *Cornicen* time to trot over to their spot, meaning that some time passed before the command to begin the assault came, and when it came, it was faint and hard to hear, although the Third Cohort *Cornicen* next to us instantly relayed the First Cohort's call. It meant that the start was ragged, and I swore I could almost hear Nerva cursing, although I also knew that he was aware that with a line of four Cohorts, it was a practical impossibility for a smooth start. Even so, it took an extra heartbeat longer for the Gotones pushing the ram, six men to each side, with their shields slid into the rack above their heads that made the ram look like it had a pair of stubby wings, to get started, and then only because Catualda, with Otmar next to him at the head of his warriors, shouted at them in their tongue. The ram lurched forward, but they were several paces behind the Cohorts on either side, and there was more shouting, though it was drowned out by another horn call, again relayed, this one the signal for the *ballistae* to begin loosing. We were too far away to make out any features, but we could see the helmeted heads of the Marcomanni lining their rampart, and I just happened to be watching in the right spot when a rock struck the wall, in between the crenellations, which in this case was just a case of every other log being sawn off a couple feet taller, but somewhat unusually, with a flat top instead of a point. The stone hit low, but it caromed upward then kept going through the gap, sweeping the warrior who had been standing there out of sight, and although we were still too far away, I knew that there would be a spray of blood and viscera that coated his comrades on either side, while I had a glimpse, more of a sense actually, that there had been another Marcomanni behind him who was thrown backward. Without knowing how wide the parapet was, it was impossible to know just how many warriors the Alaudae men scaling the ladders would be facing, but my guess was that they were at least three deep, and depending on whether or not Maroboduus planned on putting all of his men into stopping us at the wall, or offering a token resistance before falling back to the citadel, which seemed to loom larger above us with every pace. The cracking of the *ballistae* as they hurled their cargo at the wall served as the punctuation to what was a growing noise all around Alex, Canus, and me, and while it took a few heartbeats, I realized what it was, unable to stifle my groan.

"What is it?" Alex had to raise his voice to be heard, the noise of the Gotones warriors rising with every step closer to the wall.

"They're working themselves up into a frenzy," I almost had to shout. "You know, like they do when they're about to fight us."

"You are lucky we are on the same side, Roman! Otherwise, your woman would be a widow tonight!"

The warrior just in front of me had shouted this over his shoulder, then he turned and gave me a grin; I believe that was what it was meant as, but since he had either broken or filed off his front teeth so that only fangs showed, I could not be sure.

His Latin was not that bad, I had to admit, but I shouted back, "I think that's what Arminius said...just before we beat him at Idistaviso! And," I added before he could retort, "at the Angrivarian Wall!"

As soon as I said it, I chided myself, thinking, Gnaeus, you idiot. You're going to get into a fucking brawl now because you pissed all over this German's *caligae*.

Thankfully, instead, he roared with laughter, saying, "That is because the Gotones were not with him, Roman! But," he thumped his chest, "you stay behind Garivald! He will keep you safe!"

Even if I had been disposed to respond, there was no time, because we reached the invisible line that told the Marcomanni we were within missile range, a shower of arrows materializing from behind the wall. Since they were fire arrows, they were easier to track; they also all seemed to be heading directly for me, something that I have learned is a natural reaction, every man I have heard speak about it around the fires saying essentially the same thing...why are they aiming at just me? With the smoke, and with the range, tracking their flight was not only easier, it meant we had time to react accordingly, yet when they reached the apex of their flight, Catualda still had not shouted any order.

"*Form testudo!*" I bellowed this with every bit of power that I could, but only Alex reacted immediately, with Canus just a half-heartbeat behind, while I did the same, as the warriors around us simply stared in varying degrees of amazement, and amusement, still continuing to shamble towards the gate.

"What is the matter, Roman?" Garivald shouted. "Are you fright...?"

He got no further, and because his mouth was open, the gods actually showed him mercy, because the arrow that plunged down into his mouth burst out the back of his neck in a shower of blood, and I felt it spattering my right arm, severing his spine, while the rag wrapped around the shaft at the base of the arrowhead was still alight and smoking, albeit barely, a tiny flame flickering as it consumed the gobbets of flesh clinging to the barbed point. I was only barely aware of the shouts and screams around me, as Garivald's corpse, and the manner in which it collapsed straight down as if his bones had been suddenly and instantaneously removed, meant that if I had taken my normal stride, I would have stepped on it. I was just able to hop over the body while managing to hold my shield above my head, and I tried to avoid looking into his eyes, still and forever remaining open, wide with shock, with the shaft of the arrow jutting out from his mouth. Later, I recall wondering in the moment if those missing teeth might have contributed to his demise, thinking that perhaps if they had been there they might have altered the path of the arrow to one side of his spine or the other. His death, along with the handful of others who had fallen, wounded or dead, did serve one purpose, there being a tremendous clatter as the Gotones around us raised their shields, banging them together as they did so.

Taking a glance around, I muttered, "This is the worst-looking *testudo* I've ever seen. I'm ashamed to be part of it."

"I won't tell anyone," Alex replied, but when I glanced over at him, I was happy to see that his attention was on the sky, particularly because the second volley was already plunging earthward.

This time, the sound was almost universally what I was accustomed to, sounding like hammers striking wooden blocks, though with a hollower sound, but there were a couple of shouts of pain. The roof of the ram was now studded with arrows, but the green hides were doing their job, the flames quickly flickering out in small puffs of steam as the water-soaked hides extinguished the flames. From behind us, the different sound of the scorpions, which make a sharper cracking noise, was now almost constant, and if a bolt passes by closely enough, you can hear the hissing of the leather fletching as it streaks past on a flat trajectory. The Marcomanni were now either crouched down or using a crenellation for cover, but inevitably, someone would get curious, or perhaps develop a cramp from being in one position, while the scorpion crew chiefs knew this as well and were poised, waiting for the right moment. We were close enough now, at about a hundred fifty paces away, that we could hear the screams of men who had such a lapse, and one of them, for whatever reason, actually fell forward through the gap between crenellations, landing on his head at the base of the wall just a few paces from the gate. Rising above the gate, the only part of the parapet where there were no crenellations, were the heatwaves that make the air look strange, making me wonder if it was oil or pitch, and I suppose it is understandable that in that moment I recalled reading in the Prefect's account of the death of his Optio, Aulus Vinicius, who was doused in boiling pitch, and my great-grandfather's description of it looking like boiling honey. We were also close enough that the archers could loose on a flatter trajectory, and some of them climbed back up onto the rampart from where they had been loosing, protected from the *ballistae*, it quickly becoming a deadly game between them and the scorpion crews. It also meant that they began targeting the warriors pushing the ram instead of the ram itself, and it did not take more than a few heartbeats for one of the men on my side midway down to be struck by a missile that came slashing in from a point about thirty paces down the wall from the gateway, whereupon he took a staggering step away from the ram, but unlike with Garivald, the flames were not extinguished, and in fact, there was a flare of fire from his side, making me wonder if he had either refused or somehow forgotten to soak his tunic in water before donning his armor, or if it was so encrusted with grease from him wiping his fingers on it while eating that it did not matter. Whatever it was, he clearly panicked, running in circles as he beat at himself, but in a show of cruelty, not one Marcomanni archer loosed an arrow to put the man out of his agony.

"Catualda!" I had to shout his name three times before he turned about, and I pointed with my free hand, not having drawn my *gladius* yet, "Have someone kill that poor bastard!"

Whether he did not understand me or was refusing, he shook his head, and I did not need a translator to hear the men around me stop their shouting to begin muttering and know that they were unsettled, but the ram kept rattling along, and Catualda did send another man to replace the stricken warrior. No more than a handful of heartbeats had elapsed since the warrior had been struck, but the flames had continued to spread along his body, and it was now to the point that his beard was on fire, while his hands were blackened from vainly trying to beat out the flames. Not until he actually came to a stop, turned to face his comrades, his charred hands held out in obvious supplication did a Gotones I could not see hurl a spear from our midst. His aim was true, and I can still recall the expression of gratitude on the face of the dying warrior, which was now wreathed in flames as he dropped first to his knees, then toppled forward, driving the spear all the way through his torso. Since my attention was diverted, I missed a warrior on the right side of the ram being struck down, although this time, a replacement moved immediately into his spot, and I caught a glimpse of the wounded man hopping back to the greater safety of the formation, an arrow protruding from his thigh. The noise increased as we got closer, which was not unusual, but I had never experienced it from this perspective, as I was essentially now part of the howling mob of Germans instead of facing them. I did not see any signal by Catualda, but suddenly, the ram came to a stop, only about fifty meters from the gate, and when I glanced over at Alex, I could see the sweat streaming down his face from the strain of holding his shield aloft, while Canus had actually switched hands, something that he could only get away with in such a shambling mass of warriors, many of whom had dropped their own shields because their fatigue overcame what little discipline they had.

"What's happening?" Alex shouted, but I had no idea, and

despite knowing that it was a risk; stepping out away from the relative anonymity provided by the Gotones around me was a practical invitation for the Marcomanni archers to riddle me with arrows, both because of my size and that I was a Roman Centurion, yet this was also the worst time to stop, so I did that very thing in order to get an idea of the reason for the halt.

My arm was tiring as well, but fortunately, I did not have to expose myself very long, because I immediately saw why. Catualda had done essentially the same thing I just did by stepping away from the formation and from the ram, but it was what he was doing that took me a few heartbeats to grasp. Once I did, I sidestepped quickly back into the formation, where the warriors around us were now shouting their challenges, shaking their weapons up at the walls, though thanks to our scorpions, no Marcomanni were willing to expose themselves long enough to bellow their response to the challenges back.

"Catualda's sending some sort of signal," I shouted to both Alex and Canus. "He wanted them to see who it is, so get ready for the gates to open!"

In a show of defiance, and foolhardiness, Catualda, deciding his message had been sent and received, walked back behind the ram as if he were taking a stroll, where Otmar was waiting with his shield, which he handed to him. Then, Catualda turned his back to the wall, another dangerous move, although he was also close enough to the ram to be partially protected by it, the roof and every shield now studded with arrows, while a couple of the shields were burning, though the hides on the roof were doing their job. He began shouting something, which we naturally could not understand, except for "Marcomanni" and "Maroboduus" and "Gotones," along with a couple of epithets I recognized. As he exhorted his men, they were responding in kind, roaring their own responses, still gesticulating with their *gladii*, spears, and a handful of axes, all while Catualda pointed back over his shoulder at the walls. Out of the corner of my eye, I saw movement perhaps twenty paces down the wall, turning my head just in time to catch a sequence of events that occurred so quickly, even as I watched, I was not certain what I was seeing.

A Marcomanni archer, perhaps on a dare or a wager, was

leaning out between the crenellations, his body twisted so that his bow was aligned and aiming directly at Catualda, and I saw his arm sweep back, his draw hand reaching his nose, knowing that a competent archer needed barely more than an eyeblink to aim before loosing. What I did *not* see, nor could I even if I had known to watch for it, was the scorpion bolt streaking through the air, striking the archer in the middle of his chest before, barely slowing down, it vanished in a spray of blood, while the archer's missile went flying up almost vertically. Most of the Gotones were paying attention to their leader, but enough had been drawn by the movement, concentrated mostly towards the rear of the thousand men, and they let out a roar of what I suppose was appreciation to their Roman allies, however temporary we may have been. When I returned my attention to Catualda, he looked startled, but then Otmar shouted something to him, I guessed an explanation judging by the manner in which he nodded, smiling as he did as if this was a sign from the gods, which I supposed it might have been. Apparently deciding this was a good time to stop, he bellowed something, which I did understand, a single word, the name of his tribe, and almost immediately, it became a chant.

"*Gotones! Gotones! Gotones!*"

I saw Alex shouting something, but I could not make out the words, so I leaned over so I could hear him.

"I hope they fight as well as they shout!"

I laughed, but what I was about to say, something I was sure would be witty in the moment, was instantly forgotten when there was a flurry of movement, not down on the ground but up above the gateway, where the shoulders and heads of a pair of men who appeared to be holding something between them given how they were facing each other and not us materialized, moving in a manner that indicated they were swinging something heavy back and forth in order to get enough momentum to throw something.

"*Catualda! Move!*"

In retrospect, it was not only a useless warning, it could have been dangerous, because while he picked my voice out from among the chanting, he clearly did not understand it, freezing him in place long enough that if it had been a threat, it could have harmed him, or worse. It *was* a threat of sorts, just not one that was an immediate danger; it was a body, the pair of Marcomanni heaving it up and out away from the gateway, the body's limbs flailing as it sailed through the air before landing with what would have been a sickening thudding noise if we could have heard it over the din. The body—the man was obviously either unconscious or dead—landed about thirty paces in front of the ram, bouncing slightly and with enough momentum that it rolled him over so that his face was visible.

I had only seen him from a distance, but the split beard was impossible to mistake, although it was soaked in blood from where his throat had been cut, and I heard my voice say, "Chariovalda!"

Just that quickly, we learned that Catualda's ruse had failed, and that we would have to fight our way into Casurgis.

Chapter 6

To his credit, Catualda did not hesitate, spinning about to bellow at his warriors to resume moving, while Otmar dashed to the ram, which did immediately begin moving, but I saw Catualda's face and how ashen it was, which I took as the sign he at least partially understood the ramifications of what had just taken place. There had been something of a pause in what was taking place around the gate, and I believe I can be forgiven for most of my attention being focused on what was happening around me, but as we resumed moving the final distance to the gate, I looked to my left, and saw that all three Centuries of the Third and, off in the distance, the First were either at the base of the wall, or were already beginning to scale the ladders. This did not bode well at all for Catualda now that we were going to have to fight for the gateway, and I wondered if he had outsmarted himself by refusing to mention Chariovalda and his Marcomanni to Nerva, because I could see a case being made that Nerva would not have committed to an assault of the walls if he had been aware that the gate was going to be opened. Certainly he would have been prepared to do so, but if he could avoid casualties to his own men, I knew that if I had been in his *caligae*, I would have been content to wait to see how matters developed. None of which mattered, and I returned my attention to our own situation, just in time to see the ram lurch, making me think that it had been struck by something, though I could not imagine what it might have been. I got my answer soon enough, and as many things as I have seen in battle, the corpse of Chariovalda after it had been crushed under the wheels of the ram to this day ranks as one of the most gruesome. Hardened warriors these Gotones may have been, I heard more than one man retching at the sight, while I was thankful that the corpse had been crushed by the righthand wheels so that my view was partially obscured by the legs of the warriors next to us.

When I saw Alex's head begin to move, I shouted sharply, "Don't look!"

Thankfully, he listened; Canus, however, either did not hear or his curiosity overcame him, because he immediately began gagging, and I just barely heard him gasp, "His eyes popped out of his skull!"

If Canus thought this was the worst thing he would see, he was quickly disabused of that belief, because the instant that the ram reached the gate, what I assumed were the same pair of men who tossed Chariovalda's corpse out reappeared, each one holding a stout piece of wood that was threaded through the handles of a large cauldron that was smoking furiously. Moving as quickly as they dared, they placed one end of their piece of wood on the outer edge of the horizontal log that formed the lintel, then with an obvious effort, pushed the opposite end of their stick forward, thereby tipping the contents of the cauldron. Just as they did so, a scorpion bolt came streaking past, transfixing the Marcomanni on the left, and while it was not in time to stop the cauldron from being tipped onto the roof of the ram, it did mean that not all of the contents landed on its target. The first two men pushing on the left side, which had already lost one of their original number, certainly did not view this as fortunate, because while they were partially protected by their shields from above, when what turned out to be boiling oil struck the hardpacked surface of the roadway right next to them, it splashed up and onto the two Gotones, immediately transforming them into a pair of screaming, terrified men out of their minds with pain as the substance boiled and instantly blackened every inch of exposed skin. This time, at least, nobody needed to be reminded, and a flurry of short throwing spears quickly put them out of their misery, but it was the ram that needed the most attention as the green hides began smoldering, creating a thick, choking smoke.

"They need to get that fucking gate open now before that thing goes up!"

I do not remember saying this; Alex told me later that it was me, although I do recall what I was doing, and that was moving at a run when I saw that none of the substitutes standing just behind the ram were moving to take up the vacant spots. Not for the first time I cursed my size, thinking that even a Roman shield, which is one of the largest I have ever seen, still does not provide enough cover for a man my size, so I hunched my shoulders tightly together as I rushed to the left side of the ram and the first spot. The shield that had belonged to that man was now burning, but there was an edge that was not yet on fire, and I grabbed that to yank it out of the way, whereupon I had another reason to curse, this time aiming it at Titius, who had been thoughtful in creating the rack specifically for the flat shields of the Gotones. In simple terms, a Roman shield would not fit, and I was faced with a horrible choice of not even attempting to jam it into its spot on the rack and discarding my shield...so I did not make it. As quickly as I had been cursing my size, now I thanked the gods for my strength, because I kept hold of my shield in my left hand, using only my right hand on the stout handle that protruded out almost three feet, although I had to drop into a deeper crouch than the other men because of my height.

"Push, you bastards!" I bellowed, and while the smoke was choking me and my eyes were filled with tears, my ears were working, yet I was still completely unprepared to hear Canus' voice right behind me shout back, "We are, Centurion! At least," he amended, "I am."

However, the ram did begin moving, although at first, I felt certain we were the only ones doing so, though in less than a heartbeat, I felt the others putting their weight into it, and the ram resumed moving, picking up speed so quickly that it gave me an idea.

"Keep going! Don't stop!" I shouted, then immediately realized how unlikely it was they would understand the words, let alone my intent, but then I recognized Catualda's voice shouting in their tongue.

Despite not understanding the words, I felt certain that he had repeated what I shouted, and we were going about as fast as it was possible to move a ram that size when we slammed into the gate. Because of my position at the front, over the general crashing sound of the ram's head, then the front of the frame smashing into the iron-bound wood of the gate, I heard a deeper crack that indicated we had damaged the locking bar. Because the ram itself was slung on ropes so that it swung freely, it was pushed backward so that the ram's head was flush with the frame and not protruding out the three feet it normally was, and I heard Catualda take over, shouting a command that became apparent when, using the ropes trailing behind the frame, the ram was pulled even farther backward by some men hauling on the ropes.

My shield was still above my head, but remembering that the shield above Canus had been on fire, I turned my head to check on him, just in time to see him begin to step away, and I bellowed at him, "Don't move, Canus! We need all of our weight to keep the frame against the gate!"

"That shield is about to fall on my fucking head, Pullus!"

That, I saw, was true, and I also saw that it was too heavily ablaze for anyone to be able to yank it out of the rack without being burned, so with a curse, I said, "All right, but get behind the ram. And keep your shield up!"

He disappeared from my sight, just as Catualda shouted the order to release the ropes, and out of the other corner of my vision, I saw the bronze ram's head swing forward, picking up speed so that it struck the gate with a force that shook the body of the frame, which I felt through the handle, which I was still pressing against with most of my strength. There was another cracking noise from the locking bar, but this was also when I noticed another noise on the other side of the gate, one that did not make any sense. Is that...fighting? I wondered. The ram was being pulled back into position, making it marginally quieter, and I strained my ears as much as I was using my body to keep the frame of the ram firmly pressed against the gate. In the span of a couple heartbeats before the ram came swinging forward again, I was certain that my initial impression was correct; there was already a fight going on inside Casurgis. The ram's head struck a third time, and this time, there was an explosion of splinters from the wood of the gate, though I was fortunate this time that I was not struck, and in the brief span of time where it was not crucial that we kept the frame pressed against the gate, I straightened up and turned away from the gate to look down the wall, seeing that, while there were Romans on the rampart, the leading Centuries still had men standing at the base of their ladders, meaning that there was no way that it was men of the Alaudae who had come down from the rampart and reached the gate to fight for it. I turned back and threw myself against the handle just in time for the ram to crash into the gate, and this time the damage done by the ram's head was more extensive, the locking bar breaking, not all the way through but enough that, because we were throwing our weight into it, the frame of the ram nudged the gate partially open, creating a crack just wide enough that I could see into the town. What I saw was enough for me to stand up, though not forgetting to keep my shield above me, and take a step to the side away from the ram so that I could backpedal a few paces, whereupon I called for Catualda.

Who, I was angry to see, did not move, shouting back, "What is it, Centurion?"

"You need to see this!" I pointed back to the gate.

He came, though clearly reluctant to do so, holding his shield above his head, although by this time, the archers had been neutralized by the presence of the first line Cohorts now on the rampart, while the Gotones under Catualda were close enough to hurl their javelins and short spears at anyone foolish enough to try and replace the pair of Marcomanni directly above the gateway. Still, it paid to be careful, which was why I continued to hold my own shield in a similar position while leading him to my spot; I pointed, and again it appeared to me that he might not move into it, as if he suspected some trickery at play and if he leaned over to peer through what he could clearly see was a large crack, he might get a spear through the eye. I was about to grab him and shove his head into position when he finally did so, and his reaction was immediate, jerking back upright to stare at me with an expression of amazement and hope.

"There are men fighting for me! Chariovalda's death was not in vain!"

Before I could say anything, he hopped past me and went running back to where his warriors were waiting, shouting something that I could guess because of the reaction, a huge cheer from his men. Otmar had momentarily stopped the ram from battering the gate, but he resumed, and within another three strikes, the locking bar finally gave way, the final strike of the ram sending the gates flying open. Normal practice calls for the ram to be pulled out of the way so that the gateway is unobstructed and as many men as possible can be fed through it; that did not happen here, and I am afraid that I am the one responsible for that, though it was not completely my fault. In another mark of their collective inexperience, my temporary comrades pushing the ram seemed unaware of what they needed to do next, standing up straight and not moving the ram out of the way, and because of this, I began moving, into the town. Drawing my *gladius*, I stepped around the front of the ram, becoming the first man inside the walls of Casurgis, although I swear on the black stone that was not in my thinking at the time; in simple terms, I saw fighting going on, and I responded accordingly. What I did not know until a short time later was that, seeing me enter the town, the next two men inside the walls were also Roman, as Alex came rushing forward from his spot in the mass of Gotones, while Canus followed him, not having seen me rush inside, and this was something that would cause me some grief.

It would not be until the next day before we learned exactly what happened; all that I knew in the moment was that I instantly understood that there was no way to tell which Marcomanni were foes and which were friends; it was Alex who provided the answer.

"If they attack us, they're with Maroboduus," he shouted. "If they don't, they're with Catualda."

Even with everything going on, I felt quite foolish, but while this was certainly true, it quickly proved to be easier said than done, because at first, we were largely ignored, but we also were standing there just inside the gateway. Therefore, I began stepping over the bodies that were scattered around the gate, not ending those men who were still alive since I did not know who I would be dispatching, friend or foe, trying to ignore the uncomfortable feeling of leaving a foe behind you that might have been pretending to be dead. I got about ten paces inside the gate, which was possible because the fighting among the Marcomanni had moved away from the gate, with essentially three fights going on; one between what was about sixty warriors whose backs were to us down the muddy street next to the wall to our left, a larger fight with at least a hundred warriors doing the same in the opposite direction, and then what was clearly the main fight down the street that ran deeper into the town. The truth was that we seemed to be largely ignored, but that changed in an eyeblink when, from what was too narrow to be a street that intersected with this main street running from the gateway, four Marcomanni appeared, stopping for a heartbeat to gape at us, then with one of them roaring what had to be a command, they came rushing our direction.

"Get behind me!"

Even as I shouted this, I realized how unlikely it was that Alex would obey, so I took two sudden and large steps towards the onrushing warriors, but it was not hubris, it was fear that he would choose to put himself on my shield side, which I knew would actually put him in greater danger. I have said it before; being a paid man meant that I never had occasion to train with a shield, and while I had done so in the intervening time, I was acutely aware that I had not put as much effort into it as I could have, choosing instead to focus on fighting with *gladius* and *vitus,* or just *gladius* alone. Because I could not figure out a way to carry my *vitus* on this day, I had left it behind, or I would have discarded the shield the moment we entered Casurgis, but it was also the fatigue I felt from holding the shield above my head, and while I brought it up into position, I felt the tremors along my entire arm.

One of the four seemed more eager than the others, armed with a spear and shield, but I do not believe that he was eager to die, which was what he did when I turned aside his thrust by twisting my left wrist so that his spearpoint hit my shield at an oblique angle and slid off, then used his own momentum to dispatch him with a third position thrust behind his shield as he went stumbling past me. Not surprisingly, this stopped his three comrades from making a headlong charge, though I doubt that it was because they were expecting to be reinforced, which was what happened as they conducted a quick discussion on how to attack the giant Roman and his two comrades, suddenly joined by three more Marcomanni from the same alley. This gave Alex time to reach my side, except that he placed himself to my right, while Canus sidled around to our left, but putting himself slightly apart from us, and I instantly saw that it was a cunning maneuver on his part. It did not buy us much time, however, as a pair of Marcomanni detached themselves and approached Varro's man, while the other four began shuffling towards Alex and me, two of them armed with spears, the third with an ax, and the fourth with a long *gladius*. If it had just been me alone, I could have predicted how they would attack me, with the spearmen on my flanks, using the longer reach of their weapons in an attempt to force me towards the warriors armed with ax and *gladius*. How they intended to attack the two us was something that we would never learn, because Catualda and his men chose this moment to arrive, having dragged the ram out of the way, and we heard their roar behind us as they rushed into the town.

Not surprisingly, the Marcomanni facing us, without hesitation, turned and fled, but their reprieve did not last longer than it took for some of Catualda's Gotones go sprinting past us to run them down from behind, hacking them to death before they could reach the parlous safety of their comrades down the main street. Canus, however, managed to draw blood, despite the fact that his two opponents did the same thing, except they chose to try and dash down the street next to the wall to the south, but Canus was too quick, cutting one of them off. The stranded Marcomanni shouted desperately for his comrade to come to his aid, but the man gave him a bare backward glance and did not slow down. Moving with the same speed I had witnessed before, Canus feinted a low attack with his long dagger, dodged the desperate wide slicing swing from the spear the Marcomanni carried, then slashed his opponent's extended arm, causing him to drop the spear, then finished him with a thrust deep into his side. He paused long enough to wipe the blade on the man's tunic then performed a thorough search, ignored by the Gotones who were now flooding past us. At first, I did not think Catualda would acknowledge me, clearly angry that I had entered Casurgis before he could, but he stopped a few paces past where I was standing with Alex and Canus, snapping orders to Otmar and two other warriors, whereupon his cousin shouted for most of their group to follow him down the street leading deeper into the town, while the other two men went trotting in opposite directions down the street paralleling the wall, presumably to take control of the Marcomanni warriors fighting for Catualda.

"Centurion," Catualda said, and there was no mistaking the cold anger, "if I did not know better, I might think you were trying to steal some glory for yourself."

"Your men are undisciplined," I almost said "rabble," but I managed to use, "warriors, and they were standing there with their thumbs up their asses waiting for orders which didn't come. You," I pointed at him, but managed to avoid poking him in the chest, "were rattled because your man out there," I used the same hand to jerk a thumb back over my shoulder, "got his throat cut."

"That," he allowed, "is true, but we did not know the situation inside!"

"Which is why I brought you to the gate so that you could see," I retorted. "And we could hear there was fighting going on before we broke open the gate, which means that there were at least a few Marcomanni who remained loyal to you, and they needed us to reach them sooner rather than later." For the first time, I saw the sudden flash of doubt across his features, so I was not about to ease up now, and I asked the question I should have asked long before this, "How many times have you commanded this many warriors, Lord Catualda?" He did not reply, but the shake of his head was all I needed. "And have you ever assaulted a town before?" Another shake of the head. "I've lost count of the number of towns we've taken," I continued, ignoring Alex. "The most important thing is not to hesitate."

"I...understand, Centurion," he said, then paused before he added, "and I...agree that I hesitated. But," the coldness returned to his demeanor, and his voice, "Centurion, you are not to do that when we take the citadel, or I am afraid I will have to make a complaint to *Quaestor* Varro. Is that understood?"

Oh, how I wanted to snatch him up and give him a good shaking, at the very least, my normal response to being threatened, but somehow I managed to say, through clenched teeth, "I understand, Lord Catualda."

I did refuse to say I would obey, and I worried that he knew enough about how the Legions worked that he might know I was saying only half of the customary reply, but he just nodded.

"I need to go find Otmar and see how many of the Marcomanni loyal to their new king are still alive," he said, and it was not the words as much as the way he said it, but before I could say anything, he turned and strode off.

"How many towns have you actually been part of taking?"

I knew that he knew the answer as well as I did, but I was unwilling to say that, in fact, it was a small number indeed, so instead, I replied, "I was talking about the Legions in general, not just me."

"Ah," he nodded, "I see." Then, he burst out laughing, earning him a shove.

Canus joined us, and asked, sensibly, "What now?"

"Now," I decided, "we wait for Nerva and his boys to clear the rampart, and then we regroup like the Primus Pilus said. And," I finished with a shrug, "we see what's next."

And, what was coming was that my father saved not just my life, but those of the Alaudae and Catualda's force.

What became clear fairly quickly was that, while Maroboduus had devoted a substantial number of men to defending the wall, the Marcomanni king had either planned ahead, or seeing the futility, very quickly withdrew his men up the left-hand hill. With nothing much to do until Nerva had his *Cornicen* sound the assembly for senior officers, the three of us walked south along the street lining the wall, with Canus wanting to stop to search the corpses of the dead until he discovered that Catualda's men in this part of the fight had already done a thorough job of it.

It was Alex who commented, "There are a lot of barrels and crates under the rampart."

At first, I gave it barely a glance, and even when I did, I did not think much of it. Now that we were inside the walls, what we suspected was confirmed, that the rampart was actually wood, jutting out about twelve feet and supported by stout wooden pillars that created an undercroft, which was where the barrels, crates, and assorted sacks were stacked, all along the wall down from the gate. The sounds of fighting were fading, but we were cautious, checking around the corner of the buildings at every intersecting street, but as expected, none of them ran straight enough to see more than a block or at most two, although all we saw was the backs of Catualda's warriors chasing terrified townspeople who had been cowering in their thatched huts until the last possible moment.

"They're probably heading to the citadel," Alex commented, adding another piece to a puzzle, though I still did not know it.

We were still a couple hundred paces from the Third Cohort standard when we heard, from beyond them, the signal that informed us that the Primus Pilus' *Cornicen* was sounding the assembly of senior officers.

"Maybe we should have stayed with Catualda," Alex said. "Will he recognize the call and know he's supposed to be there?"

"Pluto's cock," I muttered, though before I could say anything else, Alex was turning, but I stopped him. "Take Canus with you. I don't want you to get caught out by yourself."

Sketching a salute, Alex went trotting off, with Canus in tow, but I did not need to warn them to stop at the first corner again, worried that since we had just done so, they would think it was safe. Pausing just long enough to peer around the corner, they quickly vanished back towards the gate, leaving me temporarily alone, though it did not last long, because coming from the direction Alex and Canus had just gone came the second and third line Pili Priores at a trot. It was about that same time that I caught a whiff of smoke, finally spotting a single column back in the direction of the main gate but deeper into the flat part of the town, just my side of the cleft between the hills. As long as it did not grow, it would not be a problem, but I reminded myself to keep an eye on it, and once the Pili Priores reached me, we hurried to meet Nerva, reaching the Third Cohort standard just before he arrived from the opposite direction, huffing and puffing with his face streaked with sweat.

"Report!" He did not bother with the formalities, addressing the Quintus Pilus Prior.

"We've relieved Lord Catualda's men..."

"Then where is he?" Nerva snapped, leaning over to look past us, but before I could point out the reason for his absence, he grunted, "There he is."

Turning my head, I saw him moving at a quick trot, weaving around the bodies, then saw Otmar and the other Gotones a fair distance behind him, moving at a slightly slower pace, and I was able to pick Alex and Canus out from among them by their Alaudae shields.

Once Catualda arrived, Nerva proved that he was not as ignorant of Catualda's secret ally as the Gotones noble, or I, thought, asking bluntly, "How many men do you still have counting those Marcomanni?"

If his goal was to catch Catualda by surprise, he achieved it, the nobleman's mouth opening and closing a couple of times before he managed, "While I have not made a full count, I have about fifteen hundred warriors."

"How many of them are from your original group?"

Catualda hesitated, then admitted, "I do not know exactly, Primus Pilus, but I believe that I still have eight hundred Gotones."

"That won't be enough," Nerva replied without hesitation.

"Fifteen hundred men is more than enough, Primus Pilus," Catualda began, but Nerva cut him off.

"Surely you're not planning on using those Marcomanni to help take the citadel!" He sounded shocked. "How do you know you can trust them after what happened at the gate?" I did not blame Catualda for looking immediately at me with an accusing expression, but Nerva assured him, "Pullus didn't say a word to me."

He indicated the Tertius Pilus Prior, Sextus Agricola, who did not look happy, but he did not hesitate to explain, "My

Hastatus Posterior had just gotten on the wall and saw the fighting, and I sent a runner to the Primus Pilus to let him know."

"Those men fought for me at the gate," Catualda replied, sounding stubborn. "Why would they not fight for me when we take the citadel?"

"Because their king is up there," Nerva countered. "And they may have second thoughts about betraying him with you and your lot outside the walls of the citadel." Shaking his head, he said flatly, "I'm not taking that risk."

"It is *my* decision," Catualda shot back, truly angry.

"Not if you want my men here." Nerva did not shout; in fact, he did not raise his voice, but anyone could see that he was deadly serious...and Catualda knew it.

His shoulders sagged in a sign of defeat, and he closed his eyes to say, "As you said, Primus Pilus, if you refuse to allow my Marcomanni to fight, I do not have enough men to take the citadel now that we know Maroboduus did not commit even half of his warriors to defending the wall. What do you propose?"

"The First will take part," Nerva replied immediately, but he held up a hand to forestall Catualda, "in support. You and your men will bear the brunt of the assault." In something of a surprise, he turned to me to ask, "What's the condition of the ram?"

"It's too badly damaged to use," I replied. "It was badly burned by some oil, and I heard the frame cracking the last couple of strikes."

In response, Nerva turned to Agricola, ordering, "Send a couple sections to retrieve the second ram and bring it here." Turning, he indicated back along the wall. "There's a street that goes straight up the hill, but it looks like it dead ends about five blocks short of the citadel. I'll send men to scout a way to get to the citadel gates beyond that."

"What about the second hill?"

This was from the Quintus Pilus Prior, not Petronius' replacement, but his replacement's successor, which explained why he was not as hostile towards me as some of his men, and I knew why he was asking; so did Nerva, who gave him a grin.

"Go ahead, it's yours and the third line Cohorts. But you greedy bastards know the rules about loot!"

Catualda cleared his throat, but one look from the Primus Pilus stilled whatever protest he planned on making, which if I had to guess was to try and claim at least a part of the proceeds the Cohorts were going to gain as they took the second hill, which as I have mentioned, appeared to be the home of the wealthier inhabitants, especially nearer to the top, which was the same as in Rome. And, I was equally certain, what Catualda planned on demanding would be a percentage much higher than any man of those Cohorts, their Centurions, or their Primus Pilus would be willing to give up.

"What about searching these hovels?"

"We don't have time," Nerva replied to the Secundus Pilus Prior's question. "We'll do it later. I want to hit the citadel as quickly as possible." He scanned the faces around him, then spotted the Octus Pilus Prior, Numerius Pusio. "Pusio, you and the third line Cohorts are going to help Lord Catualda keep his Marcomanni here by the wall. Don't be obvious about it," he cautioned, "but make sure that you've got them hemmed in by you and the other third line Cohorts."

There was a lot going on; Catualda reacted immediately, turning to shout a summons to Otmar, who came trotting up, just as we heard the rumbling sound of the ram being pushed down the street before we saw it, scattering the packed mass of men, both Roman and Germans, out of the way, with four rankers dragging the corpses out of the way, a good thing in my view, the grisly memory of Chariovalda and his crushed skull still fresh in my mind. Catualda presumably informed Otmar of what Nerva was ordering, which in turn prompted Otmar to begin shouting and gesticulating wildly, pointing between the Marcomanni, identifiable by the colors woven into their tunics, the citadel looming above us, and Nerva. I remember thinking that it would have been a good idea to have Herminius with us, but this had been as haphazard an endeavor that I had been a part of, so I was not surprised that he was likely still sitting on his horse outside the walls, wondering what was happening. Naturally, there was a lot of noise, particularly when the Marcomanni began to understand that the

Romans who were now maneuvering into place, blocking off
the street we were on next to the wall in both directions were
not doing so randomly, nor were the Centuries positioning
themselves in the cross streets that allowed access to the rest
of the town.

For the span of a couple dozen heartbeats, it appeared as
if Catualda's Marcomanni were seriously considering fighting
us, as a warrior about my height, though of a leaner build, with
a high, conical helmet and a beard that was dyed blood red, or
perhaps it was dried blood from a slain foe, began haranguing
his comrades. Whatever it was, it was enough to send both
Catualda and Otmar hurrying away from us, reaching the
Marcomanni, whereupon it was Catualda's turn to make all
manner of gestures, though these were clearly in an attempt to
placate the warrior and his comrades. Next to an actual battle,
this was one of the most chaotic situations I had experienced
and, between the possibilities in the offing and the noise, it was
next to impossible to think; I offer this up simply as a way of
saying I have no idea how I was able to do so, yet I somehow
did, as all of the small moments came together in my mind.
Alex's comment about the large quantities of barrels and crates
under the rampart; the rampart being made of wood; the
civilians all fleeing uphill to the citadel...and Primus Pilus
Nerva deciding we did not have the time to perform a thorough
search of all of the dwellings, shops, and barns here in the flat
part of the town. It was as if I was in a trance, because when I
returned to awareness, Catualda was already leading his men,
with a new set of warriors pushing the ram, up the
perpendicular street that Nerva had designated, the ramparts
now packed with the Alaudae of the Second and Third Cohorts
in order to make enough room to maneuver, while I caught a
glimpse of the eagle standard just as it vanished from view as
the First Cohort began ascending the hill using the next street
over from the Gotones. More importantly, I did not see Nerva,
but when I asked Alex, who had been standing with Canus, a
bemused expression on his face, he quickly pointed in the
direction of the eagle. I had to shove my way through the
jammed mass of the other Centuries of the First, ignoring the
curses as I pushed men from behind, but I finally rounded the

corner and spotted Nerva's white crest next to his *Aquilifer*.

"*Primus Pilus! Stop! Stop the advance!*"

I do not know how many times I yelled this before Nerva whirled about, a scowl on his face, though he did grudgingly walk in my direction, descending the street as I made my way towards him.

"What the fuck are you doing, Pullus? Didn't you hear me say we need to move, *now*?"

"Primus Pilus," I spoke quickly, knowing that I had precious little time, just as I knew that I could not tell him *why* I was trying to stop the assault. "There's something that we need to check before we go up to the citadel."

"Check? What do you mean, check?"

Deciding to act rather than explain, I turned and once again had to shove my way the half-block down to the street next to the wall, counting on Nerva to follow me, if only out of anger and an opportunity to chew on me for delaying. Thankfully, he actually did, though he was not happy about it.

"This better be for a really fucking good reason," he growled, but as certain as I was, my heart was still in my throat when I ordered a ranker from the Fourth of the First to stand up and away from the barrel he had been leaning against while he waited to begin moving.

"Use your *pugio*, and open the top of that barrel," I ordered, though I was not surprised when he glanced over my shoulder at Nerva, who said from behind me, "I think he's mad, but do what he says."

Drawing his *pugio*, the ranker began to pry the top open, but he only got it open a crack before he recoiled from the smell.

"It's oil!" he exclaimed, and while I felt vindicated, I was not through, pointing to the crates stacked next to the barrel, ordering him to open the top one. As he did this, I addressed Nerva over my shoulder as I pointed, "Do you notice anything about how these barrels and crates are arranged, Primus Pilus?"

He did not reply for a moment; I was watching the ranker, but he must have been examining the scene, because I heard a gasp.

"Pluto's *balls*, there's no way this is random."

By this time, the ranker had pried the top of the crate off, and I thrust my hand into it, pulling out the contents to show Nerva.

"Dry sawdust," I said, though there was no need since he had eyes. "That *cunnus* Maroboduus plans to burn his own fucking city down...with us in it."

Nerva did not hesitate, spinning around to search for his Secundus Pilus Prior, finding him standing with Agricola, and while he did not indicate for me to follow him, I did so, just in time to hear, "I'm rescinding my last order. You and Agricola are going to secure the town between the hills."

"Oh? Why the change, Primus Pilus?"

Nerva was within his rights to tell the Secundus it was none of his fucking business, but to his credit, he did no such thing, saying instead, "Because thanks to Pullus here, I have reason to believe that that cunning bastard has a fair number of his boys hidden away down here. And," he turned and, though he had to move slightly to get an unobscured view of the wall, he pointed out, "see all of those barrels and crates? Notice anything?"

Frankly, I was happy that it was Agricola who noticed first. "There's a barrel, then crates, then barrel, then crates. That," he concluded, "is too Roman. Barbarians are never that organized."

"And we opened one of the barrels, and a crate," Nerva said grimly. "They're full of oil and dry sawdust."

"You mean Maroboduus was going to burn down his own town? Just to kill us all?"

"It certainly looks that way," Nerva agreed. "Although," he added with a grim humor, "I think it has more to do with Catualda than us. We just happen to be in the way."

"So, you were in error telling us we didn't have time to search," the Secundus said, making me wonder if this was the happiest day of his life; given his demeanor, I had to believe it was.

Once more showing great restraint, Nerva replied simply, "Yes, I was." I understood then that the Primus Pilus knew the Secundus far better than I did, because the Pilus Prior looked absolutely crestfallen as Nerva continued, "We're going to resume our advance on the citadel. I know I can count on you two to be ready for however many men are hidden in that fucking rat maze." Returning their salutes, Nerva turned away, beckoning to me to follow him. Waiting to get out of earshot of his nemesis, he asked quietly, "How did you know about that?"

That, I thought, is a good question, although by this moment, I at least understood the answer. Was it a happy accident that the night before I was thinking about my father's account of his time as Primus Pilus of the *Legio Germanicus* when they took Raetinium in what would be the last gasp of the part of the Pannonian revolt that Germanicus had been charged with suppressing by his adoptive father Tiberius? That I remembered how the chieftain of the Maezaei, Dodonis his name, chose to burn down his last stronghold in an attempt to destroy his Roman foes by stacking all manner of flammable material underneath the wooden rampart, hiding a large number of his warriors in the dwellings around the walls? Or, was it the gods or the shade of my father reaching across that invisible barrier between our worlds to intervene on my behalf?

Aloud, I only said, "I guess Fortuna loves me, Primus Pilus."

He gave a short, sharp bark that might have been a laugh, although he surprised me by agreeing, "I've known that for some time, Pullus. Now," he turned serious, "I have a favor to ask."

Before he was through, I was certain of two things: I did not want to say yes, but I knew that I could not say no. And, as much as I hated to admit it, what he was asking not only made sense, I was the only Roman who could do it at this point.

Nevertheless, I felt it wise to force him to be more specific, my suspicion being that he was being deliberately vague, which was why I said as much, and while he clearly did not want to, he said irritably, "Don't let Catualda harm Maroboduus. Now," he held up a hand, "if the old bastard refuses to surrender or something like that and wants to go down fighting, don't risk your own ass trying to take him alive. But if he does surrender, you *cannot* let Catualda kill him."

I was about to ask why; more specifically, I was going to ask by whose order this was, but I realized that I did not really want to know the answer. As I saw it, the less I knew the better, and I could always say that I assumed that all of what we were doing was at the behest of the Imperator, and not by Sejanus, through Varro.

Consequently, I saluted, saying as I did, "I understand, and will obey. Although," I hesitated, something occurring to me, "do you think I could borrow a *vitus* from one of your Centurions?"

It turned out that none of them were willing to give up their own, but I found an Optio who, as is their habit, used a turfcutter handle that he was willing give up. I was just reaching the rearmost ranks of the Gotones with Alex and Canus behind me, about halfway up to the top of the hill when, from down below and to our right in the direction of the gate, a sudden roar arose, stopping all of us. Between the haphazard arrangement of the buildings, and the height, I only had to move a few paces down the nearest cross street to look down and, while my view was partially obscured, it was enough to see that my father's warning had been needed. Warriors wearing Marcomanni colors had swarmed out of a row of buildings about three blocks inside the flat section of the town, running directly into a Century of either the Second or Third Cohort, it being too far away to read the standard, but who had been ready for such an attack.

"You were right," Alex said beside me, but I only nodded, not taking my eyes of the scene below.

Then, knowing there was nothing we could do but trust that the men of the Second and Third managed to keep any Marcomanni from reaching the flammables and igniting them, I resumed pushing my way through the Gotones, finally spotting the ram, which had stopped moving. Because of my height, and it being higher up the hill, I immediately saw why, unleashing a string of curses.

"It's fucking stuck!"

"What?" Alex had to stand on his tiptoes, but because of the helmeted heads of Catualda's warriors, he could not see.

"How?"

"This street narrowed down and those stupid bastards pushing it tried to force their way between the buildings, and now it's wedged!"

I was still moving as I shouted this over my shoulder, finally reaching Catualda and Otmar, who were in the process of screaming at a gap-toothed warrior of about forty, who had clearly been in charge of moving the ram.

Spotting me approaching, Catualda made a gesture at the warrior that I suppose was a sign of his disgust, and asked me with barely disguised hostility, "What are you doing here, Pullus?"

"Oh," I lied, making sure to grin, "I didn't have anywhere else to be." Before he could make an issue of it, I indicated the ram. "What happened?"

"This oaf here is what happened." Catualda pointed at the warrior. "He thought he could just push these houses down, and instead of stopping once it did not happen, he told them to keep pushing. And now," he actually kicked a wheel, "it is stuck."

Personally, I did not fault the warrior as much as Catualda did; just looking at what, even for a prosperous tribe like the Marcomanni, and in their capital, was only a little better than the kind of hovel we ran into on a regular basis east of the Rhenus made it seem a distinct possibility that it could be pushed down.

"Get some of your axemen," I suggested, "and search some of these houses for some kind of tools that can help tear it down."

I was not sure how to feel about the look of almost pathetic hope on his face as he asked, "Do you think that will work?"

It took a great deal of effort for me to remain patient, pointing out, "There's only one way to find out. Besides," I thought to add, "do you want to only use ladders to try and get into that citadel?"

This had the desired effect, and very quickly, a dozen Gotones with axes were hard at work, chopping away at the wattle to get to the columns and supporting beams of what appeared to be a combination shop and home of some sort of tradesman, who, thank the gods, was nowhere to be found. In fact, the buildings on the citadel hill were completely empty, which made me even more certain that they were sheltering in the citadel; it would be one of the only things I was wrong about on this day. Naturally, it seemed longer than it was, but finally, the building on the left side of the street was a pile of wreckage, with just enough space for the ram to resume moving, while Catualda had sent men up the street to make sure this did not happen again; it did not, but when they returned and gave their report, Catualda informed me of yet another complication, one that was potentially devastating.

"We will have to make a hard left turn two blocks up," he said, and just by his expression, I knew that he was aware of the problem.

While Titius used the frame of a wagon for both rams, he did not also use the front wheel assembly upon which the frame of a wagon sits that allows the wagon to turn. For the original ram, it was not an issue, since we just lined the ram up with the outer gate, but it could be argued, successfully in my mind, that someone should have thought about this for the citadel, given the labyrinthine nature of the streets, which we could plainly see from outside the walls given the hill.

"We have enough men to muscle it," I said with as much confidence as I could muster, adding a shrug that I hoped conveyed my lack of concern. "We'll just pick up the front end and move it around."

Nobody was more shocked than me that, when the moment came, that was exactly what we did, although our problems were far from over. Because of the orientation of the streets, despite starting from a spot at the base of the hill where the citadel's gates would be directly ahead of us, we were now at a spot just below the top of the hill, but with the citadel to our right; however, either Maroboduus or one of his predecessors had made sure that there were no buildings close to the walls, giving us an open area of more than fifty paces where we could once again muscle the ram into position so that the double gate was directly ahead of it. Of course, we had to do all this while within range of Marcomanni archers, and if they had more boiling oil or pitch, which I thought highly likely, we could expect more of the same treatment we received at the outer gate, and given there was nowhere for these Marcomanni to fall back to, with more vigor. The more I thought about it, the more I began to think that using ladders might not be the worst idea, though not in a straightforward assault. This was when the notion came to me, but before I broached it with Catualda, I pulled Alex aside, telling him my idea. Frankly, I was expecting him to tear it to pieces; perhaps it is more accurate to say that a part of me was hoping he would.

Instead, he rubbed his chin, a sign he was deep in thought.

"That," he said slowly, "could work. Although," he added, "can I make a suggestion?"

Naturally, I agreed, and when he finished, I realized that, as he always does, his suggestion was not only an improvement, I will cross the river certain that it spelled the difference between success and failure.

I wish I could say that Catualda immediately understood and appreciated what we were offering, but his first reaction was to shake his head and say flatly, "That is madness." He pointed at me as he reminded me, "You were the one who said that using ladders was foolish!"

"I did," I agreed, seemingly, "but I was talking about that being the only assault." It was my turn to point, at the ram. "That is going to be what they're worried about, as long as that's all they see. And I'm not talking about using all of the available ladders and every one of your men on the eastern wall of the citadel."

For the first time, he showed a glimmer of interest, asking warily, "How many men?"

"One hundred," I answered, which was one of Alex's suggestions, because I had initially thought only fifty would be needed. "Going up five ladders on the northern wall, while you're moving the ram into position." Thinking that it would help, I squatted down and, using my finger, I drew a rough rectangle in the dirt. "Five ladders is only twenty men per ladder, meaning that we can get up fast, and if we place them here," I indicated a point next to the corner that represented the junction of the northern and western wall, "we suddenly show up with men in their rear, away from the ram."

"With only a hundred men?" Catualda was still doubtful.

"Which is why we need one hundred of your best." Without any warning, another thought burst into my consciousness. "Besides, didn't you say that Maroboduus' hall is almost up against the western wall since there's no way to approach from that side?"

"Yes."

"And do you think he's going to be on the eastern wall? Or is he going to be in his hall?"

"He will be in his hall," Catualda's face split into a smile, but it was a cruel one. "Cowering like an old dog." Suddenly, he stood up, and said, "Your plan is accepted. And," he said this more loudly than necessary, especially since he was speaking in our tongue, "I will lead the way."

This was most definitely not what I had in mind, but when I opened my mouth to suggest that he should be with the bulk of his men, Alex grabbed my elbow, squeezing it, and I saw the slight shake of his head out of the corner of my eye.

"Lord Catualda," I tried to sound humble, which set my teeth on edge, "I request the honor of accompanying you and your chosen men."

"Of course, Centurion," he said graciously.

He's trying to sound like a king already, I thought with a sour amusement.

"I'm coming with you," Alex whispered, then before I could say anything, Canus spoke up, "So am I."

"Well, I suppose it will be one hundred and three men." Catualda laughed.

The change in his demeanor was striking; just a matter of heartbeats before, he had been close to despondent, yet now he was behaving as if victory was assured. How much of this is a performance for his men? I wondered. Following on the heels of that thought was me chiding myself, Does it matter? If his men believe him, that's all that's important. Calling Otmar and a handful of other subordinates, Catualda quickly explained the new plan, and judging by the manner in which his officers received the news, his enthusiasm was necessary. While I could not hear what he was saying because of the noise, there was a moment where Otmar and the others as one turned and looked at me, and judging from their expressions, it seemed likely that Catualda was telling them this was my idea in the event it failed. Catualda's men were getting restless, and while most of them took care to remain hard up against the buildings, I suppose it was inevitable that with such a poorly disciplined bunch, men either forgot or got careless, stepping out into the street, and a sharp-eyed Marcomanni archer up on the ramparts took advantage.

Since we were actually spread out along three streets, two that ran east/west on the northern side of the citadel, and the one running north/south in between, I did not see the handful of men who were struck down, hearing either their shriek of pain, or the angry bellows of the stricken man's comrades. I know that it would not seem this way to the man who had been hit, but arrows rarely kill a man outright, although given what I had seen with the Gotones and their standard of caring for the wounded, the chances of the wound corrupting with one of their warriors was much higher than with us. Nevertheless, it made moving about more difficult, and while Catualda and his officers were selecting the warriors he wanted with us, three of them were hit by an arrow, although one man who was struck by an arrow through his forearm barely glanced down at it, then with an impassive expression, shoved it through until the point was protruding from the other side several inches, his only sign of the agony he must have been in a groan when one of his comrades grabbed the shaft right behind the iron head and snapped it. Withdrawing the rest of the shaft, the warrior allowed his comrade to wrap his arm, then he said something to Catualda that I took to be his assurance he could still fight.

"I'm glad that bastard is on our side," I heard Canus mutter to Alex, and I had to agree.

While Catualda was doing this, Otmar had taken over getting the ram into position, while the warrior I supposed was the third in command led a group of men down to the base of the hill and the eastern wall to retrieve five ladders of those that had been left behind by the First. We did not want to draw attention to where we intended to place the ladders, making it difficult to see just how heavily defended the rampart along the northwestern corner of the citadel was, but for this to work, the surprise had to be complete. This also meant that we had to wait to move into position until the Marcomanni were convinced that the ram was the main and only effort, which made it even more difficult to endure. It was Alex who thought of something that might have destroyed our chances of success.

"If they don't see Catualda near the ram, mightn't they get suspicious?"

As usually happens when he says something of this nature, before he was finished, I knew that he was right, and I went off in search for Catualda; thankfully, I found him with Otmar as he gave his cousin last-moment instructions. To his credit, his reaction was the same as mine, and the pair exchanged helmets, since Catualda's had a pair of raven's wings, along with their cloaks, while their mail shirts, while not being identical, were close enough in appearance that it was unlikely any Marcomanni would notice. Their familial resemblance helped a great deal, although Otmar's beard was just a bit longer, and he wore it in plaits, but this was quickly taken care of, and after a brief examination, the pair silently appointing me as judge, I nodded.

"I can barely tell you apart," I lied, though it was a matter of degree; I was confident that no Marcomanni up on the rampart would notice, especially with everything else going on.

With this last detail taken care of, the pair embraced, whispering to each other, leaving me to stand there awkwardly, but then Catualda walked over to me and, being careful to stay pressed up against the buildings, we headed to the spot two streets away from the cleared area around the citadel, which was the same around three sides, except for the western, because the citadel had been built right up to the edge of the steep drop-off down to the river on that side. Since the citadel was clearly visible from our camp, we had been surprised to see on our arrival that there was no ditch around the base, but Catualda had explained that, although there had been one there when he was a child visiting his aunt, Maroboduus had ordered it filled, though he had no idea why, which was convenient for us. There were a series of fire-hardened stakes buried in the foundation that protruded outward, but those would not take long to remove, although every heartbeat of time was precious. I was pleased to see that Catualda thought of this on his own, calling on the dozen warriors for whom the ax was their primary weapon, placing them ahead of the men who would be carrying the five ladders. However, when I saw that he did not take the time to assign a group of men to a specific ladder, which was carried by four men, I stifled a curse before I tapped him on the shoulder. To my relief, rather than snap at me about it, he looked chagrined and immediately rectified the matter, finishing just when there was a massive roar from the eastern side of the citadel.

"The ram's moving," I commented, needlessly, since Catualda was already hurrying to a spot where he could peer around the corner and see the rampart two blocks and another fifty paces away, remembering to remove Otmar's helmet before he did so.

It was frustrating to have to rely on Catualda relating what he was seeing, but very quickly, it became clear by the noise that the battle for the gate was now raging, yet Catualda did not move, remaining crouched down so that his head was not at the normal spot a sentry would look if trying to determine they were being watched. Between the structures and the distance between our position and the gate, while we could hear, the sound was understandably muffled, but then there was not one but several high-pitched shrieks of what had to be unimaginable pain, jerking our attention in that direction, just in time to see a roiling column of black, oily smoke rising above the thatched roofs.

"They've hit the ram." Alex, who was just behind me, sounded understandably grim, and we stood, our eyes fastened on the smoke, watching to see if it grew.

I was not alone in breathing a sigh of relief when we watched it slowly dissipate, the sign that either the green hides had done their jobs, or Otmar and his men had managed to control the flames. Suddenly, Catualda stood up, looking over his shoulder at me, his eyes alight with a fire of their own.

"About half of the men have disappeared," he informed

me, already moving to a spot where he could be seen by the men with the ladders. "They all headed to the front of the citadel."

This was good, but half was not all; I also understood that if we waited for the perfect moment, when the wall would be deserted, we would likely miss our opportunity. Consequently, I glanced over my shoulder at Alex.

"Ready?"

"Right behind you," he assured me.

I cannot say why, but then I looked over at Canus, and while I did not say anything, he correctly interpreted my gaze, giving me a nod, which was also when I noticed his chin thongs were not tightened enough.

"Tie those," I pointed to them, "tighter. You don't want to lose your helmet, or worse, have it come down over your eyes."

This also made me look at Alex, but he had already done so, and with this, I held up my hand to them to wait as the axemen turned onto the street that led to the wall; our assault had begun.

From this moment, everything was about speed, and it was clear to see that Catualda had either impressed this upon this chosen group of warriors, or being experienced in their own right, they implicitly understood, because while we did not move at a run, it was close. The axemen burst out into the open area, but to our pleased surprise, they were almost halfway across the fifty paces before we heard a shout from up on the rampart, my assumption being that the remaining sentries were more interested in what was happening near the gate, understandable yet still a serious error. And, for a couple of them, it was the last one they would make, as about a half-dozen Gotones hurled the light javelins that some of them carried in a sheath strapped to their backs. One of them was hit twice, once in the chest, then just as he toppled forward over the waist-high rampart, which was not crenellated for some reason, a second javelin struck him in the back on his way down, and he landed just in front of a pair of axemen, one of whom stumbled over the body and was only saved from impaling himself on one of the sharpened stakes by his alert comrade, who grabbed one of his arms, altering the endangered man's track so he managed to slam into the wall in between a pair of stakes instead of onto one and impaling himself. Otherwise, the teams of axemen made it to the relative safety at the base of the wall, while those Marcomanni sentries armed with bows shifted their attention to the men carrying the ladders. Each file was preceded by four Gotones who had been selected by the size of their shields; at least, this was how it appeared to me, and proving that they were not completely incapable of working with the kind of precision necessary to protect their ladder carrying comrades, two men dropped into a crouch, while the other two men stood just behind them, leaning over at the waist and with their arms extended, thrusting their shields forward so that the bottom rims of their shields touched the top of the pair in a crouch. Naturally, it was impossible to move as quickly as possible like this, and every heartbeat was crucial, especially when I saw a man, though he was beardless and was probably in his teens, turn and begin running down the rampart, towards the gate. Before he had gone a dozen steps, at least a half-dozen javelins went streaking in his direction from behind me, with all but one missing; thank the gods the one that hit him was enough to stop him in his tracks.

"Hurry! Faster, you bastards!"

Even as I roared this, I felt slightly foolish, and yet, either they understood or, more likely, my tone seemed to spur them on, each pair clearing a swathe four stakes wide so the ladders could fit and the men could stand just around the base without having to worry about being skewered. In truth, I doubt that even my own 1st could have timed it as well, as the warriors with the shields who were leading the way, each of them with at least a half-dozen arrow shafts protruding from them, reached the base of the wall just as the axemen finished. And, even more importantly, the four men of the ladder team moved quickly, with three of them pushing upward on the ladder, while the fourth man dropped to the ground in a sitting position with his back to the wall, grabbing and bracing the bottom of the ladder, although I did have to correct the man whose ladder I would be ascending, showing him that he needed to move his hands from the horizontal rung he was grasping to the vertical supports so that his fingers were not crushed. I was acutely aware that Catualda, who would be ascending the ladder next to me, was watching the progress of our respective teams, yet even knowing that it was foolish, I could not seem to help myself, actually shoving the last Gotones aside whose position had been closest to the base while hopping up onto the second rung, with nothing else in my mind other than getting to the rampart first. Catualda actually used his shield to shove his bottom man aside, but then in his haste to catch up with me, his foot slipped and plunged through the space between the rungs.

"Gnaeus," Alex warned, and I felt the vibration that told me he had just put a foot on the ladder, "don't do anything stupid! Let him win!"

I *knew* he was right; it was not only the wise thing to do, it was probably the safest thing to do, if only because he had a shield, which he was holding above his head, and all I had was the turfcutter handle, and I swear on the black stone that I did hesitate...for a moment. But, I was also angry, and I had become convinced that Rome would rue their choice in Catualda, although I still could not have explained why I felt this way in concrete terms. Consequently, I did not slow down, craning my neck upward, seeing that there was a shield resting on the parapet, which explained why the wall was not crenellated; that, and whoever built this probably did not think that it would ever really need to be defended. I did not recall doing so, but my *gladius* was in my hand, and because of the accident of my size, I am one of the few, not of just Romans but most men of every tribe I have run into, who can still grasp the rung at the same time. Still, I was at a disadvantage, especially when, to my left, another Marcomanni warrior materialized immediately next to the man whose shield blocked my progress. I learned he was armed with a spear when, leaning out slightly, he launched a vicious thrust out and down at me, but I was able to knock it aside with the turfcutter handle so that the point shot past me over my shoulder. Now, I had to decide the best way to attack the defender directly above me, but I had an instant's warning of what was coming when the bottom of the Marcomanni's shield lifted from the wood of the parapet, followed by a sudden thrust, also with a spear. Because I had just used my turfcutter to knock the first attack away, and I was grasping both my *gladius* and a rung with my other, I had no choice but to throw myself flat against the ladder. The move saved my life, although I cannot say I was all that appreciative in the moment because the point of the spear struck my helmet a terrific blow, and while it was at a shallow enough angle that the point skipped off the metal; later when we looked at my helmet, there was a gouge just under the crest on the left side that came within a whisker of penetrating all the way through, and while it would not have punched through my skull, there is no doubt it would have dazed me even more than I already was.

The world in front of my eyes exploded in a burst of light, but more confusingly, I was not sure whether my eyes were open or closed, and in that instant, if the spearman who initiated the attack executed another thrust, I would not be here to dictate this. For whatever reason, he did not, for which I will be forever thankful, but I was still in grave danger, which was why I did what I did, and it is something that I doubt I will ever do again, despite how it worked out. While dazed, I retained enough of my senses to understand that the spearman above me was going to repeat his attack, except this time, when I saw his shield lifting off of the parapet, I had just wrapped my left leg around the vertical support so that I could let go of the rung with my right hand, and while it was over my head, and without any power except from my arm, I blindly thrust my blade through the gap, something that we are trained never to do, yet feeling the resistance as my point punched into his body, able to tell just from experience that he was wearing a boiled leather cuirass, and with gritted teeth, I shoved my arm forward until I felt the handguard strike his cuirass. The reason that I would not perform this maneuver again if the situation arose was because of what happened next; it began with a shrill scream of pain that only increased when, with as much power of my wrist as I could muster, I twisted my blade before withdrawing it, and while I was prepared for the warm shower of blood and offal that drenched my hand, what I did not anticipate was him moving his left hand out and away from the parapet, not much but enough that, when it slipped from his hand, the heavy wooden shield dropped onto my head, striking the crown just in front of my crest. Because I was already dazed, I believe that the effect from the impact was even worse than it would have been otherwise, but as stunned as I was, I still could feel myself falling backward so that for the span of perhaps a heartbeat, the only way I was still attached to the ladder was because of my leg wrapped around it. This was another moment where my size threatened to betray me, as the weight of my upper body along with my *hamata* bent me backward so that I felt the strain on my left leg, and even through the fog I remember thinking that, at best, I could expect a broken leg if I kept falling backward. Suddenly, and without any warning, I has struck in the back by something solid, only vaguely aware that there was a protuberance on its surface that would end up leaving a round bruise on my back, but it was Alex's grunt that came from the effort of supporting the weight of my upper body on his shield that he was holding above his head that brought me somewhat back to a state of awareness.

"If...you...don't straighten up...I'm...going to..." Alex was gasping, but it did get me moving, and I did as he said, pulling myself back erect, albeit with difficulty.

While this all happened much more quickly than it takes to describe it, I was still in a horribly vulnerable position, but I was aided by the fact that, once the spearman dropped his shield onto my head, he had slumped over the parapet, blocking any of his comrades from immediately moving into his place. Further helping me was that the spearman who had attacked me first had been frozen behind his shield by one of the Gotones with javelins, seeing two protruding from his shield, and he had just ducked a third that sailed high. Now that I was upright and with my head clearing, though even in that moment I could tell I would have a headache, I was faced with the choice of pulling the body off in my direction so that I could clear the parapet, but I had seen what happened when a body came tumbling down a ladder, so instead, I used the turfcutter handle to push the corpse back in the opposite direction and onto the rampart, then dropped into a crouch, and using my left hand, which was now on the parapet, as the pivot point, leapt up and over it, swinging my legs over. By doing it in this manner using my left hand, it made it natural for me to face the first spearman, and my right arm was already moving in a thrust at my foe, who was now forced to decide whether to move his shield to block me while exposing himself to another javelin, or to try and dodge my thrust and keep his shield resting on the parapet. He decided on the latter, and in that first span of eyeblinks, it seemed as if he made the correct choice, though it was because I had forgotten that I would not be landing on the wood of the rampart, but on the corpse. More accurately, I stepped into the guts of the slain Marcomanni since he had landed on his back, and I suppose it is easy to imagine that this is not as stable a platform from which to thrust from any position; in this case, I launched from the first, but when I twisted my hips, the shift in weight made my foot slip inside his stomach cavity, the point striking nothing but air without requiring any effort on his part to dodge my attack. However, now that I was standing there, the spearman had no real choice but to turn his attention to me, and he pivoted on his right foot as he moved his shield from the parapet to block me, but before I could respond, I barely caught the streaking blur of the javelin that struck the Marcomanni in his side. It was not a mortal wound, but my thrust, this time from the second position and more extended than I would have liked because my foot was still trapped, still had enough power to pierce the side of his neck.

Because of the placement of our ladder, this was the last Marcomanni on the rampart on the eastern side, and I divided my attention between extricating my foot while trying to choke down the bile from the sight, sound, and smell as I did so, and looking down the length of the rampart to see if any of the Marcomanni who I could see crammed onto the eastern rampart was looking in our direction, although to that point, they had not. For a moment, I thought about giving Alex the all clear to climb up and let him suffer the same fate I had, but since I did not want to hear about it later, I bent down, grabbed the dead man by one arm, and heaved him off of the rampart, which I could now see was a bit more than seven or eight feet wide, enough for a man to brace a comrade with barely enough room for a third man to move along the rampart, provided they turned sideways to do so. Once that was done, only then did I turn my attention to Catualda's ladder, and while I was disappointed to see that he was already on the rampart, I also noticed that the pair of Marcomanni lying at his feet both had javelins protruding from their bodies. Beyond the Gotones nobleman, I saw that the fighting for the rampart was not going as well, so once Alex and Canus were with me, I hurried over to Catualda, who seemed more concerned with wiping his blade down with the hem of one of the slain men's tunic, and when I glanced down, I saw that along with the javelin, the Marcomanni had been stabbed, though at the same time, I noticed that most of the blood leaking out onto the wooden platform was not from the stab wound, an indication that the slain man had been dead when Catualda stabbed him.

Seeing where I was looking, Catualda said, "He was still alive, so I finished him."

"You're blocking the ladder," I told him, earning me a blank stare before he muttered something, though he did step aside. "The faster we get more men on the rampart, the better," I admonished. "And," I pointed back towards the main gate, "we can't count on none of those bastards looking in this direction, so you're going to need to keep some men down on the ground and up here on the rampart in position to block them in the event they head this way."

"I do not need lessons from you, Centurion," he snarled, but then he turned and shouted at the handful of men who had reached the rampart from the ladder next to his, and they immediately headed over.

This was the first moment I had to actually examine the interior, and I saw that Catualda had been accurate, that it was almost a small village inside the larger town, with several long, low buildings about a dozen paces away from the wall, and across from them on the southern side were identical structures, although one of them was higher and larger, which I identified as the barn. Finally, to our right was the largest of the buildings, Maroboduus' hall, with a high, peaked roof, though it was made of thatch as well, which I thought odd given that it was hard up against the western wall, but I assumed it was a mark of confidence that the western slope of the hill was so severe, no attack would come from that direction. And, I knew, if it was like a normal chieftain's hall, the building itself would be defensible, with heavily reinforced doors, though right then, I could only see the roof from where we were standing. Catualda, while he had moved out of the way and the men using his ladder were now scrambling up, seemed content to watch his men at the other three ladders fight their way up without any help from the men already on the rampart.

This was too much, and I snarled a curse as I shoved Catualda aside, snapping to Alex, "You two follow me since we're the only ones who seem fucking interested in giving this bastard his crown!"

Catualda shouted at me, and I understood that he was calling my mother a whore, which almost got me to spin about and keep Maroboduus on his throne, but I managed to restrain myself, although it did serve to rouse the beast in my stomach, and I could feel the shifting deep within me that I had learned was a sign. There were five Marcomanni around the middle ladder, with only one of Catualda's men on the rampart, but with his back pressed against the parapet and, more importantly, blocking the next man on the ladder from joining him. He was doing what he could with his ax, swinging it at the pair of Marcomanni on my opposite side to keep them at bay, while thrusting his shield at the enemy whose back was turned towards me, his own hip hard up against the parapet. Because they formed a semicircle, one of the Marcomanni on the other side facing in my direction saw me coming, and clearly without thinking shouted a warning, and also without thinking, the warrior next to the parapet spun about. There would be debate later, good-natured, between me and one of the Gotones, the axmen who was first up the middle ladder, who struck the killing blow, but what mattered is that the standstill at the middle ladder was quickly solved, and I made sure there was no question about who slew the warrior next to the first Marcomanni, dispatching him after blocking his spear thrust with a feinted first position that dropped his shield to block the attack that never came, then whipping my blade around in a semicircle to his left to take him in the throat.

The second Gotones up the ladder literally threw himself at a third warrior, a youngster whose eyes I saw go wider than one would think possible as he fell backward under the weight of his attacker. Their struggle was so wild that it actually sent the fourth Marcomanni staggering backward until his heels were hanging over the inner edge of the rampart, which somewhat unusually did not have a lip on it, enabling Alex, who had just arrived, to use his shield, bashing it against the Marcomanni's own protection, sending him falling backwards as he discarded both spear and shield to windmill his arms in that unthinking reflex we all possess when we fall backward. It was not all that far, perhaps about eight feet, but it was the Marcomanni's misfortune that there was a water trough directly underneath him, and he hit the edge, snapping his back about midway between waist and shoulders. The final Marcomanni began swinging his spear, wildly and in a wide arc that did manage to keep us at bay, but it did not protect him from the thrust to his back from one of the Gotones who had gotten up the fourth ladder. This seemed to send a signal to the dozen or so Marcomanni still on the rampart as, on some unheard or unseen signal, they turned and leapt off the rampart, some of them landing well, others awkwardly, while one man snapped a bone in his leg, consigned to trying to crawl towards Maroboduus' hall. Immediately, three of the Marcomanni scrambled to their feet and began running back in our direction, clearly intending to rush to the eastern end of the citadel.

"We can't let them go!"

I was already moving as Alex shouted this, and even in the moment, I knew that if I had stopped even for a heartbeat to think about it, I would never have done what I did, which was to begin running down the rampart, also heading towards the gate, then timed my leap off the rampart for the fastest Marcomanni with nothing other than a vague thought of landing on him, and with the equally vague hope he would soften the impact with the hardpacked dirt. My aim, at least, was true, both of my *caligae* striking him squarely in the back, and the sounds of the air rushing out of his lungs, and the cracking of his ribs as all of my weight drove him down into the ground happening almost simultaneously. I suppose his body did soften the impact, but it also guaranteed that I landed clumsily, and I went stumbling forward, then just as I got my feet under me, I was struck a terrific blow from behind that sent me reeling and struggling both to regain my balance and my breath, but before I could turn to confront my unseen attacker, which I suppose I was dimly aware had to be the second Marcomanni, who was just behind my target, he stabbed me, his spear striking me low on my left side, just above my kidney, and with enough force that I felt the tip penetrate my body, sending a lightning bolt of agony through me. And, if he had retained his wits, or perhaps if he had been more experienced, he would have continued driving the point all the way through my body, but I believe that he was more intent on getting past me and reaching his comrades who were clearly furiously engaged with Otmar and the bulk of the Gotones, and perhaps even the First Cohort by this time. Consequently, he let go of the spear as he rushed past me, yet somehow, despite the bolt of agony it caused, I managed to lunge for him, extending my left hand, though I still grasped the turfcutter handle, with the intent of shoving him off balance by using the end of it, but I was only partially successful, staggering him so that he stumbled for a couple of paces though he did not lose his feet. The spear, still lodged in my back, was not embedded deeply enough that it stuck straight out from my body, which was a good thing, but with the butt end sagging and hitting the ground, which was not a good thing at all. There is no way I can describe the agony of the next few heartbeats, yet I had a secret ally that helped me, as the beast that dwells deep within me roused itself, and truly that was the only way I was able to sprint the few paces it took to overtake the fleeing Marcomanni, even as the butt end of the spear bounced off the dirt with every stride, making me feel as if Jupiter was sending a bolt of lightning throughout my body. I used the handle again, except this time, I was close enough to thrust it right between the shoulder blades of the Marcomanni, and with enough force that he lost his feet so quickly that he did not get his hands out in front of him, slamming into the ground face first and sliding for a few feet, shattering his teeth and crushing his nose. He was unable to roll over before I ended him with a thrust, but I heard pounding footsteps behind me, and without thinking, I began to turn, certain that it was the third Marcomanni, my arm already moving into a first position. How Alex managed to block my thrust neither of us will ever know, but there is not a day that goes by where I do not think about this moment and offer a prayer to the goddess Fortuna that he did.

In the moment, however, I am somewhat ashamed to say that I was actually angry that he did so, which I attribute to the beast within me, and Alex must have seen in it my expression, because he shouted, "Gnaeus! It's me! Alex!"

"I know it is," I gasped, and I had to fight an almost overwhelming urge to drop to my knees, yet I retained enough of my wits to know that it would not ease the agony of having a spear hanging from my back. Instead, I told Alex, "Get this fucking thing out of me." Not surprisingly, he hesitated, but I snarled, "You're trained as a *medicus*, so do your fucking job!"

"I don't want to cause more damage," he protested, but he sheathed his *gladius* and grounded his shield, and if I had been in a better frame of mind, I would have laughed at the manner in which he approached me, clearly prepared to leap out of the way.

Since it was difficult, and painful to twist my torso to try and watch, I returned my attention to the eastern end of the citadel, seeing that some of the men on the rampart nearest to the northeastern corner had dropped down to the ground, but to my relief, they were all universally facing south, in the direction of the gate, their posture such that told me they were waiting for orders to enter the fray.

"The good news," Alex spoke with a careful tone that was as instructive as his words, "is that the spearpoint isn't very deep, maybe a bit less than two inches, but between your *hamata* and undertunic, it probably didn't penetrate more than an inch or so, and while it's still bleeding, it's not bright, so it didn't hit a vessel. The bad news..."

"Is that you won't know if there's anything in the wound until you examine me," I finished for him, not out of concern for his feelings but from impatience. "Well, you can do that later. Now, you need to get that thing out of me."

"Gnaeus..." he began, but I was in no mood.

"Get. It. Out."

I wish I could say that even a part of me regretted my harsh tone, but in fairness, I had just seen one of the Marcomanni down at the eastern end glance in our direction, and as often happens when someone does so for no particular reason, turned his head back to the front. For a brief moment, I hoped that he had not been paying close attention, but then his head whipped back around to stare, and from my perspective, he was doing so directly at me, and I saw him reach out to grab the warrior directly in front of him, then point in our direction when Alex withdrew the spear. I have never completely understood why the sensation when a foreign object in the body is removed from your body is not one of relief, but a stab of even deeper agony, yet that was what I felt then, to the point I thought my legs would give way. It sounds odd, but the sudden movement of what I counted to be about thirty Marcomanni detaching themselves to begin coming in our direction at a trot did more to clear my head than anything I might have done.

"Catualda!" I bellowed over my shoulder, though I did not turn my attention away from the Marcomanni. "We need a line of spearmen here, now!"

"Gnaeus," Alex said quietly, "Catualda isn't here. He's already headed for the hall." I began to turn around, a foolish thing to do, but I was sufficiently astonished to forget that as I spun about, also forgetting the bolt of agony the movement would cause.

However, my gasp was not from pain, but at the sight of the almost empty space behind us, except for the last fifteen or so Gotones still hopping down from the rampart, while just beyond them, I saw the tail end of the rest of our force turning the corner of the last building.

"*Stop right there!*" Having no way of knowing how many of these stragglers spoke Latin, I relied on my tone, and whether it was the order or my voice, what mattered was the men stopped, although several of them were clearly reluctant.

Now, it was a race to get them formed up in a line to block these Marcomanni from falling on Catualda from the rear, and

I knew the prudent course of action would be to retreat myself, meeting them where, to their credit, on seeing this new threat they were beginning to form a line, but the beast was roused, and I was in no mood to retreat. I did not make a conscious decision about any of this; it was just that my legs suddenly started moving, except they were taking me forward, not backward, and my last memory of the moment was hearing what sounded like a beast snarling, which I suppose it was in a sense as I went charging at the oncoming Marcomanni. As usually happens, I remember very little of what took place, although there were more fragments in the immediate aftermath; having Alex, and Canus, present meant that I heard about what took place, which may have much to do with me recalling more than I normally do. The reason I am still alive is because neither of them hesitated in following me in my headlong rush at the Marcomanni, who were understandably caught by surprise by the sight of a large Roman rushing them, armed with nothing but his *gladius* and a sawed-off turfcutter handle, and I will leave it to Alex to fill in the gaps I do not remember.

As is always the case when a group of men go rushing into battle, some do so with more abandon than others, which meant that Gnaeus, who had broken into a sprint that left us more than a dozen paces in his wake, would not immediately be confronted by overwhelmingly superior numbers, while the speed with which he closed the distance sowed further confusion; I suspect that the look of fury that I knew was on his face also helped. There were a pair of Marcomanni leading the others by perhaps a couple of paces, and they would have been wise to cut their strides to let their comrades catch up, but they did not, nor did Gnaeus slow down. His speed clearly caught them by surprise, and they just barely managed to both get their shields up, not that they helped much, and while they were both armed with spears, the man to Gnaeus' left rushed his thrust, which I believe was what caused his comrade to delay his, meaning that one spear was already extended, which Gnaeus knocked aside with his turfcutter handle, while the second was only just beginning its thrust and consequently had little power behind it. While his aim was true, striking Gnaeus in the chest, his own momentum in the opposite direction knocked the spear flying out of the Marcomanni's hand a fraction of an eyeblink before Gnaeus slammed into their shields, which as they are trained to do, they had overlapped with each other, consequently sending both men flying off their feet a couple paces backward. Both of them landed on their backs, the wind knocked from them, but Gnaeus barely slowed, ignoring the pair and reaching the next closest Marcomanni, armed with a long gladius, *which he brought down in a brutal overhand swing. Since I had reacted to Gnaeus' sudden move and was trying, vainly, to catch up to him, I had just reached the pair of Marcomanni on the ground, the one on the right nearest to me, so I had to look away from Gnaeus to dispatch this warrior, who had just rolled over and was pulling himself to all fours while shaking his head in an attempt to clear it. Just before I killed him with a thrust to his back, I heard a shriek of agony, but I could tell it was not Gnaeus, and I kept my eyes on my foe as I drove the blade down between his shoulder blades, "looking" my blade in to where I wanted it to go in the manner Gnaeus' father had taught me, ending his life as he collapsed facedown with nothing more than a breathy moan.*

"What is he doing?" Canus shouted, enabling me to place him just to my left and slightly behind me, just as he was reaching the second man who had not even managed to roll over from his back to get to his feet. "Is he mad?"

"Just stay behind him and watch his left flank!"

I was moving again as I shouted this, my attention back on Gnaeus, where he had already stepped over the warrior he had just dispatched, and while I did not see how he did it, the result was obvious, with the Marcomanni's severed hand still clutching his gladius *next to the body, while his head was several feet away from the rest of the corpse. Gnaeus was still moving, his blade glinting with the blood he had already spilled, though no longer at a run, and this was the instant I heard the clash of metal behind me and to my left, the sign that Canus was engaging with the other Marcomanni Gnaeus had knocked down, though this time, I did pause just long enough to glance over, in time to see Canus follow up his parry of his foe's spear thrust by making a short, hopping move to the side that placed him on his opponent's weapon side, and before the Marcomanni could bring it to bear, Canus' blade shot out in a seeming wasted move, because the point punched the air just behind his foe and below his waist, but then in a move that was so quick I am still not sure that I saw it, he brought the blade back towards him, but with the Marcomanni's right leg between him and his blade. Only Gnaeus has the strength to sever a man's leg in this manner, but that was not Canus' intention, only to rob his enemy of half of his support, the warrior giving a shrill scream of pain, and because of my position, I could clearly see the look of despair on his face as he collapsed to his knees, while in one continuous motion, Canus pivoted so that he was standing behind the Marcomanni, and with a fluidity that was as daunting as it was impressive, drew his dagger across the man's throat. All that I just described took perhaps two heartbeats, but even in that short span of time, when I returned my attention to Gnaeus, it took me a moment to find him, because he was nowhere near the last spot I had seen him. This was also partially due to the fact that he was now surrounded by five Marcomanni; when Canus saw this, he gave a shout of alarm.*

"He's gotten himself surrounded!"

"Yes, but that's not a mistake," I assured him, although I was also moving again, this time at an angle to draw closer to Canus so the pair of us could work together. "We still need to help keep those other bastards occupied!"

I pointed to a half-dozen Marcomanni who were slightly separated from the wild melee that Gnaeus had instigated, yet while to his credit, Canus did not hesitate, there was no missing the look of resignation on his face as the pair of us moved at a quick walk towards the second group of Marcomanni, who had paused to discuss how they could best insert themselves into what was a brawl, with two of their number already on the ground at Gnaeus' feet, one writhing in pain and the other in the immobile shapelessness of death, though his blood was still pooling on the ground around him. Then, in the fraction of a heartbeat before we got within reach of the enemy spears, there was a great shout behind us as the Gotones who Gnaeus had ordered to stay with us and not join Catualda finally arrived, although I know that in real time it was perhaps fifteen or twenty heartbeats. Later, we would learn that there had been a bit of a debate among these fifteen men, but then one of them managed to persuade the others that, as formidable as the big Roman was, with only the two of us to help him, it was a virtual certainty that these Marcomanni would be falling on their own rear. With their help, we sent the Marcomanni reeling, yet to our surprise, they were not reinforced, although now that we were closer to the eastern gate, we could tell that a rare fight was going on, though it was impossible to tell who was winning. Gnaeus, however, did not need our help, leaving me, Canus, and the surviving Gotones; two men were now dead, another four wounded, one of them seriously, as spectators as Gnaeus, having vanquished four of the Marcomanni who, just a matter of a handful of heartbeats earlier, had been sure that their superior numbers would be enough, discarded his turfcutter handle so that he could yank the last Marcomanni's shield from his hand, tossing it aside much like his son did with a cup when he was feeling petulant. The warrior, who actually looked experienced, with several knuckle bones tied into his beard, tried to stab Gnaeus with his spear, but Gnaeus knocked it aside with an ease that was an eloquent expression of his contempt, then his left hand snatched out to grab the Marcomanni by the throat, the warrior immediately dropping his spear to grab at Gnaeus' hand with both of his, trying desperately to pry Gnaeus' little finger loose, using the traditional method to break a man's grip on your throat by snapping the smallest appendage.

"He's wasting his time," I commented between gasps as I tried to get my own breath back, feeling a bit of sympathy for the Marcomanni despite myself, and the Marcomanni quickly reached that conclusion, abandoning this to start hammering on Gnaeus' hand and wrist, again with both hands.

Gnaeus did not intend to strangle the man, or perhaps this was his original intent, but then, with more effort though with nothing near what it should have taken, even for Gnaeus, he lifted the Marcomanni up off the ground until his feet were dangling several inches off the ground, and with his great-

grandfather's gladius, *he thrust the point into the Marcomanni's body, just below the breastbone, his mail vest as if it was nothing more than his tunic, the blade bursting out of the man's back in a shower of blood, while the Marcomanni's eyes bulged out so much that I was certain they would pop out of his skull, his already purple face suddenly turning, not pale perhaps, but certainly a lighter shade. Nor did his eyes pop out, but they did roll back in his head, and for the first time, we heard Gnaeus saying something intelligible; up to that point, it had been something between a snarl and a feral kind of growling low in his throat.*

"You thought that you could kill me, you cunnus, *you barbarian piece of* cac*?" His voice rose in volume with every word, ending with his bellowing so loudly that I imagined that it could be heard throughout the entire citadel.* "I am Gnaeus Volusenianus Pullus, Centurion of Rome's 1st Legion, and there's not a fucking man alive that can kill me!"

He punctuated this declaration by flinging the dead Marcomanni, his head now bent backward to a degree that only the dead can achieve, with so much force that his body slammed against the northern wall, then bounced off to collapse in a heap at the base, while Gnaeus' shoulders suddenly slumped, his head dropping to his chest and his eyes closing. Canus made to rush to his side, but fortunately, I was close enough to grab him by the arm.

"Don't," I warned. "Don't touch him, not yet." Then, I released him, telling Canus, "I know what to do."

This was not exactly true; while I had been present when Gnaeus had what we refer to as his divine fit, at least on those few occasions he will speak of it, I was never certain how he would react, but I had developed the belief that it was best to try to speak to him before touching him.

Consequently, I made sure to stand just out of his reach, then called to him quietly, "Gnaeus? Can you hear me?"

He did not respond, though his eyes opened and he began staring blankly at nothing that I could discern; I was about to call his name again when his head moved, slowly, to look at me.

"My back hurts," he said with dull surprise, reminding me

that he usually had no real memory of these moments, although I also was aware that he had been stabbed a couple of heartbeats before he went into his fit.

"You were stabbed," I reminded him, then thinking this was a good moment to do so, I approached him and said, "Let me look at it."

"Stabbed?" He frowned. "In the back?" For the first time, he showed some life, his voice rising slightly. "How did I get stabbed in the back? I didn't..."

He could not finish, but I did not need him to, understanding.

"No, you didn't turn your back on the enemy." The thought made me laugh. "That will never happen. But one did manage to get behind you."

He was turning so that I could examine his wound, although I had already seen that it had stopped bleeding, the blood only barely reaching his tunic below the bottom of his hamata, *when we were interrupted by a shout, though not from the eastern wall but the opposite direction. We both turned to see a lone warrior sprinting towards us without his shield, the sign that he wanted to move as quickly as he could, but it was his waving arms that gave us the first hint that this was not just important, but potentially dire.*

"Do you recognize him?" Gnaeus asked, but I shook my head.

He shouted something when he was about fifty paces away, but it was a name, that of one of the warriors who had stayed behind, who went running to meet his comrade. Gnaeus had started moving as well, ignoring me and my attempt to check his wound, leaving me to run over and pick up his discarded turfcutter handle.

Despite the delay, I was close enough to hear the Gotones warrior the new arrival had summoned, and understood why when he gasped, then spun about to address Gnaeus, in broken but understandable Latin, "Centurion, Lord Catualda requires us! He is now trapped between two forces outside Maroboduus' hall and needs our help!"

Alex's informing me of the cause of the pain in my lower

back ironically helped clear my head a bit, but as always seems to happen after these...episodes, I was almost overcome with exhaustion and wanted to do nothing more than find a safe spot to sleep. The arrival of Catualda's courier and his alarming message helped to restore my energy somewhat, but even as I forced myself into a run, with the surviving Gotones who had actually heeded my call to stay behind following me, my legs felt as if they had been filled with lead. I sensed Alex pulling up even with me, and I prepared myself for a scolding, but while in a sense it was coming, it was not what I expected, which would have been him grousing about not checking my back.

Instead, what he said was, "Shouldn't we leave some of these men behind in case the Marcomanni come back and try to get behind us again?"

It was a sensible suggestion, but we had just reached the last building that blocked our view of the hall, and before I answered, we turned the corner.

After taking it in for a heartbeat, all I could think to say was, "I don't think we have that long."

It was only when we pieced it together later that Maroboduus' plan became clear to us, beginning with the fact that there were more Marcomanni warriors inside Casurgis than we had believed, and that the king had not devoted a significant number of those warriors to defending the town's outer walls. In essence, the wily old king lured our forces into a trap of his making, although thanks to my father's account, we had managed to thwart part of his plan, the Second and Third Cohorts stopping the Marcomanni warriors hidden in the flat section of the town from reaching the flammables lining the walls. This was only part of his plan, however; just as Catualda understood that the goal was to capture or kill Maroboduus himself, so too did the Marcomanni king recognize that killing Catualda was the key to retaining his throne and, quite likely, his head. To that end, he had hidden men away in the double row of buildings, but I am certain that he had expected Catualda to try and bash through the main gate, then advance down the center of the citadel in between those buildings.

Our own change in tactics had forced his hand, yet to his credit, and despite the fact that he was barricaded in his hall, he had not hesitated, managing to signal his warriors to come pouring out into the muddy street that bisected the citadel, with the gates lined up with the doors to the King's hall. As we had seen on the northern side, the buildings on the southern side were constructed so that, while there were gaps between them, they were not wide enough for even a small man to navigate, effectively securing the flanks of the warriors who now blocked the street. From our vantage point, I could not see through the throng of Marcomanni now packed into the space, while Catualda's men were desperately trying to maintain their position in front of the hall. Naturally, the double doors were closed, while hard up against the hall were three ranks of Marcomanni, their backs to the hall, with the Gotones now in between. Despite being unable to see, I could tell by the sounds that Otmar, and the First Cohort were effectively pinned down at the gate, although I could just see the top of the gateway and that the inner doors were sagging off their hinges, but the roofs of the buildings blocked my view of the walls. This took about three or four heartbeats, but while I realized that we needed to act, I did not really know what to do, so I sidled around the back of the mass of Gotones to get closer to Maroboduus' hall, both to get a different view and to find Catualda, since he was not wearing his familiar helmet. I finally spotted him, shouting at his men around him, but while I would not have been able to understand him, it was not difficult to see that he was exhorting them to push the Marcomanni back away from the doors to the hall. Glancing over my shoulder to make sure Alex and Canus were with me, I began shoving my way towards him through the Gotones crammed together, half facing east, and the other half facing Maroboduus' hall. As I reached Catualda's side, he glanced up, his face shining with sweat, but it was the expression of relief that seemed odd given the last time we had been together.

"Centurion, I need your help!" He pointed, not towards his men fighting but at the ground, and it took me a moment to understand what he was pointing at. "We need to use this to batter down the doors, but we do not have room to use it!"

From somewhere, his men had found what looked like a support beam, or perhaps a column, and they had rigged it up with ropes, but he was right; there was not any room to use it. The most immediate problem was the ranks of Marcomanni with their backs to the hall, wrapped around both sides all the way to the wall and who were fighting with a double incentive; not only was their king inside, but they were effectively trapped. However, either because Catualda was overeager, or the pressure by the Marcomanni previously hidden in the buildings were now squeezing the attackers, the press was simply too great, not only to employ the ram, but for either side to do much more than shove their shields against their opponent's and glare over them, spitting curses, or literally spitting at each other, yet another example of how, in this kind of fighting, their spears and long *gladii* were next to useless. Ultimately, it meant that Catualda's men were not whittling the Marcomanni defending the hall down; in fact, I saw perhaps a half-dozen bodies lying in the dirt out of the fifty or so men defending the hall, though this was not the only unusual thing happening. There was a level of the noise that, while not missing altogether, was more muted in the clashing of metal on metal and the thudding when a spear or *gladius* thrust was blocked, consequently making the dominant sound the curses and shouts of men who at least understood each other. At this rate, I thought, this will be decided by the men with the most endurance, and the truth is that in this situation the attacker is always at the disadvantage, having to exert themselves to get to this point, while the defender has the advantage of conserving their energy. It was this thought that got me thinking of other ways to break the impasse, and I suppose it was still in the back of my mind that Maroboduus had wanted to burn us to death, even at the cost of his own capital that got me to not look around but look up, at the thatched roof. Alex, seeing where my gaze went, immediately understood, but he did not agree.

"Surely you're not thinking what I think you are," he began, but rather than get into a protracted discussion, or what passed for one given the circumstances, I simply asked, "Do you have a better idea?"

It only took him a couple of heartbeats, where he scanned the area around us, taking in the situation, and I saw in his expression a look of resignation then.

"No," he admitted. "But what about Catualda? He'll never..."

"Because I'm not going to tell him. But," I took a breath, knowing what I was asking, "he'll notice if I disappear."

"All right." He did not hesitate. "I need to find something I can use to make torches. I'll use four, no," he corrected, "five."

When he did not mention him, I said, "Take Canus with you."

He nodded, then after a brief exchange with Canus, who I noticed did not look surprised, the pair pushed their way back out of the crush towards the northern wall. As they did, I was struck by a sudden thought, or more accurately, a fear, that some Marcomanni had either come looking for their comrades that we had dispatched, or were looking for a way to get into the fight, and I regretted my haste in not leaving any Gotones behind. As was I pushing my way to Catualda, from the eastern side of the citadel came the sound of the *cornu,* and I paused to listen, recognizing the call by Nerva for the Fourth Cohort to join the fight. My first thought was, There's not enough room for another Cohort in here, but I also could not clearly see the situation around the gateway and that end of the citadel, which was about a hundred fifty paces away.

When I got back to Catualda's side, he demanded, "What was that horn, Centurion? What did it mean?"

"Primus Pilus Nerva has summoned the Fourth Cohort to join the First."

"He needs to allow Otmar and my men to resolve this!" he shouted up at me.

"They're not making any headway," I countered, though even as I spoke, I was watching one of his men with their back to the hall facing the gate take advantage of what he saw as a lapse by the Marcomanni across from him, the man actually taking a step back and dropping his shield, not much, but enough that Catualda's man thought to take advantage of it. And, just as I had perceived in my glance, it was a trap, having seen the expression on the face of the Marcomanni to this warrior's left, who was waiting for the Gotones to make a lunge with his spear before swinging his ax down, severing the Gotones outstretched arm at mid-forearm. His scream pierced the underlying noise, one of the few cries of pain during this part of the fight, but Catualda did not even glance in the man's direction.

"I know that!" he snapped. "But have you come up with an idea on how to change that, Centurion? You," he began to point at me, but since he was holding his *gladius* he must have thought better of it, "are the expert in war, are you not? *We must get to that dog, and we must do it now!*"

Before, while Catualda had certainly been excited, there had never been the tinge of hysteria that I was certain I heard now, and judging from the sudden glances of the men around him, they heard the same thing I did.

Feeling decidedly odd doing so, I used the same kind of tone I would with Latobius when he had been startled by a small animal darting across our path, telling the Gotones nobleman, "I have come up with something, Lord. You and your men need to be ready."

"What is it? What do you have planned?"

"It doesn't matter, does it?" I countered.

As I hoped, this shut him up, though I knew it would not be for long. A sudden increase in the noise, originating around the gateway, signaled the arrival of the Fourth Cohort, and above the crowd of helmets, I spotted the Cohort standard just inside the gateway, but while the *Signifer* advanced to a spot roughly even with the eastern edge of the double row of buildings, he got no further, which did not surprise me. With no room to maneuver to either flank, the men jammed so tightly together, and with Otmar and the Gotones facing the Marcomanni, I was concerned that this could last all day. Like all barbarian tribes who thought of themselves as warriors and not as part of a larger unit, they did not have a rotation system that allowed fresh men to take their place, essentially trying to kill each other until one of their foes made a mistake. The First was jammed up against the rear of Otmar's men, and while I had missed it during our move to the northwest corner of the wall, they had already expended their supplies of javelins, drawing blood, but not enough to cause significant casualties, not with what we would count later as three thousand Marcomanni within the citadel's walls. With no way to swap out the Gotones for Nerva's Alaudae, we were at a stalemate, and while I was confident that what we were about to do would break it, I was equally sure that Catualda would not like it; the only question would be how much.

Alex and Canus reappeared from around the corner, waving that they were ready, and while I very briefly considered warning Catualda, I quickly dismissed it, not wanting to risk him intervening, instead raising my turfcutter handle in the signal to go ahead. When I did so, however, I was stricken with a pain so severe that I almost dropped the handle, which reminded me that I had been stabbed in the back...what? I wondered. A third of a watch ago, if that? The stab of agony did have one salutary effect, helping dispel the feeling of lethargy that I had been struggling with, yet in the back of my mind was the niggling fear that the cause of the pain was less from the wound itself, Alex having assured me the spear had not penetrated very deeply, but because there was scrap from my undertunic, or worse, a link from my *hamata* still inside my body. I knew just how quickly the corruption of the body could begin, and in the moment, I thought that this might have been one factor in my reasoning for what Alex and Canus were about to do.

My view of them was partially blocked because they were behind the ranks of Gotones who were across from the Marcomanni who had wrapped themselves around the side of the hall, with the western wall protecting their left flank. This was also the moment when it occurred to me that we could have put some men up on the rampart, and bombard those Marcomanni with missiles, but they had since been expended, just another mistake on a day that seemed filled with them. Shielded from view by the Gotones surrounding that side of the hall, the pair disappeared from my sight as well, it taking a heartbeat to recognize they had crouched down, but then I saw a thin line of smoke an instant before they both stood erect, each holding a torch, and in almost the same motion, they flung them over the heads of the combatants, tumbling end over end, trailing smoke and sparks, but even as they landed in the thatch, I cursed bitterly because I could see that the flames enveloping the cloth they had wrapped around what I learned later I correctly guessed were broken spear shafts had been extinguished by their flight through the air, although they were still smoking.

"Wait for them to catch better!" I shouted, even as I knew it would do no good; there was no way for them to hear me.

Even worse, it got Catualda's attention.

"What are you saying, Centurion?" He tried to laugh, but it failed miserably. "What are you trying to catch?"

"Nothing, Lord," I actually moved slightly to try and block his view, but now that I was facing him instead of the hall, I saw his eyes widen as they followed the tracks of the next pair of torches.

"*What are you doing?*"

The hysterical note returned in full force, and I risked a quick glance over my shoulder. My initial reaction was of disappointment because, while there were two spots on the roof that were smoldering, one near the peak and another farther down but closer to the front, there were no flames.

I sensed more than saw Catualda moving then, and while he did not try and shove me aside, it was clear he was trying to get around me, while shouting in his own tongue what I was certain was a command to try and extinguish the flames. Knowing it was a risk, I still reached out and, none too gently, grabbed him by the neck of his armor, arresting his progress and while I did not intend to, almost yanked him off his feet.

"*Get your hands off me, you Roman dog!*" With his *gladius*, he pointed where, at that instant, Canus was tossing the fifth and final torch, now fully ablaze, while the smoke from the thatch had thickened and, most importantly, I saw the first flickering flames consuming the thatch. "*You are burning my hall! I did not...*"

"*It's not your hall yet!*" I bellowed with just enough power to overwhelm his own shouting but not enough to draw attention beyond the immediate circle of men, although I did release him. In a slightly quieter tone, I continued by pointing out, "You told me to come up with something. And that," I pointed again, "will do it."

Even in this brief moment, the fifth torch, which had landed higher up near the first one near the peak, had already caught, the smoke now becoming thick enough that I could see the heads of the Marcomanni in the rear of the group who were facing Otmar and his men turning to stare up at the roof.

"I did *not* tell you to do that," Catualda snapped, then made to resume moving, but this time, I did not try and stop him, as some of the men around us, now that they had seen what I intended and, even if they did not understand Latin, could see that their presumptive king was unhappy about it had shuffled into something of a protective cordon around him.

I could also see that most of their hearts were not in it, reminding me that these were the most experienced warriors of his warband, and they knew that this was the best, if not the only way to break the deadlock. Five of them followed him as he stalked away, shoving his men aside, but I did not see what he could do to stop it; the roof was now smoking furiously, the flames clearly visible, while the Marcomanni defending the hall were now noticeably alarmed, shouting and gesturing up at the thatch, though none of them along the side moved. I did hear a hammering noise, and when I located the source, I saw a pair of Marcomanni using the butts of their spears to pound on the double doors of the hall, but while they remained closed, they began shouting, though it was too noisy to hear if they were engaged in an exchange with the men inside. I was struck by a sudden thought; a fear, more accurately, that the reason Catualda had summoned men to go with him was that he intended to punish Alex for acting on my orders. This got me moving, and I was none too gentle shoving the Gotones in my path aside, while in my imagination, they were being deliberately slow in moving, but when I spotted Alex and Canus, they were still standing behind the last ranks, with Catualda and his men seemingly nowhere around. When I asked the pair, however, they pointed back towards the eastern wall, and I turned to see the Gotones gathered around a barrel about fifty paces away; it was then I recalled noticing the three barrels that were used to gather rainwater spread along the northern wall of the citadel.

"Pluto's balls," I groaned, "he's going to try and put the fire out."

"Do you want us to stop him?"

I tried to hide my surprise, and pleasure, that it was Canus who asked this, but I did not hesitate to shake my head.

"No. Let this be on his head. He wants to be King," I gave the pair a grim smile, "he's going to have to live with his decisions."

Chapter 7

In what is still one of the most ironic moments in which I have been a part of to this point, when Catualda later declared that it was the decisions he made at Casurgis, and specifically when storming the citadel, that brought him victory and the crown of the Marcomanni, he was actually correct. And, I confess, I should have thought about it myself; while I was counting on the fire to drive Maroboduus and his royal bodyguard inside his hall out into the open, I should have put more faith in the smoke doing the same while doing less damage to the hall. When Catualda had his men throw buckets of water on the thatch by ascending the rampart and running down it to a spot where they were in range and at roughly the same height, while it doused the flames, it also created a thick, choking smoke that within probably no more than a hundred heartbeats, caused the doors and the windows on both sides to be flung open, and while the Marcomanni defenders outside the hall had not moved, the very sight of the doors opening infused Catualda's men with the kind of energy that is so crucial in the final and critical stage of a fight. Almost literally scenting victory, the Gotones closed with their foes, and I must give Catualda credit; he had returned to his spot and was leading the way. Unfortunately, smoke is indiscriminate in its victims, and when it came roiling out through the open doors, it struck both sides with crippling effect. In fact, it was a bit worse for Catualda and his men because, facing the hall as they were, they took the full force of the smoke, and the embers, some of them catching on warriors' tunics, and in at least two cases I saw, men's beards, causing them to drop their weapons and shields as they beat frantically at their face. The other change was in the noise, as men started choking and coughing even as they were now thrusting and swinging wildly at an enemy only half-seen as their eyes filled with tears, and while there is no way to know, I suspect that the casualties from this part of the battle was just as likely inflicted by a friend as a foe, on both sides.

Once I made sure that Alex and Canus were unharmed, the three of us went back to around the front of the hall, but removed to the side of the door just enough that we did not get the full effects of the smoke that boiled out in a horizontal column before turning upward into the sky, yet despite pulling up my neckerchief to cover my mouth and nose, I was still coughing, while my eyes burned and streamed, just not as badly as those in the direct path of it. Nerva's warning to me, to stay close to Catualda and, more importantly, to protect Maroboduus from being killed if possible, was foremost in my mind, so I did keep my eye on him as, for the first time, he showed a real eagerness for battle, pushing his way to the front of his men, hacking and chopping away at any Marcomanni who stood before him. From behind us, out in the open area between the buildings, the noise level had increased as well, and I risked a glance in that direction, though it was as much to blink away the tears so my vision cleared as to see why, but I was just in time to see Roman javelins arcing through the air, telling me that Nerva had ordered the Fourth Cohort to pass their javelins forward since the eagle was in the same spot it had been just behind Otmar's force. And, this time, amidst the screams, curses, and the hollow thumping of missiles caught by Marcomanni shields, I saw a rippling of movement back in my direction as the Marcomanni faltered. This elicited a roar from our combined forces, and I did manage to spot Catualda's raven-winged helmet on Otmar's head moving forward, his bloody *gladius* thrust into the air. This, I understood, was *the* moment, that moment when the battle hangs in the balance, and this spurred me to move as quickly as I could to reach Catualda. Perhaps the gods decided to do me a favor, because just as I reached a spot behind him, he slew a Marcomanni, and for a brief instant, there was no enemy warrior between the Gotones nobleman and the doorway. The interior should have been visible between the open doors and the fact that the windows had been thrown open, but the smoke was sufficiently thick enough that it resembled a dark cave, the situation practically screaming for caution, yet I was not surprised when Catualda went rushing into the hall. Nevertheless, I was a step behind him as he plunged into the darkness, and to our left, I sensed a rush of movement, but it was the piercing scream of a woman that stayed my hand, although she was little more than a darting shape in the gloom. It did not stop Catualda, however, from pivoting to face in her direction, and I saw the glint of his blade as he plunged it into her body, cutting her off in mid-scream, which turned into a breathy moan as she collapsed onto what I noticed was actually a wooden floor, though it was covered in rushes. She had barely hit the floor when there was a bellow of rage, but this one came from the right side of the hall, and there was no way that Catualda could have turned and brought his shield up in time.

Since I was still facing the rear of the building, I actually left my feet by taking a hopping step while twisting my body to land directly in the path of what I could now see was a burly warrior, older than me but with several arm rings and armed with a *gladius*, though not the longer Gallic style with a more rounded tip that most Germans used. Indeed, it looked very much like a Spanish *gladius*, which made sense, and made it more dangerous, in the closer confines of the hall, and his shield was also much smaller than normal for a German, round and about the size of a platter, with a spike protruding from the boss. A random thought struck me that he looked like a gladiator, and within less than a heartbeat, he demonstrated that it was more than appearance as he began his attack not with his *gladius* but with the shield. I am also somewhat ashamed to say that he caught me by surprise, and while I managed to dodge the thrust by twisting at the waist so that the point only nicked the inside of my right arm just below the edge of my *hamata* instead of where he aimed in the center of my chest, the pain from the slice to my bicep was a shade compared to the unexpected stab of agony to my lower back caused by the sudden motion. Perhaps my bellow of pain, along with the gloom and our stinging eyes led him to believe that he had inflicted more damage than he actually had, or perhaps the habits formed during his time in the sand, since he was later identified as a Chatti who had escaped from a *ludus* a couple years earlier, made him decide that I was ready for the kill. Whatever the reason, I am grateful for it, because instead of launching an immediate thrust while I was vulnerable, he grinned at me.

"I will enjoy killing you, Roman," he taunted me, in surprisingly good Latin. "I have killed *many* men bet..."

If the hall had not been so dark and the smoke so thick, maybe I would not have killed him as easily as I did...but I do not believe that is the case. I think that if we had been outside, I would have still moved more quickly, and because he was slightly distracted with his boasting, he still would not have gotten his shield over in time, although I will say that if he had been using the standard-sized shield favored by the German tribes, he might have blocked it, or at the very least knocked the point of my *gladius* aside so that it did not pierce his heart. I did not bother twisting the blade, knowing that my thrust was fatal as much by the feel as anything, and I needed to return my attention to Catualda, who had just stepped over the corpse of the slain woman, barely giving her a glance as he peered into the darkness towards the back of the hall. We were still on the other side of the large fire pit in the center, and the hall was of a sufficient size that it was hard to make out any details beyond it, other than there was a line of warriors, standing on a raised platform, upon which sat a high backed chair where a lone figure stood, and I caught the barest glint of some sort of metal in the area of the figure's head, assuming that this was Maroboduus and the gleaming metal was his crown. The hall behind us was now filling up with Catualda's men, as most of the Marcomanni had retreated to the far side of the firepit, forming a double line just ahead of the men I was certain were members of the royal bodyguard, though several warriors were cut down before they could join their comrades. Outside, the fighting was reaching its height, though I did not shift my gaze away from the scene before me because Alex was just behind me, murmuring to me about what was taking place.

"It looks like the Marcomanni outside are about done," he informed me. "And I can see the eagle has gotten next to Otmar and his bunch. It looks like they finally moved aside."

That was a welcome development, but inside, the noise had gradually died down, although Catualda still had to raise his voice near a shout. Naturally, all I understood was "Maroboduus," but I also heard the lack of deference, or even courtesy in his voice, just the harshness of a man who knows he is the victor. Interestingly, whatever it was he said clearly angered Maroboduus' bodyguards more than it seemed to do to the Marcomanni king, and now that I was closer, I could see his features more clearly, though I still had to wipe my eyes regularly. He was in his late forties, with iron gray hair that was pulled back, and a beard that, somewhat surprisingly, was neatly trimmed, and without any kind of adornments like knuckle bones. I was not surprised to see that, even with his age, he was still powerfully built, with a chest that, though not as large as mine, was still impressive, while his arms were just beginning to sag a bit, something that Bronwen loves to tease me about, how she looks forward to the day when I begin to sag in places.

"Then," she likes to say with a wagging finger, "you will have an idea of how it feels to be a woman after she has borne children!"

It was, I confess, an odd thought to have in the moment, and I almost laughed, but I managed to refrain. Maroboduus did not speak until Catualda stopped, and when he did, I was surprised at how his voice did not match his appearance, sounding much younger, more vibrant and powerful. When he began speaking, he did not sound defiant but matter-of-fact, though I noticed that he kept indicating the men standing in front of him, each of whom looked ready and willing to continue the fighting, but when he pointed at the corpse of the slain woman, for the first time he seemed truly angry, while Catualda's response was to mutter something in their tongue, while the shrug that accompanied his words communicated his indifference. In the moment, my assumption was that Maroboduus' anger stemmed from the idea of killing a woman; I would be learning differently shortly.

Suddenly, and without any hint he was about to do so, Maroboduus suddenly pointed at me, and asked in even better Latin than the man I had slain moments before, "What is your name, Centurion? And are you with the 5th Legion out there?"

Despite my surprise, I replied immediately, "My name is Gnaeus Volusenianus Pullus. And no," I shook my head, "no, I'm not in the 5th. I am..."

"You are in the 1st Legion," Maroboduus cut me off, and I felt my mouth drop in astonishment, but I was premature because he was about to surprise me even further. "You are the Centurion commanding the Fourth Cohort, and your father was Titus Pullus, also of the 1st."

"H-how did you know that?" I managed to gasp, barely noticing the sudden look of alarm on Catualda's face, while in the back of my mind was the urge to correct him, since that was my old rank, though it was a bit much to expect him to know something that was just a couple months old.

Either my words or the surprise with which I uttered them actually elicited a chuckle from the Marcomanni king.

"How could I not know that?" he countered. "You are a giant among Romans, you are a Centurion, and," he shrugged, "your father was famous, even among the tribes you Romans call the Germans. I saw him once, though it was long ago, and you favor him in your face as well as your size." His expression turned grave, and he inclined his head in what I took to be a show of respect. "I heard that he fell when you were rescuing Segestes and taking Herman's wife hostage. I offered a sacrifice to Tyr in his name when I heard." There was no way to know if this was true, especially given what was about to happen, but I chose, and choose to believe that he was sincere. Turning his attention to Catualda, Maroboduus continued, his tone changing to one of unmistakable scorn, "As I am sure you know, my...nephew," he managed to make the familial term sound like a curse, "is demanding that I surrender my kingship to him. And," for the first time, his mask slipped, and I could see the bitterness and, even worse, the helplessness that comes from recognizing the inevitable, "he swears that I will be allowed to live, and to depart to wherever I choose to go." Catualda, now that the conversation seemed to be back on his concerns, began nodding emphatically, but Maroboduus was not through. "I do not believe him," he said flatly. "I believe that at the first opportunity, he will cut my throat," he swallowed hard, then turned at the waist to indicate the space behind him, "and those of my wives and small children..." suddenly, he thrust a finger to point, not at Catualda, or me, but at the dead woman, "...just as he slew his own aunt." I heard someone gasp, only dimly realizing that it was me, although Alex said later that he did as well, and it was only then I also realized that there were several people, three adult women, and six children of varying ages, huddled behind the raised platform.

"That is *not* true!" Catualda protested. "I did not recognize her because of all the smoke! I just saw someone rushing at me, and I reacted as any warrior would! I give you my word that..."

"Your word!" Maroboduus cut him off with lacerating scorn. "Your word is worthless, Catualda!" Pointing again, not at him but outside the hall, "I knew about Chariovalda and his treachery weeks ago! I knew that you had bribed him and those thirty-two other nobles, after I gave them lands and honors, and it will be to their family and clan's shame that they listened to you and betrayed their king! No!" He spat on the floor to emphasize his point. "Your word cannot be trusted!" Turning back to me, Maroboduus asked, "Centurion Pullus, do you swear on your Legion eagle that you will protect my family and myself from my nephew?"

What other answer can I give? I thought with more than a little dismay, and I desperately wanted a moment to confer with Alex, but in a moment that proved how well he knew me, I heard him whisper, "You don't have any choice but to give your word, Gnaeus."

"I do." I was about to add "Your Highness," but I had the sense that this might prove too much for Catualda to bear, and he was already staring at me with a poisonous hatred. "I will make sure that you and your family remain safe, and will be escorted from Casurgis."

"Then," he drew himself up, and despite myself, I was impressed with the deposed king as he said with a ponderous dignity, "I will order my warriors to lay down their arms."

I was about to bring up the need for Maroboduus to ensure the safety of his warriors, but Maroboduus understood better than I did there was no need, although perhaps it was for my benefit that he still addressed Catualda in Latin.

"I do not believe that I have to ask you to spare my warriors, and that you will treat them fairly, do I...*nephew*?"

"No, Uncle," Catualda assured him without hesitation. Then, again I believe for my benefit and as a way to assuage my concerns, he pointed out, "We still have to worry about Herman, do we not?" Perhaps he felt a twinge of guilt and wanted to offer a sop to Maroboduus, or who knows? Perhaps he was being sincere when he said, "I can only hope to make him pay as much as you did, Uncle. I have heard that he is not going to budge from the Sudetes because you made him pay a heavier cost than he wanted."

For a moment, the old king's hostile mask slipped, and he sighed. "My warriors fought bravely, but we were severely outnumbered." I saw a sudden glimmer in his eyes, and his voice took on a pleading quality. "You must keep Herman from moving, Catualda. He *cannot* take any more of our land!"

"I swear it, Uncle," Catualda replied, and for the first time since I had been in his company, he at least seemed to understand the gravity of the moment, and the burden of kingship.

It did not appear to me that Maroboduus was convinced, but he lowered his voice to address his men, and while it was clear they did not like it; one man actually argued for a couple of heartbeats, gesturing emphatically at Catualda, which made me wonder if I would be faced with the choice of putting myself in between this bodyguard and the Gotones nobleman, and how, while I would do it, my heart would not really be in protecting Catualda. Maroboduus listened, then placed a hand on the warrior's shoulder, his voice and expression grave, but what mattered was that his words had the intended effect, the bodyguard's head bowing and, most importantly, dropping his *gladius* onto the floor. This sent a signal to the others, creating a clattering racket as weapons were surrendered, and Catualda snapped an order over his shoulder that sent his men hurrying to gather them up off the floor, which created another dispute. For a long moment, as the volume of the squabbling rose and became more pointed, I braced myself for one of Maroboduus' men to try and snatch his weapon back from one of the Gotones who had confiscated it. Catualda intervened, and there was another exchange that seemed to ease the tension; more importantly, the confiscation resumed.

While he obviously did not want to, Catualda deigned to explain in Latin, "Some of Maroboduus' bodyguards were concerned that their weapons would not be returned to them, and they are valuable to these men, both because of their quality and they have been passed down from their fathers or grandfathers." He did smile then, but it was more ironic in nature, which I understood when he added, "You can understand their concern, can you not, Centurion? Given that." He pointed at my *gladius*, which was still in my hand and I had not yet wiped down, saying nothing more.

"Yes, I can."

It was all I could think to say, although it did prompt me to walk over and, as is the custom, though I have no idea why we do it, made sure to wipe my blade clean on the tunic of the German I had slain, despite the fact that the body of the woman belonging to Catualda was closer, and there was more fabric to her gown. Again, I did this without thinking, so I was unable to completely stifle my groan as I bent over, and I realized that I was stiffening up more with almost every passing heartbeat. Despite the pain, my eyes also went to the arm rings, which again by custom were mine, this one not just unique to Romans but one that is commonly held by warriors of all nations and tribes that I have encountered or heard about, yet something caused me to glance over at Catualda, and I saw him fixedly staring at me, seemingly oblivious to everything and everyone else. I confess that there was a part of me that wanted to take the rings, but I restrained myself, standing erect while biting my lip so I didn't groan again. The weapons had been collected, and the hall itself had fallen deathly quiet, which made for a jarring contrast compared to the fighting outside. Since I had not looked in that direction for some time, I was shocked to see how much closer our combined forces had gotten; the Alaudae eagle was no more than fifty paces away from the doorway to the right, and I spotted Otmar's borrowed helmet just a bit farther away to the left. How, I wondered, is

Maroboduus going to get his men to stop fighting? On the heels of that came another thought: What if his men do not listen?

I moved to stand next to Alex and Canus, watching as Maroboduus walked, slowly, down the center of the hall, around the firepit then to the doorway, though he did not immediately step outside. His head moved as he scanned the jumbled mass of combatants, making me think he was looking for someone, which he confirmed when he cupped his hands to his mouth, and shouted a name. Naturally, several heads of the men not currently engaged turned, and some of them were within my line of sight and I saw the expressions of surprise and shock, which quickly transformed into one of dismay as men saw that Maroboduus was not alone, Catualda standing just behind him but off to the side so that he was plainly visible. The warrior he summoned, who was only a few years younger than the Marcomanni king, had to shove his way through the mass of men to reach Maroboduus. Watching his face was instructive, but when he opened his mouth, clearly intending on arguing, Maroboduus cut him off with a sharp word, whereupon the warrior briefly closed his eyes before offering a deep bow, then turned about and began bellowing. Suddenly, I realized that I had a role to play by getting Nerva's attention and somehow signaling him that Maroboduus was surrendering. Looking around, I saw an overturned bench, ran over to it, and with Canus' help, dragged it to a spot just outside the doorway and immediately behind Maroboduus and Catualda, hopping up onto it then almost falling back off because of the sharp stab of pain. I managed to stay on, and now I towered over everyone, yet I still held my *gladius* up in the air and began waving it back and forth as I willed Nerva, who I spotted by his white crest standing next to his *Aquilifer*, to see me. At the moment, he had his back turned, and I glimpsed a Centurion with a black crest facing him, and he was actually the man who spotted me first, then I saw Nerva turn as the Centurion pointed. A heartbeat later, he raised his *vitus* in the signal that he saw and, more importantly, understood my purpose in signaling him something important. Making the movement slow and deliberate, I turned my *gladius* from its posture pointing at the sky, then slowly rotated it so the point was aimed at the ground, then lowered my arm, again doing so slowly, making the symbolic gesture of dropping my weapon. My reward was the sound of a *cornu* a couple of heartbeats later, and between Maroboduus' man shouting the same thing over and over and the Legionaries who were engaged with the Marcomanni taking a step backward, while keeping their shields up of course, breaking off their assault, the noise level began dropping, until about fifteen heartbeats after the *cornu* sounded the call, the noise of fighting ceased altogether. Casurgis and its citadel had fallen, Maroboduus was no longer the King of the Marcomanni, and I now had another challenge facing me, because I was certain that Catualda would try and kill Maroboduus.

The reign of King Catualda began in an inauspicious manner, when he announced that the men of the Alaudae would not be allowed to take any spoils, which unsurprisingly was not a popular decision on his part, and for about two parts of a watch, it appeared that his reign would be cut short by an angry Roman Legion. Finally, he agreed to pay a sum that equaled three hundred *denarii* per man, a thousand for the officers, but while Nerva refused to discuss it, I am certain he got substantially more. One mystery was solved; my guess that the citizens of Casurgis had fled to the citadel was wrong, but neither were they cowering inside their own homes, although as always with a few thousand people, there were a couple hundred who had refused to leave their dwellings, most of these people dying. The cleft between the two hills actually ran all the way between them to the river, the flat ground between them gradually narrowing until it was a narrow defile that could not accommodate more than four people standing side by side, and hidden away behind a stand of trees between the riverbank and the defile were a few dozen boats. These had been used to ferry the citizens across the river, where they had settled and waited to see the fate of their homes; it also explained why Maroboduus had at least appeared to be willing to burn his town down around us.

The force of Marcomanni hidden in the dwellings and shops in the flat part of the town had numbered five hundred warriors, and they had been slaughtered by the Second and Third Cohorts almost to a man, with only a few dozen prisoners taken, but it was the question of the other, larger number of warriors who had been defending the citadel that was the second crisis of the new King's reign. It began with Maroboduus' bodyguards, who were being held in the hall now that the smoke had cleared out, although the odor of burned thatch still hung heavy in the air, there now being several ragged holes in the roof through which sunlight came streaming down, making it brighter in the hall than it had been in some time, I was sure. Alex, Canus, and I were still inside, and for the moment were being largely ignored, while Nerva and his Quartus Pilus Prior had entered, along with Otmar, the two Gotones embracing and talking excitedly while Maroboduus, now with his wives and children out in the open, looked on impassively, impressing me with his self-control. His three surviving women, who ranged in age from a woman who was close to Maroboduus' age to one I felt certain was barely out of her teens were not so circumspect, although the eldest and the one I guessed was now the senior wife by default, was more composed than the other two, who clutched each other, sobbing on the other woman's shoulder, while the younger children huddled around their mothers, the youngest who was a bit older than Titus and toddling about, clutching the younger wife's gown with one hand, while the thumb on his other hand was stuck in his mouth.

The dispute began when Catualda gave orders to some of his men still in the hall; the bulk of his men were now outside the citadel, ostensibly to secure the town and relieve the men of the Alaudae, but I suspected that this had been the work of Nerva, who wanted to separate the Gotones from Maroboduus' warriors while passions were still high, something that he confirmed later. What those orders were became clear when some of them began to try and separate Maroboduus' bodyguards from their king, and it quickly became heated, while Maroboduus did and said nothing; to my eyes, he looked disinterested in the whole affair. The volume of the dispute between Catualda, Otmar, and their men and the warrior I had identified as the commander of Maroboduus' bodyguard rose as the other men on both sides began adding their voices, the gestures becoming more emphatic. Since the bodyguards were disarmed, it would be a slaughter, and I continued looking to Nerva, but he looked more bemused than anything, and finally, I could not refrain.

Clearing my throat, when this did not work, I just interrupted, addressing Catualda, "What's the issue, Lord Catualda?"

I should have known better, and Catualda snapped, "Do you not mean *King* Catualda, Centurion? Or," he added in what I am certain he thought was a magnanimous gesture, "Your Highness if you prefer." There was no way that I was going to do the latter, though I did manage to force an apology through my teeth, then repeated my question. "Oh," he gave a dismissive wave at the bodyguard commander, "he's reminding me of the oath that every man of a royal bodyguard must make to never leave their king's side. And," he added crossly, "I reminded this oaf that Maroboduus is no longer king, *I* am, so he is no longer bound by that oath."

Without thinking, I turned to address Maroboduus, and while I was sorely tempted to address him as "Your Highness" just to irritate Catualda, I managed to refrain, but I did speak respectfully, "Have you told your bodyguard commander that you are under my protection now?"

I got my answer in his expression of chagrin, though he admitted, "No, Centurion Pullus." He actually gave a tight, humorless smile. "I suppose that it slipped my mind." Turning to the commander, while the warrior and his men clearly did not like it, by the time Maroboduus was through speaking, this crisis was averted, but it also reminded me that Nerva had not been present for the surrender, and I had not had a chance to speak to him about the condition.

There was one final exchange between Catualda and Maroboduus, and we learned what it was when the new king, his cousin, and several men walked directly to the platform, but rather than sit on it, Catualda had the throne lifted off the platform, it taking two men to handle the heavy, ornately carved wooden chair, but he was not through. The next task took a full half-dozen men to move the wooden platform;

naturally, this made us intensely curious, and I found myself standing next to Nerva, every Roman present having moved to within a few feet, standing just on the far side of the firepit. Our position gave us a perfect view of the yawning hole underneath the platform, down into which led a set of wooden stairs, the darkness in the hole obscuring what lay beneath the hall.

"Pluto's thorny *cock*," Nerva breathed. "That must be their treasury."

Since the torches and hanging lamps had been extinguished, there was a brief wait as some were struck into life, and as we waited, I glanced over at Maroboduus, now almost completely forgotten, yet his face gave nothing away, and I wondered what it must feel like losing everything but one's life in the space of a day. Unsurprisingly, Catualda insisted on leading the way, but equally so was Otmar stepping in his path, shaking his head as he pointed down into the cavern, undoubtedly reminding Catualda that he must begin thinking like a king, and no king would venture into the unknown first. This did make me wonder if perhaps one reason Maroboduus did not seem overly perturbed was that, down below, he had one final surprise waiting, but another glance at him did not offer any clue. Nevertheless, when Catualda relented and Otmar descended the stairs, which I could see were broad enough for two men to negotiate side by side, I realized that I was holding my breath. However, when the cry came, it was not of alarm but of amazement, and awe, prompting Catualda to snatch another torch and dash down the stairs, while the Gotones remaining up above all crowded around the entrance, waiting for their king to give permission to descend, I supposed. A glance at Nerva earned a shrug, along with a grin that communicated we were of a like mind, and we both sidled up to stand behind the Gotones, with Alex and Canus right behind us, although I was the only one of us who could see much, but what little I did see caused me to let out a low whistle, which of course startled the Gotones warriors, the one directly in front of me whirling about. When he saw that it was me, however, and I recognized him as one of the men who had helped me repel the Marcomanni attempt to get behind us, he gave me a gap-toothed grin.

In heavily accented Latin, he said, "We are rich, Roman. Very, very rich."

Judging from the iron-bound chests stacked two high that stretched out into the darkness beyond the edge of Catualda's torchlight, this was true; the uproarious and delighted laughter of Catualda and Otmar just made it that much clearer.

Unsurprisingly, no Roman was allowed to descend into the cavern, but from Maroboduus, we learned that it was even larger than the hall above it, and as Catualda had assured me weeks earlier, was crammed full of wealth, in the form of gold, silver, jewels, and jewelry, the result of generations of raiding and trading.

"It is a natural cavern that has been enlarged over time," Maroboduus explained, his tone flat and emotionless, making me wonder if what was clearly a state of shock would wear off, and if it did, what he might do then. "It was one reason my ancestor and first King of the Marcomanni chose this hill to build his hall on. Casurgis," he shrugged, "grew up around this citadel."

With Catualda understandably preoccupied gloating over his new wealth and status, after consulting with Nerva, and explaining to him that I had agreed to take on the responsibility for protecting Maroboduus and his family, the Primus Pilus decided that this would be a good time to escort the deposed king and family out of Casurgis and back to our camp.

"I'm giving you a section as an escort," Nerva informed me, "but I'm going to have to stay put and make sure the boys don't do anything stupid and make sure they know they're not going away emptyhanded. And," he finished with a sigh and a sidelong glance, "that they don't get greedy."

He did not explain any further, but there was no need for him to do so; I understood both his words and his concern completely. Yes, the news of a cash bonus would help assuage his men, but that did not mean that they would not try and sneak choice bits of loot from the dwellings, either behind their officers' backs, or almost as commonly, with the promise of sharing the proceeds of what they found. As time passes, and given who will be reading this in the coming years, I would be remiss if I did not at least mention that, at that time, it was only three years after the revolt of the Legions of the Rhenus and Pannonia, and there was an argument put forth during this period that this behavior was a holdover from the anger and resentment that the rankers felt that led to the mutiny. I had not been under the standard all that long when the mutiny occurred, and if I had not been exposed to the wisdom of my father and Marcus Macer, both of whom had been in much longer than I at that point, I would probably have accepted this explanation. However, it was actually reading the words of my great-grandfather the Prefect that enables me to say with confidence that this is an excuse used by apologists, because he made it clear in his account that this attitude predated the mutiny by decades. More than anything, I remember hearing my father say something that, at the time, I had wondered where he had gotten it from, and I learned where by reading the Prefect's words.

"Legionaries are only concerned with fairness when it's to their advantage," he had said first, and my father had repeated more times than I can count, both verbally and in his own account.

And now, young Titus and whatever future brothers you may have, you are hearing it from me. Regardless of the origin, it was something that I understood very well, and we left Nerva at the ruined citadel gate giving orders to the Centurions of his Cohort with an agreement that he would return to camp as soon as he could. I ordered the Sergeant, of Nerva's Tenth Section, to send a pair of men ahead of us with instructions to warn of us of any possible trouble spots, my concern being that there might be Marcomanni warriors who had yet to be rounded up and escorted under guard down to the flat part of the town, where they were being held in the only open area large enough, the market square. Seeing their king under guard by only a section of men, even if they were Roman, might prove a tempting target for a rescue attempt, hence my caution, yet something quite different took place. For the most part, the dwellings and businesses that occupied the citadel hill appeared undamaged, but most striking was the lack of bodies, another sign that Maroboduus' strategy had been to put up an initial resistance along the eastern wall, then immediately withdraw up the hill to the citadel. Oh, there were a few doors that were either sagging on their hinges and hanging open, or had been knocked down, and there were items scattered about in the mud streets, indicating that a home or shop had been ransacked, all of which Maroboduus took in with a stony expression, for the first time showing a hint of anger, though I did not have much sympathy for him. I was tempted to ask him how many towns and villages had he and his Marcomanni had sacked, how many homes had they invaded and taken anything of value that was now stuffed in chests up above us in his hall. I did not, partially because I did not want to elicit a reaction that could cause us issues, but also because, even in our short association, I realized that I liked Maroboduus; in fact, I already liked him more than I liked Catualda by this point, and not for the first, nor would it be the last, I wondered if Drusus' judgement about Catualda had been faulty. None of which mattered, I reminded myself, and by this time, we had descended down to the flat part of the town, where for the first time the scene looked more like a town taken by assault.

There was still a pall of smoke hanging in the air in between the two hills though there were no active fires from what we could see, but it was first the sound, then the sight of what *was* taking place that brought us to a standstill. It began with a clearly feminine shriek of terror from the building on the opposite corner of the intersection we had just reached, eliciting gasps from Maroboduus' women, and moans of fear from the children, but then things became infinitely worse when a pair of Legionaries emerged from the building, one of the few two story structures, the sign that it had belonged to someone of means, each of them grasping the arm of a struggling woman. I say she was a woman; if anything, she was the same age as Maroboduus' youngest wife, perhaps a bit younger, with golden hair and a fair complexion, and even though her face was contorted with terror and smeared with dirt, a tactic women often use to disguise their looks, it was clear to see that she was a rare beauty. And, as I knew every adult present was aware, what the pair of rankers had planned gave this Marcomanni girl good cause to be out of her mind with terror, yet when I stepped out into the intersection so they could clearly see me, not only did they not release the girl, or even look guilty about being caught, they both actually gave what could only be called an insolent grin as they continued dragging her in my direction.

"Gnaeus," Alex called out quietly. "Look behind you."

I did, and to my shock, I first saw the red crest of a Pilus Prior before I recognized that it belonged to the Secundus, facing my direction and giving no sign whatsoever that he intended to intervene, although I waited for the pair of rankers to take their prize past him, watching as he ignored the girl's pleas to him, clearly understanding that he was of some importance. For a moment, I thought that perhaps they were actually taking her to the market square, which was in the general direction they were headed, but then they reached the next intersection, and ducked out of sight to the right and away from the square.

Stalking up to the Secundus, I did not bother saluting, nor was I particularly respectful when I confronted him, saying, "The Primus Pilus gave explicit orders that all civilian prisoners were not to be molested...in any way."

"Really?" He not only shrugged, but then gave a yawn as if this was of such little notice that he was actually bored. "I've received no such orders."

"I saw him send runners to each of his Pili Priores," I shot back, which was not a lie exactly, though it was an exaggeration, but this did not seem to faze him.

"Oh? I haven't received any runners, from the Primus Pilus or anyone else." The smile he gave me was so smug that I actually felt an itch in my palm that made me want to ball my hand up into a fist and punch him in the face. "Besides, how do you know those rankers are mine? You haven't been with us long enough to recognize every man and what Cohort they belong to, Pullus."

"That's true," I acknowledged, but his smile vanished when I said, "and maybe it's different in the Alaudae, but a good Centurion in the 1st wouldn't let any ranker violate the orders of the Primus Pilus. But," now it was my turn to shrug, "maybe you do things...differently."

I am fairly confident that he was the one who wanted to take a swing then, although we both knew he would never do that, yet I also knew there was nothing I could do either, so I spun about and stalked back to the party. We resumed walking, and there was no way to avoid the bodies of the Marcomanni warriors he had left behind to try and spring his fiery trap.

"Thank you for trying to save that maiden, Centurion," Maroboduus broke the silence. "That was an honorable thing to do."

I could almost hear the unspoken part, "for a Roman," but I nodded in recognition that I had heard him.

Then, completely on impulse, I asked him, "Would you really have burned your capital down around us just to kill us all?"

He did not seem surprised at the question, and given the manner in which he responded, I suspect his thoughts had been running along the same lines, yet I was still startled when he answered, "I do not know, Centurion." He sighed heavily before he continued, "I know that a leader must never make a threat that he is not willing to carry out, and I will say that when I gave the orders, I meant them to be carried out. Not," he added bitterly, "that it mattered." We continued in relative silence for a few paces, with the top of the eastern wall and main gate now visible over the roofs and save for the quiet sobs of Maroboduus' women and children, forced to confront the sight of the bodies of their own warriors, although there were a fair number of Gotones corpses present; the Roman wounded and whatever dead there were had already been removed. Suddenly, he asked in a tone that I took to be genuine curiosity, "How did you know what I had planned, Centurion?" I glanced at him just in time to see his features twist into a bitter grimace. "Did that faithless dog Chariovalda manage to get word to Catualda somehow?"

I was about to lie and tell him he had guessed correctly, or perhaps offer something noncommittal that could be taken either way; instead, I heard myself saying, "Actually, no. You could say that it was my father."

Naturally, this intrigued him, although I saw he did not

believe me, but I was honest about it, telling the story of Raetinium and how that had been on my mind, which in turn led me to recall reading about it.

Once I was finished, he considered this for a moment, then said honestly, "I do not know how I feel about that, Centurion, but I suspect that if we ever meet in the afterlife, I would thank your father for saving me from a decision I would likely regret the rest of my days."

We had reached the main gate by this time, the discarded ram still smoldering next to the remains of the heavy wooden gates, and when we exited Casurgis, he stopped again, turning to look at it, and for the first time, there was no mistaking his deep hurt and sadness.

"I wonder if I will ever see Casurgis again," he said in Latin, then turned and murmured something in his tongue to his family, whereupon they collapsed together, huddling around him in an awkward and extended embrace, leaving the rest of us to stand there, unsure what to do.

We resumed our journey to the camp then, reaching the *Porta Praetoria,* where I released the Tenth Section to return to report to their Primus Pilus they had accomplished their task, while I realized that I had no idea where to lead a deposed king and his family. Ultimately, I took them to our tent while sending Alex off to Nerva's to make arrangements with his clerk to find some shelter for them, and we settled down inside to wait for the return of the Alaudae.

The sun was setting when the Alaudae marched into camp, minus the third line Cohorts, one of which Nerva had ordered to remain behind in Casurgis to supervise the return of the Marcomanni civilians from across the river, this having begun about mid-afternoon, and the other two guarding the Marcomanni warriors who had remained faithful to Maroboduus, in a hastily constructed enclosure taking up the market square. Nerva and his men did not come emptyhanded, but along with the chests loaded into two carts, there were two more loaded down with wine; Nerva told me later that Catualda had also offered a quantity of mead, but the Primus Pilus had, wisely in my mind, turned it down. It is not just that mead is more intoxicating; there is something in it that unleashes a wildness in men that makes every man wearing a transverse crest or the white stripe of the Optio regret it when one of their men manages to get their hands on a supply. This was one of the few times I actually was somewhat disappointed at the lack of mead, thinking that it would help dull the pain in my lower back that seemed to intensify almost by the moment, and as soon as Alex returned from hurrying off to make sure that Maroboduus' women and children were fed, with his help, I got my *hamata* off, then tunic and undertunic, yet despite bracing myself for bad news, I was even more unprepared for what he actually said.

"There are no links missing," he told me, although at that moment, he was still concerned because all of the bouncing around the spear did when I continued running, tearing not just the muscles of my lower back but the fabric of both tunic and padded shirt, making it next to impossible to match the edges cleanly, the primary method *medici* use to determine whether there are pieces of fabric in the wound, but it was not until he examined me, ignoring my moans of pain for the most part, other than snapping at me to stop behaving like one of the children who were watching wide-eyed, before he pronounced, "It will take about ten stitches, but I'm about as sure as I can be that it's clean and there's nothing in it."

"Then why is it so sore?" I grumbled, but he was not sympathetic in the slightest.

"Because you *did* get stabbed with a spear and continued moving after you were hit. And," he added wickedly, "you're not getting younger." He did not say anything else, yet he must have made a face, because suddenly, Maroboduus' children began giggling, but when I glared down at him over my shoulder, he looked unrepentant. "I'll wrap it tighter than normal," he said. "That should help support it and help the muscles that were torn by the spearpoint bouncing around to heal. But," he warned, "you need to let me know the instant you feel feverish."

"I thought you said it was a clean wound!" I protested.

"And," he replied tartly, "I might be wrong. Unlike you, I don't have a problem admitting that."

"Oh, go piss on your boots," I growled, though it was with an expression and I said it in such a way that, as I hoped, made the children giggle again.

While the women still seemed in a daze, all three of them refusing food, like all children, the youngsters had been quickly revived by sustenance, and were clearly intensely curious about the camp around them, especially now that the novel event of seeing the huge Roman getting patched up was over, and it was not long before, after catching the oldest girl trying to sneak out of the tent, I gave Canus the job of watching them as they wandered around the camp, clearly not thinking it through very well. If he had looked nervous before the assault, now he looked almost terrified, while Alex, who had been standing opposite of Varro's man and out of his eyeline, stared at me in open incredulity, but I did not change my mind.

Instead, I said, only half-jokingly, "You're forbidden from tying them down, Canus. And," I added without thinking, "don't kill any of them."

This was the moment we learned that at least one of Maroboduus' wives understood our tongue, because from behind us came a sudden moan of terror, and when I turned around, I saw that it was the middle wife who was clutching one of the children to her, staring up at me with horrified eyes. Thankfully, Maroboduus, who had heard the exchange, understood the rough humor I was employing, and he stepped in, soothing his women with an assuring tone, undoubtedly telling them that I was only jesting, even if it was in poor taste. With my wound tended to and the children gone, I finally was able to eat my own meal, but just as the spoon was about to reach my mouth, the *cornu* sounded the call for all senior officers to meet with Nerva. I confess that I thought about ignoring it since I held no post in the Alaudae, but not only had I been attending all such meetings, there would undoubtedly be a discussion of what came next, so I dropped the spoon into my bowl, knowing myself well enough that actually eating a bite of food would only make my hunger worse, cursing Nerva and the Fates as I did so. Snatching up my *vitus*, I left the tent, and the first thing I saw was a line of children scampering down the street towards the forum, with Canus following behind, shouting at them to slow down.

He glanced over his shoulder and saw me, scowling at me as I called out cheerfully, "Remember, Canus, don't kill them. I took a count, so I'll know if one's missing!"

He did not think this was humorous, while even chuckling hurt me, so I did not continue with my fun, watching as he dashed behind them, and I remember thinking in that moment that, while I still did not fully trust him, I acknowledged that I had perhaps judged him too harshly. After all, I had not walked in his *caligae*, and what little I knew of life as a Head Counter from a place like the Subura meant that his path was even narrower than for a man like me; however, neither did I forget what he had done to Florus, and more importantly, the manner in which he had done it, yet at the same time, I could not forget the actions I had taken in the past that were similar. We were both men who lived with violence, and used it as a tool to achieve our ends, and while I would argue that what I had done was in service either to Rome and the Imperator, or to my family, I also was certain that he would make the same argument, at least as far as serving Varro was concerned. This was all the thought I gave the matter since I had reached the Primus Pilus' tent, and I was waved in, entering his private quarters to see that I was not the last to arrive, although the third line Pili Priores had been excused. The last pair of Pili Priores arrived, and the mood was celebratory, though fairly quickly, it became clear that not everyone was happy.

"Three hundred *denarii* is fine," Agricola said as we were settling down, "and tell Catualda the wine is appreciated. But, Primus Pilus," his lips twisted into what can only be described as a leer, "you know that we need something...more than just money and wine."

I was not surprised that there was almost unanimous agreement to this, earning them a scowl from Nerva, though as we learned, his ire was not aimed at his Centurions.

"I know that," he replied, then shook his head. "But when I asked Catualda to hand over some women, he refused. He said that now that he is King of the Marcomanni, he can't be seen handing over his subjects to us."

This unleashed a torrent of indignant abuse by the

Centurions, and through the babble of voices, I heard the Secundus saying, "He wouldn't *be* king if it wasn't for us!"

He was certainly not the only one who uttered this sentiment, he was just the first, but suddenly, Nerva turned his attention on the Secundus as he raised a hand for silence, while I sat there thinking this was another example of how fairness was only important when it was to our benefit.

Once the others subsided, still staring at the Secundus, Nerva continued, "Actually, he said that he might have considered it except for an incident that he was made aware of just before I went to speak to him. Apparently, a young Marcomanni girl was reported missing, but she wasn't the daughter of just a random townsperson; her father was an important man and member of their nobility. Catualda actually sent that cousin of his, Otmar, along with other Gotones to search for her." He paused then, seemingly to take a sip from his wine, yet I saw that his eyes never left the Secundus, and now the others noticed as well. I glanced over at him, and I noticed that he suddenly seemed more interested in inspecting the nails of one hand.

"And? Did they find her?" the Sextus Pilus Prior, Numerius Longinus, asked.

"They did," Nerva nodded, then after a pause, and with a grim tone, said, "hidden away in a stable in the flat part of town, naked with her throat cut, and with blood on her thighs." Then, his eyes still on Secundus, he asked bluntly, "Does anyone know anything about this?"

It took a conscious effort on my part not to look at the Secundus, but out of the corner of my eye, I saw his head shaking, just like the others around him. Nerva's only reaction was a slight lifting of his upper lip in an unmistakable sneer before he shifted his gaze away to look at each of his Centurions, one by one, as I sat there hoping he would not look at me, recalling how often I have been told my thoughts are easy to read.

"You said she was important," Agricola spoke up.

"Yes," Nerva nodded. "At least, her father was to Catualda. It was that Marcomanni lord who they threw over the wall at us after they cut his throat." He gave a harsh chuckle.

"Appropriate, I suppose, that his daughter died the same way. What was his name?"

"Chariovalda," I supplied, earning another nod.

"Yes, that was it."

"But why does he think we have anything to do with it?" Agricola countered. "Her father may have been important to Catualda, but he would have been seen as a traitor by the other Marcomanni. I know that we did a good job of cleaning those *cunni* out of that part of the town, but you know as well as I do there are always leakers." He used our slang term that describes enemy who evade capture when we sweep through an area, like a town. "It's more likely that it was one of them than one of our boys."

"That's what I told Catualda," Nerva replied, "and he agreed. Which is why he was willing to let the entire matter drop." To my eye, he looked anything but happy about this, strengthening my suspicion that he knew that the Secundus was involved, even if by association. "However," he finished, "he wasn't willing to...lend us any women." Before anything more could be said, he moved on. "I've looked at your butcher's bills, and they're even better than I hoped, but we're still going to stay here for at least the next five days, mainly to help Catualda establish himself as the new King of the Marcomanni." At this, he turned to me. "Is Maroboduus settled in his new accommodations?" He offered a sour smile at this, saying, "I know that he doesn't have the comforts that he's become accustomed to, but I'm sure the Imperator will make sure that he's comfortable wherever he's going to be settling."

"He is, Primus Pilus" I replied, then added, "although I don't think he's really noticed his surroundings. His women," I chuckled, "are another story."

"Well, his safety is your responsibility until we get back to Mogontiacum," Nerva reminded me, despite the fact that there was no need since I was the one who had made the promise, and I had been the one who informed him. "But," he allowed, "I think that once we get away from here and that bastard Catualda, you'll both be able to sleep better." Slapping his desk, he stood up, smiling for the first time, "Now, let the boys get drunk and tell them their Primus Pilus is proud of the job they did. And," he promised, "tomorrow, we'll be handing out their bounty."

It was not surprising that the Centurions supported this idea, and they all came to their feet as well, but as they were filing out, this time, Nerva did not wait to signal me to stay behind. Once we were alone, he examined me for a long moment, his face impassive, until I began growing uncomfortable.

Finally, he broke the silence by asking, "How's your wound?" I do not know why, but I was surprised that he knew, and when I made that known to him, he snorted. "I'd have to be blind not to see the way you're moving. But," he admitted, "I heard about it. And," he regarded me steadily, "I heard other...things about what you did today."

"How?" I gasped, not needing him to expand.

A sudden thought occurred to me; there were only two Romans present during that moment, but I did not even consider Alex, settling on Canus as the likely suspect.

I do not know if Nerva guessed where my suspicions were heading, but he held up a hand as he explained, "I heard it when I was with Catualda." He suddenly shook his head. "There's no fucking way that I'm going to call him 'Your Highness'," he muttered, and I would have heartily agreed, but I did not want him to think that I was licking his ass. "Where was I? Oh, yes, I was with him when one of his men, some bastard with a missing tooth came up to him, and while they talked in that gibberish of theirs, I heard your name. So naturally," he shrugged, "I demanded to know what the bastard was saying, and that's when I learned about...what you did." An expression I had never seen came over his face then, and while I could not identify it with any kind of precision, I could tell he was feeling awkward about something; I got an idea about what it was when he blurted out, "It's the same thing that happened with your father, and has happened to you before, like we talked about, isn't it?" Something in my own expression must have confirmed it, because he slapped the desk and exclaimed triumphantly, "I *knew* it! I *knew* when that *cunnus* talked about it that's what happened. Pluto's cock," he laughed, "I would have known if he hadn't told me in Latin just by the look on the bastard's face. That's what it was, wasn't it? That...divine fit? That madness?"

I cannot say that I cared for the manner in which Nerva characterized what is a profoundly personal, and still to this day, disturbing thing that happens to me, yet at the same time, I had to force myself to acknowledge, to myself at least, that the Primus Pilus was, in his own way, giving me a compliment of sorts.

Still, when his tone turned wistful and he said, "I wish I had been able to see it with my own eyes," I was unable to stop from snapping, "It's not some sort of entertainment, Primus Pilus! It's something that happens to me that I can't control, and it only happens when either I or the men around me are in grave danger! I have no control over it, and..."

"*Pax*, Pullus, *pax*!"

Nerva actually looked genuinely embarrassed, and while he had no need to do so, nor would many men in his position, he said with what I believed then and believe now was utter sincerity, "I didn't mean to cause you any offense, Pullus, truly I didn't. It's just that you Pullus men are famous under the standard. I don't have to tell you that, do I? And there aren't many men who can say that they've been present when Mars comes down to Earth among us mortals. I," he finished quietly, "just wish I could have that much and be able to tell my children I saw it with my own eyes."

How, I wondered, did he know that this was what men close to those of us bearing the name, the size, and the profession under the standard, claimed happened, going all the way back to the first man who described it thusly, Sextus Scribonius, more than sixty years ago? Was it really that commonly a held belief? Naturally, this was the first thing I asked Alex when I returned to the tent to relate what had taken place, and I had been shocked by his reaction, which was to look at me in surprise.

"You mean you don't know that's what men say?"

"No!" I exclaimed, stunned and quite shaken at the idea.

"Well, it is," he had assured me.

Now, in Nerva's tent, I was still trying to grapple with the larger meaning of this, so I focused instead on what Nerva said.

R.W. Peake

"I'm the one who needs to apologize, Primus Pilus," I said. "It's just that it's not something I like talking about...to anyone."

"Well," he replied in what I took as a tacit acceptance of my apology, "all that matters is that you stopped those Marcomanni from falling on your rear. But," he pointed at my side, "even if I hadn't heard about it, I can tell that you're hurt. How bad is it?"

"It's not bad at all," I assured him. "Alex was able to close the wound up with a few stitches, and it didn't penetrate nearly as deeply as we thought. And," I added the most important part, "nothing was driven into the wound."

"Well," Nerva replied, "I know that your man Alex will keep an eye on it. And," he added, "you. I know that you trust him, but we have some good *medici* with the Alaudae, and it wouldn't hurt to have them take a look at it. After all," he tried to make a joke of it, "you're going to have to be on your toes and keep your eyes open, because I think that Catualda isn't happy that Maroboduus is still alive."

This was definitely the impression I had gotten as well, but I did not think it would hurt to ask Nerva, "Did he say anything to you that might be useful? Any hint he might have given?"

"No," Nerva shook his head. "Not really. Although," his face creased into a frown as he thought about it, "he did say that he needs to speak with Maroboduus before we leave. I suppose he could try something then."

"I don't think he'd be that stupid," I replied immediately, then I was struck by a thought, and I asked Nerva, "Was he still there when his man told you about what I did?"

"Yes." He nodded. "He heard every word. In fact," he chuckled, "I think he turned a bit paler, although that may have been because his man was...descriptive about what you did."

"Then as long as I'm there," I grinned at him, "I think we don't have anything to worry about."

Nerva nodded, then added, "And if he tries to send you away, we'll know he might try it. Still," he allowed, "Maroboduus doesn't look easy to kill."

Now that I had been in his presence and witnessed his cool

318

demeanor during the fighting in his hall, I wholeheartedly agreed, but I was still going to make sure I was there.

"I need to go join the boys." Nerva stood and began heading for the partition, but I stood there, trying to think of a way to broach the subject still on my mind.

"Primus Pilus," I began, "about that girl. There's something I think you should know..."

"I know," Nerva stopped me, his face grim. "That girl was raped and murdered by two of Secundus' men. Although," he amended, "not in the First. They're Third Century men, and Frontinus is his minion."

"You're certain?" I gasped, and he nodded, prompting me to ask, "What are you going to do about it? Surely you're not going to just let it go!"

I could see that I had irritated him, though his tone was even enough if a bit defensive, explaining, "It's complicated, Pullus. The Secundus has...friends." The look he gave me then was shrewd. "Don't tell me that you don't have men like that in the 1st." This was something I could not deny, and I did not try to do so, although I said nothing. Taking my silence as an admission, he went on, "But there are other ways to deal with a problem, as I'm sure your own Primus Pilus would tell you." Then, he did something unusual, clapping me on the shoulder, and said, "Now, go get some rest, Pullus. You need to heal up, and I doubt that Catualda will try something tonight. He's got other matters to tend to right now."

With that, we left his tent, and I could hear the raucous cheers as men were informed by their Centurions about the drink and money coming their way, and I reminded myself to send Alex to procure at least a jug, amending immediately that two would be better. When I reached the tent, Canus was back, looking more exhausted than immediately after the fight in the citadel, but someone could have toppled me with a simple push, so shocked was I at the sight of one of Maroboduus' children, one of the little girls, who had fallen asleep sitting next to Varro's man and toppled over so that her head was in his lap.

"I can't move," he whispered, with such a hapless expression that it actually hurt my back to make the effort not to roar with laughter. "This is the quietest she's been, and if I wake her up, she's going to start chattering again. And," he did smile then, not one of his normal, leering grins or one tinged with cruelty, but a genuine smile that, had I not known the circumstances, I would have said was that of a proud father, "she asks *so* many questions, even though I don't understand a fucking word."

What, I thought, do I say to that? The rest of the children, along with Maroboduus and his women, were gone now, sharing another tent, and I was reminded of Nerva's comment about how different the accommodations would be, not to Maroboduus, perhaps, since he was a warrior in his own right. Alex was gone, but Canus did not know where he was, and I lowered myself onto my cot, trying not to groan as I did, not wanting to wake the girl, though not long after that, her mother appeared, and while she was clearly nervous, she gave Canus a grateful smile as she relieved him of his burden, the girl only stirring slightly as her mother picked her up, laying the girl's head on her shoulder. I did not say anything, content to watch as I thought about how, although this girl was older, about four years old, she resembled Titus when he fell asleep on his mother's shoulder, and before I could stop it, there was an ache in my heart to go along with the one in my back. Thankfully, Alex showed up carrying two jugs of wine, handing me one while he and Canus shared the other, and while I thought about having him give me a quick oiling and scraping, I was too tired to get up. I finally got to consume my meal, not bothering to have Alex reheat it, then had a couple cups of wine, so I fell asleep quickly, before the call to retire, the sounds of the celebration of the Alaudae acting as a soothing lullaby.

I had a hard time rousing myself the next morning, coming perilously close to calling for Alex to help pull me up off my cot, though I somehow managed to get to my feet. The Batavians were back, having played no real role in the assault, other than being sent out by Nerva on a wide circuit around Casurgis looking not only for any possible Marcomanni reinforcements, which was not deemed likely, but for signs that Arminius had resumed his advance southward from the

Sudetes. None of us were disappointed to learn that they did not find any sign of either, but Herminius informed me that Nerva was sending them out again at noon, but this time to the west, in preparation for our withdrawal from Casurgis and return back to the Rhenus. Alex changed my bandage, informing me that the wound was no redder than it should have been, dismissing my complaint about the continuing soreness as whining, which I suppose it was. In retaliation, I had him give me a good rubdown and scraping, and he was wise enough to be gentle around the stitches, actually taking time to knead the muscles around the wound which, while it was certainly painful, did make the area feel a bit looser. At the beginning of second watch, a runner came from Nerva to inform me that he was about to return to Casurgis, ostensibly accompanying the Cohort that was relieving the one that had taken the first daylight watch, a nonnegotiable demand by the Primus Pilus, and he required my presence, though while the runner did not explain why, he did say I should be in armor. It was Alex who suggested that I wear all of my decorations, including Vergorix's torq.

"You've carried it all this way," he had said with a grin, "it would be a shame not to wear it at least once." More seriously, he went on, "If I had to guess, I think that Catualda is going to try and make a show of being a new King, and he's likely to try something to demonstrate his status. Wearing your decorations," he shrugged, "is a good way to counter that."

I agreed, but it turned out that the difficulty I had was wearing my *hamata*, which had been cleaned and repaired overnight, because even with the padded shirt, it was extremely painful. Alex solved it by fashioning a second pad that he placed over the bandage, then wrapped more bandage around it, and while it helped the pain, he said something that almost got me stripping back down.

"With that extra bandage, you look fat," he observed critically, having to actually restrain me from pulling the *hamata* off, and it did not help that I had to use a different notch of my *baltea*. "You're worse than a woman," he muttered, but soon enough, I was fully outfitted, my *phalarae* in place, the arm rings around my biceps, and the torq fastened at the neck, just in time for me to meet Nerva and the Sixth Cohort in the forum.

When I saw the Primus Pilus wearing his armor but without his decorations, I braced myself, certain that he would send me back to my tent, but instead, he looked a bit abashed.

"I should have thought of that myself," he mumbled, but he did not delay us so that he could run to his quarters. As he let the Sextus Pilus Prior march the Cohort, he apprised me of the latest developments. "Catualda is up at the citadel, holding court and putting on airs, from what I've been told. Supposedly, he's interviewing the Marcomanni noble prisoners one by one to determine whether he can trust them." He gave me a sidelong glance, asking, "You know what that means, don't you?"

"Probably he's squeezing them for every *denarius* they've got, saying it's proof of their loyalty," I answered, which earned me a snorting laugh.

"So you *do* know what's what. But yes, that's what he's been doing, although I suppose he might be done by now."

Reaching the gateway, I was somewhat surprised to see that there was a work party busy repairing the gates, although not that this was happening, but that there were Alaudae *immunes* who, from what I could see, were doing most of the work in repairing the gates as the men Catualda had designated for the task stood there watching in bemusement. They scrambled out of the way as the Cohort marched through, but since I was with Nerva, who was actually walking behind the Sixth, I was unprepared for the sight that greeted me. I cannot say that Casurgis was back to normal, but considering that just the day before I could have counted on one hand the number of civilians I spotted, alive at least, the town was almost bustling. The second thing I noticed was that, while there was still a guard on the market square, it had been reduced to a mixed force of just one Century, the Sixth of the Sixth stopping there to relieve the Sixth of the Fifth, and about a hundred Gotones, a handful of whom I recognized. More strikingly, the number of prisoners had been halved at the very least, giving the remainder enough space to lounge on the hardpacked dirt.

"I guess that enough nobles paid Catualda and were

allowed to get their warriors," I commented.

"Maybe," Nerva grunted. "Or," he did not say anything, instead drawing one finger across his throat as he grinned at me.

Frankly, I did not think this likely, but I just murmured something vague. The reason that I did not think it likely was that none of the civilians, many of whom were loitering around the edge of the market square, talking to some of the prisoners, seemed agitated or worried about the fate of their loved ones. But, I acknowledged to myself, I could be wrong, because there was no telling what was happening in Catualda's head. By the time we began climbing the left hill to the citadel, we were down to two Centuries, and I was surprised at how steep it was, having no memory of it the day before, although my wound probably did not help matters. Nerva sent the last two Centuries to the southern wall, while the citadel gateway had actually already been repaired, though the gates were open, but when we entered, the place was packed, mostly with men, though I saw a handful of women in the crowd.

"They're here to plead their man's case," I guessed, pointing out the women and Nerva nodded grimly.

For a moment, it appeared as if some of the men were not disposed to step out of our path, but then I gently moved Nerva aside and led the way, noticing that he did not complain. Once I was leading, I cannot say that men scrambled out of the way, but none of them tarried, yet it was the expressions on their faces that I noticed, as if I was an object of curiosity, and perhaps a little fear. That gap-toothed *cunnus* told anyone who would listen for a cup of mead. Well, I hope he's got a horrific hangover, I thought sourly, but chose to look on the bright side that I did not have to push my way through the crowd. The doors to the hall were open, as were the shutters, so once we got within a dozen paces or so, we could dimly make out Catualda, though he was standing on the platform, which had been moved back over the entrance down into the cavern, and not seated on his new throne. His arms were crossed as he listened to what I assumed was a Marcomanni, who was standing in front of the platform and I did not need to speak their tongue to hear the impassioned, pleading tone, the man making emphatic gestures then pointing at a pair of men standing in the ring of men surrounding him, most of whom were in a pose similar to Catualda, with arms crossed. They did not appear to be hostile towards the speaker, yet there was definitely something there, an air of skepticism perhaps, though they were attentive. About midway through his speech, I noticed some heads nodding, and a ripple of murmurs that seemed to bode well for him, but his eyes never wavered from Catualda. Once he finished, the new king began to pace back and forth on the platform, which meant he walked about two steps before turning back, and repeated the process, while he stroked his beard with one hand. It was, I remember thinking, as if he was behaving in a manner that he thought a king should behave; deep in thought on a weighty matter, with an air of artifice about it that, in my view, made it a performance and not something genuine. Stopping suddenly, he turned and said something; it was not much, only two or three words, but it roused a chorus of gasps from the audience, while the man actually staggered backward, and when he turned towards the men he had indicated earlier, I could see he was paler than he had been just moments earlier. Then, to my astonishment, and from my view, to the audience's as well, the man dropped to his knees, going from pleading to begging, and whatever sympathy he had among his fellow tribesmen evaporated. Now, the looks of disgust and contempt were impossible to misinterpret, and Catualda was clearly unmoved, shaking his head, then making a dismissive gesture, but when the man continued his importuning, he glanced over at Otmar, who was standing to his left just off the platform. Catualda's cousin stepped forward, going to the man, yet somewhat to my surprise, he did not handle the man roughly, just pulling him gently to his feet, then turned him around and led him out of the hall. As the pair passed me, the Marcomanni looked right at me, yet I could tell that he did not see me, and I felt a prickling up the back of my neck that I interpreted as the sign that I was looking at a condemned man being led away to his fate. Catualda turned his back to the audience, but it was only to snap his fingers, summoning a young and very pretty slave, who hurried over to hand him a wooden cup, which he drained before turning back. This seemed to be a signal as another man came from the crowd to stand in front of the throne, but Catualda held up a hand, his eyes now on Nerva and me, and the smile he offered us got nowhere near his eyes, though his tone was cordial enough.

"Centurions! Welcome to the first full day of my reign!" He paused, and I realized that he was waiting for one or both of us to offer our wishes that it be long and prosperous, but I was not about to, and I prepared myself to argue with Nerva later about how that was his responsibility as the Primus Pilus, yet he remained as silent as I did. Catualda's features darkened, the smile fading, but he hurried on, "Yes, well. I wanted to thank the both of you for the help you gave in removing Maroboduus from the throne." He surprised me then, because he said, "And Maroboduus was a great king of the Marcomanni, in his day, but," he shook his head as if he was saddened to say it, "his day has passed, and he is too old and set in his ways to see it." He stopped, but it was Otmar who spoke, in their native tongue, and it was not much of a guess that he was relaying Catualda's words. I tried to appear as if I was still looking at Catualda while I studied the faces of the audience, trying to determine how they were accepting what I was certain would be the new version of Catualda's usurpation, that he was forced into it by circumstances. Once Otmar finished, he resumed, "Primus Pilus, I assume that your men are pleased with my gift to them? Although," he allowed, trying to sound regretful, "I know that they were upset they did not have any...companions for their revelries last night."

While I had caught it, I hoped that Nerva had not, a hope that lasted for the time it took him to growl, "Gift? What gift? The Alaudae *earned* that money with their blood! And," he pointed his *vitus* at Catualda, "*we* are the only reason you're standing where you are as King!"

"Do not forget," Catualda snapped, "that I *am* King of the Marcomanni. And while we are not as powerful as we should be, I am going to remedy that, Primus Pilus. You would do well to remember your place!"

"Why, you jumped-up, miserable piece of..."

"Lord King," I cut Nerva off, seeing how Otmar's hand

had dropped to the hilt of his *gladius*, which signaled others in the hall to do the same, including men behind us from the rustling sound, and while I was not overly worried that they would try to strike us down, it only takes one fool to turn a tense moment into a brawl, and as outnumbered as we were, a brawl into a slaughter, "while it's not my place to apologize for Primus Pilus Nerva, nor do I feel the need, I would also point out that the two of us represent far more than just the 5th Legion. After all," I pointed to myself, "I'm not in the Alaudae, but here *I* am, and I don't think I have to remind you exactly how you're standing there...do I?"

Oh, he did not like it, that was plain to see, but neither could he deny the truth of what I was saying, and a heavy silence fell over the hall.

"No, Centurion Pullus," he said finally. "You do not have to remind me. And," he turned to address Nerva, and while it was through clearly gritted teeth, he said, "I would like to apologize to you, Primus Pilus, for misspeaking. As you said, your men earned the money from my treasury in blood, so it was no gift." I began to relax, but then he added, "Of course, my men would have been able to take Casurgis without any help, but our losses would have been much heavier."

It did not help that his men who spoke Latin began nodding their heads, and I braced myself, praying silently that Nerva would not explode at this, not that I would have blamed him.

To my shock, he simply shrugged and replied, "If you say so, Lord King." Before Catualda could respond, he went on, "But we're here at your request. You said you had some matters to discuss?"

"Yes, I did," he agreed, then addressed Otmar, who in turn said something to the assembly, and while they clearly did not like it, they began shuffling out of the hall. Once it was empty and the doors were shut, he sat down on his throne, another affectation, and he began with Nerva. "Is your plan still to stay here for another four days, Primus Pilus?"

"It is," Nerva replied, cautiously, then added, "although it looks as if we could move our wounded as early as tomorrow."

"Then you should do that," Catualda replied.

"I thought you needed us for a few days," Nerva countered. "Until you have a...firmer handle on the Marcomanni."

"I thought so as well," Catualda admitted. "But things are going better than I expected. It turns out that there are many Marcomanni who welcome this change. They no longer trust Maroboduus to be the leader he was in his younger days."

How much did that cost you? I wondered, but I kept that inside my head. And, if I was being honest, I had noticed that there was an air of apathy, not just among the Marcomanni, but with Maroboduus himself, as if his struggles with Arminius and stopping him had sapped the last of the strength he needed to rule during dangerous times.

Nerva did not say anything for a moment, then with a shrug, he said, "Ultimately, if you don't think you need us, I would be just as happy leaving sooner rather than later." He thought for a moment, then informed Catualda, "We will be leaving day after tomorrow."

Catualda did not say anything, just inclined his head in what I believed was another piece of theater, as if it was what he thought kings did in this moment, then he turned to me.

"Centurion, I would like to speak with you privately, if you do not mind?"

I was not expecting this, nor was Nerva, but when he glanced up at me, I nodded as I answered Catualda, "Very well, Lord King."

I saw his lips thin down, confirming that he wanted to hear the more flowery "Your Highness," but he was also asking something of me that I could turn down.

"I'll be waiting outside," Nerva murmured. "Yell if you need me."

Now it was my turn to be irritated, but I thanked him and said nothing else, waiting while Otmar, the only other man still in the hall, escorted Nerva to the exit, but after the door shut, I heard his footsteps approaching, telling me that "private" was a relative term.

Evidently, Catualda saw and correctly interpreted my expression, sounding apologetic for the first time.

"I am afraid that Otmar and I are still somewhat at odds

about what it means to be the commander of the royal bodyguard. And," he laughed, "as he pointed out, Bertilo never let Maroboduus out of his sight either."

I was reminded of the warrior who had been here in the hall the day before, and before I could think it through, I asked, "And what happened to Bertilo?"

Otmar chuckled, a harsh one tinged with cruelty, while Catualda shifted on his throne, saying vaguely, "We were unable to come to an...understanding, unfortunately."

"So he's dead," I said flatly.

"He was a fool!"

Otmar said this just as he passed me to resume his spot at the base of the platform, and he made sure to give me a hard stare as he continued, "He was given the choice of taking a holding and retiring from court. He refused the King's generous offer. So," he sneered, "I took his head."

I was certain that this was more than just boasting on Otmar's part, that there was a veiled threat there; within a couple more moments, all doubt was gone from my mind.

Choosing to ignore Otmar, sending a message that I did not consider him important enough to waste my time on, I pointedly turned my attention back to Catualda to ask, "What was it that you wanted to discuss, Lord King?"

I must give him credit; he did not hesitate, though it took a couple heartbeats for me to comprehend his meaning.

"How much?" he asked quietly, but said nothing else.

"How much?" I repeated, and I was about to ask what he meant when it came to me. "Ah," I said softly. "How much will I take to let you kill Maroboduus? Is that it?"

"Yes," he replied simply. He sat back, resting his elbows on the arms of the throne, placing his outstretched fingers together fingertip to fingertip with his pointing finger touching his chin as he regarded me. When I said nothing, he continued, "Your *Quaestor* Varro gave me some information about you, Centurion, information that I found interesting." As alarming as this was, I was not about to respond; when he saw this, he went on, "It concerns your family, and their status. Specifically, how you were once a member of your Equestrian Order?" I actually relaxed slightly, because I had been prepared for him to bring up the truth about my parentage, although this was somewhat related, so I nodded. "He also told me the amount in *denarii* it requires to be elevated, one hundred thousand, yes?" Again, I nodded. "Now," he held his hands out in a helpless gesture, "I cannot offer you the full amount, but I could offer you one quarter of that amount, in exchange for you simply doing nothing when Otmar here comes to the camp."

Somehow I managed to avoid gasping, but internally, I was reeling. *Twenty-five thousand denarii*? With what I had saved, and what my real family back in Arelate had already assured me they were willing to contribute, I would have an amount very close to what I would require for elevation. However, and thankfully, hard on the heels of that thought was the other requirement that any man needs for elevation, and that is a sponsor. And, I understood almost immediately, if I took Catualda's money and looked the other way and allowed Maroboduus, and at the very least probably the two boys among his children if not the entire family to be slain, while I was no longer certain exactly who wanted Maroboduus kept alive, even the least powerful Roman among the list of men with an interest in this matter, Varro, was highly placed enough to retaliate against not just me, but in a manner similar to what I felt confident Catualda wanted to do to Maroboduus' family. Honestly, the temptation offered by this staggering sum lasted perhaps a heartbeat, and even if it had been more of a factor, I am certain when I say that my answer would have been the same, for a more fundamental yet equally powerful reason; I liked Maroboduus more than I liked Catualda by this point. Consequently, I actually hesitated for a couple more heartbeats to make it seem as if I was seriously considering before I shook my head.

"I'm afraid I must decline your offer, Lord King. I gave my word as a Centurion of Rome, which," I pointed out, "was acceptable to you."

"It was," Catualda nodded, "at that moment. But it is no longer acceptable to me."

"You are really willing to die for that old man?" Otmar sneered. "Because you *will* die, Roman, I swear it!"

I surprised even myself by how quickly I was able to move, and in the moment, I did not even remember feeling any pain in my lower back, yet despite Otmar already having his hand on the hilt of his *gladius*, he barely got out half its length before the tip of my own was pressed against the base of his throat, and I would have drawn blood if he had not taken a stumbling step backward, which I closed immediately.

"Do you really think you could defeat me, Otmar?" I asked quietly, then I was struck by an idea. "Didn't you hear what I did yesterday?" He refused to answer, but when I pressed a bit harder with the tip, drawing a tiny drop of blood, I felt him swallow hard, then he nodded. "And how many men did you hear I slew?"

He must have understood that I would not allow him to remain silent, because he answered, or tried to, stammering, "I...I do not know exactly, but I heard it was many."

"Actually," I admitted cheerfully, "neither do I. When I get like that, I really don't remember much. All I *do* remember was that there were a lot of bodies around me. Now," I changed again, snarling suddenly, "are you trying to say that you're better than seven, eight, or nine men, all on your own, you *cunnus*?"

Oh, how he wanted to draw his *gladius* the rest of the way, the hatred he felt for me almost a palpable force radiating from him, but as enraged as he clearly was, he was also no fool. From behind me, Catualda spoke, his voice calm and almost gentle.

"You have made your point, Centurion, and you have given me your answer in a way that there is no way to misinterpret." In a slightly sterner tone, he addressed Otmar. "Take your hand off your hilt, cousin. Do not give Centurion Pullus the excuse he is clearly looking for." Otmar's hand dropped from his hilt, then he held both hands out from his sides in a clear sign of surrender, though his eyes told a much different story, something I actually understood, knowing how I would feel in his *caligae*. Once he did that, I dropped my *gladius* from his throat, but I did not sheathe it, and when I turned to face Catualda, I did it in a manner that kept Otmar in my line of vision. I was not surprised that any sign of amity was gone from the new king's expression, and he said coldly, "We have no need for further congress, Centurion. You have made your answer clear, so you are dismissed." Despite the fact that I was expecting this kind of treatment once I gave my answer, I was not prepared for Catualda to sound, if anything, sympathetic, though he waited until my hand was on the door before he said, "Centurion, I give you my word as King of the Marcomanni that no harm will come to you from any of my people." This caused me to turn to face him, realizing that I should say something, and I mumbled a thanks, but then he said, "I would just warn you that neither you nor Maroboduus are out of danger just because you are safe from us."

At the time, I thought he was just trying to rattle me and did not think much of it, though I did tell Nerva once I was outside and we were descending the hill, but his reaction was much like mine.

"He's probably hoping that the Chatti try something on our way back," he said dismissively. Then, he added with a grim smile, "Let 'em try. The assault on Casurgis was easy, but it got my boys' blood up and they're spoiling for a fight now."

I did not reply, mainly because my back had decided to remind me that I had been wounded just the day before, and I occupied my mind thinking about how strange it was that, when I had actually made a sudden movement just moments earlier when drawing my *gladius*, I did not even notice. When we returned to the camp, I headed for our tent, and once again, I was met with a sight to which I was still unaccustomed, Canus being led by the hand by the same daughter of Maroboduus, except this time, the pair were trailed by the other children, and she appeared to be pulling him towards the area of the stables, which in turn reminded me that I had not visited Latobius since the morning before. Varro's man did not see me coming, mainly because he seemed absorbed in what the girl was saying, so when I called his name, his head swiveled, saw me, and immediately, he assumed a sheepish expression.

Changing course to intercept them, when I got close, the other children, while not overtly friendly, seemed to view me as more of a curiosity than anything else, but I could not help noticing that when I got to Canus, the little girl actually moved to his opposite side, grabbing his other hand and putting him between me and her. It is silly, and I knew it in the moment that it was silly, but I felt hurt by her actions; I suppose I was thinking of my *de facto* niece Iras, who was a bit older but had never behaved in this manner with me.

"*Oy!*" Canus chided her. "Don't act like that with the Centurion. He won't bite." He grinned at her as he added, "At least I don't think he will, anyway."

This unleashed a torrent of chatter from her that neither of us understood, and he gave me a ruefully amused glance.

"Is she always like this?" I asked, but I was looking at her and smiling, hoping my tone would put her at ease. "So quiet?"

This made Canus laugh, then reply, "I think the only time she's quiet is when she's asleep. And," he grimaced, "she doesn't sleep much."

"Do you even know her name?"

"Actually, I do," he answered, then used his free hand to point behind him. "I learned it from one of them. Her name is Goda."

"*Salve*, Goda," I started to bow, but my back kept my gesture to a bow of my head. Pointing to myself, I said, "My name is..."

"Pullus," she said before I could, surprising me a great deal, then began chattering again, though this time, she made several gestures, one of them pointing back over her shoulder in the general direction of the tent she was sharing with her parents and siblings.

"She says that our father told us who you are."

This was said in Latin, albeit halting, and from the oldest of the other five children, a boy who looked to be about eleven, with a sullen expression that told me that he was old enough to understand the circumstances that brought them to this Roman camp. He impressed me when he did not look away after I locked eyes with him, actually drawing his shoulders back as he stared at me defiantly.

"And, young Lord," I asked with exaggerated courtesy, "what is your name?"

"Mardobus," he replied, and I asked, "Are you the oldest son?"

"Yes," he nodded, then I saw an expression flit across his face, one of pain, which was explained when he finished, "I am now."

"Ah," I nodded, feeling awkward. "I...am sorry to hear that."

He shrugged, while I realized there was not much to say, although I did make a note to have Alex find out more about Mardobus' older brother and how he might have died. We were at the stables now, such as they are in a marching camp, and any idea that I might have escaped my horse's notice was dispelled by his whinny when he picked up my scent. Since he was a stallion, he was picketed separately, and now that Tyr was no longer in the camp, having been retrieved by a representative of the new king, it was clear my horse viewed himself as the leader of the herd, and I headed over to him, happy that I was actually wearing my *hamata* since I did not have anything to offer him. When I mentioned this to Canus, Mardobus overheard me, and he called to his sister, who dashed over to him and the other children, who had huddled around Mardobus. I understood why when, with varying degrees of willingness, three of the children produced two apples and a hunk of bread that they had squirreled away. Mardobus handed them to Goda, then pointed at me, speaking to his sister with the kind of sternness I have witnessed used by the oldest sibling. She gave a short but piercing squeal of delight, reminding me that little girls possess this, their secret weapon in the form of an invisible but painful awl that they can plunge into the ears of an unsuspecting adult. Her shyness also evaporated in the amount of time it took her to skip back to Canus and me, although she could not bring herself to look me in the eye as she offered the treats to me.

I shook my head, pointing to my horse, who was straining against the picket rope, and I said gravely, "I think he would like to get them from you more than me."

As I hoped, she understood, and proving that she had been around horses, she approached Latobius, holding one of the apples out by placing it in the palm of her hand with her hand flat, but what Goda did not know is that Latobius is not only fond of children, he knows they must be treated differently, and after a good snuffle of her hand and arm, which made her giggle, he delicately took the apple, crunching it placidly as he lowered his head to allow Goda to stroke his broad forehead.

"She has really taken to you, Canus," I remarked as we both watched, while the other children either watched or wandered over to some of the other horses who appeared friendly.

"I suppose," he replied vaguely. He was silent for a moment, then said, "She reminds me of my girl."

I could have been knocked over with a feather, and I was unable to muffle my gasp of astonishment, nor to keep from staring at him.

"You have a child?"

"No." He shook his head, but the corner of his mouth twitched, then he grinned. "I have children, Centurion. Two, to be exact. Although," he allowed, "from different mothers." He shifted a bit, and I do not think it was a coincidence that he looked over at the other children as he said, "I don't see them very often. And," he said with a sigh, "I haven't been the best father."

It was becoming ever more difficult to think of Canus as an enemy, even as I heard Alex's warning in my mind, yet even with that barrier, I am not certain I would have known how to respond other than as I did, saying lamely, "Well, there's always time, isn't there? Are they both in Rome?"

"One is," he replied, still looking away. "The boy. He'd be..." his face screwed up as he thought, "about that lad's age," he indicated Mardobus. "The girl is a little older than Goda here, though not much."

"Where does she live?" I asked, but he shrugged, then said simply, "I have no idea. The last time I saw her was a year ago, and the next time I came to see her, the neighbors said her mother had taken up with another man, and they had moved away. Nobody knew where."

That, I thought, is why he's so attached to Goda, who, by this time, had just given Latobius the crust of bread, but when she was about to hand him the final apple, I gently stopped her.

"Two apples doesn't agree with him," I said, which of course she did not understand, so to distract her, I swept her up and set her on Latobius' back.

Thankfully, her initial shriek of fright turned into a squeal of happiness as she settled on his broad back, her short legs barely able to straddle his chest, and on impulse, I pulled Latobius' picket pen so that I could lead him around by the bridle. The reserve shown to me by the other children almost immediately evaporated so that, before I could say no, it was Canus' turn to look on in amusement as I led all but Mardobus around on Latobius' back, the boy steadfastly refusing to participate, watching with what I suppose he thought was an indifferent expression at his siblings, arms folded.

It was as we were walking back that Canus said suddenly, "Maybe I will go to see my boy after this. That is," he added gloomily, "if I can."

"Varro is going back to Rome at some point, isn't he?" I asked. "You might have to wait until he does, but then you'll get your chance."

"I suppose." Clearly deciding a change in subject was in order, he asked, "So, what did that *cunnus* the new King of the Marcomanni want?"

I hesitated, not sure I should answer, but then I decided that it was not likely to remain a secret, so I told him.

"That's no surprise." He laughed. "He *really* wanted to kill the old man yesterday, and I can't say that I don't understand why."

The truth was that I understood it as well, but I thought it could not hurt to probe Canus a bit to see if I was missing anything, so I pretended to be surprised.

"Really? Why do you say that?"

"Anyone with eyes and sense can see that, while that Marcomanni might be old, there's a reason why he's been king for so long. And Catualda," his lip lifted in a sneer, "is now Maroboduus, or he thinks he is, but it's a show that he's putting on. That's another thing anyone can see. Which," he looked up at me then, a strangely intense expression on his face, "I think Catualda knows deep down. He knows that he's met a better man, and just that thought alone is enough to make a man like Catualda want to send Maroboduus to the afterlife."

Suddenly, I was not so certain we were speaking about

Maroboduus and Catualda, though I did not say as much. We were almost back to the Marcomanni's tent, where Maroboduus was actually standing outside, arms crossed as he spoke to the older woman, but even with all that was taking place to upend his life, the sight of his children heading for him made the deposed old king smile. I also saw that Goda was, if not his favorite, was certainly well-liked by the king, and that Goda was not the offspring of the senior wife, who made no secret of the fact that she was glaring at the little girl, then said something sharp to him, which in turn earned her a rebuke from her husband, something she clearly did not like.

"Catualda swore that there would be no attempt by him or any Marcomanni on Maroboduus," I said to Canus. "What do you think?"

"I think he's telling the truth," Canus answered immediately, and without any doubt in his voice. "I think that he's going to be forced to accept that getting Maroboduus away from here will be the best he can hope for. And," he added, almost as an afterthought, "I think he's going to have his hands so full that he's going to be forgetting about the old king."

"What makes you say that?"

Canus did not answer right away, then spoke carefully.

"I think," he said slowly, "that Catualda is more in love with the idea of being a king than in actually ruling his people. And," he chuckled, "he's as greedy a bastard as our patricians."

I was impressed, perhaps because his views aligned with my own insight into the new king. That is probably why, on another impulse, I asked, "Do you think Catualda was telling the truth about not recognizing his aunt? You were there, too. It *was* smoky, and hard to see."

He did not answer immediately, just giving me a sidelong glance before, instead of answering, posed a question of his own.

"What do you think?"

Without hesitation, I replied, "I think he knew exactly who she was."

"So do I," he answered grimly, then with a shrug, he added, "although I don't suppose it matters."

This, I understood, was true, and we said no more. Since

we reached our tent first, Canus left me there to let Alex know what had transpired.

"What are you going to do until we leave?"

I considered Alex's question, then shrugged and said, "I guess I'm going to be sleeping outside Maroboduus' tent for the next two nights."

"You know I'll stand watch with you," he told me, but then when Canus returned and, hearing what I planned, volunteered as well, Alex flatly refused.

To my surprise; in fact, almost shock, Canus did not argue, nor did he bristle at the implication, and that should have alerted both of us, but it did not.

Chapter 8

Nothing happened that night, nor the next, other than I did not get my accustomed amount of sleep, and sleeping on the hard ground aggravated the pain from my back, which made me irritable, and of course I took it out on Alex. The night before we broke camp was naturally the worst, but there were no attempts by any Marcomanni to penetrate the camp. In fact, on the day the Alaudae departed, the new King of the Marcomanni could not be bothered to see us off, sending Otmar out instead to offer a stiff and completely insincere thanks for handing his cousin the throne. Throughout it all, Maroboduus displayed a demeanor that would have done any Stoic proud, but when we fell into our column of march, he was naturally part of the command group, and was mounted. Surprisingly, it was on his own personal mount, which Otmar had brought with him that morning, a dun stallion with a black mane and tail, tossing the animal's reins into the dirt before he wheeled his own mount and went trotting back to the gates that we had repaired for them. The eastern wall was lined with people, but we were too far away to tell if they were making any kind of demonstration, either of farewell, or bidding good riddance to their former king. Until, that is, we began moving, when, across the open ground, we heard a noise that it took a few moments to understand.

"*Mar-ob-du-us! Mar-ob-du-us!*"

"Oooh, Catualda is *not* going to like that!" Alex laughed, yet while I found it amusing, I was also intently watching the man whose name they were chanting, sitting stiffly erect in his saddle, and I was close enough to see how he was struggling to maintain his composure.

Thank the gods his family is in a wagon, I thought, because I knew how I would have felt if Bronwen was present to watch what had to be an extraordinarily painful moment, or even worse, Titus if he was old enough to understand, like Mardobus. During the brief amount of time we had had to converse, I had learned that Maroboduus had become King after his father died in battle, not against Rome, but against the Chatti, back before Rome arrived. He had been all of nineteen years old, and he had been King for twenty-seven years, until someone in Rome had decided his usefulness to the Princeps was over, and while he never indicated as much, quite wisely, more than once during our return to Mogontiacum, I was struck by the thought of how bitter it must be that Maroboduus now relied on the very people who were responsible for deposing him to keep him and his family safe. Yet, if this bothered him, he did an admirable job of hiding it, although he was not very talkative for that first day, as the twin hills of the capital of his former kingdom slowly receded in the distance. With his permission, and I suspected at the tireless pleading of Goda, she was actually riding with Canus, sitting in front of him and, as always during our short association, talking away and perfectly content that Canus' responses were in the form of an occasional grunt. Alex and I, riding behind the unlikely pair, spent the first part of the first day's march talking about getting back to Mogontiacum, and whether it would be encased in the first real snowfall of winter. Perhaps it seems odd, but what we did not talk about was what might be awaiting me, although we did discuss the possibility that our women and children were still with my mother at her villa, which was what I preferred.

"I understand that, and in some ways, I agree," Alex had said. "But I also worry about them there more than I would in Ubiorum."

He did not say why, but he did not need to; Varro was there in Mogontiacum, waiting, and probably growing impatient for our return. Nevertheless, we were still happy to be heading west, although Nerva insisted that the men march in their *segmentatae*, though he allowed them to carry helmets and shields strapped to them. The Alaudae's casualties had been light, but as I knew from experience, the comrades of the hundred thirty-seven men who were now in urns on their Cohort wagons, along with the couple of dozen men whose wounds meant they were still in danger of either dying or being cashiered out did not view it that way. Every loss is keenly felt in a Legion, by the men of the section the fallen belonged to, their Optios, their Centurions, their Pili Priores, and all the way up to the Primus Pilus. Nevertheless, spirits were high, buoyed in part by the coins jingling in Legionary purses and the prospect of how quickly they could change ownership to the whores and purveyors of other vices, something that I would have been partaking in myself not that long before, yet I had, and have no regrets. In fact, as I get older, I recognize how much of my debauching was because of the expectation that is based on the fact that most Centurions started in the ranks, and I was acutely conscious of my status as a paid man, and once the *vitus* was removed from my ass—one of my father's more memorable comments about the problems Gnaeus Volusenus brought with him to the 1st—it was a way to prove to my men that we were not so different. Now, all I could think about was seeing Bronwen and my son, and I did not have to ask Alex if he felt the same way.

We had been riding in silence, and I was struck by a thought, turning to ask, "Did you ever think that we would..."

Proving how well he knows me, and how often our thoughts run along the same lines, he finished, "...That we'd be more concerned with seeing our families than getting drunk?" He laughed at my astonished expression, admitting, "I was just thinking the same thing." Shrugging, he jerked a thumb over his shoulder where the First of the Third was marching behind us, prattling away about who would get the drunkest, who would bed the most whores, and who would make the most money at dicing. "It's hard not to with all that going on."

The Primus Pilus had decided, with resistance from the Secundus and a couple other Pili Priores, to take the most direct route back to Mogontiacum, the argument against it that it took us through the heart of Chatti lands, while Nerva pointed out that the likelihood that the Chatti had not already determined what we were doing, that it had nothing to do with them and that we posed a threat so low as to be nonexistent. Ultimately, it was a short discussion, and the first three days was a process of retracing our steps threading our way back through the mountains, albeit without the tension. Maroboduus slowly became less withdrawn, and while he was never overly voluble, I found in him a man as interested in affairs of war as I was, which meant that we passed the miles discussing the campaign against Arminius, who, I was not surprised to learn, Maroboduus hated just as much as we Romans did, even if it was for decidedly different reasons.

What did surprise me was when he sighed then admitted, "It was not always like that with Herman. In many ways, I admire him."

"*Gerrae!*" I exclaimed, forgetting that he was not a native Latin speaker. "He's part of the reason you're..." realizing there was no good way to end what I had started without thinking it through, I finished lamely, "...here."

He gave me a bitterly amused look, and he assured me, "Oh, I do not hold any warm feelings towards him any longer, Centurion. But," he shook his head, "I do not believe that any man could have united the tribes that he did, and kept them together as long as he did." This was not a new sentiment I had heard expressed, although none of them had come from as lofty a personage as a former king of a German tribe. Going on, he said something that caught my attention. "Although I believe that Herman has finally made a fatal mistake in his attack on my kingdom."

Perhaps if I had not actually liked Maroboduus, I would have reminded him that it was no longer his kingdom, but instead, I asked, slightly incredulously, "Are you saying that you think Catualda can defeat him?" I did not add "when you couldn't," though I could tell there was no need to, the Marcomanni hearing the unspoken part.

Maroboduus' mouth twisted into a half-sneer, half-grimace at my question.

"Catualda couldn't defeat Herman on his best day, and Herman's worst. No," he shook his head, "I believe that Herman has finally alienated himself with his fellow Cherusci. My spies told me that there was a great deal of resistance to his idea of attacking me, but he went ahead anyway. And," he smiled, but it was without humor, "while he forced me to retreat from our northern border, the last battle we fought damaged us both, which is why he will not come south now."

I did not particularly feel like rubbing salt in his wound, but I felt compelled to point out, "Couldn't he just be regrouping and is even now making preparations to assault Casurgis? Although," I allowed, mainly because I was struck by a snowflake, looking up to see flakes drifting down, "campaign season is over."

"I do not believe his fellow tribal leaders are going to allow that to happen," Maroboduus replied confidently, making me wonder how much he knew, and how he knew it. "In fact, I will not be surprised if Herman is dead by this time next year."

In that moment, I put this down to wishful thinking on Maroboduus' part more than any kind of realistic assessment of the political situation, yet I also remember cautioning myself to not underestimate the Marcomanni, and that his understanding of the political situation between and within the tribes of Germania far surpassed mine. Nevertheless, I still found it next to impossible to fathom the idea of Arminius being murdered by his own people, not after all that he had achieved for them, even with the last two defeats we had inflicted.

When we reached the narrow part of the valley that had been our cause for concern on our approach to Casurgis, I asked the Marcomanni, "If you hadn't been dealing with Arminius, would this be where you'd try and stop us?"

"Do you mean if I was willing to go to war with Rome?" he countered, clearly amused, but he also understood that I was asking this as a simple question of tactics and not with any larger political questions in mind, because he shook his head. "We are close, but no, this is not the place." He pointed to a stand of trees that began on the slopes of the hill to our right, and extended out onto the flat ground for perhaps a quarter mile. "You are looking at this as the most likely place for an attack, yes?" He was right, and I nodded. "But that is why I would not choose this spot, because you are expecting it."

While this made sense, I also tried to think of another location that provided the kind of cover that came close enough to the track where a sudden attack would not give us enough time to drop our packs and orient ourselves into an open formation, but he refused to say anything, forcing us to ride in silence for another couple of miles. Finally, he broke it as he pointed to a rocky outcropping that jutted out so that, from this direction, it appeared to block our path, but then I recalled how the track curved around it, though I could not remember what the terrain on the other side looked like, reminding me of how different things can look when coming the opposite direction. From this way, however, the outcropping looked far too steep and craggy to be useful as a spot from which to launch an ambush, but as soon as we rounded the outcropping, I saw that the western side of it was more gradual, just enough to help an ambushing force pick up speed, though not so much they would be careening in our direction and out of control, and the slope was wooded.

I felt his eyes on me as I studied the slope, and he guessed correctly that I was not overly impressed, saying, "So you see this and think that you would be prepared for an attack from this direction, yes?" When I nodded, he said suddenly, "Follow me," and wheeled his horse, going to a trot to the left side of the column, where the ridgeline that formed the southern barrier of hills and low mountains terminated less than a mile away. Once I caught up with him, he pointed to the trees and undergrowth that were now bare of leaves, reminding me, "This would not have been as bare when you marched in this direction, yes?" That was true, although the leaves had begun falling, but I had to acknowledge that it would have been harder to see men weeks earlier, particularly a tribe of Germania who wears muted colors specifically designed to blend into the background. However, he was not through. "You also have only yourself, your Roman friends, and six Batavians as your cavalry, and..." He stopped speaking, reining his horse down to a walk, then slowing even more, and I understood why when, without any kind of warning, I felt one of Latobius' hooves sink, and while he immediately pulled it out, I heard the sucking sound, while Maroboduus said, "Yes, I would have my cavalry up on the slope behind us, but I would have my missile troops here, and they would attack first. And," he asked with a smile, "what would you do, Roman?"

I thought for a moment, realizing that because, as he had

pointed out, we only had ten mounted troops, including me, Alex, and Canus, who could hardly be called a horseman, Nerva would undoubtedly send out one of the Cohorts to drive the missile troops back out of range.

"We'd pursue with one of our Cohorts," I answered, but felt compelled to point out, "but while this ground is soft for horses, that doesn't necessarily mean that it's too soft for the Legion."

"It is," he replied without hesitation, "but if you doubt me, you can always dismount and find out for yourself." I laughed at this, assuring him I believed him, reminding myself that he would know every inch of his tribe's lands. He continued, pointing towards the southern slope, now about three hundred paces closer, "This soft ground extends for about a hundred paces beyond here, and it is because of a stream that runs just beneath the ground. The source is up there." He pointed halfway up the wooded slope, then moved his finger down a bit. "I would have had my armored warriors waiting there just up from the base of this hill, waiting for your men who are pursuing my missile troops. Your men would be winded from being weighed down by their armor and shields and the muddy ground when my warriors attack." His voice had changed, the tone turning flat, and grim, while I found it all too easy to envision his description. "I would not try to destroy this force, but to pin them down and force Primus Pilus Nerva to commit more of his Cohorts to come to their assistance." He paused, and while I did not look at him, I sensed that he was waiting for some signal from me to continue, which I gave with only a nod, and he went on, "Once he did that, and those men were almost to reaching their friends, that is when," out of the corner of my eye, I saw him turn in the saddle to point back to the outcropping, "I would lead my cavalry in an attack to the part of your Legion that was not engaged, and my cavalry would significantly outnumber three or four of your Cohorts. That," he finished, and I heard the note of satisfaction there as he almost undoubtedly envisioned the scene in his mind and liked what he saw, "is what I would have done, Centurion Pullus."

Frankly, there was not much I could think to say, and I followed him as he trotted back to the column, for the first and what I am sure will be the only time I thanked the gods for Arminius and his attack on the Marcomanni. Would he and his warriors have been able to shatter the Alaudae and stop us? Honestly, I do not think so, but it is close enough that I freely admit I could be wrong; what I *was* certain of was that, even if we had repulsed the Marcomanni, it would have been at a much heavier cost than what the Alaudae had suffered taking Casurgis. Only later did I realize something; not only did Maroboduus never mention Catualda and his Gotones as a factor in this imaginary ambush, they did not cross my mind either, and I am not sure what that says.

Once we were beyond the mountains that marked the western border of Marcomanni territory, a change came over the party of Marcomanni; even Goda became withdrawn, choosing to ride in the wagon with her siblings, though I believe it was more because that was expected of her. Canus tried his best to seem indifferent to her absence, but it was clear that he missed her company, even if he could not understand anything she was saying. The men of the Alaudae were beginning to chafe, both in a literal and figurative sense over Nerva's orders to remain in armor, especially once we returned to the open, rolling countryside where it would be next to impossible to ambush a force of our size. And, with every mile that drew us closer to Mogontiacum, in one way, I began to relax, only realizing after the fact how tense I had been when the possibility of some sort of attempt on Maroboduus' life seemed possible, yet in another, as we neared Mogontiacum and my mind began to grapple with the possibilities of what might await me, the tension returned in subtly different but noticeable way. It is impossible to count the miles that I barely noticed passing as Alex and I discussed the possible outcomes, and what my response would be. More out of desperation than because either Alex or I thought it was a good idea, I actually approached Canus, hoping that our mutual distrust, if not completely gone, had subsided enough that he would be willing to offer some insight into what Varro might have planned, yet he insisted that he had no more idea than either of us.

"I gave up trying to figure out what Varro is up to," he said once, and I could hear the exasperation there, making me wonder if it was aimed at me, or if he was in a similar situation, trying to determine what his superior had in mind for Canus. "All I do know is that he's a clever bastard, and there is literally nothing he wouldn't do if he thinks it will bring him some advantage."

At least twice a day, once during the first half of the march, then again shortly before the end of the day before we made camp, I made it a point to walk with Nerva, leading Latobius, both as a way to find out if he had gotten any kind of warning from Herminius and his Batavians, who were now on their own as far as me being part of the scouts. Honestly, it was a case where I did not volunteer, content to have Nerva ask me, but he never did, so I was happy to stay with the column, for the most part anyway. I did take Latobius out for a gallop, but always within sight of the column, just enough to keep him, if not entirely sated, then at least satisfied enough that he did not try and throw me. The pace, while not leisurely, was such that men were able to leave the wagons and rejoin their comrades on the march, albeit without their *furcae* and pack for the first couple of days, although there were the inevitable relapses that sent some men back to the wagons. Simply put, it was a normal march for an army returning from campaign, and I know now, as I did immediately after what took place, that I had been lulled by that routine. Perhaps it was the announcement that we were now a week away from Mogontiacum, and had put Marcomanni territory sufficiently behind us that Maroboduus roused himself from his lethargy and resumed riding his horse again. The next day, he began letting his children ride with him, except for Mardobus, but when I asked the deposed king why, he smiled and shook his head.

"Because he says that he is not a child any longer, Centurion, or so he tells me. He is at a difficult age." Suddenly, he laughed. "Although he is not nearly as bad as his brother was."

Even with the laugh, I heard the pain there, but as curious as I was, I did not pry, and he went trotting off with another son, this one about eight and with the black hair that identified him as the son of the middle wife, and who rode behind him instead of in front, in what I took to be his own sign of independence, rather than riding in front like his sisters did. I felt a pang then, thinking of a few years from that moment, when Titus would want to ride behind me instead of in front, although it had been a struggle just for Bronwen to allow me to hold him with both arms as we just sat on Latobius, but that was a battle that had been worth it, if only because of his obvious joy at being so high up and seeing a brand new world, along with the feeling of his strong little body between my arms. Maroboduus would take each of the children out for perhaps a sixth part of a watch, roaming out around the column, though I noticed that he avoided entering the forests and completely disappearing from sight, which I took to be more the habit of an old warrior than any real concern of an ambush. I noticed that he saved Goda for the last ride of the day, and they would stay out later, and I wondered how her siblings took this sign of favor, although from everything I had seen, it was the senior wife, Frida, who seemed to object to it the most.

This routine lasted for a few days, until we reached the Moenus (Main) River, which signaled that we were three days away from Mogontiacum, and when the black-haired boy approached his father at what had become the accustomed time shortly after the first rest break, Maroboduus rebuffed him. I had noticed that Maroboduus seemed to be relapsing back into the mood that had enveloped him immediately after departing Casurgis, which I could understand, but when he went trotting away, I made no attempt to follow him, thinking that I would give him some time to himself. After all, I thought, we're far away from Catualda, and there was nobody marching with the Alaudae that had any reason to do Maroboduus harm. Consequently, Alex and I picked up our conversation from earlier, while men sang marching songs, and despite the leaden skies that threatened either a freezing rain or perhaps snow, it was not unpleasant, even with the small cloud of vapor hovering over the entire column created by the men talking and singing. I suppose I had noticed that Maroboduus had been heading for a line of trees, but I also knew that there was a stream that was responsible for the heavier vegetation, overhearing Herminius when he reported as much to Nerva earlier, so I did not think that much about him disappearing from sight. Now, as far as why I happened to glance over my shoulder not long after that, I have no idea; it certainly was not because I was concerned about the Marcomanni, or that I suddenly wondered about Canus' whereabouts. However, the result was the same; I did glance over my shoulder, looking to my right to where Canus normally rode, right behind Alex, and when I saw the empty spot, I cut Alex off.

"Where's Canus?"

Alex started, then twisted in the saddle, frowning, but he did not sound alarmed. "I don't know. Maybe he stopped to piss."

That, I realized with some chagrin, had not occurred to me, but I moved Latobius out of the column to scan the area between the column and the trees.

I did not see him, but then Alex suggested, "Maybe he had to *cac*."

On its face, this made more sense; whenever possible, men prefer a bit of privacy when they squat, and although no Centurion would allow one of his men to vanish when the nearest cover was more than a hundred paces away, being on horseback, and not under anyone's orders, could explain why Canus had vanished.

I turned Latobius and trotted back to rejoin Alex, since the column had not stopped marching, whereupon Alex resumed what he had been saying, but I do not recall what it was, because without any thought, I actually yanked Latobius' reins, kicked him, hard, launching him into a gallop as if he had been shot from a *ballista*. Alex shouted something, but the wind was already shrieking in my ears, and I am afraid that, for the first time that I could remember, I smacked Latobius on his rump so hard that it made my hand numb, the only thought in my mind being a prayer that I was wrong.

The story was told in the line of tracks that pointed me directly to where I fervently hoped I would find nothing alarming, with those made by Canus' horse angling from where he left the column to intersect with those created by

Maroboduus' stallion about fifty meters from the line of trees. Prudence dictated that I should slow Latobius before I went crashing into the underbrush, but I did no such thing, although I did loosen my hold of the reins, sending him the signal that I was relying on him to weave a path around the trees because he was better at it than I could ever hope to be. This strip of forest was not that deep; I could see the open area where the stream ran just about fifty paces away, and we came bursting out of the undergrowth more quickly than I had anticipated, costing me a valuable heartbeat or two that could have been fatal. Latobius had veered slightly from the path he was on when we entered the trees, and since he cannot speak, I never learned if he somehow knew the perfect spot for us to appear, but all that really matters is that he did so. The scene that greeted me I suspect will be burned in my memory for the rest of my days; Maroboduus on the ground, seated but leaning back on his hands, his horse more than a dozen paces downstream where his reins had been tied to the branch of a tree, with Canus standing over him, but with perhaps a half-dozen paces between them, his long dagger in his hand, spinning about in surprise at my sudden appearance behind him. Latobius, again without me touching the reins, slid to a stop, his front hooves splashing up mud and water, while I dismounted not in my usual manner, but by swinging my left leg up and over his neck so that when I landed, I was facing him and Latobius was behind me, though there was no need to guard my rear.

"What are you doing, Canus?"

I surprised myself by how calm I sounded, and at first, I thought that the Canus I first met was back, his lips drawn back from his teeth as he snarled, "My fucking job, that's what!"

My surprise deepened to shock as my mind tried to wrap itself around this sudden and completely unexpected development.

While I was intensely curious, it was more to buy time that I asked, "But why? Why would Varro want to kill Maroboduus now that he's gotten what he wants with Catualda?"

For the first time, I thought I detected a crack in Canus' demeanor, and I was certain I heard the frustration as he cried out, "I don't know! I swear I don't! I just know that Varro told me that if it looked like the old man was going to survive the march back, I was to take care of him!"

The subject of this conversation decided to try and get his feet under him, moving slowly, but I had been around Canus and had seen him in action enough to know this was a bad idea, yet I could not shake my head to warn him off.

There was no need, because without turning towards him, Canus snapped, "Don't do anything stupid, old man."

I was not altogether surprised to see this had no effect on Maroboduus, although he did stop moving, the former king scoffing, "So you expect me to sit here and just let you slaughter me, Roman? I would rather die on my feet..."

"You'll die either way," Canus said flatly, though his eyes stayed on me.

"You don't have to do this, Canus." I tried to keep my voice calm, and reasonable. "Just tell Varro that you never had the opportunity. Tell him," I shrugged, "that I never let the king out of my sight, and the only way to get through him is through me." Realizing how this might be taken by him, and acutely aware of the pride a man like Canus, who I had come to understand was a warrior in his own way and how he might interpret it, I added hurriedly, "Tell him that you didn't think that he would want all of the scrutiny that would come from killing a Centurion."

The look he gave me was one of bitter amusement...and something else, which I understood when he gave a humorless chuckle.

"Oh, Pullus, trust me. Varro wouldn't be upset about that, not at all. In fact, he told me that he's almost positive that someone in Rome would be *very* happy if you managed to get yourself killed. If it was helping that *cunnus* Catualda so much the better. But no," he shook his head, "that's not something that worries Varro."

"Canus, do you really think you can defeat me?"

Anger flashed across his face, but more than that, I saw the knuckles gripping the hilt of his long dagger whiten, and I subtly shifted my weight as I anticipated what his opening move would be. Then, he exhaled a sharp breath, his shoulders sagging slightly.

"No, Pullus," he replied quietly, and despite myself, I felt a pang of sympathy; who better than me to understand what kind of soul-lacerating thing it is for a warrior to admit such a thing? "No," he repeated, "not after what I've seen you do. But," his face contorted, and he shouted, "*I have no choice*! Surely you understand that!"

"I understand duty," I agreed. "But this isn't an official act by the *Quaestor*, and you know it."

He did not reply immediately, and it seemed as if he were considering something, then he broke the brief silence just as Maroboduus managed to draw one foot towards his body without Canus noticing.

"I didn't tell you the truth about something," he began, then stopped. I was about to urge him to continue when he did so. "It concerns my son and daughter. I *do* know where they both are. And," he closed his eyes, "so does Varro. In fact," he gave a barking laugh, the kind that one makes when there is nothing really funny, "they're at one of his villas outside Rome."

For the first time, I looked directly at Maroboduus, and I saw the startlement first, followed immediately by understanding, while I returned my attention to Canus as I spoke slowly, untangling the meaning, "And if you don't kill him," I indicated Maroboduus, "Varro will kill your children."

I was surprised when he shook his head, but I was almost immediately sickened, realizing that there was a worse fate than death.

"No, he won't kill them," he said flatly. "He'll make them his...pets." His mouth twisted into an understandable combination of helpless fury, contempt, and hatred, though he sounded emotionless as he continued, "The *Quaestor* has a...fondness for children. Both girls and boys. Until," now his voice started shaking, "he gets bored with them. Then, he has them...disposed of."

I made a decision then that I would not ask the obvious about who it was that did the disposing, both because I was certain I knew the answer, and because it might have ignited my own rage, which to this moment, I had kept in check.

Instead, I nodded my understanding of his dilemma, and asked softly, "So what are you going to do?"

"Do I have any choice?" he asked bitterly.

"Roman," Maroboduus spoke up, "may I say something?" Canus did not reply, but did give a curt nod. "I know this may mean nothing to you, but I swear on my honor as..." his face twisted, and I believe he was about to refer to himself by his former title, "...a noble of the Marcomanni tribe that I will do everything within my power to get your children away from *Quaestor* Varro."

"You?" Canus looked incredulous. "What could you do? You're broke! That *mentula* Catualda has all of your money now!"

Despite myself, I winced, but Maroboduus nodded, seemingly unperturbed by this reminder of his newfound poverty.

"I am not as wealthy as I once was," he agreed. "But I am not destitute. And," he added quietly, "I am not without influence in Rome."

While he did not appear altogether convinced, Canus clearly was more open to the possibility, while I held my breath hoping that Varro's man did not think quickly and spot the obvious, and many holes.

"I...I appreciate that, Lord," he muttered finally.

"So, what now?" I asked.

When I cross the river and I search out Gaius Fonteius, I will thank him for making certain there was no way that I could misinterpret what he was about to do. I will also say that he died well, without flinching and facing the great unknown of life among the shades straight ahead without any more fear than any other man I have seen, and that I learned Canus' real name as he died in my arms; this is all I will say about this moment.

We brought his body back to the column, slung across the saddle, where we were met by Alex, who had waited long enough for the pair of Batavians riding at the front of the column to join him. On our return and before we were reunited with the others, Maroboduus and I talked about what had transpired.

"He could have killed me, Centurion."

Misunderstanding, I assured him, "Canus is...*was* good, but I wouldn't have let him get to you, Lord."

Maroboduus shook his head.

"That is not what I meant. I mean, before you arrived. He had me at a total disadvantage." He sighed. "I am afraid I was not paying any attention. I had dismounted and was sitting there on that rock, watching the water flow past and feeling sorry for myself, and I did not even hear him approaching. He was just...there." He shrugged again.

"Then why didn't he strike?" I asked, still perplexed, then thought to ask, "And why were you on the ground like that?"

"Oh, I stood up," Maroboduus replied, "and was walking towards him because I did not know what he intended. And," he admitted, "he knocked me down, then told me to stay down, but he did not threaten me." He fell silent then, and I happened to glance over at him and saw him frowning; I understood why when he went on, "Then he said something that only makes sense now."

"What?"

He turned to look at me steadily, "He said, 'We are waiting for Pullus.' And when I asked him why he thought you would come, he just shrugged and said that he knew you would because you swore an oath to me." He surprised me then, because he veered closer to me so that he could thrust out his hand. "And I am very glad you did, Centurion."

This was flattering, but I was also certain about something myself, and I replied, "He wasn't going to hurt you, Lord."

"What makes you say that?" he asked, and I could tell he was genuinely curious.

Pointing in the direction of the wagons at the rear of the column, now about a hundred paces away, I replied simply, "Because of Goda."

I expected him to dismiss this, or argue, but instead, he regarded it for a few heartbeats before he nodded, then said solemnly, "I believe you are right. And," he sighed, "I do not look forward to telling her that he is dead. She was very fond of him."

Our conversation ended because Alex and the two Batavians came cantering up, and I saw my friend's eyes go to Canus' body then going wide, which was understandable.

"What happened, Gnaeus?" he gasped, but when I opened my mouth, I really did not even know where to start.

"Canus made a choice," was all I could think to say. "He chose honor." Without any warning, and completely unexpectedly, I felt a lump form in my throat, so I just barely managed to get out, "And he died well. Like a Roman."

Alex regarded me for a long moment, then turned Lightning and fell in beside us, after dismissing the Batavians, Arnfrid and Wigmar, who, despite being obviously curious, went cantering back to the front of the column. Naturally, our return attracted attention from the men, and I could see their faces turned towards us, knowing that the speculation that was going on right now would be replaced by wagering within the span of a few heartbeats. Seeing the men pointing and chattering away reminded me of something, and I handed the reins to Canus' horse to Alex.

"I need to tell Nerva." I turned to address Maroboduus. "Lord, will you come with me?"

He naturally agreed, while Alex, a bit perplexed, asked, "What am I supposed to do with him?"

"Take him to the baggage train, and hand the reins to a slave," I decided. "Once we stop to make camp, we'll send him on his way."

Parting ways, with Maroboduus and me heading for the Alaudae eagle, the second Cohort in the column, and Alex heading in the opposite direction to the wagons, only then did the two of us realize something, although it was Maroboduus who swore softly.

"Alexandros will have to go by our wagon," he murmured, his expression morose. "And Goda will see Canus."

"Not necessarily," I replied, though not with much conviction. "She might not look out of the wagon."

He gave me an amused look then, that of a father who knows a child.

"Goda is a delightful child, Centurion, but she is also a frightful busybody. No," he sighed, "she will hear Alex passing by, and she will stick her head out to see."

As we learned later, this was exactly what happened, and it upset Alex almost as much as it upset the girl, but it could not be helped, I suppose. Nerva saw us coming, and he stepped out of the column, *vitus* in both hands as he looked up at us, his customary scowl in place.

"Lord," he bowed his head slightly, then nodded to me, "Pullus. I saw you galloping off like Cerberus was after you, and I was about to send a Century. But," he made a show of examining both of us, "you're clearly fine."

Where do I begin? I thought, but I was saved by Maroboduus.

"Primus Pilus, Centurion Pullus became concerned about my absence. And," he glanced at me, an inquiring expression on his face, and I nodded for him to continue, "he had cause to be. The *Quaestor*'s man Canus had followed me, and," he sounded abashed, "he caught me by surprise." He paused, while Nerva looked baffled, which was understandable, but the Marcomanni took a breath before he continued, "He was there to kill me. But," he indicated me, "Centurion Pullus arrived before he could."

"*What?*" Nerva gasped. Then, as it sank in, I could see he was experiencing the same thing I had, shaking his head as he asked, "But, why?"

I was about to tell him, but Maroboduus cut me off before I could.

"He was paid by Catualda," Maroboduus lied calmly. "Before we departed Casurgis, Catualda approached him and offered him a large sum to murder me before we returned to Mogontiacum."

Somehow, I quelled the urge to speak and inform Nerva this was not true, though Nerva looked doubtful as it was, rubbing his chin as he thought about it.

"That would be a huge risk for a man like Canus to run," he said slowly. "Running afoul of his employer, not to mention Drusus and the Imperator?" I saw Maroboduus stiffen, and suddenly, my dilemma about whether or not to dispute Maroboduus' version of events did not seem so major. Obviously unaware that he had inadvertently mentioned there was a connection to Maroboduus' plight and Tiberius and Drusus, Nerva mused, "It would have to be a huge sum to tempt him. Although," he allowed, "that bastard was certainly throwing a lot of money around before we left." Shrugging, he asked, "So what happened? Where is he now?"

"His body is back with the baggage," I spoke for the first time, and Nerva started, his eyes widening a bit as my words registered, but it was fleeting.

"Well, I can't say that I'm surprised at the result." Then, he added carelessly, "I'll have him disposed of when we make camp."

"No," I said sharply, then immediately softened my approach by adding, "please, Primus Pilus. I'd like to have him cremated and ask for an urn."

"Why would you want to do that for him?" Nerva asked irritably, but then his eyes narrowed. "What aren't you telling me, Pullus?" He looked over at Maroboduus, but he just shrugged; I believe his thoughts were elsewhere, so it was left to me to answer, partially honestly, "He watched my back when we went over the wall at Casurgis, Primus Pilus. I just feel like I owe him that much."

Since the column had continued marching, Nerva had devoted all the time he was willing to, so he waved a hand and muttered, "Fine, don't tell me. Go ahead and burn him, and you can have an urn."

He was already turning to trot back to his spot, leaving Maroboduus and me relatively alone, and I braced myself for the inevitable questions about what Nerva meant when he mentioned two of the three most powerful men in Rome, yet to my surprise, he said nothing. Falling back into our own spot, he seemed content to ride in silence, then we were joined by Alex, who reported that Canus had been taken care of before he turned to Maroboduus.

"Lord, I'm sorry, but I'm afraid that young Goda and one of your other children peeked out the back of the wagon when I passed by, and she saw Canus. She...didn't take it well."

"That does not surprise me," Maroboduus murmured. He reined up, then turned his mount. "I will go comfort her."

Once he was safely out of earshot, I related Nerva's

clearly unintentional mistake in mentioning Tiberius and Drusus in the context of Maroboduus' deposing by Catualda, but Alex was not as certain as I was that Maroboduus was surprised by this.

"Did he say anything?" he asked. "After what Nerva said?"

"No," I admitted, "but he got a strange look on his face."

Alex thought for a moment, then shrugged and said, "I'm almost certain that Maroboduus has already figured out that the only way a Roman Legion would be involved with Catualda's plot to depose him is proof that Tiberius or Drusus is involved. Besides," he pointed out, "that is so far above us that there's no point in worrying about it."

Which, I understood, was true, and it was quickly forgotten as we talked about Canus.

"I misjudged him."

"Not as badly as I did," Alex countered. "I didn't trust him even a little bit, and was waiting for him to plunge that fucking dagger into your back any chance he got."

"I'm glad you did," I surprised him by saying. "Because it put my mind at ease." I sighed. "I just hope Maroboduus can do something about his children."

"Do you think he meant it?" Alex asked me; I had informed him of the former king's promise. "Remember, he is still a king, at least in terms of thinking like one, especially at a moment like that, and they make promises all the time that they have no intention of keeping."

It was a fair question, and I considered it for a moment, then I surprised myself slightly by nodding.

"I think he did, and he does," I said, but I also was honest. "But he's not a king anymore, and while he said he's not destitute, I don't know how much money he could have sewn up in his cloak." We were quiet for a bit, then I voiced the nagging thought that had been lurking in the back of my mind. "Do you think that, if what Canus said was true, that Maroboduus is safe?"

"I do," he answered immediately, the sign that he had thought about it. "If only because it will help keep Catualda obedient to Rome, him knowing that Maroboduus is still alive.

And," he grinned, "what Tiberius grants, Tiberius can take away."

This had been my thought, but it helped having confirmation. That evening, while the Legion was making camp, Nerva assigned some slaves to build a pyre, and we purified Gaius Fonteius, who I will always think of as Canus, with fire, burning the entrapping flesh away so his soul could fly to wherever the gods and the Fates have destined for him to go. And, I like to think, the presence of one small mourner, who was clearly grief-stricken, would have made Canus happy.

It was when we reached the stretch of the Rhenus that runs east and west that marked we were now one day away from Mogontiacum, thirty miles away; more importantly, we were about to hit the paved Roman road. Not surprisingly, neither Alex nor I found it easy to sleep that last night, but what had surprised me was noticing the absence of Canus in our tent; even Herminius and Arnfrid commented on it. Unlike their two Roman comrades, however, none of the Batavians were dreading the idea of returning to Mogontiacum, all of them spending that evening talking excitedly in their tongue about the delights awaiting them in the part of the city that catered to the non-Romans, although a fair number of men under the standard who had developed a taste for the exotic found themselves wandering over there. The next morning, the routine was the same as always; camp was broken, everything packed up, although Nerva had stopped ordering ditch and walls two days earlier, meaning that it was a bit more leisurely since there was less to do. And, as I had been doing for the entirety of the march, I joined the Pili Priores for the marching orders, while Maroboduus was present as well, though nobody was surprised that, as was customary on this final day, the First Cohort was in the vanguard. The Legion eagle and Cohort standards would be garlanded with ivy, announcing to all who saw the Alaudae that they had been successful in what they had been sent to do, although I had my doubts that Tiberius wanted this action announced publicly. We had been gone from Mogontiacum for more than six weeks, while Alex and I had been gone from Ubiorum, which we both thought of as our real home, for almost a year, and never far from my mind was the possibility that I might never return to the 1st at all. Alex was in a slightly better situation given his position with the army, yet neither of us wanted to be faced with the prospect of being separated, although I would not hesitate to force him to do so if it meant keeping his freedom. My first indication that something different was happening was when I saw Nerva exchange a quiet word with Maroboduus, who, like me, had dismounted for the meeting; my second was the manner in which some of the Pili Priores behaved as they dispersed, even if it was nothing more than a nod, or some murmured statement I could not quite make out, while some of them, like the Secundus Pilus Prior, behaved as they always did.

"Pullus, stay behind for a moment," Nerva called to me, just as I was mounting Latobius.

Maroboduus did mount, guiding his horse past me, saying, "Once the Primus Pilus is finished speaking with you, I would like a word as well."

As soon as the Pili Priores had left; I noticed that the Secundus lingered a bit, until a glare from Nerva sent him scuttling away, I walked over to the Primus Pilus, but instead of speaking to me immediately, he first barked at one of his Sergeants, reminding him to check a ranker's canteen to make sure that it was filled with water and not wine, and despite the circumstances, I had to fight a grin as I thought, the job is never done. However, he did not turn to look at me, choosing instead to keep watching his Century, which did not help my anxiety.

Then, without warning, he said, "This is where you and Alex leave us, Pullus." My first thought was that he was essentially abandoning us here, but he continued, "It's not going to be safe for you in Mogontiacum, for either of you."

"But my family is there!" I gasped. "So is Alex's! I won't leave them there, Primus Pilus!"

For the first time, he looked up at me, yet his face was expressionless.

"You won't be," he replied. "Because they're not there. They're back in Ubiorum."

This did not make sense to me, and frankly, I did not believe him, but I managed to avoid saying that, instead asking in disbelief, "How can you know that?"

His expression altered then, and while I was not sure, it seemed as if he was embarrassed, but he answered with one word; more accurately, a name.

"Barvistus." I still did not understand, and he said impatiently, "I sent Barvistus ahead to Mogontiacum, with instructions to go to your mother's villa." Suddenly, I recalled that, in fact, I had not seen Barvistus for the past few days, but when I asked Herminius, he had given some vague explanation that he had been sent ahead by the Primus Pilus. "He waited until your family was packed up and ready to leave, then rode with them to Confluentes before he returned to the Legion." I did not know what to say, and even if I had, I doubt I would have gotten the words out, my emotions threatening to shame me.

"T-thank you, Primus Pilus Nerva. I can't tell you how much it means, to both of us."

It was all I could think to say, while he looked embarrassed, shuffling his feet about.

"Yes, well," he mumbled, "it's the right thing to do." He looked up at me then, and while his expression was hard, I thought I saw a glint of humor in his eyes as he said, "And, if you ever tell Tiberius, I mean Sacrovir, I said this, I'll deny it with my last breath. But," he took a breath, "I was wrong about you, Pullus. I thought that you were another paid man who just happened to have a famous father, and that you used his accomplishments, and," he indicated my body, "your size and strength to gain honors that you didn't deserve. But now?" He shook his head. "I've seen how wrong I was. In fact, I think that you're destined to be a Primus Pilus yourself one day. Although," he gave a snorting laugh, "I'll be long gone by then. And," he said seriously, "if you manage to keep yourself from getting killed by one of those patrician bastards in Rome."

As sobering as the words were, and as moved as I was by the sentiment, knowing how hard it must have been for Nerva to utter the words, I could not stop myself from grinning down at him.

"In case you haven't noticed, Primus Pilus, I'm hard to kill." Then, before he could think that I was ungrateful, I said hurriedly, "But thank you for your words, Primus Pilus. And," I continued sincerely, "I have to confess that my feelings about you have changed as well. I'd be proud to serve under you as my Primus Pilus." Then, I had to add, grinning again, "Of course, only if it was in the 1st."

As I hoped, this pleased and amused him, but his businesslike demeanor quickly returned, and he withdrew a scroll from his *baltea* that I had not noticed.

"Give this to Primus Pilus Sacrovir," he said, and though he did not need to, he explained. "It's a summary of what we did, your role in it, and my assurance that if there's any trouble coming your way, I'll be available to do whatever I need to, to help stop it."

Without waiting for my response, which I suspect was on purpose, he thrust his arm out, which I took, then I saluted once we broke our clasp, rendering it freely, which he returned with the same solemnity.

"May the gods protect you, Alex, and your families, Gnaeus."

It was the last thing he said to me, and so far, it is the last we have spoken. Leaving him, I mounted and trotted back Latobius down the column, just as the *cornu* sounded the alert, followed a couple heartbeats later by the order to advance, and I saw Maroboduus sitting on his horse next to the column, waiting. Signaling that I would join him in a moment, I cantered over to Alex, telling him what was happening, and he hurried down the column to find our pack animal, being led by a borrowed slave.

Only then did I ride over to the Marcomanni, who surprised me by saying conversationally, "I wanted to say goodbye since you are leaving us."

"How did you know that?" I asked.

"Primus Pilus Nerva and I discussed it last night. He asked my advice."

On its face, this seemed unlikely, but now that we had had exposure to the Marcomanni king, I know that I had been impressed, and I had sensed that Nerva felt the same way. Some of this was probably due to our coming to know Catualda, and the contrast was striking, but whatever the case,

I could envision that Nerva sought his input on the matter of whether I stayed with the Alaudae.

"And?"

"And," he shrugged, "I agreed with him that you are not likely to be safe, especially now that Canus is dead."

This had not occurred to me, but there was another aspect that bothered me, and I heard the coolness in my voice as I pointed out, "But the only people who know how Canus died are me, Alex, you, and Primus Pilus Nerva. Neither Alex nor I are going to talk about it, and I don't see Nerva doing so."

If he heard the implication there, he gave no sign that he was offended, simply pointing out, "How many men saw me ride off, Canus follow me, then you galloping to my rescue?" I did not reply; there was no need to because, given the flat, open ground, everyone on the left side of the column would have seen us. He smiled then as he went on, "And when they saw the two of us return to the column, with Canus' body, how many men do you think would wager on it being me who killed Varro's man, Centurion?"

He was right; it had been naïve of me to think that Varro would not hear about Canus from the men of the Alaudae when they were out in the city spending their newfound wealth, nor was it likely that the men would believe that, between the two men they saw riding back, they would pick Maroboduus over me, if only because of my size and reputation.

I signaled that I was setting this aside by asking, "What about you? And your family?"

He understood immediately, replying, "Oh, I am safe, as is my family. The Imperator and his son will ensure our safety because they want to keep me alive in order to make sure that Catualda does not get any dangerous ideas." This, I thought, was treacherous territory, and I was about to shift the subject, but Maroboduus continued to speak, saying in a conversational manner, "After all, they are responsible for taking my crown from me and giving it to Catualda, so I suppose that is the least they can do."

I could not suppress a gasp, which evoked a bitter smile from him.

"You knew?" He nodded, and I asked, "When? How?"

"I knew when your Roman Legion showed up outside the walls of Casurgis," he replied, and now I could hear the bitterness, which was completely understandable. "But I had heard rumors of a meeting between my nephew and Drusus a few months ago." It was the first and only time where Maroboduus referred to Catualda by his familial connection as the blood nephew of his former senior wife. Maroboduus caught me by surprise then, asking, "Why would this *Quaestor*? Varro?" I nodded. "Why would he order Canus to kill me, Centurion Pullus? While I do not understand your rank structure all that well, *Quaestor* is not a particularly high office, is it?"

"No, it's not."

"Then how could a *Quaestor* be bold enough to send a man after me? Is that not a terrible risk for him? And to what purpose?"

I thought about how forthcoming to be, but it was only a brief struggle, and I went on to explain what I knew, about Sejanus, his influence over the Imperator that had caused Germanicus such concern before he was sent East, and how Varro was one of Sejanus' creatures. Maroboduus seemed to appreciate this information, and once I was finished, he cleared his throat, and said awkwardly, "Yes, well I just wanted to thank you again for intervening with Canus, and that I bear neither you nor the men of the 5th Legion any animosity for your role in deposing me. You were only doing your duty, and I consider you a man of honor among Romans. I also wanted to let you know that I was sincere with Canus about doing what I can for his children, although," he gave a self-conscious laugh, "I have no idea what that might be. Once I reach Rome, I should at least be able to learn more of their...situation."

Similarly to Nerva, he offered his hand, not in the Roman manner where we clasp arms, but hand to hand, and I accepted it, then we turned our mounts and I headed to where Alex was waiting. At the time, it certainly seemed reasonable, and likely, that Maroboduus would be going to Rome, but we learned very quickly that this was not to be; as of now, he is in Ravenna, and there is no sign that he will be leaving there any time soon. I think about him surprisingly often, especially once Catualda began displaying his true colors as King of the Marcomanni, which did not take long at all.

Naturally, we gave Mogontiacum a wide berth, adding a bit of time to our journey. Reaching Confluentes late in the day, we briefly discussed pressing on, but now that the weather had turned, neither of us were particularly enamored of the idea of spending a night out on the cold ground for the ten more miles we would have made before being forced to stop. Neither of us spoke of it, but I am certain we were of a like mind; knowing that our families were back in Ubiorum with our Legion made it an easier decision. Stopping early also gave Latobius and Lightning extra rest, and we left before first light the next day, planning on a hard day's ride and reaching Ubiorum after dark but early enough for the city gates to still be open. Neither of us talked much, both absorbed in our own thoughts of a reunion with our loved ones; it also meant that neither of us were paying much attention to the weather, although the clouds had been leaden and threatening since it had gotten light enough to see. And, when the first flurries of snow began falling, I barely noticed, but within a third of a watch, the road, now a fully paved, good Roman road, was impossible to see, while visibility ahead of us was down to about fifty paces.

"We're going to have to stop at Rigomagus," I had to shout to be heard, both because of the wind and because I had pulled my winter neckerchief up over my nose and mouth, and Alex nodded agreement.

If we had been able to make it to Bonna, then we would at least have been able to get news about the Legion, since there is a fort there manned at all times by one of the third line Cohorts, while Rigomagus is manned by a Cohort of auxiliaries. The civilian settlement that had grown up around the auxiliary fort was crammed full of people, travelers who, like us, had decided against pressing on, packing the lone inn. Fortunately, a Legion Centurion can be assured of a spot in the auxiliary camp, and we were blessed that there was an officer's hut available because one of the auxiliary Centurions had died of a fever a couple weeks earlier and had yet to be replaced. Even so, we did return to the inn for our meal, just to listen to the inevitable gossip that is as much a part of a traveling inn as the fare on offer, but we were to be disappointed in this as well, since the consensus was that affairs in the province had been dreadfully boring.

"Not even a cattle raid," I overheard one man sniff, sounding as if that was the worst thing in the world. "The Germans have been fully pacified, it appears."

His companion, a man with narrow-set eyes that never seemed to rest on one thing for more than a heartbeat, shrugged and mildly disagreed.

"I think it's too early to say that, Cornuficius. I think that they're as tired of all the fighting as we are, but they're just resting."

I naturally tried to act as if I was not listening, but I did not miss Alex regarding me with an amused expression.

He did think to keep his voice low, though it was hard to do so because of the buzz of conversations like that one.

"Try not to look so disappointed, Gnaeus. We could use a little peace and quiet for a bit."

I knew he was teasing, but I also was aware that he had good reason to say this, because that was exactly where my thoughts were, thinking, Gods, I *hope* not! Yes, I would be perfectly content to have a nice, quiet winter, without the need to rouse the Legion, or just the First Cohort for that matter, but come spring, the idea that we would not be marching did not make me happy at all, something that I would never openly admit to Bronwen. Otherwise, it was a pleasant evening hearing the chatter, with a warm fire, and the prospect that, barring a blizzard, with only thirty miles left, we would be home the next day. When we retired to the auxiliary camp, a slave had already stoked the fire in the stove, making it quite snug, and we both fell asleep quickly.

Waking to the *bucina* call the next morning, I held my breath as I opened the door of the hut, but to our relief, while there was about a foot more snow on the ground, it was not enough to significantly impede our progress. We had purchased an extra loaf apiece at the inn, and we ate quickly before saddling our mounts and repacking our baggage on our packhorse. The sun was visible only as a hazy sphere obscured by gray clouds, its light weak and not offering its normal warmth, but we were both accustomed to the weather, and prepared for it. I was wearing the fur-lined *sagum*, along with my double thickness *bracae*, and my father's fur-lined leather gloves that had caused him some heartache when he had purchased them when he was still a young *Gregarius* in his second full year under the standard and as his father liked to joke, the "richest family of the Head Count" after Divus Augustus' unjust and petty demotion of the family after the death of the Prefect. It is not lost on me that, in order to keep the Pullus name by accepting my father's posthumous offer of adoption, I lost the status of Equestrian that the Prefect had suffered and sacrificed so much to attain for his family's posterity, and I have often thought of the day when we meet beyond the river, wondering what he will say about me doing so. Even so, I still have no regrets about my decision, and in fact, I think an argument could be made that, given my interactions and conflict with Prefect Sejanus, my relative unimportance in the rigid hierarchy of our society marks me as less of a danger than if I had been in both the Centurionate and still in the Equestrian order. None of which was in my mind that morning, beyond the thought about the gloves, and I found myself smiling at the memory of reading from my father's account when he and my grandfather had clashed about a pair of gloves, when my father had quipped that it was not about flaunting the family wealth but about keeping his hands warm and able to hold a *gladius* should the moment come. His satisfaction at rendering Gaius Porcinianus Pullus speechless and unable to offer a counterargument ranked as one of his happiest moments, something that I could identify with quite easily, remembering my own smugness when I had done the same to him.

The going was a bit slower than it would have been without any snow on the road, but we were not the only ones out, and since the traffic was both ways as the day progressed, our pace picked up as the snow was packed down. It meant that it was still daylight when we spotted the walls of Ubiorum first, then the walls of the camp, which used to be exactly a mile west of the town, which fronted the river, but was closer now since Ubiorum had expanded, the walls being extended almost three hundred paces west some years before. Even in the relatively short period of time I had been in Ubiorum, now going on seven years, it has grown immensely, while my father, who transferred into the 1st from Pannonia their first year at Ubiorum, had seen it grow from a shantytown occupied by the camp followers and sharp operators that follow a Legion into a town of about six thousand inhabitants. Now, without either of us saying a word, we both drew up, staring at the southern wall, and the scattered dark shapes on the road ahead of us, some moving towards us, away from Ubiorum, others going towards it like we were.

"You know," I remarked, "there was a time or two this past year that I wasn't sure I would ever see this place again." Alex did not say anything, but I saw him nod in agreement. "And," I laughed, "I never thought I would be this happy to see it."

With that, we nudged our horses onward on the last mile of our journey home.

There was a feeling of unreality as we entered through the southern gate, continuing as, without needing to guide them, both Latobius and Lightning carried us into the town, turning at the proper corner and in the right direction that took us to their stable where they spent most of their time. There was a bit of a problem because the owner, a retired veteran from the Gallic cavalry, had rented out their normal stalls, and Latobius in particular obstinately refused to enter the new stall. Thankfully, the veteran was willing to swap out the occupant of my horse's old stall, a gelding belonging to a merchant who had arrived during our absence, whereupon Lightning balked at the idea of being separated from Latobius since they had always been near each other. This cost a few coins, but soon enough, our mounts were settled in, rubbed down and fed; then, hefting our packs, we walked the two blocks to the building where, unlike the villa in Rome, we had apartments that were on the same floor. Given the time of day, and the habit formed over the time we had been together, we knew that our families would be in the same apartment; the only question was whether it would be mine or Alex's. Ascending the stairs, we stopped at the landing to have a whispered argument about who should be knocking on the door.

"The last time you did it, Bronwen fainted!" Alex argued, which was true enough, but when I pointed out that if it was Algaia who opened the door to see her husband showing up unannounced, it was likely to end the same way, he scoffed, "When is the last time you've seen Algaia faint?"

That, I recognized, was true; she had been held hostage by my uncle and maintained her presence of mind, so I stood aside and gestured up the stairs. He decided to head to my apartment first, rapping on the door, but there was no answer. Then, before we could turn our attention to his apartment, the door to it opened, and it was Bronwen, standing there, eyes wide and with Titus on her hip, who I am certain was responsible for his Mama keeping her feet, although she reached out and grabbed the edge of the door as she reeled slightly. I was already moving, as much to grab Titus and her to keep them from falling as to embrace her.

"Is it really you?" she murmured as she wrapped one arm around my neck, while Titus, finding himself once more being crushed between his parents, had the same reaction as the other times, howling in protest.

The next few moments are a bit of a blur, as Alex rushed into his apartment, pushing past us to find Algaia, who had been in the other room and was hurrying into his arms, with all the adults talking at once, laughing, crying, and celebrating our reunion. I did not see Iras coming, but I felt her legs wrapping around my legs, after she kissed her father of course, then Bronwen handed me my son, so with my free hand, I swept her up, her little arms going around my neck, while Titus drooled on me, and I realized there was only one thing that could have made me happier, yet before I could ask my wife, my prayers were answered.

"Welcome home, my son."

I turned, my vision clouding instantly at the sight of my mother, standing in the doorway leading into the other room; only then did I finally feel complete, knowing that every person I loved who was in Germania was safe and under one roof.

"We had to wait until it got dark to slip out of the villa," my mother explained as we sat at the table in my apartment, where she was sleeping. "The *Quaestor* has had a man watching ever since you and Alex left with the Alaudae. But," she smiled, though it was a kind I could not recall seeing before, with a hardness to it, "he didn't think that, being the women we are, we would dare set foot outside after dark, so he didn't bother keeping a man on watch after the sun set."

I felt a rustling sense of disquiet, and I actually thought it might be better not to ask; of course, that was what I did.

"How did you know that he wasn't keeping a man on watch?"

"Because, I went to visit Lucius a couple of times," she replied, looking me in the eye as she did so, which I understood was a challenge to say something about it, and if I am a judge of my mother, she was slightly disappointed when I did no such thing. She continued then, explaining, "So, when Primus Pilus Nerva sent Barvistus, he told us that you and Alex were fine, and that you had been successful in whatever it was you were sent to do." She frowned in irritation. "And Barvistus refused to tell us what it was! That was quite infuriating!" I glanced over at Bronwen, expecting her to look as amused as I felt, but it was clear that she shared my mother's indignation, asking me with a scowl, "Was that your idea, Gnaeus? Did you tell that Batavian not to let your wife and mother know why you were risking your life?"

"I had nothing to do with it!" I protested, yet they did not seem to believe me, so I said, "We didn't even know that Nerva had sent him ahead!" I turned to Alex, demanding his support. "Did we?"

"No, we didn't," he assured them. "We didn't find out until two days ago, when we were just outside Mogontiacum."

"So you didn't go into the city?" my mother asked. When I shook my head, she sagged in relief. "I was hoping you wouldn't. *One* reason I went to see Lucius," she emphasized the first word in another clear message to me, "was to learn as much as I could about what was going on. While he didn't know, he did say that Varro had begun behaving more...erratically."

"Erratically?" I frowned. "Was he more specific than that?"

"Not really," she shook her head, prompting a snort from me, which earned me the sight of flaring nostrils as she glared at me. "He's not a spy, Gnaeus! And," she pointed at me, "he was doing it to help me, yes, but it was also for you! I was trying to get an idea of what you could expect when you returned."

Now it was my turn to glance over at Alex, but he, understanding, shook his head at the idea of telling the women about Canus. However, I did not see how I could completely ignore something that would be an important factor in the *Quaestor*'s mood once the Alaudae returned with Maroboduus, and without Canus.

"I don't think that things went like the *Quaestor* would have wanted. Not," I added, "completely, at least."

"Then it's probably a good thing that you didn't go into the city," my mother decided. Then, she added in a thoughtful tone, "Actually, I *do* recall something Lucius said that I didn't think much of at the time, but he said that it was as if Varro was waiting for something big to happen, and the pressure of waiting had made him increasingly raw. Then, when Barvistus came to the villa, it was just after he had reported to the *Quaestor*, and he said that Varro asked him questions about what you had been sent to do, but when Barvistus reported that all had gone according to plan, that it seemed to enrage Varro instead of making him happy."

Without knowing what Barvistus told him, it was hard to know, but later when Alex and I discussed it privately, our thoughts were running along the same lines.

"Barvistus would have told him that Casurgis fell, but also that Maroboduus had been unharmed."

"And he was supposed to be dead," I nodded, but then pointed out, "although when Nerva sent Barvistus ahead, it was the day before Canus...died."

"He probably was expecting Canus to do it sooner and not waiting until the last moment," Alex commented. "Which would explain why he was so irritable."

"Then I'm glad we're not around to see what he's like now," I said fervently.

At the table, my mother continued the story.

"Barvistus came to get us after it was dark a few days ago, and escorted us to Confluentes. We left with a cart and a mule." She smiled again, but I did not.

"That's not nearly enough to haul your possessions, Mother!" I objected. "Who's guarding the villa? Just Grimhilt?"

"No," she assured me. "Carissa and Mandalonius returned from attending to her sister's affairs a week before. And," she gave me a rueful smile, "I didn't have the heart to dismiss Grimhilt."

While this was a relief, I had to laugh at the idea of Carissa, who was as formidable in her own way, and Grimhilt establishing the hierarchy under my mother's command. Still, I was happier that Carissa's man Mandalonius was there more than Carissa, who was not particularly intelligent, and was generally docile, but as a former gladiator, knew what he was about if things got violent.

"Besides," she continued, and with a firm tone, "this is only temporary. I'll be returning to Mogontiacum as soon as I can."

"Mother Giulia," Bronwen put a hand on my mother's arm, "you know that you are welcome to stay as long as you like. Baby Titus loves having you around, and so do I!"

"And I adore the both of you," my mother assured her. "But, my dear girl, this apartment is *not* made for this many people in it, and that is without my own things as it is. No," she shook her head as she said firmly, "as soon as it's safe to do so, I'm returning to Mogontiacum."

The rest of our time that day was spent on lighter topics, but I confess that I scarcely paid attention, and judging from our time together later, Bronwen was of the same mind, both of us wanting to celebrate our reunion in a more personal manner.

My reunion with the 1st, and with my Century, was in many ways the antithesis of that with my family, and it started as soon as I was ushered into the private office of Primus Pilus Sacrovir.

"It's about time," he grumbled after our exchange of salutes, though there was a smile on his face, but it did not last long. I proffered the scroll from Nerva, which he accepted, muttering as he did so, "There's a lot going on here as well." I opened my mouth to ask what that meant, but he held up a hand, his eyes going to the scroll, moving along the lines, leaving me to study his expression intently for some clue. His eyes opened more widely, not much but noticeably, at one point, then at another, he glanced up at me. "So, Casurgis is taken, Maroboduus was removed from the throne, and," he had to refer back to the scroll, "and Catualda is on the throne, while Maroboduus and his family are safe and back in Mogontiacum for the moment." I nodded, hoping that he would not ask for details, which lasted for the amount of time it took him to ask, "So? What was the assault like? Was it bloody?"

I spent the next few moments describing what had taken place, and I could not help noticing that Sacrovir seemed to be paying only partial attention, his eyes back on the scroll.

When I finished, he regarded me for a moment, then asked, "Is that all?"

I had not been entirely forthcoming, but I knew there were two possibilities, neither of which I cared to divulge, although for different reasons, yet I could tell that Nerva had mentioned something that would lead him to ask.

Deciding to take a guess, I said, "I did have something to do with getting Maroboduus to surrender by guaranteeing his safety back to Mogontiacum."

My heart sank at the sight of his eyes narrowing as he stared up at me, though his tone was level enough as he said, "Primus Pilus Nerva didn't mention that." I was afraid he would press for details, but instead, he said, "But that's not what I'm talking about." His tone softened fractionally, "I think you know what I'm referring to, Pullus."

"Yes, sir, I do," I acknowledged. "But there's not much I can tell you about it."

His expression altered, not much, but becoming markedly less stern, and he said, "Ah, I see. You don't remember?"

"No, sir." I shook my head, which was true; I did not mention I had been told about it later.

"Well," he sighed, "the reason I brought it up is because I have some news that I'm afraid might cause...whatever it is that happens to you Pullus men to happen again." My heart began pounding, the first thought racing through my mind being that the 1st was marching back across the Rhenus, though I had no idea for what reason; however, the truth is that I would have never guessed the real reason. "Your Century is out of control, and unless you can get them in hand within the next couple of days, the way things are going, I'm going to have to order some of your men to run the gauntlet before they're back in hand."

I desperately wished he had offered me a seat, and I was standing too far away to grab the edge of his desk, feeling as if I had been punched in the stomach.

"But...why?" I finally managed to gasp.

The look he gave me was almost pitying, but his answer took me a moment to understand.

"Florus."

Chapter 9

"The men blame me for not saving Florus," I told Alex as we walked to what would be our new quarters, since we had never actually made it to Ubiorum, except that we took a more circuitous route so that I could explain to him what we were walking into. "They think I could have and should have done more to save him, but since we weren't with the Fifth, they've run roughshod over Bibaculus since we left." Alex's reaction was much like mine had been, a strangled gasp, but I told him grimly, "Wait. It gets worse. According to Sacrovir, the ringleader of the troublemakers is Vinicius."

"Vinicius!" he exclaimed, then asked hopefully, "You don't mean the..."

"Yes," I answered tersely, "the *Tesserarius*." The Fifth Century had another Vinicius in the ranks, though he was no relation to the *Tesserarius*, and I did not blame Alex for thinking it was the ranker, since that was my first thought as well, mainly because it was wishful thinking. "Not the ranker."

"Pluto's thorny *cock*!" We walked a few steps more before he asked, "And what has Bibaculus done about it? Anything?"

"Nothing effective," I spat. "Sacrovir says that he's spending most of the day inside his quarters."

As I knew he would, Alex got immediately to the nub of the issue.

"And what's Sacrovir doing about it?"

"He made a mistake," I answered, then hurried to add, "and that's coming from him, not me. He said that he thought we would be getting back sooner than we did, and he wanted to wait before he stepped in. Now," I sighed, "he's given me three days to get the men in hand."

"*Three* days?" Alex gasped. This was bad enough, but my heart sank when he asked, "So, what are you going to do?"

"I was hoping you'd have some idea," I snapped ill-naturedly, even as I knew it was unfair.

"You just told me about it!" he protested. "Give me a few moments to think about it!"

I waved a hand in apology, but came to a stop at the intersection of the First Cohort, just around the corner and out of sight.

"The men are restricted to their huts," I told Alex. "So at least they'll be easy to find." I took a breath, feeling the uncoiling in my stomach, and I reminded myself about Sacrovir's comment warning that the beast inside me might be roused. Not yet, Gnaeus. "But we're starting with Vinicius."

"Do you want me there?"

I thought for a moment, then shook my head. "No, go on ahead to our quarters and get settled in. And remind Euphemios that you're still my chief clerk, just like before. I know he's been doing your job since we've been gone, but you know what to do." He nodded, since we had discussed this, deciding that paying Euphemios fifty *sesterces* extra was the best approach and would smooth things between him and Alex, not that I cared that much. We parted ways as he bounded up the steps to our new quarters, which I knew were actually the size of a Pilus Prior's quarters, but the extra space was devoted to the front half of the hut, needed because of the size of a First Cohort Century. The Optio and *Signifer*'s quarters are next to the Centurion's; during the time of the Prefect and my grandfather, the Optio, *Signifer, Tesserarius* and *Cornicen* shared quarters, but now the *Cornicen* and *Tesserarius* share a hut or a tent, and it is on the opposite side of the Optio and *Signifer's*. I paused for a moment, thinking that I would talk to Bibaculus first, then decided against it, not wanting to be near the limit of my control before I confronted Vinicius, so I continued to their hut, stopping outside. While I did not kick the door in, neither did I knock with my *vitus*, the customary method; instead, I grasped the latch, twisting it slowly so it did not make noise, then slammed into it with my shoulder. The effect was not quite as violent or noisy as kicking it in, but it was close, and I did remember to step into the doorway to avoid having the door shut in my face, which has happened to many a new officer...including myself, when a more experienced Centurion, namely my father, "forgot" to warn me of one of the more embarrassing things that can happen. Since this was my first time in their quarters in Ubiorum, I did not know who I would confront first, since the occupants are allowed to choose which half is their own, though I was not surprised to see Macrinus lounging on his bunk. His eyes went wide, and he started to swing his legs onto the floor, but when he opened his mouth, I shook my head and put my finger to my lips.

"Macrinus! What the fuck was that?" Vinicius' voice was muffled by his closed door, "Why are you making such a racket? I'm trying to sleep! I've got a fucking hangover, you know that!"

I crossed the room in three long strides, and this time, I did kick the door open, but because of the cold, he had shuttered the one window, and the daylight from the doorway was not as strong, so I do not believe he recognized me. I was wearing just my tunic, having handed Alex my *sagum* to take into our quarters, not wanting any kind of hindrance in my movements, while he let out a cry of alarm as he scrambled to his feet, but in the dim light, it was hard for both of us to see, for him to dodge and for me to grab a handful of his tunic. I managed to be successful, snatching him off his feet, which was not all that difficult because Vinicius is short and of a slender build, balding and with several teeth missing, grabbing him with my right hand since my left held my *vitus*, though I did not strike him with it.

Instead, with his feet dangling inches off the floor, I said in a conversational tone, "It appears that we have some matters to discuss, *Tesserarius* Vinicius."

It was when he tried to speak and only a choked squawk came out that I realized I had grabbed a large handful of his tunic up around his throat, making it impossible for him to talk, or to breathe, so I dropped him back to the floor, then waited as he rubbed his throat. Even in the dim light, I saw him glaring up at me, which was unusual in itself; in my limited time on the march from Rome, he had never struck me as having a defiant streak.

"Yes, we do, Centurion," he began, but got no farther because I slapped him hard across the face, sending him staggering back with enough force that he crashed into the wall, knocking the jug on the small table over, spilling the wine in it.

"That's Primus Hastatus Prior, you *cunnus*," I snarled at him, and I was gratified to see the fear in his eyes. Oh, he was still angry, but now he had another emotion competing for his attention, and I closed the distance so that I could tower above him. "It seems like you've forgotten yourself, *Tesserarius*. Or," I said menacingly, "perhaps I should refer to you by your future rank...*Gregarius Ordinarius*."

His eyes went wide, and all signs of defiance vanished from his demeanor, yet I could see he felt obligated to provide some sort of defense.

"The men are...upset with what happened to Florus, sir," he began. "But you had left, and when we went to Bibaculus, he refused to take our concerns to the Primus Pilus."

"Concerns? What concerns?" I asked.

"*Gregarius* Florus wasn't allowed the process due to him as a Legionary of Rome," Vinicius replied, and I confess my heart sank a little, because this was true.

However, I also felt it necessary to point out, "His guilt wasn't in doubt, Vinicius. There were too many witnesses in The Happy Legionary who saw what happened, and the woman in question has a...reputation for inciting this kind of thing."

"That may be true, sir," Vinicius said stiffly. "But that doesn't mean Florus should have been deprived of his rights by regulation."

It was this moment when I felt a niggling sense that not only was this a bigger problem than I had thought, but, when it came to the form of the matter, the men of the Fifth Century had a legitimate grievance. All of the men in the First Cohort, no matter the Century, or the Legion for that matter, are veterans who have been under the standard for long enough to have been present for the mutiny now more than four and a half years earlier, and along with the pay and length of enlistments, probably the third most important thing on the list was the arbitrary nature of punishments meted out by their superiors. And, as I knew all too well, the scars from that period of time were still fresh, and there are always men, both in the ranks and among the officers, who hold grudges longer than their comrades, and these men, of all ranks, had been complaining about the concessions made by Tiberius ever since the mutiny ended, saying they did not go far enough. It was, I realized in that moment, something that I should have seen coming before I departed, although at the same time, I had no idea on Gaia's earth what I could have done about it, nor did I have any idea that I would not be staying with the Fifth.

Without thinking it through first, I asked Vinicius, "And what do *you* think about it, Vinicius? Do you agree with the men who are saying this?"

"Yes, Hastatus Prior," he answered immediately, without hesitation, and my respect for him went back up a notch, reminding me that *Tesserarius* is the one rank that is elected by the men, although with the Augustan reforms, the Centurion has the right of veto over it, but I had never heard of it happening in the 1st.

It was certainly not in my plans to do so, at least not unless I was forced into it, either by Vinicius' obstinance or by Sacrovir; I had just intended to slap Vinicius a bit and put the fear of Dis, and me, into him, but before I could talk myself out of it, I heard myself asking, "And, what do you think I should do about it, Vinicius?"

He was at least as startled at being asked as I was for asking, and he stammered, "I...I...it's not my place to say, Hastatus Prior."

"Don't hand me that *cac*!" I snapped. "You're an officer in this Century, and while I know that I haven't been in command of the Fifth for very long, and have been away for almost two months, I also know that before he had his...problems, Hastatus Prior Varo would have expected every one of his officers, down to the section Sergeants who came to him with a problem also provide a solution to it. Otherwise, you're nothing but a bellyaching complainer just like most rankers! Or, am I wrong about Varo?"

Vinicius actually closed his eyes, I assumed to break eye contact with me so that he could admit, "No, sir. You're not wrong. Hastatus Prior Varo had the same policy." He opened his eyes, which took on a shrewd look. "If I tell you what I think, will you swear on the eagle that the boys will never know that I said what I'm about to say?"

It rubbed me the wrong way, yet I also acknowledged to myself that I had initiated this, and being honest, I could see why an officer would want that kind of assurance, especially with matters as they were in the Century.

Still, the words did not come easily, but they did come, as I intoned, "I swear on the eagle of the 1st that the Century will never know this came from you."

He was clearly satisfied, and for the next few moments, keeping his voice low in the event that Macrinus might be pressing his ear to the door, which I had closed, he gave me his thoughts. When he was through, it made me regard Vinicius thoughtfully, the germ of an idea planted, though I was not anywhere near ready to broach it with him.

"You've given me a lot to think about," I told him. "But first things first." Turning to go, I opened his door, then as I walked out of the hut, I told them both, "You're still confined to quarters, but Macrinus, be ready to come to my quarters when I send someone for you."

Once again, I did not stop at Bibaculus' quarters, because my confrontation with Vinicius had sufficiently unsettled me that I wanted some time to think matters through. When I entered, Alex was leaning over Euphemios' shoulder, who was clearly uncomfortable, though I could not tell whether it was just Alex's proximity, or he was anticipating Alex's reaction at what he was reading.

Glancing up, Alex said simply, "The Century diary."

"How bad is it?"

"Worse than it was before you took over," he replied grimly. "Just from this," he indicated the diary, "we have almost a hundred men who would rate an entry in the Legion diary for punishment. It," Alex shook his head, "is bad, Gna...Centurion."

This time when I wanted to sit down, I could do so, and I staggered over to a stool and dropped down onto it, the wood screaming in protest, though I did not suffer the added ignominy of it collapsing and sending me to the floor, however poetically appropriate that may have been.

"What happened while we were gone, Euphemios?" I demanded. When he hesitated, I assured him, "Nothing you say will leave this office."

With that, he did not hesitate, nor did he spare my Optio, although he did begin by qualifying his condemnation, "Honestly, Hastatus Prior, I do not believe that even if Bibaculus had more experience, he would have been able to stop this from happening." Clearly understanding how that sounded, he added quickly, "And by that, I mean that I do not believe one man could have kept the Century under control. At least," he smiled, and I tried to ignore the ingratiating, oily quality to it, "no single man who is not you." I stared at him stonily, and his smile faded. "Yes, well," he fumbled, "I think that your predecessor had let things go, because of his own problems. And," now, he glanced up at Alex, which I found curious, but my friend, and Euphemios' superior, nodded, "I do not believe that our march back here from Rome lasted long enough to completely get the men under your control."

I understood, both what he meant and why he glanced at Alex, that not only was this an accurate assessment, he had discussed this with Alex while I was with Vinicius. Now that it was out in the open, there was the next obvious question, which I directed at Alex.

"What do we do about it?"

Now, Alex looked uncomfortable, glancing over at Euphemios, though he still replied, "I think that's something we should go into your quarters to discuss. Besides," he said, not unkindly, "I interrupted Euphemios in putting today's report together, and Melander is undoubtedly waiting for us to hand the report to the Primus Pilus."

If anything, the other clerk looked relieved at being excluded from the discussion, another sign of just how dire matters were, so I got up and walked into my quarters and private office, seeing that Alex had not had time to do anything other than dump my gear on my cot. The one piece of good news was that word of our return had preceded us in enough time to have a jug of wine and cups brought, and I had Alex pour us both a cup while I moved behind my desk and sat down. It was bare, though that would change quickly enough, starting with the records of the worst offenders, and I was certain that those men would be the same ones who I dealt with when I took over the Century more than three months earlier now, so I had Alex dig out the tablet containing those names. This, I would quickly learn to my astonishment, was a mistake. Oh, there was overlap between that list and those entered in the Legion diary by Bibaculus, but the overlap was nowhere near identical. In fact, and most distressingly, there were a number of names in the Legion diary belonging to men I had put onto the good book that every Centurion carries in his mind of those men who he believes he can count on during dangerous or tough times, including almost half of the section Sergeants. This was so disheartening that I sat back in my chair, seriously thinking of going to Sacrovir and telling him that this was beyond my ability to handle, and that the only way to reassert control over the Fifth Century was Sacrovir's solution, which would shatter the Fifth Century and finish it for the foreseeable future as an effective fighting unit. At least, I thought miserably, then I could rebuild the Century from the ground up, yet even as I thought about this, I also shuddered at the thought, because I would have to watch my back in the event that we went into battle, because Rome would not care that one of their Centuries in one of their Cohorts, even if it was in the First Cohort, in one of their Legions was not ready to go to war. And, I reminded myself, Arminius is still alive, and yes, Maroboduus might have weakened him to the point he was unable or unwilling to resume offensive operations against us, but that was certainly nothing I would wager my life on.

"Gnaeus, you know that you can't let Sacrovir get involved in this," Alex said quietly.

"I know," I agreed before I asked miserably, "but what can I do?"

He did not answer, so we sat in silence, sipping from our cups until, at last, Alex set his down.

"I have an idea," he began. "But you might not like it."

"At this point, I'm open to anything."

"Remember what you did in Rome? With the Praetorians?"

My first reaction was confusion, and I pointed out, "I did a lot of things with them."

"When you faced them in the square, with the *rudis*."

At first, I could only stare at him, it taking a long moment before I found my voice to gasp, "Are you fucking *mad*? You want me to face a First Cohort Century? The only way I made it through the Second back in Rome was because you brought me the Prefect's elixir, and I was sore for days. And," I pointed out, "they were *Praetorians*, dress-up soldiers and not veterans of the Rhenus and men of a First Cohort!"

"I didn't say it would be easy," Alex replied with a straight face, but I saw something in his eye that might have been interpreted as hopeful, though he quickly became serious. "Nor am I suggesting that you face the entire Century, or all at once. Sacrovir gave you three days."

"Counting today," I interjected. "And we're about to turn in a daily report that looks like *cac*."

"I don't think he's counting today," Alex countered, then went on before I could argue, "but even if he is, do you really think he wants to order men executed by their comrades? That," he reminded me, "makes a Primus Pilus look almost as bad as the Centurion, and when it's a First Cohort Century?" He shook his head to emphasize the point. "No, I think he's going to be willing to give you one, or maybe even two extra days."

"All right," I acknowledged grudgingly, "I can see that. But how is this going to help? You know what my father said about how you can't beat men into a better frame of mind."

"Yes, I remember," he said with a wistful smile that, even now, years later, was tinged with pain, one of the occasional reminders of how much longer their association had run than our own, knowing my father since his childhood as he did. The smile changed into a grim one, as he reminded me of something else my father said. "But while you want your men to respect you out of regard for your ability and the fact that you're looking out for them, what's most important is respect, and..."

"...If you can't get it that way, you have to get it out of fear," I finished for him, beginning to get a glimmering of an idea of where he was headed. Suddenly, it came to me. "You want me to do what I did to Petronius, but to several men and not just one."

"Yes," Alex nodded, "something like that. Although," he added quickly, though needlessly, "not to quite the same degree. I don't think Sacrovir will fault you for putting some men in the hospital, given the alternative is to have some of them executed."

It was a daunting prospect, to put it mildly, but as I thought about it, I saw that it might work; however, there was one aspect that I added on my own that, later, Alex said made all the difference. He might have been just trying to make me feel good, but I prefer to take him at his word.

"All right," I slapped the desk as I stood up, "go get Macrinus to sound the assembly. I've got some things to say to the Century."

I was not surprised that the men of the Fifth assembled in our street slowly enough that it would have normally earned the laggards a swipe of the *vitus*, but given what was in their future, I forestalled punishing any of them. Instead, I stood there, impassively but with the slight curl of the lip that the Prefect likened to the expression worn by a man who has a *numen* waving a steaming, hot turd right under his nose. I also was not wearing my *sagum* despite the cold, but had chosen not to put on my armor since it was too late to begin what we had planned, nor did I want to give these men the impression I was worried about my own safety from them, forcing myself to stand there without shivering or giving any sign that I was cold. It had not warmed up sufficiently to melt the snow, so the street was now a hardpacked surface of dirty light gray, the men's hobnailed soles making a crunching sound as they shuffled into their spot in the formation. This was also the first moment I laid eyes on my Optio, which I now realized was a mistake to not speak to him before I had summoned Macrinus to sound assembly, and he did his best to avoid my gaze as he chivvied the ranks, mumbling to the men to move slightly this way and that so that, should I choose to do so, I could stand and look down each rank and see only the men immediately next to me. I did not do so now, preferring instead to wait for him to move from the first to the fifth rank, which was required because the width of the street does not allow for ten ranks of sixteen men. Watching him as he finished, then began walking towards me, I was certain I could see him shaking, and since he was wearing his *sagum*, as all the men were, I knew it was not from the cold. What he had no way of knowing was that, at this moment, I was actually a mass of indecision about what to do with Bibaculus, because the truth was that I found it hard to blame him for what had taken place, yet at the same time, I knew I had to make a decision, and a reckoning about whether or not I trusted him to be my Optio. At the moment, my instinct was that the answer was no, he was not, yet there was enough doubt there that I was questioning myself, and as he approached, I actually offered a silent prayer to the gods for some sign from them that would make my decision easier. None of this was visible to Bibaculus as I watched him come to an abrupt halt, a pace from me, hearing the heel of one *caliga* smack into the heel of the other as he came to *intente* then saluted.

My sense that he was shaking was confirmed by the quaver in his voice as he at least tried to sound professional. "Optio Bibaculus, reporting to Primus Hastatus Prior Pullus that the men of the Fifth Century, First Cohort are either all present or are accounted for, sir!"

I had already seen there were men missing by the ragged ends of the opposite end of the formation from where Lentulus stood in his spot as *Signifer*, although he had not brought out the standard, so I was prepared for the alternate wording when men from the current strength were missing. When we reached Mogontiacum, the Fifth Century consisted of one hundred twenty-nine effectives, thirty-one men short of our full complement, although there had been eight men left here in Ubiorum when the 1st left for Rome and had since recovered enough to rejoin the Century, leaving us twenty-three short, which Sacrovir had informed me would be corrected on our return here. Since all First Cohort Centuries are plumped up from the lower Cohorts, thereby ensuring that the First is always composed of veterans, we did not have to wait for the winter replacement draft, but for obvious reasons, Sacrovir had put this on hold for the Fifth and for the entire Cohort. Then, in Mogontiacum, we had of course lost Florus, but Sacrovir had informed me earlier that day that he had managed to save the lives of Paterculus, Dentulus, and Serranus, although Paterculus had been flogged fifteen lashes, five of them with the scourge, Dentulus and Serranus having been confined to camp, fined, and put on barley and water for a month. All of this meant that we should have been three men short, but just a glance told me it was more than that.

"What's our effective strength, Optio?" I asked, part of the ritual.

One peculiarity about Bibaculus was the abnormally large lump that all men have in their throat, and I saw it bob down then back up before he answered, and I understood why he had to swallow hard.

"One hundred twenty-nine, Hastatus Prior."

While this was bad, I had also guessed that it was something close to this just by judging the length of the ranks, so I was somewhat prepared, but again Bibaculus swallowed, and I lost my patience.

"Well?" I snapped. "What's the status of the seven missing men?"

"We have four in hospital, sir," Bibaculus replied, then listed their names before finishing, "all from injuries sustained in fights out in town."

I felt the stirring in my gut, and I tried to prepare myself as I said tightly, "That's four, Bibaculus, and the total is seven. Where are the other three men?"

"I...I...they're out of the camp, sir."

"Out of the camp?" I echoed, and I confess that I was actually clinging to a stubborn hope, which was what prompted me to ask, "Does that mean they're on some sort of work detail, perhaps? One that you forgot to mention?"

Bibaculus actually closed his eyes, I believe from the shame of admitting, "No, Centurion. They're not on a work detail. They're...out in town."

"'They're out in town,' you say," I repeated. "But since the Primus Pilus told me earlier this morning that the Century is confined to quarters, they clearly aren't out in town with permission, are they?" Bibaculus did not reply verbally, just shook his head, which I should have reprimanded him for, but I did not. Instead, I frowned as I pretended that I was trying to remember something as I said, "Yet, as I recall, you reported that all the men were accounted for...didn't you?"

"Yes, sir. But," his tone changed to a mixture of earnestness and pleading, "the reason I said they were accounted for is because I know where they can be found, sir. The men in all three of their sections told me where they can be found, so as soon as you give the order, I'll go into Ubiorum and bring them back, I swear it!"

By the time Bibaculus was through, his fate was sealed, his time as my Optio done, as the one nagging question about whether I was judging him too harshly was answered. For a variety of reasons, I neither informed him, nor did I indicate this, instead nodding.

"Very well, as soon as I'm done with the Century, I'll send you and Vinicius out to bring them back."

"Vinicius, sir?" He frowned, then I suppose he realized this was neither the time nor the place to argue, saying only, "I understand and will obey, Hastatus Prior."

He stiffened and saluted, which I returned, then said, "Go take your post, Optio. I'm going to talk to the men now."

He hurried to his spot, while I studied the faces of my men as they watched Bibaculus trotting past, and what I saw there was yet another reason I knew he could no longer be my Optio. Once he was in his place, I took a deep breath, then began speaking.

Without any warning, I asked, "How many of you believe I didn't do enough to save *Gregarius* Florus?"

I expected the looks of startlement, and anticipated there would be some hesitation, but what surprised me was how little there was, and how quickly men began raising their hands, while I looked on with what I hoped was an expressionless face. Of the officers, Vinicius was the first to raise his hand, followed by Macrinus, but to my relief, Lentulus did not, nor did Bibaculus, although frankly, I did not care or count him since he had no future in the Fifth. Alex was inside the Century office, but as we had agreed, he was peeping through the shuttered window that faced the street, and with Euphemios' help, were writing down the names of men whose hands were raised as quickly as they could. Once I saw how many men raised their hands, I realized that it would be faster for them to just write down the men who did not; thankfully, Alex saw and did exactly that.

"Put them down," I ordered after a moment where I made sure that every man who was so inclined to raise their hands did so, but as daunting as it was, I also knew that some men who were late in raising their hands had done so more because of what their more adamant comrades might think of them if they did not.

"Do any of you have any doubt that Florus killed the *Gregarius* from the Alaudae?"

This *did* surprise them, which was my plan; more importantly, I saw the kind of hesitation I had hoped to see with my first question, and since the men were at *intente*, I saw their eyes darting to either side as they tried to use the edge of their vision to determine what their comrades were doing. Weren't expecting that, were you? I thought with a grim amusement. They were not the only ones in for a surprise, because suddenly, I recognized the voice of Vinicius speaking up from his spot in the middle of the third rank.

"No, Hastatus Prior, at least I don't." He paused, and I guessed that it was to wait for the muttered chorus of agreement that took a couple of heartbeats to come. I suppose he realized he was not going to get more than that, so he continued, "But as I told you before, no matter what he did, he had rights, and those rights were ignored!" Now his voice was joined by a ragged but clearly audible chorus of agreement, and men were nodding, which I could have bellowed at them to stop since they were at *intente*, but I did not. With this demonstration of support, the *Tesserarius'* voice grew stronger. "Florus may have killed that bastard from the Alaudae, and he *may* have deserved to be executed, but we'll never know, because he wasn't allowed to speak on his behalf, or to call witnesses because he was murdered himself, by that *mentula* they call Canus! And," Vinicius turned his head now, making it clear that he was addressing his comrades, though I still said nothing, "where is *that* bastard now, eh? Back in Mogontiacum with his master, no doubt, sharing the *Quaestor*'s oysters and larks tongues!"

This was the moment I realized that the men of the Fifth did not know about Canus' death, and this was also when I saw a possible way out, but first, I had to lay some groundwork. I held up my hand in the signal that I wanted the men to quiet down, because Vinicius' words, and his reminder about who was responsible for their comrade's death had roused their ire to the point some of them had begun shouting at me.

"Vinicius is right! That Canus murdered Aulus! What are you going to do about it?"

"This is why we mutinied! To stop this kind of thing from happening, but it looks like Rome and Tiberius didn't listen! Maybe it's time we got their attention again!"

Unfortunately for this ranker, I happened to be looking in his direction, but the reason I spotted him was by the sudden, uneasy reaction of the pair of rankers on either side of him, telling me they understood just how dangerous a thing this was for any man to say no matter what the circumstances, and I felt certain that he had counted on the bodies around him to protect his identity. What's his name? I thought, not for the first time cursing the challenge of a First Cohort Century with twice the men, and the fact that we had been together barely more than a month before I left with the Alaudae. Clodianus! I recalled, that was it, and along with his name came the other information, and it was with an effort that I did not smile at him as he watched, suddenly nervous since I was looking in his direction. While he was not at the top of the list Alex and Euphemios had compiled, he was close enough to it that I now bumped him up as the first man for what I had planned. And, once I told Sacrovir what Clodianus had said, I felt confident that I would be protected for almost anything except killing him. None of this showed in my face, however, and finally, the men quieted down so that I could speak.

"First," I began, "I was there when *Gregarius* Florus died." Just from their surprised reaction, I saw they had not known this. "While a *medicus* was summoned, even if he had gotten there earlier, there was nothing he could have done, because one of Florus' ribs punctured his lung."

"All the more reason that Canus needs to be brought to justice!"

"That," I said mildly, "will be hard." It was probably not wise given the consternation, but I could not help pausing for a heartbeat before I explained, "Because he's dead as well."

As I expected, this caused even more of a stir, but now I could see the confusion on the faces of most of the men, though not all of them. It was the misfortune of a ranker in the first rank, who I immediately recognized and remembered, to be a heartbeat late as the others quieted back down.

"So he says," I heard him mutter. "I wager he's just saying that to shut us up."

I did not move quickly; in fact, I was almost at a leisurely pace as I crossed the distance between us to stop in front of the man, who, as men usually do, unconsciously leaned backward in response to my towering over him.

"Are you calling me a liar, *Gregarius* Hybrida?"

Hybrida, who was actually the Sergeant of the Second Section, blanched, probably as much from my reference to a lower rank as our proximity, shaking his head vigorously. "N-no, sir." Then, realizing that he was in fact doing that very thing, he said weakly, "I didn't mean it, sir. I was just talking." With the fervor of a man grabbing on to a log floating past as they are both hurtling downstream on a raging torrent, he said, "It's just that we're still upset about Florus, Centurion, that's all." He turned to the man to his right, Isauricus, also in the Second Section. "Isn't that right, Publius?"

"Quite right, Sergeant," Isauricus agreed, but I noticed he was still looking straight ahead, his eyes nowhere near me.

I pretended to consider this, then shook my head.

"No," I said, my tone flat and hard. "I think that's a load of *cac*. I think you just called me a liar, Hybrida." I put the tip of my *vitus* against his chest, but rather than strike him, I just softly tapped him with it. "But you and I will be discussing that later."

With that, I had the second name on my list, while Isauricus wisely kept his expression blank and his eyes straight ahead as I stepped back and returned to my spot.

"Clearly, some of you doubt me when I tell you that Canus is dead," I resumed. "But I assure you he is...because I'm the one who killed him."

There was another uproar at this, and I noticed that we had now drawn the attention of the other Centuries of the First Cohort as they returned to their huts from the duties of the day, which during this time of year were either construction and repair projects, or some sort of training outside the camp. It was an oversight on my part, but it could not be helped, and I confess that it was as much out of a desire to get the men off the street and back into their huts so that I could prepare for the next day as anything else.

"I can prove it," I assured them. "I can show you the urn carrying his ashes." I offered a small prayer of thanks to the gods at my admittedly spontaneous decision to take Canus' ashes, mainly because I was certain that the urn would simply be tossed aside when the Alaudae returned to Mogontiacum, either by Nerva, or by Varro. "And," I decided that a small lie was in order, "Alexandros Pullus witnessed it. Will you accept his word?"

This was a gamble, but in my mind, it was not a large one; Alex was new to the Fifth of the First, but his reputation among the clerks of the entire 1st Legion, and his actions at the Long Bridges were well known by them, which in turn meant that the men of the ranks had heard of him by this point, and for the first time, I saw heads moving in the right direction.

"Yes, Hastatus Prior, this will be acceptable to us." For the first time, Lentulus' voice was heard, the *Signifer* stepping away from the formation and turning to face his comrades. "Isn't that right, boys?"

It was ragged and it was not unanimous, but there was no mistaking the assent, and I had to make an effort not to show any sign that I was relieved, and I indicated the onlooking men of the other Centuries. "Then that's enough for today. You're still restricted to your quarters." Before there could be any protest, I barked, "Optio Bibaculus, *Signifer* Lentulus, *Tesserarius* Vinicius, attend to me in my quarters! Century dismissed!"

Turning on my heel, I marched straight to the door of the Century office, using my ears to determine that the men were doing what I had ordered, and I heard my officers, recognizing among them Hybrida's voice calling to their comrades to obey me. That, I thought, went better than I expected, but we still had tomorrow to get through. Before that, however, I had to talk with the officers.

It went against my inclination, since I was still angry at the men for being in this situation in the first place, but a quiet word from Alex persuaded me to offer the three men a cup of wine in my quarters. However, I was pleased to see that they were all visibly nervous as they sat on the stools in front of my desk, and I did not offer the traditional toast, knowing that they would interpret this correctly, that I was still unhappy.

I began by asking, "If you and the rest of the Century are satisfied that I'm telling the truth, that the man who killed Florus is dead, and that it was at my hand, will that be enough to get the men back in hand?"

None of them wanted to answer, that was clear, but once again, I noticed that my current Optio and Lentulus looked at Vinicius, who shifted on his stool, clearly uncomfortable.

Despite this, he replied, "It will certainly help, sir. But," I saw his eyes narrow, "I think it would also depend on why you killed the bastard. Was it because of what he did to Florus?"

I had anticipated this question, and dreaded it, but I had decided that another partial lie was in order, and since I was prepared for it, I replied immediately, "Not totally, no. I also swore an oath to protect the Marcomanni king who we helped the Gotones nobleman Catualda depose. By," I added, "orders of the Princeps." Or someone close to him, I thought to myself; the truth was, and still is to this day, I have no idea why we did what we did, or who ordered it, even now that I know the result. "But," I continued, "as Alex will attest, I had my own...plans for Canus."

Naturally, all eyes went to my friend, who nodded and said gravely, "The Hastatus Prior saw what Canus did to Florus, and he knew that something had to be done about him." He hesitated; he told me later he was trying to decide just how far he could go and still have a chance of being believed. "The problem was that there were other factors that the Hastatus Prior had to take into account given who Canus worked for, and what we were there to do that meant he couldn't act immediately."

None of the officers spoke, although I saw Vinicius and Lentulus exchange a glance that I was sure was some form of communication, but I also noticed how they both pointedly ignored Bibaculus. Once more, it was Vinicius who spoke.

"You said there were other reasons for what you did with Canus. May I ask what they were, sir?"

"You can ask," I snapped, not thinking it through, "but that doesn't mean I'll tell you." By design, Alex had taken a seat at the table, which was across the room from my desk, putting him behind the officers, so I was able to catch his glare at me, which I correctly interpreted. Still, I know I sounded grudging as I added, "But I will. As I said, I gave my oath to King Maroboduus to protect him." Realizing that it would make more sense, I briefly explained what had taken place at Casurgis, our assault on his citadel, and Maroboduus correctly understanding that Catualda wanted him dead. Deciding that it would help my cause, even if it did hurt my pride a bit, I explained with, "What I didn't realize at the time was that Canus posed a threat to Maroboduus because of who Canus worked for, mainly because I couldn't imagine Varro going against something arranged by the Princeps through his son."

As soon as I said it, I understood I had erred, and all three men gasped in unison, although it was Alex's grimace that forewarned me.

"Are you saying that *Quaestor* Varro ordered that bastard to kill Maroboduus?" Lentulus got it out first, but I cut him off.

"No!" I said sharply. "That's *not* what I'm saying, at all, and," I pointed at each of them, "this better be the last time I hear a fucking *whisper* about it! That is *not* something you want to be associated with if Varro hears men saying that! Now," I continued more calmly, "I *will* tell you the details, but not until you swear on the eagle that none of you will ever utter a word that connects the *Quaestor* to what Canus tried to do. After all," I pointed out, "Canus is replaceable, and I know that as soon as Varro heard about Canus from Primus Pilus Nerva, he went out and found a man to replace him, if he didn't have one already."

To my relief, they all agreed readily enough, but I made them intone their oath individually, and honestly, considering what was in Bibaculus' future, I worried the most about him breaking the oath out of anger and a desire for revenge against me.

Once they did so, I used Maroboduus' lie. "Catualda bribed Canus to kill Maroboduus, and" I embellished a bit more, "an offer of a spot as part of his royal guard in the event that he needed to leave Roman territory." Shrugging, I finished the tale, "I don't know if he didn't make up his mind for several days, or the fact that we were just a couple days away from Mogontiacum meant that he decided he couldn't wait until we got back because he'd decided to take Catualda up on his offer. Either way, I stopped him, and in the process," I reminded them, "I avenged what he did to Florus."

Alex cleared his throat, and when the three turned on their stools, he pointed to the urn that he had retrieved from our baggage and was now sitting on the table, and they all stood and walked over to examine it, whereupon I learned of another mistake on my part, one of omission in not mentioning something before.

I saw Vinicius frown as he looked down at the urn, but it was Lentulus who asked, "Who's Gaius Fonteius?"

For a brief moment, it appeared as if everything had been in vain, but when I replied, "That's Canus' real name," they seemed to accept this without any questions about how I knew this.

Once I gave them time to look at the urn, I repeated my initial question, hoping for a different answer. "Now that you know everything, will this be enough to get the men back in hand?"

For a second time, the other two men of the trio looked at one man, and for the second time, it was not Bibaculus; that Bibaculus looked to Vinicius as well was even more telling.

"It will help," the *Tesserarius* spoke carefully. Shaking his head, he admitted, "But, no, sir. I still don't think it will be enough."

While this was what I expected, it was still a disappointment, which I expressed in the form of speaking harshly.

"Well, they're going to have two fucking choices." It had not been my original intent, but I felt I had no choice but to tell them, "Primus Pilus Sacrovir has given me two days to get the Fifth back under their standard and acting like Legionaries and not a fucking mob of Germans, or he's going to take steps of his own."

"Floggings," Lentulus sighed, closing his eyes, while Vinicius added grimly, "With the scourge no doubt, considering what happened to Paterculus."

I laughed, though without any humor.

"Wrong," I replied flatly. "He's not going as far as requesting a decimation, mainly because that has to be decided by a man of Legate rank, and it would raise questions he has no desire answering, but he has five men he plans on executing, which he can do on his own authority, and I'm guessing that you know who most of them are."

"Caelius," Bibaculus spoke for the first time. "He has to be at the top of the list."

This time, Lentulus and Vinicius were the ones who looked at their Optio, but I could not immediately identify their expressions; if forced to guess, I would have chosen a combination of sympathy and a level of disdain, as if they were thinking the same thing.

"If you were decent at your job, you would have settled Caelius' books a long time ago."

Like the other officers, Marcus Caelius, a *Gregarius* in the Ninth Section, quickly placed himself at the top of my mental list of men who needed to be dealt with, and I had planned on doing so as soon as we returned to Ubiorum, although my plan had been to unload him on one of the third line Cohorts. It was not just that he was slovenly, shirked duties, and was a troublemaker both in camp and out in town; he was universally loathed by his comrades, to the point that he was one of the few men who did not have a close comrade, Vinicius holding his will in his role of *Tesserarius*. When I asked Bibaculus about this, he was succinct in his reply.

"Because there's nobody in the Century who can put up with him. And," he added meaningfully and in a manner that he knew I would not mistake, "they don't trust him *anywhere*."

Given who this is being written for, and depending on when they read it, this statement may not need explanation, but in the event that it does, what Bibaculus was telling me was that Caelius was a man who could not be trusted to stand in the ranks with his comrades when it came time for us to do what we are paid to do, killing Rome's enemies.

Now it was time for me to make my final move, beginning by asking Vinicius and Lentulus, "Do you agree with Optio Bibaculus? That if the only way to avoid outright executions is to make a demonstration to the Primus Pilus that the Fifth Century is capable of handling its own business, and making sure that the men most responsible for where we are right now are punished...severely, that *Gregarius* Caelius has to be one of them?"

While there was hesitation, it was not much, both men nodding, then when they saw I required more than that, murmuring their assent. Without waiting, I moved on, bringing up the names of the ten men that Alex and Euphemios had supplied, and one by one, the three officers agreed, albeit with varying degrees of willingness. I was not surprised that the further down the list, the less enthusiasm there was, but when I added an eleventh name, the atmosphere immediately changed, with Vinicius and Lentulus exchanging a glance that conveyed something close to alarm.

"But, why Hybrida?" Vinicius asked. "He's the Second Section Sergeant! What has he done?"

Before I could answer, Lentulus did, which made sense since he was closer to Hybrida earlier.

"He said the Hastatus Prior was lying when he said that Canus was dead," he explained.

"Oh." Vinicius suddenly looked uncomfortable. "I see." I thought this would be enough, but he was not through, "But what if he apologized for doubting you? Especially once we tell them we've seen the proof?"

Under other circumstances, this would have been enough,

but I was angry that this was necessary in the first place, so I was not in the mood to change my mind. With the eleven men selected, all that remained was how they would be punished, but I had not divulged my intentions yet.

It was Bibaculus who, clearing his throat, asked nervously, "What did you have in mind as far as their punishment, Hastatus Prior?"

I was opening my mouth when Vinicius spoke, a grim smile on his face.

"I think I can guess," he said. Pointing at my harness hanging from the stand behind me, "Does it have to do with that?"

Knowing he meant my *gladius*, I nodded, although I did assure them, "I'll be using a *rudis*, but yes."

"When?"

"Tomorrow morning," I replied. "I've already sent Euphemios to the *Praetorium* to reserve the training ground."

With that, I dismissed Lentulus, leaving Vinicius and Bibaculus, who both looked nervous.

"I told Bibaculus this earlier, but I want the two of you to go into town and bring those three *cunni* back."

Since all three of them were on the list, they knew who I was talking about, but when they rose to leave, while I considered holding Bibaculus back to inform him this would be his last duty as my Optio, I decided against it. Then, a minor miracle occurred.

Bibaculus murmured something to Vinicius, but since his back was to me, I could not hear, though I did hear Vinicius say he would be waiting outside, glancing at me over the Optio's shoulder before closing the door to my quarters. I saw Bibaculus' shoulders pull back just before he turned about and returned to my desk, while I regarded him silently, until the silence was such that I opened my mouth to break it.

He beat me to it, but I was completely unprepared to hear him say, "Hastatus Prior, I don't deserve to be your Optio, and I'm formally requesting that I be relieved of my post." As my father liked to say, we could have heard a gnat fart in the silence, and there is no real way to describe my shock, feeling my mouth dropping open, yet nothing came out. Bibaculus apparently took pity on me, adopting the kind of tone I might have when trying to soften the blow. "I'm not doing a good job, am I, Hastatus Prior?"

"No," I replied, softly but without hesitation. "I can't say that you are, Bibaculus."

"I told Centurion Varo that I didn't think I was ready," he said glumly.

This was the first I had heard this, and I was about to question him about why he accepted the post if he knew that he was not ready for it; fortunately, I stopped myself, knowing how unfair it would be. It is so rare that I have never heard of it, a man telling his superior he was not prepared or qualified to hold a position that is one step up the ladder of responsibility, so Bibaculus would have been the first. That is why I did no such thing.

Instead, I asked, "What did he say?"

"That I'd grow into the job," he answered unhappily, then gave a mirthless laugh. "But I think he saw his son in me." Seeing my look of confusion, he explained, "Tiberius and I were close comrades when we were *Tiros*, and he was my best friend." He sighed. "I took his death almost as hard as the Hastatus Prior, but when he told me that he was promoting me, I knew I wasn't ready, but I didn't want to disappoint him. Not so soon after...that."

My respect, and my regard for Bibaculus grew immeasurably in the time that it took for him to offer his explanation. It did not affect my decision that he could not continue as my Optio, but this was the moment when I decided to speak to Sacrovir on Bibaculus' behalf.

"Thank you for your honesty, Bibaculus. I do appreciate it. And," I hesitated, though not because I was having second thoughts, "I'm going to speak to Primus Pilus Sacrovir and see what we can do. At the very least, I'll do everything in my power to ensure that there's no kind of adverse entry in your record." I stood up, which he correctly interpreted, but just as he was about to leave the office, I felt compelled to add, "Bibaculus," and when he turned to face me, I said quietly, "that took a lot of courage on your part to admit that. Trust me, I know."

I cannot say he looked pleased, but I did not really expect him to, and he left my quarters, giving me my first chance to take a breath. Summoning Alex, I told him about Bibaculus and how he had essentially resigned his post.

"When are you going to tell Vinicius?" he asked, then added, "I'm assuming that he's your choice?"

"He is." I considered for a moment, then shrugged. "I suppose as soon as they get back from retrieving those three bastards from town. And yes," I held up a hand to forestall Alex pointing something out that, frankly, was in the forefront of my mind, "I know that Sacrovir blames Vinicius and thinks he's behind it all. But, I'm going to talk to him, and tell him that Vinicius was just being a good *Tesserarius* and listening to his comrades." Sighing, I finished, "Hopefully, that'll be enough."

I walked over to the table, grabbing up the jug to pour myself and Alex a cup, which he saw and came to take his seat, but I was just handing it to him when there was the sound of the outer door opening again, and I paused, hoping that it was nothing that required my attention. That was a hope destined to last for a pair of heartbeats, when Euphemios rapped on the inner door. Muttering a curse, I bade him to open it, but I was in for yet another surprise, although this one was more pleasant.

"Optio Bibaculus and *Tesserarius* Vinicius are back, Centurion."

"*Gerrae*! They just left!" I exclaimed. "All right, let's hear what this is about."

The clerk stepped aside and the pair entered bearing identical expressions that I thought made them look somewhat sheepish, but Vinicius deferred to Bibaculus, who explained.

"We were about to leave camp, but Numerius thought it might be a good idea to check the huts. And," he shrugged, "all three of the bastards are back in camp now, Hastatus Prior."

While it is not an easy thing to do to sneak into or out of a Legion camp, for veterans, especially men like these who seem to take pride in thwarting the regulations, it is not all that difficult, and while I was mildly curious about how they did it, if only so that if there was anything I could do about it I could take action, it was not sufficient to make me talk to them. Their time, I thought, is coming soon enough. However, their unexpected reappearance this soon made me realize that I should not put it off any longer, and I turned my attention to Vinicius, when once more Bibaculus came to the rescue.

"Hastatus Prior, I already told Numerius that I'm relinquishing my post. And," his chin lifted slightly, as if he was ready to be challenged, "my opinion may not mean much to you and it's not my place to say so, but I think that the best choice to replace me is standing right here next to me."

"You're right," I looked at him and replied coldly, "it's not your place." I paused, more out of a sense of drama than for any other reason. "But as it happens, I do value your opinion, at least in this matter." I could not stop myself from grinning. "Probably because I also happen to agree with it." I returned my attention to Vinicius. "Since Bibaculus already told you the first part, I'm now telling you the second. You're the new Optio of the Fifth Century," then thought to add, "pending the approval of the Primus Pilus, of course."

It was unfair to both men to do it in this manner, and I knew it, but the truth was that I was tired of dealing with this mess, while I also knew that I needed to get some rest before the next day, and I still had to report back to the Primus Pilus. Besides, I told myself, these were veterans, and as such, they knew better than most that, under the standard, very little of our life is fair. There is duty, and there is honor, neither of which are particularly fair for anyone desiring something resembling a normal life in our world.

"I...I...I understand, and will obey, Hastatus Prior," Vinicius stammered. "I will do my best to never make you regret your choice."

"Just do a better job than me, and you'll be fine, Numerius," Bibaculus whispered, though he had to know that I would hear, but I said nothing, and Bibaculus saluted. "With your permission, Hastatus Prior, I'll go pack my gear and get out of Vinicius' way."

"That can wait." I waved a hand. "My suggestion is that you go get some rest. Tomorrow will be a big day."

Now they both saluted, which I returned and dismissed

them, leaving me and Alex, but as desperately tired as I was, my day was not over. Nor, I realized, would I be returning to my apartment.

"I need to go inform the Primus Pilus of where things stand," I began, and I knew he would not like the task I was about to give him, yet I still had to fight the urge to grin. "While I'm doing that, I need you go to the apartment and let Bronwen know I'm spending the night in camp."

The look of horror he gave me I would liken to that of a man who had just been told he would be facing an entire tribe of Germans on his own, and without any weapons of any kind. It was a look I completely understood, and I did feel a flicker of shame, but it was not strong enough to change my mind; besides, I reasoned, only I could talk to the Primus Pilus about all that had taken place.

"You planned this beforehand!" he accused.

"What?" I laughed. "Are you really that scared of my wife?"

"Why aren't *you* doing it?" he challenged. "You could go talk to Sacrovir and *then* go tell *your* wife you're not coming home tonight!"

"I could," I agreed. "But I'm the one who's going to be in the square tomorrow. And," I grinned, "I don't want to already be wounded."

"Ha! So you *are* scared of your wife!"

"Of course I am." I laughed. "She's *my* wife, after all. She's not likely to throw anything at *you*."

"Saying she's not likely to isn't the same as saying she won't," he grumbled, but he was doing it as he left my quarters.

Picking up the tablet with the names of the men who I would be facing in the morning, I followed him out of the office just as the *bucina* sounded the end of the official day, and I was pleased to see that my Century's part of the street was deserted. I chose to take it as a good sign, that the men of the Fifth realized that their Centurion was back, and a change was coming. If all went as I planned, there would be no doubt about that before the noon watch tomorrow.

My conversation with Sacrovir did not take as long as I

feared it would, but I cannot say that I was particularly happy at the result. However, when I related what he had said to Alex after he returned without a mark on him, sheepishly telling me that Bronwen's response had been that she had assumed this would be the case given the problems, my friend quickly saw the positive aspect of what Sacrovir had said.

"He's actually doing you a favor, Gnaeus," he said, without hesitation or any doubt. "By being there in the morning, he's sending our boys a message that this isn't something you're doing unilaterally, and that at the very least, the Primus Pilus sanctions it. And," he mused thoughtfully after taking a sip from his cup, "I wouldn't be surprised if he has the word spread that you're actually saving the Century from a bigger punishment involving more men."

As we would learn the next day, this was exactly what Sacrovir did. I was not surprised to find that sleep was hard to come by as I tossed and turned, worrying about what the day would bring. The wound on my back had healed cleanly, Alex removing the stitches more than a week before we reached Ubiorum, but I could still feel the muscles that had been cut, especially when I made a sudden and violent twisting motion, as I undoubtedly would be in the morning. Somehow, I managed to fall asleep, because the *bucina* call was a surprise, jerking me awake with a hammering heart, and I swung my feet to the floor, thankful for the thick carpets that came from Alexandria as part of what we purchased during our short stay. As much as I enjoy the peppercorns and the *kinammon*, on cold mornings, these carpets have proven to be the best bargain here in Germania on cold mornings like this one. Stepping outside to head to the latrine, I was slightly dismayed to see more snow had fallen, about a foot, which would make traction more difficult, though I quickly decided I would use the men to tamp it down in the square we would be using. I say square as if it was some sort of arena, yet while it is such, its boundaries are created with the bodies of the men, but ask any man under the standard, and they will know exactly what is meant, and the rough dimensions. When I returned, Alex had just entered with my food, steaming hot and, most importantly, with a fresh loaf and not just a chunk left over from the night before. My appetite is largely unaffected by external events, and this morning was no exception, though I might have eaten a bit more quickly than normal, then sent for Macrinus.

"Sound assembly," I told him. "The Optio should have gone to every section hut by now to let them know to be in full armor and with their training weapons."

Macrinus saluted, then hesitated, and while I anticipated his question, I did not save him from asking it, "Sir? Is it true that Vinicius is our Optio now?"

"Yes," I answered tersely, hoping that my tone communicated this was all I intended to speak about it.

It only lasted as long as it took him to ask, clearly nervous, "What about Optio Bibaculus? I mean, Bibaculus?"

"That," I said coldly, "isn't up to me; it's up to the Primus Pilus. And," I pointed to the outer door, "you have a job to do, Macrinus, so get to it."

I was slightly tempted to tell him that I had asked Sacrovir to find a spot for Bibaculus in one of the lower Cohorts, but since I had not seen him since I made the request, I did not want to curse it. With Alex's help, I got into my own armor, twisting at the waist a few times in both directions, increasing the speed and force so that I could get an idea of what to expect in terms of the pain, pleasantly surprised that, while it was painful, it was only when I moved most violently, and even then it was manageable.

The assembly had sounded when I began preparing, making it just the right time to leave my quarters, but before I exited, Alex held up the padded sleeves. "I'm sure I know the answer, but just in case you got some sense while you were sleeping..."

I gave him my answer in the look I offered, and with a sigh, he followed me out, but I did surprise him by stopping and retrieving my *sagum* from the hook next to the door.

Seeing his face, I explained, "I just want to stay warm before I get to work."

He muttered something under his breath, but I did not catch it, and I stepped out into the street, which was already full, not just with my Century, but with the others of the First; unlike the others, however, we were not marching to the forum to receive our orders for the day, having gotten permission from Sacrovir to get started as early as possible. Mainly, I wanted to rattle the men by doing something out of the ordinary, beginning with Vinicius' first official act as Optio of informing them that, unlike their comrades, they were to muster in armor, with their *rudis* hanging from their *baltea*, the only part of their training gear the men kept with them. The wicker shields, along with the padded sleeves and wicker faceguards, were already out at the training ground, transported there by some of the section slaves, led by Euphemios. Vinicius was standing in my spot; Bibaculus was nowhere to be seen, but I knew that he was in his old quarters, packing his gear since Vinicius had graciously offered the excuse that he would not be ready to move into his new quarters, allowing Bibaculus to spend one last night. Since the Fifth was the only Century attired in their armor and wearing their helmets, it was natural that we were the object of curiosity, while some of my men were looking about uneasily in the moments they had before being called to *intente*, which Vinicius did before marching up to me and rendering his salute.

"Hastatus Prior, the Fifth Century is all present and accounted for, sir, with one hundred thirty-two effectives."

Since both Bibaculus and Vinicius had come to inform me that the three miscreants out in town had returned to camp, while the four men were still in the hospital, I had expected this, simply returning his salute. There was one difficult and somewhat embarrassing moment when, without thinking, I gave the command to the men to face in the direction that would lead us to the training grounds by the most direct route, while the Centuries to our right, the Fourth through First, had faced in the direction of the forum, meaning that if I had given the order to march, we would have collided. While I quickly corrected myself, resigned to taking the longer way to the training ground, I heard the snickers from not just the men of the Fourth and Sixth, but from my own Century, yet rather than anger me, I actually smiled, relishing the sudden flicker of unease on the faces of my men as they began wondering what the day held in store. If I do this right, I thought with grim amusement, nobody in my Century will be laughing, and in some ways, more importantly, no man in the other Centuries will be, either at my Century, or their Centurion. We did have to wait for the Legion *Cornicen* to sound the command to march, but as soon as we reached the first intersection, while the rest of the Cohort marched straight to the forum, we took a right, heading for the *Porta Principalis Dextra*. Just as we reached the gate, I heard someone shout my name, turning to see Sacrovir's Optio trotting up, and I called the halt.

Keeping his voice low so the men could not hear, he said, "The Primus Pilus wants you to wait. He's parading the Cohort to watch."

My first reaction was that this was a jest, though for the life of me, I could not think of why he would make one like this. Nevertheless, I assured him that we would do that, and we resumed our march, exiting the camp, marching the couple hundred paces to the spot just beyond the rows of training stakes jutting up from the ground, their appearance made even starker by the clean white blanket of snow that was marred only by the tracks of the cart and mule, while Euphemios and two of the section slaves were standing next to it. This was the moment most of the men realized what the day held in store for them, the ranks buzzing as they told their slower-witted comrades what should have been obvious to them as soon as they got close enough to see the wicker shields stacked in the cart. I was aided in my need to wait by the fact that the area where the sparring would be held had to be packed down, which was accomplished by the men of each rank forming the square marching back and forth, so that by the time all four sides had done it twice, I was satisfied that the footing would be firm and, most importantly, hard. Even so, I was forced to wait, but I took Vinicius and Lentulus aside, telling them quietly why we were waiting, and I noticed that my new Optio turned a shade paler, although Lentulus did not look much better.

"Any idea why, Hastatus Prior?"

I had an idea, but I was not confident enough that I was right to communicate it, so I just gave them a shrug, saying only, "We'll find out soon enough."

A few moments later, the First of the First emerged, the

men all in their tunics and *sagum*, but I spotted the white crest of the Primus Pilus first, then saw him leading the way in his armor, which was unusual as well. I was unsure whether I should walk to meet him, then decided to wait since they were heading in this direction, choosing to spend the time studying the expressions of the men of the First as they approached, wondering if they were aware of what was happening.

Sacrovir reached me, returning my salute as I reported, "The Fifth Century is ready for punishment, Primus Pilus."

I said this more loudly than necessary, wanting my men to hear what was about to take place, and I was rewarded by a ripple of gasps and muttered exclamations, knowing that now that they understood the purpose, their next task was trying to determine what form it would take. From what I could tell a few moments later when it was revealed to them, none of them guessed correctly.

"Very well, Hastatus Prior," Sacrovir replied, the volume of his voice matching mine, "but first, I'm going to address your men...if you don't mind."

Assuring him that I had no problem with this whatsoever, I stepped aside so that he could take my spot, although he was facing the Century, while I called out the permission for them to go to *otiose*, so those who needed to do so could all pivot on their left foot to face in our direction.

Just before he began, he murmured to me, "The problem with Bibaculus is solved. Rutilis will take him to replace the Optio of his Fourth Century. He's a drunkard, and is about to be busted down to the ranks."

Since this caught me by surprise, I could not hide my expression of relief; part of my struggle the night before getting to sleep was the normal anticipation of what I was about to do, but it also had to do with Bibaculus, who I had become convinced had been thrust into a position that he was not currently ready for by a grief-stricken man who should not have been making decisions.

"Men of the Fifth Century!" Sacrovir began, and I could see that his greeting was not lost on them, since he normally opened such moments using "Legionaries" or "Comrades," but I was also certain they were not prepared for how bad it was going to be; they were not the only ones in for a surprise. "First, let me be clear. I'm here against my better judgment, because without the intercession of your Hastatus Prior, I would be recommending to the Legate that, because of the egregious and unlawful behavior of the Fifth Century over the last several weeks, that *the worst offenders be executed by running the gauntlet*!" He roared the last few words, and the effect on my men was as one might imagine. "However," his voice, while it was still harsh, softened, if only fractionally, "despite the fact that Hastatus Prior Pullus was absent for the worst of your behavior, he came to me and accepted full responsibility. And," he looked up at me as he continued, "he asked me to allow him to choose the method of your punishment." This was true, but he was not finished. "And he guaranteed that if the Fifth Century puts a man on the punishment list, for an offense that warrants anything other than extra duties or fines, he will resign his post, and those men who should be executed will have their sentences carried out." Now, *that* was not true; I certainly made no such offer, nor did Sacrovir make any mention of it, which made it a bit of a struggle to appear as if I was not hearing anything new. He finished addressing my Century by saying, "Your comrades in the First Cohort are here to witness the punishment that Hastatus Prior Pullus has devised." Then, he turned to me, his voice ringing with the authority that comes from being a Primus Pilus of a battle-hardened Legion of Rome for half a decade. "Hastatus Prior Pullus, carry out the punishment."

I saluted, then walked, deliberately slowly, to the cart, unbuckling my *baltea* and laying it on the drivers bench then made a show of selecting a *rudis* from the spares that we carry. My back was turned to the men, which was a good thing, or they would have seen my grin at the chorus of groans and gasps as they finally understood what was happening.

All told, I faced ten men by the time that, to a man, the Fifth Century begged me to stop, and swore on the eagle standard that I would have no cause for complaint. My cause was helped by the sight of Clodianus, who as I had promised, was the first man I faced, holding his shattered right elbow joint, being dismissed to walk to the hospital under his own power, unescorted in as potent a sign that his time not just with the Fifth but as a Legionary was over, no longer being worthy of even that scant attention. That this was neither by accident nor that I would be satisfied with just Clodianus was demonstrated by what I did to Caelius, and if anything, his fate was even direr, which was actually my goal. Just as with Clodianus, I took his measure within a matter of a couple of heartbeats, knowing that I could finish him whenever I chose, but at least Clodianus had attempted to put up a fight.

Caelius confirmed his cowardice when, to the hoots and jeers of his comrades, the instant Vinicius blew his bone whistle to start, he threw down both his wicker shield and *rudis*, dropping to his knees as he screeched, "I yield! I yield!"

I did not answer, verbally anyway, his lack of shield and weapon just making it easier to shatter both of his wrists with enough force that the bones pierced his skin, spattering the snow with his blood in a rough arc around his body as he writhed in agony. A glance over at Alex told me what I wanted to know, though he only offered me a grim shake of his head, which prompted me to speak for the first time.

"I hope you have some money saved up, Caelius, because you're going to need to pay someone to hold the sponge to wipe your ass. There's no way that the *medici* will be able to save your hands."

His only answer was to continue shrieking, and I was finally forced to signal for Euphemios to come and half-drag, half-carry Caelius out of the square, while his comrades looked on, mostly in silence, and if I was any judge, without any sympathy, reminding me what Bibaculus had said about him. One by one, the men on the list were shoved out into the square, but while they all put up more of a fight than Caelius had, the result was the same, although the degree of injury lessened. A couple of the men did a creditable job, which I noted and, while I did not make it obvious, their injuries were accordingly less severe, putting them in the hospital for a few days, though as they would learn on their release, none of them were given light duty after that. I never wanted them to be under the impression that this was anything but what it was, a punishment for their crimes, yet I was also relying on my new Optio to perform a dual role as both Optio and *Tesserarius* to work behind the scenes to convince the men of the Century that this was actually a better alternative, reminding them of what our Primus Pilus had said. As usual, I eschewed the sleeves and face guard while using my *vitus*, and I was reminded that this was, after all, a First Cohort Century full of veterans, earning a pair of painful and unsightly bruises, one across the outside of my left forearm, while the other was visible only to Alex and Bronwen, both of whom chastised me for it.

"If that had been in battle, you would have been in serious trouble," had been Alex's pronouncement, which was true enough, while Bronwen had been more succinct, if not as accurate.

"I would be a widow," she had sniffed, then pointed at our son, suckling at her breast. "And he would be without a father!"

The truth was that the bruise along my ribs was almost a foot long, and was the result of a wild slashing blow, by Hybrida, the only man I had given a choice, although it was not much of one.

"You called me a liar, Hybrida," I said conversationally if still a bit out of breath, choosing him as the last man immediately after the rest of the Century gave their oaths. "But, thanks to," I pointed at Vinicius first, then Lentulus, "these two, they convinced me to offer you a choice. You don't have to face me if you don't wish to," I waited until he heaved a sigh of relief, "but if you don't, you're back to *Gregarius*."

"*What?*" he gasped. "But...but that's not...!" He stopped himself; I learned later it was because Vinicius, who was standing just behind me, gave him a nonverbal warning by glaring at him. What I saw was him close his eyes, swallow hard, then reply bleakly, "I understand Hastatus Prior...and I accept your offer."

Hybrida proved then why he was a Sergeant in a First Cohort Century, putting up a spirited fight that, while I did not admit it until just this moment, pushed me harder than I had been pushed in sparring in some time. And, while I scoffed and said that it was luck at the time, the truth was no matter how it happened, he caught me out when I overextended with my *vitus*, raising my arm a bit more than was wise, and giving him the opening to strike me with a slashing blow that barely missed my elbow. That served to light my own fire, and within a dozen heartbeats, he was flat on his back with the point of my *rudis* at his throat, causing him to drop his own, along with his training shield, then falling bodily back onto the snow. However, despite the fact that I was still angry, and hurting, I held out my hand, his look of suspicion cheering me a bit, but I promised that the bout was over, then pulled him to his feet.

"Get back in ranks...Sergeant," I said, though my face was a mask; only when he turned and limped off, unable to lift his left arm, did I smile.

Regardless of my own feelings, the man that mattered was standing there, arms folded as they had been the entire time, and I marched to him, stopped, and rendered a salute. I did not speak, mainly because I did not know what to say.

He was the one who broke the silence by saying, "As impressive as always, Pullus. And," he lowered his voice, "I'm happy to see that you took my...hint about Caelius and Clodianus. It's good to know that those two rocks in my *caligae* won't be showing up on my report anymore. Although," he said severely, "if you ever repeat that, I'll deny it, and you'll think those two were blessed by Fortuna."

While I had no doubt that Tiberius Sacrovir was perfectly capable of doing such a thing, if not by himself then sending enough men to make it happen, I was not particularly worried about it; in fact, I grinned and asked innocently, "Hint? What hint, Primus Pilus? I have no idea what you're talking about."

He only grunted, but I saw one corner of his mouth twitch upward. Turning serious, he continued, "But you know that your men will have to be on their best behavior for a long time, Pullus. Although," he added, "I'm not particularly worried about it. I watched them while you were...doing what you do, and I think that you made quite the impression. Yes," he finished, clearly pleased with himself, "I think that was quite a good idea I had."

"I completely agree, sir."

I knew when it was time to apply the honey; besides, I agreed with him, for reasons that should be obvious. We exchanged another salute, then he said, "We'll wait here while you march your boys back to camp. I've got some things I want to say to the rest of the Cohort. They," he gave me a grim smile, "didn't need as much of a reminder as your boys did, but it's always good to give them one."

Just as we both hoped, the misbehavior of the Fifth Century stopped that day; what I was not so happy about after the winter passed was the lack of anything for the Legions to do, at least when it came to what most of us consider our real job. Consequently, most of our time was spent on construction projects, which included the construction of an aqueduct, the first such structure that we ever worked on. It originated in a line of hills that ran roughly north/south about fifteen miles west of Ubiorum, its source a series of springs that originated in the hills that converged to form a stream. Frankly, it was long overdue, but the rumor was that it had been scheduled for several years, dating all the way back before the mutiny the year Divus Augustus died, but other events, especially the campaigns against Arminius, had intervened. Whatever the reason, I actually found it fascinating, igniting an interest in me that I had not realized was there, watching in something close to awe as the men belonging to the *Praefectus Fabrorum* sketched out the form the aqueduct would take on their wax tablets, using arcane formulas that I only dimly understood, and that was because back when I was a spoiled and pampered wealthy Equestrian lad, I had had a private tutor, engaged by the man I thought was my father. I did not apply myself, to any of it, frankly, and only much later did I understand why Quintus Volusenus did not seem all that upset that I did not.

Because we did not have to go far afield, I rode Latobius back to Ubiorum quite often, and would tell Bronwen about the day's events and I suppose my admiration and envy must have shown, because one night, she asked suddenly, "Why are you so interested in these things? You have never showed any before."

It was true, but I had never thought about it before this, and I considered for a moment before I replied, "Because," speaking slowly since I was forming the thoughts as I went, "long after I die, and our children, and their children are gone, this aqueduct will be here, as a sign of all that Rome has accomplished. It," I shrugged, "is a good feeling, I suppose, knowing that. And," I smiled at the thought, "one day soon, I'll be able to show Titus the aqueduct, and he'll know that his father helped build that."

"You mean that you stand there with your *vitus* and yell at your men to work harder," she teased, "not that you got your hands dirty."

I laughed, admitting cheerfully, "That's true. But he doesn't need to know that."

However, before we began working on the aqueduct and shortly after the Kalends of December, I was summoned to the Legion office, where I was immediately waved in to Sacrovir's office, who pointed to his table as he rose from his desk, which I had learned was the sign that this was not official business.

Melander poured two cups, but I noticed that the Primus Pilus waited until the clerk left before he said, "I've got some news from Mogontiacum that you're going to be interested in." Thankfully, he did not torment me by waiting to take a sip from his cup. "Gaius Silius is back from his time with Germanicus, *and*," he gave a smile that held no humor, "he's in need of a new *Quaestor*."

I did not immediately take his meaning, pointing out, "Usually, they're appointed at the same time and are in their post for the same length." I gasped, "Wait, are you saying Varro *died*?"

He gave a barking laugh, shaking his head.

"No, nothing like that. Now," he cautioned, "this is secondhand, so I'm not certain this is true, but it comes from a source who would know. What his message said was that word came that Silius was on his way back to Mogontiacum after stopping in Rome, and was only a couple days away, and," he spread his hands, "Varro was nowhere to be found the next morning."

"He deserted his post?" I exclaimed, yet I almost immediately dismissed it. "That doesn't make sense, sir. Varro doesn't strike me as the type who would just flee, not if he's as powerful as I think he is."

"That's all I know," Sacrovir answered, somewhat tersely, as if I was questioning him, or perhaps his source, which was not my intent. "But what matters is that Varro is gone, so the immediate threat he posed to you for what happened with his man is gone."

Honestly, I did not think that, if the now-former *Quaestor* was inclined to exact some sort of vengeance on me, it would be because of what I did to Canus, but that I had somehow thwarted whatever plans he had, however inadvertently. It was a risk, but not one that I lost any sleep over. And, about three months later, we heard that Varro was back in Rome, with nothing ever coming of his abrupt departure. The most important development that came of this news from Sacrovir was that I finally deemed it safe enough for my mother to return to Mogontiacum; while her claim that I was holding her in our apartment against her will was a joke, given that she loved spending every moment with baby Titus, I confess that I had been serious in my effort to convince her to remain in Ubiorum on our return, arguing that it was not safe. Now, with this news of Varro's departure, there was a tearful farewell three days later, but I suspect that my mother was as secretly relieved to be returning to her home as I am certain Bronwen was to see her go, since our apartment was simply not made to accommodate three adults.

Chapter 10

There was another momentous event that winter, although it was of a personal nature, when Bronwen told me over our evening meal, "I am with child again."

Titus was now toddling about, and had begun talking, albeit in a mishmash of Latin, his mother's native tongue, and one that only he understood, though both his parents pretended they did as well, nodding sagely as he babbled.

I sat back in my chair, awash in emotions, some of them in direct conflict with each other; the happiness at the prospect of another child...and the fear that, as I had learned from the Prefect's and my father's account, has dogged three of the four Pullus generations, the exception being my grandfather. Gaius Porcinianus Pullus was actually the Prefect's blood nephew, adopted posthumously by the Prefect, a very common Roman practice that, to this day, Bronwen still does not understand. My grandfather Gaius was quite tall, but with a slenderer build than either his maternal uncle or his oldest son, my father, and with his wife Iras, they had seven children, five of them living to adulthood.

Despite my smile, Bronwen understood, leaning forward to touch my arm, assuring me quietly, "I survived Titus, I will survive this babe, my love. Besides," she said without any visible doubt, "this will be a girl child."

"How can you know that?" I asked, then teased, "Are you a Parisii witch, woman? Did I marry a sorceress?"

"Oh, did I forget to tell you that?" She laughed, "But no, I am having a girl child. I consulted a midwife here in Ubiorum who is Ubii, and she concurs. And," she finished simply, "Algaia agrees as well. We are having a girl."

"Well, who am I to argue?" I held up my hands in mock surrender; though I truly did not believe that this was anything more than a guess, I also knew when it was better to surrender, and this was one of those moments.

Her expression changed, subtly but noticeably, warning me of something, yet there was no way I could have anticipated what she was about to say.

"I have already thought of a name, if you agree." She said this so meekly, as if she were anticipating my response and guessing that I would not like it that I braced myself to hear some name used by her people, wondering how much of a fight I should put up at that moment, or wait for another time. I saw her breasts rise as she took a breath, let it out, then said, "I would like to name her Giulia."

This was a moment I was just happy that we were alone, and none of the men of the Fifth Century could see their Centurion crying; naturally, I agreed. Proving that men, or at least I have no business arguing with the women in my life, my daughter Giulia was born three days after the Ides of September, in the year of the Imperator's third and Germanicus' second Consulship. To the mutual relief of his parents, Titus was instantly enamored with his baby sister, and from her first day displayed an almost fierce protectiveness over her from which no one other than his mother was, or is secure; even I was subjected to a fierce scowl from my son as he eyed me holding his sister in a manner that he did not consider sufficiently gentle.

"I won't have to worry about driving any suitors away," I recall joking to Bronwen once, after enduring a tongue-lashing from Titus, or so I believed since he was still speaking his mishmash of tongues and his own gibberish. "He's going to handle that job quite nicely. And," I teased, even as I knew the reaction it would elicit, "it's good training for when he's a Centurion like his Tata."

"Our son will never be under the standard, my love," Bronwen said sweetly, and while she was smiling, I was not fooled. "He is destined for greater things."

It will probably not surprise anyone reading this, particularly you, my oldest son, that this was not the first, and it would be far from the last Bronwen and I clashed on this topic; indeed, I suspect that by the time you are old enough to read these words, you will be heartily sick of hearing us bickering about it. On this occasion, however, I decided to let the proverbial sleeping dog lie and remained silent and enjoy the moments of domestic contentment, though I freely confess that, when the squalling became a bit too much, I retreated to camp, although matters were disgustingly quiet across the Rhenus, at least as far as we were concerned. This is not to say that things were peaceful, at all; the tribes of Germania proved that their period of unity under the rule of Arminius was the exception that proved the rule that their intertribal jealousies were every bit as potent as those among the patrician families of Rome, with hatreds for the other tribes that extended back to a time before Rome was a dusty village. The turmoil in the Cherusci tribe was growing bitterer almost by the day, at least according to the spies who took Roman coin and were invariably traveling merchants who used their mobility and access to the tribes farther east of the Rhenus who were greedy for Roman goods to keep us at least somewhat apprised of matters. Indeed, I had met more than one of these men in the *tavernae* frequented by the Legions who cheerfully admitted that they made far less money peddling their wares than they did peddling information to Rome, and, most of us had little doubt, some of them were peddling information about us to the German tribes. If they noticed the looks of distaste, they were either smart enough or were making enough money not to make an issue of it, and while I admit to being one of those men who found what they did disreputable, I am not blind to the fact that they are doing Rome a service, and by extension, men like me who are under the standard. What these men related varied only by degree, but unanimously the information was the same, that there was enough turmoil within and between the tribes that there was no prospect of the Legions marching in the near future. While I did not view these developments with much favor, something that I never mentioned but I now know never fooled Bronwen as to my true feelings, I suppose it did come at a good time in a personal sense.

Since I just mentioned *taverna*, I suppose that this is the moment that I have avoided, and I know that my scribe feels the same way even if we have never discussed it, because it is painful for both of us, though it is far more so for Alex since it concerns his brother, Diocles' youngest son, named for the Prefect. My father had brought him to Ubiorum from Arelate after learning from his mother Birgit that young Titus had gotten mixed up in a *collegia* in Arelate, when he was about twenty. Honoring his mother's request, (*It was not a request, it was a demand by mother, made to Gnaeus' father and expressed in no uncertain terms)* to help her youngest son find a trade, my father had set him up as an apprentice to a smith, Decimus Scrofa, the best smith specializing in weaponry, not just in Ubiorum, but in the entire province, whose blade I carried before I was bequeathed the Prefect's *gladius*, and while it is still no match for the Prefect's, despite it being fifty years old and is now on the fifth handle, it is a blade that no Tribune would disdain carrying. Unknown to any of us was that my father, using the money that, as my grandfather liked to joke, made the Pullus family the richest members of the Head Count in history, purchased the building, while Titus was still apprenticed to Scrofa. By all accounts, Titus showed a real talent for the work, but he also fell in love with Scrofa's daughter, which apparently created some tension between Scrofa and Titus. The end result was that Titus had approached my father about backing him in starting his own business, but on Alex's advice that Titus was not yet ready, turned him down. Titus, unaware that he was a beneficiary of my father's will, had essentially resigned himself to working for Scrofa, but as always in the affairs of men and women, there was a second complication of which I was only vaguely aware at the time, having come late to the party, as it were, and that was the situation between Titus, his brother...and Algaia, for which he is glaring at me right now, though his stylus is still moving. It was not until I read my father's account that I fully understood the situation; put in simple terms, before Algaia fell in love with my friend and scribe, she had feelings for Titus that predated those she held for Alex.

Titus actually has known Algaia longer than Alex, although he originally knew her as Juno, the name that my uncle Gaius had given her when he bought her as a slave to use for purposes that need no explanation if one laid eyes on her. When my father left Arelate during his mission to find Germanicus the year of Augustus' death and the mutinies that followed, he took Algaia from Gaius, took Titus with him as well, and during the trip, the pair entered into a relationship, though only one of them took it seriously. After my father's death, and I was given leave to return his ashes to Arelate, Alex came with me...as did Algaia, having become Alex's woman shortly after their coming to Ubiorum. Despite the fact that Titus was involved with Scrofa's daughter, it turned out that his feelings for Algaia had never changed, and he had believed, or perhaps hoped, that she would choose to remain behind in Ubiorum rather than go with Alex. When my father bought Scrofa's building, he had also purchased the forge and anvil, but had actually overpaid for everything, giving Scrofa more than enough money to find another spot, along with purchasing a new forge and anvil. However, it turned out that as much as Decimus Scrofa may have enjoyed his craft, he enjoyed drinking wine even more, and in a staggeringly short amount of time, he had managed to drink a substantial portion of the money away and was unable to restart his business. And, completely unfairly in not just my opinion but the opinion of everyone aware of the situation, Scrofa's daughter placed the blame on the one blameless person, Titus. Her spurning of him happened just a couple months before I was transferred to the Praetorians, and in the period of time we had been away, Alex's brother had spiraled downward on an eerily similar path to his former master, preferring to spend his time drinking rather than running his business. This was technically none of my concern, nor was it my problem; my father had bequeathed the building, first to Alex, to hold it in trust until Titus turned twenty-five, but now that we were back and he had learned all that had transpired, Alex was not disposed to transfer control to his brother, though he was still more than a year away from turning twenty-five. Where it *was* my business, and my concern, was where Titus chose to spend most of his waking hours, at The Dancing Faun, mainly because I planned on going to speak to my successor, Pilus Prior Licinius, about my intention of opening The Dancing Faun to my new Century.

One day, when we both realized we could not put it off any longer, Alex and I went to The Dancing Faun to speak to the veteran who had been the prior owner, but as he had with Scrofa, my father had been extremely generous in his purchase price, giving Aulus Turbo the ability to start another *taverna*, or if he chose, to live out the rest of his days in modest comfort. However, like so many old soldiers, Turbo had nowhere to go, and he had made the transition from owner to manager quite smoothly, but within a matter of moments after we arrived, just after he had opened his doors before the *bucina* signaled the end of the day in camp so that there were already a handful of regulars from the town, it was clear to see that he had something on his mind, yet he was also clearly reluctant to broach it.

"So, what can I do for you two fine young men?" he began as soon as we were seated at the table nearest to the counter. Snapping his fingers to get the attention of the serving girl, he continued, "If you're here to look at the books, I can assure you that everything's in order, without a *sestertius* missing!"

"That's not why we're here, and it never even occurred to me that's a possibility," I assured him, which was true; Alex, who possesses a much more suspicious nature than I do, is a separate proposition. "We're here to talk about some changes that are coming."

A look of relief flashed across his face, but neither of us were prepared for him to exclaim with real feeling, "Thank the gods!" Surprising me somewhat, he actually addressed Alex, "I mean no disrespect, Pullus, I truly don't. But," he shook his head, "I was at my wit's end about what to do with him, because the gods know it can't go on like this much longer."

I was completely bewildered; a glance at Alex told me he was of the same mind, but since Turbo had addressed my friend, I let him reply for both of us, which he did by asking in bemusement, "'Him'? Him who? What are you talking about, Turbo?"

The old veteran's eyes widened slightly, and he glanced over at me, but all I could do was shake my head. He licked his lips before he answered, "I...I'm talking about your brother

Titus. Now," he added hurriedly, "I don't mind the occasional free cup, but he insists that because his family owns the place, he's entitled to as much as he wants! And that," he held up a hand, "wouldn't be so bad, but he also thinks that he should have a say in how I run my...I mean *our* business!"

"Pluto's thorny cock," I groaned, but whereas Alex was clearly perturbed, he also kept his focus on the important issue, asking, "What specifically is he doing that he shouldn't?"

When put this way, it forced Turbo to think about it, though it did not take him long, admitting, "Mostly, it's just his insistence that friends of his get free drinks as well, and," his voice dropped, and he glanced around, "let's just say that he's not keeping the best company."

Now it was Alex's turn to groan as he sat back, then muttered, "Not this again." Then, more to himself than to either of us, he said, "That's why we got him out of Arelate." Addressing Turbo, he asked, "Do you know any of these men?"

"Oh, I do." the old veteran nodded vigorously. "I'd wager most people here in Ubiorum have at least heard their names."

He proceeded to name three men, but I only needed to hear the first one to understand why my two companions were disturbed.

Alex glanced at me, but I said nothing, hoping that my expression was communicating how unsettling this was, and how displeased I was about it, but before either of us could say anything, Turbo made it worse, and more urgent, telling us, "And, if I'm being honest, I could live with it if it was just that bunch, but now *they've* invited the other men of their *collegia*, and they're not mixing well with my regular customers."

This was not unexpected, since it was the men of my former Fourth Cohort for whom the Faun was their *taverna*, a designation that as unofficial as it may have been, was nonetheless considered as sacrosanct as if there was an official order stored in the *Praetorium*, and men under the standard by and large view men of the *collegia* as little better than bully boys who terrorize helpless civilians and who would *cac* themselves if they faced real warriors.

"Has there been any real trouble?" I asked, relieved when

he shook his head, though it was short-lived as he replied, "No," then added, "not yet. But," his expression became grim, "it's only a matter of time. We had a close call a couple nights ago, but those *cunni* from the *collegia* were outnumbered, so they thought better of it...then."

"Have you talked to my brother about this?"

"I tried!" Turbo cried out in exasperation, and I noticed the heads of the early regulars turning, always interested in something new and worthy to gossip about, hopefully for a cup of wine from a willing buyer. "I swear it, Pullus, I've tried, but he just reminds me that his family are the owners." He paused, and I got the impression he was trying to remember something, which he did, but as soon as he said it I was certain that, while it was inadvertent, he made things worse. "He said something about how this was his due, that you two owed him." Turning to Alex, he added, "Especially you."

Suddenly, the very air around us changed, as if Jupiter was about to hurl a thunderbolt down at our table; I even felt the hairs on the back of my neck stand up, but it was the expression on Alex's face that was the most potent sign that his brother had touched on the wound that existed between them, and was clearly still raw.

Since I knew him so well, I could see that he was struggling to retain control of his temper, but his voice was flat and unemotional as he assured Turbo, "I'll take care of it. I promise you that he won't bother you anymore, and his...friends won't either."

There was no mistaking the look of relief on Turbo's face, and I decided that this was the best moment to broach the reason we had come to the Faun in the first place.

"I just wanted to let you know that I'm opening the Faun to the men in my Century," I began. "I'm going to be standing for drinks tomorrow night, and I'll introduce you to my Optio and the other officers. They'll be the men you go to first if you have any trouble from the Fifth of the First. But," I assured him, with a smile that I could see that he interpreted correctly, "there won't be any trouble, I promise you that."

I was unhappy to see his face cloud as he asked, "Have you talked to the Fourth and Pilus Prior Licinius about this,

Centurion? Does he accept this?"

Now, the truth was that I planned to do that very thing, but I heard myself saying coldly, "As Titus told you, my family owns this bar, Turbo, which means *I* own this bar since it was my father's, so whether Licinius accepts it or not, that's what's happening." Alex did not say anything, just cleared his throat, but I understood the warning, so I said, grudgingly, "But yes, I will be talking to Licinius. And, as I said, you won't have any trouble from my boys."

With our business concluded, we left the Faun, and I waited until we were a block away before I broke the silence.

"What are you going to do?"

Alex did not look at me, nor did he answer immediately, then finally, he admitted, "I don't know right now, Gnaeus. But," he said grimly, "this has been coming for a long time. I'd just hoped he would have gotten over it."

He did not specify what "it" was, but there was no need; this was about Algaia and the fact that she had chosen Alex. Given that he is sitting across from me, and we have already had more than one conversation about this, I will say that I did not have much sympathy for Titus, but it is on this subject that I have learned that being an only child means I do not really understand siblings, since the first time I voiced this to Alex, thinking that he would be happy to have my support; instead, we almost came to blows. I find this highly ironic, given all that transpired later.

We learned what course of action Alex chose when, just as we sat down to our evening meal in our apartment that same day, Algaia came bursting in without knocking, something she never did unless it was an emergency.

"Gnaeus! Please, come quickly! Alex is downstairs and he's been hurt and I can't get him up the stairs."

Naturally, this got me to my feet, as it did Bronwen, but when Titus tried to follow us, I bade her stay and keep him inside, and as I rushed down the stairs, all manner of things were running through my mind. First and foremost was the idea that, despite being back in Rome, Varro had taken his vengeance, so it will perhaps explain that my initial emotion when I saw Alex, slumped at the bottom of the stairs, was relief once I saw that he had not been stabbed. His face was swollen, his nostrils caked with blood, and he had a cut over one eye that had covered half his face with blood so that he looked like a triumphing general who had been interrupted in his preparations. My second thought was that the *collegia* men had been informed by Turbo that they were no longer welcome at the Faun, and he had mentioned Alex's name. When I crouched down next to him, he must have sensed my presence, because his eyes had been closed, and he opened one of them now, the other being swollen shut.

"Pluto's *cock*, Alex! What happened? Who did this to you?"

"I decided to talk to Titus," he replied in a raspy voice, and the sound of it alarmed me enough that I leaned forward to listen to his breathing, worried that he had broken ribs. He actually chuckled weakly, though it was without much humor. "He...didn't want to hear what I had to say."

"Where is he now?"

"Out there." He jerked one thumb over his shoulder. "I dragged him here as far as I could, but I couldn't get him inside."

Algaia had naturally come downstairs with me, and I glanced up to see her standing there, a hand on her mouth, her eyes filled with tears.

"Stay with him," I ordered, using the tone that told her this was the Centurion speaking, then went to the outer door, opening it cautiously, not thinking it likely that Titus would attack me but not wanting to take any chances.

I saw him immediately, slumped against the wall of the building, sitting in a pool of blood, instantly seeing that, as badly beaten as Alex was, he had been the victor. Titus was unconscious, the blood coming from his nose, mouth, and most ominously, from one ear, the sign that *medici* look for that a man's skull has been broken and his brain damaged. As I bent down to pick him up, I heard the wheezing rasp that I had been listening for with Alex, telling me that his ribs were broken. Well, I thought grimly, it's good that he's out cold, because this is going to hurt. Grabbing him by both arms, I moved quickly to sling him over my shoulder, trying to shut out the sudden, keening moan of pain that issued from him, his eyes fluttering but not opening. I entered the building, where Algaia was now crouched next to her husband, who suddenly did not look quite as badly beaten now that I had seen his brother.

Suddenly, I realized I had no idea what I was doing with Titus, and I believe it was just an automatic response that I began to ascend the stairs with him. This got Algaia moving, with a truly impressive speed as she squeezed past me and climbed a couple steps before turning to block my path, hissing, "What do you think you're doing?"

The truth is that I did not know; at the same time, I did not think it right to just dump him back outside, but before I could respond, Alex said weakly, "He's taking Titus to our apartment. And then," his voice hardened, not much but enough, "I'm going to ask Gnaeus to go to camp and get Philippos," he named the chief *medicus* of the First Cohort, "to look after him."

"After what he did to you?" she spat, nor did she budge. "He clearly tried to kill you! No! He is not coming into my home! I will not allow it!"

"Actually," Alex replied in what might have been a wry tone if he did not also sound as if he was in severe pain, "it's the other way around. I started it, and," his face twisted, but while it was in pain, it was not of the physical kind, "I'm the one who wanted to kill him."

"But why?" Algaia gasped, while I suddenly wanted to be somewhere else, dreading what was coming.

"You know why," he replied quietly, and since I was facing in her direction, I saw the blood drain from her face. "He never stopped loving you, Algaia, and you know that. And," he added accusingly, "I think you've secretly liked it."

If he had slapped her, I do not think he could have had a more dramatic effect on her, as all the color left her face, and without any warning, she dropped down onto the step.

"That's not true," she whispered, but I could see her heart was not in her denial. "I have always loved you, Alexandros."

"I know you have," Alex replied, but then before he could say anything more, he was racked with a bout of coughing that, had I not been encumbered with his brother's body, would have brought me back down to his side to listen to his breathing again. Fortunately, it did not last all that long, and he was able to continue, "But that doesn't make what I say untrue, *meum mel*."

"Algaia." We all started in surprise, looking up the stairs to see Bronwen standing at the top, holding our daughter, now with a practiced ease that was unlike the first weeks of baby Titus' life. She spoke gently, "Please, let Gnaeus carry Titus upstairs. If you do not want to do it, I will do what I can for him while we wait for someone."

For a long moment, I thought Algaia would refuse to move, which would put me in an even more awkward spot than I was currently in; thankfully, she rose to her feet, then turned and put her back against the wall, giving me just enough room to pass. She refused to meet my eyes as I climbed past her, while Titus gave a soft moan, and I felt his body move in a manner that warned me he might be returning to consciousness. He did not, and when I walked through the open door, Iras was sitting at their table, eyes wide and with a trembling chin.

"Uncle Gnaeus, what's wrong with Uncle Titus?"

How, I thought miserably, do I answer that? Since I did not know, I did not try, saying as gently as I could, "Chickpea, I'm going to have to lay Uncle Titus on the table, so I need you to move, all right?"

She did not reply, but she nodded, and more importantly, rose and stepped away from the table. Because of our relative positions, all she had seen of her uncle was his rear and legs, but when I laid him down as gently as I could, I heard her gasp, then she burst into tears, immediately beginning to wail. Wait until you see your father, I thought with grim amusement, and you hear that it was your uncle who did it; we'll see how worried you are about him then. Almost immediately after laying him down, Titus began choking, and realizing that it was his own blood, I rolled him onto his side, bolstering him with a rolled up cloak that I had Iras retrieve from the hook next to the door. Once I ensured that the blood that was still trickling from his mouth was not pooling in it, I left him and hurried downstairs to help Algaia with Alex, although he was able to walk with some help.

"What happened?" I asked, but he shook his head, saying only, "Not now."

Deciding it would be better to keep them separated, although I was certain that Titus would not be rising from that table to resume their combat, we took Alex into our apartment. Fortunately, Titus was too young to have the same reaction as Iras, instead standing there looking intensely interested, having to be shooed aside by his mother, which irritated him and unleashed more of his invective, although he did it from the corner. Since Alex's injuries were not as severe, he was able to take a seat, while Bronwen whispered that she would go next door to deal with Alex' brother and to comfort Iras, leaving Algaia to gather together some rags and heat some water to begin the process of cleaning his cuts. My examination was cursory, but it was obvious that he would require stitches to the cut above his left eye, while the top half of his right ear flopped over at an angle, something I had never seen before. As gingerly as I could, though it still wrenched a gasp of pain from my friend, I moved the top part of his ear into an approximation of its normal orientation flat against his head, and that is when I saw the teeth marks, making it my turn to gasp.

"*He tried to bite your ear off?*"

This elicited a chuckle from Alex, which I was certainly not expecting.

"He's always been a biter," he explained. "Even when we were children. I remember one time my mother threatened to pull his teeth out after he tried to bite her."

"Well," I said as I examined his ear, wondering how on Gaia's earth Philippos was going to fix it, "he did a good job on that one."

"How is he, Gnaeus?" Alex asked, and while his voice was quiet, I could hear the anxiety there, and I am afraid that this was a moment where my complete lack of familiarity with having siblings showed itself.

"Who cares how he is?" I exclaimed in surprise. Pointing to his face, I said, "Do you need me to bring you Bronwen's looking disk so you can see for yourself? You're going to look like you belong in the arena after this!"

I shook my head in bafflement, but then an ally in the form of Algaia spoke up, "I agree with Gnaeus, *meum mel*. You need to worry about yourself and not Titus. He did this to himself."

Now I could see Alex was angry, and he snapped, "What? He didn't beat himself half to death. *I* did that!"

Algaia was unmoved, as was I, but she spoke first. "He brought this on himself, and you know this, Alex. Titus," she paused then, her eyes suddenly taking on a faraway look that made me feel uneasy, "is not a bad man, but he is not strong, *meum mel*." She put a hand on his shoulder as she bent over so that her face was directly across from his as she said with an intensity that I had never heard from her, "That is why you captured my heart, Alexandros Pullus. While you and your brother share many of the same fine qualities, it was your strength that made me fall in love with you."

I could see Alex was moved by her words, but as is the habit of men, particularly those of us under the standard, he chose to make light of it, mumbling, "If you wanted someone strong, you would be with that big lump of meat standing there."

I laughed, but Algaia was not amused, grabbing her husband by the chin as she scolded, "You can make a joke of it if you wish, Alexandros, but you know I am not talking about physical strength. I am talking about your strength of character, and I have never met anyone who matches you in that regard." She turned her head to look up at me, and there was a challenge in her expression, and her tone as she added, "Not even you, Gnaeus."

Under just about any other circumstance, even if I secretly agreed, my competitiveness and what some, including my own mother and wife, have called my excessive pride that borders on hubris would have practically guaranteed that I would argue that point. Not, however, when the subject was my friend, because I knew that Algaia was simply speaking the truth, and I knew it then as I know it now.

Deciding this was as good a time as any, I said, "I'm going to camp to get Philippos. We'll be back as soon as we can."

As I hurried to camp, I pondered the situation, wondering

how Alex and his brother could ever recover and reconcile from this, but I confess that more than that, I was more concerned with whether or not this had solved the problem that had led to Alex confronting his brother in the first place.

Although Titus was severely injured, he eventually recovered; the bleeding from his ear was not because his skull had been broken, but from a ruptured eardrum, from which, as far as I know, he has never recovered his hearing in that ear. The reason I say that this is as far as I know is because, about a month after their confrontation, Titus vanished from Ubiorum, abandoning the smithy, and without speaking a word to Alex...or to me for that matter. It would not be until almost four months later when we learned of his whereabouts, from my uncle Septimus, who wrote to inform us that Titus had returned to Arelate. He also told us that Titus not only refused to discuss why he had left Ubiorum, he had specifically asked that none of the family inform us here in Ubiorum of his return, a request which Septimus decided not to honor, though not immediately. While it was short on details, his message did contain one piece of information that gave Alex some comfort, and some hope, and that was that Titus was abstaining from any kind of intoxicating beverages.

"I just hope it lasts," he sighed after I finished the letter, sitting in the Century office.

The bruises had long since disappeared, while he now had a scar through his left eyebrow that was quite noticeable, and his nose, while remaining straight, now had a hump in it, the combination causing Algaia to insist that it made him look "dangerous," whatever that means. Otherwise, Titus' absence from The Dancing Faun had brought about another happy change, and that was the subsequent disappearance of the *collegia* men, although there was some friction when the three men showed up the night after Alex and Titus' brawl, but Turbo, with the help of some of the regulars, convinced them that their days of free drinking were over, and it would not be worth the trouble if they tried to force the issue. Even better, thanks to Licinius and the other Centurions of the Fourth, especially Saloninus, the men of the Fifth of the First were, if not welcomed, then at least tolerated as new additions, although this created another issue.

"Turbo came to me yesterday," was how Alex introduced the subject as we were walking to camp the next morning. "He says we have a choice to make."

I groaned, certain that it would be something bad or unpleasant, "And what's that?"

"We either need to consider buying a larger place, building a brand new one, or expanding The Dancing Faun."

This was not what I was expecting, and I actually came to a stop.

"*Gerrae*! Really?" As strange as it may sound, this was the first time it occurred to me to ask cautiously, "So the Faun is making money?"

"Gnaeus," Alex sighed, but he resumed walking, forcing me to catch up to him, "you never listen to me, do you?"

"Not when it's about the businesses," I admitted.

"The Dancing Faun is far and away the most profitable business your father bought," he explained patiently. "But now with a First Cohort Century added to the regular customers from the Fourth, Turbo is saying that we're taking in a thousand a month in profit."

"A thousand *sesterces*?" I gasped.

"No." He shook his head, temporarily confusing me more. "A thousand *denarii*."

This was a staggering sum, but it raised another question as far as I was concerned.

"If we're making that much already, why do we need to expand?"

"Because Turbo is turning customers away at the door," Alex explained patiently. "And you know as well as I do what happens if men are crammed into a *taverna*."

I did know, as did every man under the standard, that rankers live in cramped conditions as it is, and when they go out for a night of debauching, they like a little elbow room. And, as a night progressed, if they were losing at their dice game, or the whore they had picked for the night chose to go with another man first, this and the combination of close quarters practically guaranteed that there would be a brawl. If the provosts, and the Centurions whose men were involved intervened early enough, it would only be between a pair of combatants, but as often as not, matters would escalate to involve several men.

Signaling my acceptance of the argument, I asked, "What does he think we should do?"

"He wants to enlarge the Faun," he answered immediately. "He said that he had wanted to do that before your father bought the place, and had talked to the owner of the building next to him, who was willing to sell. Since then, the business the man was running failed, so it's sitting empty right now, and Turbo wants to snap it up before someone else moves in."

"What do you think we should do?"

"I think he knows what he's about," Alex replied. "That's evident by how much we're making. So," he finished with a shrug, "I think we go with his idea."

Which was what we did, and it proved to be a wise decision. There was a brief period where customers were inconvenienced, when it came time to knock down one wall of the Faun to connect what is now a *taverna* that takes up half a block on one side of the street, making it the second largest in Ubiorum, and better still, the cost of the expansion paid for itself in six months. Not quite so happy a subject was the smithy, which created some conflict between Alex and myself, because for reasons that I knew but did not understand, he refused to either sell the building outright, or lease it out to a smith, who was the only tradesman who would have any use for it. Finally, in frustration at what I saw as his obstinacy, I approached Algaia, hoping that if I could not sway her to my side, I would at least have a better understanding of his mind, and once we spoke, I did at least have that.

"He is hoping that his brother will return to Ubiorum," she had explained. "And he does not want to give Titus the idea that Alex has given up on him if he does. If Alex sells the smithy, that will do exactly the thing he is trying to avoid."

I freely confess I do not understand it, nor did Bronwen who, like me, is an only child, but such was and is our respect for Alex that I let the matter drop, and it is still sitting empty as of this moment. The year that began with Tiberius and Germanicus' Consulship passed, although not without some other events that impacted our family, and that was the announcement by Algaia that she was with child again. While this was met with understandable happiness, particularly by Bronwen, it was also tempered with caution; she had lost two babes between Iras' birth and this fourth pregnancy, but the gods decided to smile on her and Alex, with young Diocles born on the Nones of December. All in all, aside from the lack of action and the rupture between Alex and his brother, it was a good year. The lustration ceremony for the 1st Legion to begin the next year during the Consulships of Marcus Junius Silanus Torquatus and Lucius Norbanus Balbus would turn out to be the last presided over by Primus Pilus Tiberius Sacrovir, not because Sacrovir died, or retired, but because to our delight, he was offered the post of Camp Prefect of the Army of the Lower Rhenus on the retirement of Crescens, who had actually postponed his planned retirement two years earlier. Even better, at least as far as I was concerned, was who his successor was, none other than Marcus Macer. Being reunited with my first Pilus Prior, who I place above all other Centurions I've served under with the sole exception of my father, was something that felt like a homecoming. Having Sacrovir as Camp Prefect also was viewed with wide favor among the men of the 1st, although not so much by the other three Legions, yet as they learned what we in the 1st already knew, he is not one to play favorites. If anything, especially at first, he was harsher with us than he was with the other Legions, but he had warned the Centurions beforehand this would be the case. All in all, the year promised more of the same, with the tribes across the Rhenus more absorbed with their own affairs and struggles between the tribes, but there was one event that, for myself, Alex, and the men of the Alaudae like Primus Pilus Nerva was, while notable, not much of a surprise. The reign of the Marcomanni King who was known as Catualda the Usurper was destined to be short-lived, and from everything we heard, he had only himself to blame. Those suspicions that I had, that were shared by Alex, Nerva, and even Canus before he died, that Catualda's main goal was not to rule the Marcomanni but to become fabulously wealthy proved to be accurate. He was profligate in his spending, lavishing himself and his supporters like Otmar with riches, while he proved to be capricious, and vindictive, to those Marcomanni nobles he did not feel supported him strongly enough. The end result of his actions was that when Vibilius, the King of the Hermunduri, saw all that was taking place, he invaded Marcomanni lands, driving Catualda from the throne, and in an irony that still makes me chuckle to think about, the King who deposed a King was forced to beg Tiberius for sanctuary. It was granted, but fortunately for Catualda, he was sent to Narbonensis Gaul, where he currently resides at Forum Julii, and *not* Ravenna, because I have little doubt that Catualda would not fare well living in the same city with the man he deposed.

I believe that it is natural and understandable that my thoughts would be with the Prefect as I recount the one other notable event outside our family, one that rocked us personally, and the entire Roman world, although we did not actually hear about it until the Ides of Januarius of the next year during the Consulships of Marcus Valerius Messalla and Marcus Aurelius Cotta Maximus Messallinus, three months after it happened.

"Germanicus Julius Caesar is dead," Gaius Silius announced to the assembly of all the officers gathered in the camp forum.

I was just as shocked as the others; despite his best attempts to learn beforehand the reason for the summons, Alex's normally reliable contacts in the *Praetorium* had been extraordinarily tight-lipped. However, I also do not believe I am speaking out of turn when I say that, of all of the assembled officers, because of my personal relationship with him, I was rocked harder by Germanicus' death than my comrades. It also explained why Silius had threatened every clerk in the *Praetorium* with not just a flogging, but one with the scourge, followed by beheading if any of them let word of this escape in the brief period he was here in Ubiorum. He had arrived from Confluentes just before noon, and his next stop would be Vetera to inform the 14th and 2nd, and his features were drawn and tired, which was understandable. Naturally, his announcement had produced an uproar, and I got the distinct impression that he had been prepared for this, which made sense since he had presumably done this at least twice before, first at Mogontiacum, then at Confluentes. While it was possible he had stopped at Bonna as well, given that one of our third line Cohorts was there, I did not think so simply because of the time of day he had arrived in Ubiorum. Rather than try and quiet us down, he stood there, his expression as if it was chiseled from stone, but being in the First Cohort meant I was close enough to see the look in his eyes, and what I saw there was a real sadness, which I shared, but more troubling was the fear. Perhaps if I had not served in Rome and the Praetorians, however briefly, I would have dismissed that expression, believing that Tiberius was firmly in control, but I had seen firsthand how ambitious, and dangerous Sejanus was, and he had allies like Varro, although he was at least back in Rome. This knowledge meant that I understood why Gaius Silius had fear in his eyes, and this was the moment where I recalled reading the Prefect's account about the aftermath of Caesar's death. Thankfully, before my mind could run away with this, the others quieted down enough that Silius was able to continue.

"He died of an unknown but lengthy illness, five days before the Ides of October, at his villa in Epidaphnae, a suburb of Antioch. His wife Agrippina was at his bedside," perhaps it was because I was closer to him, but I felt certain I saw a flash of anger when he mentioned the illness, "as were Vibius Marsus, Gnaeus Sentius, Quintus Veranius, and Publius Vitellius." He paused again, but this time, the silence was almost total, I suppose as men tried to absorb the larger implications as I already was. Silius resumed, "His ashes were transported back, carried by his wife, who landed at Brundisium, where she was met by a huge crowd of mourners, including two Cohorts of the Praetorian Guard, sent by the Imperator." Silius had been moving his head as he spoke, a trick used by orators to make it seem as if they are speaking directly to each member of their audience, so at first, I thought it was just a coincidence that he mentioned the Praetorians when he was looking at the First Cohort, but our eyes met, and he gave a slight nod, informing me for the first time that Gaius Silius even knew who I was, and of my connection to the Praetorians; hard on the heels of that thought was remembering that he had accompanied Germanicus on the first part of his embassy to Asia, making me wonder exactly how much he knew about me and my relationship with Germanicus. I also had the fleeting thought, wondering if one of the Cohorts had been the Second, which in turn made me wonder if Creticus was still the Pilus Prior. He continued, "The Imperator is naturally grief-stricken, as is every Roman citizen." He paused, and I understood why when he warned, "I know how your men feel about Germanicus as well, and there will inevitably be all sorts of rumors swirling about concerning the manner of Germanicus' demise...and," I saw the anger come back, "who's rumored to be responsible for it. *But*," he hardened his tone, "I am counting on each of you to do your duty and keep your men in hand! We simply cannot have a repetition of what took place in the aftermath of Divus Augustus' death. Is that understood?"

There was a response from the one hundred twenty voices, although it was ragged and without much enthusiasm, but it clearly satisfied Silius, or perhaps he just understood this was the best he was going to get, and we were dismissed. Macer immediately stopped the Pili Priores from returning to our men, telling the rest of us to wait for instructions from them, which in my case meant Macer. It was moments like this I missed being Pilus Prior, despite the fact that it was just a matter of at most a sixth part of a watch before I would learn what was said, but I am not unique in that regard. However, it also gave me an opportunity, and as soon as I walked into the Century office, I told Alex and Euphemios the news, one of the rare occasions where I knew something before he did. I gave him a moment as he gasped in shock then collapsed into his chair, his face pale. Euphemios was similarly affected, though not anywhere near the degree as Alex, whose relationship with Germanicus, while certainly not as extensive, actually predated my own, going back to when he was a teenager, and Germanicus was just a few years older, and with the *Legio*

Germanicus.

Finding his voice, he managed to gasp, "But, how? What happened?"

"Silius said it was an illness," I answered, only belatedly realizing that I probably should have waited to go into my quarters so I could say what I wanted to say without Euphemios hearing, but I had learned to trust him, though not to anywhere near the same degree. Still, I went on, "But there was something about the way he said it that stuck out. So, now that the word is out, I want you to get busy and try and find out as much as you can, because I think there's more to it."

He only paused long enough to gulp down a cup of wine before leaving, and it was shortly after that when Lucco, who had made the move from the Second Cohort with Macer, although Melander remained as the chief clerk, knocked on the door then stuck his head in the office to inform me that Macer was ready to talk to the Centurions of the First. Joining the others in the Primus Pilus' quarters, Macer gave us the opportunity to express our collective grief about the demise of the most popular general any of us had ever marched for, though he was quick to shut down any talk that even remotely smacked of speculation about the true cause of Germanicus' death.

"We're going to have our hands full as it is keeping this kind of talk to a minimum," he explained. "Although," he allowed, "I don't think it's in our interest to try and shut down everything that might get them in trouble. If they want to speculate in their huts, that's fine, but it can't go anywhere else," he said sternly. "Is that understood?" We assured him that it was, and he finished with a suggestion. "Let your boys know that you're hurting about Germanicus just like they are, but the only things that can happen if they go out in town and run their mouths are all bad. Hopefully, that will be enough. Now," he stood, "I'll leave it up to each of you the best way to tell your boys, but they need to be informed before the end of day call."

"Should we keep them in camp tonight?"

Macer considered the question from the Pilus Posterior, then shook his head. "No, I don't think so, as long as you make sure you warn them about their mouths." We began to shuffle out, but Macer called me to stay, although this happened quite frequently, which was not surprising given our association, and if the other Centurions had a problem with it, they were wise enough to keep it to themselves.

"Do I even need to ask," he grinned, "about what you have Alex doing?"

"Is that your way of saying you want to know what he finds out right after I do?"

"Of course." He laughed, then turned serious, understandable given what he said. "I've already heard some whispers that there's something that smells about the story. Not," he held up a cautioning hand, "that he wasn't ill. Apparently, he was, and for quite some time. No, the questions are about what caused it. And," he hesitated, then dropped his voice even lower, "who's behind it if it wasn't just a case of the gods turning their face away from someone they have loved most of his life."

Promising I would let him know what Alex found out, I left the Legion office in a thoughtful mood, because I realized that Macer had touched on one reason why this hit us so hard. It was clear that the gods loved Germanicus Julius Caesar, but quite unusually, he was loved by every class of Roman citizen; in fact, as I thought about it walking down the street back to my quarters, I could not recall anyone uttering a bad word against the man. Starting that moment, and I suspect for the rest of my life, I began wondering what our world would be like now that he was gone. And, it is now more than a year later, and I wonder even more, given all that has taken place and what we have learned.

"Piso."

Alex spat the name like an epithet, as it would quickly become. It was now after nightfall, and we were at the table in my apartment, where the mood was quite somber, with even Titus, sensing that his normal antics at mealtime would not be appreciated or tolerated, subdued. Both Algaia and Bronwen had begun crying when we told them the news, but not surprisingly, they both insisted on being present when Alex told me what he had learned. He had paused to take a long draught from his cup of wine, his third, although I was only behind by one cup, both of us silently agreeing that we would get drunk in the soldier's way of honoring a departed comrade, but in the privacy of our own homes. Vinicius, who had proven to be an excellent Optio, had assured me that he and *Tesserarius* Hybrida would preside at the Faun, which would no doubt be packed. Normally, I would have insisted on being there as well, but the mood now that the news about Germanicus was out was unanimously sorrowful; the idea that there would be any ranker drunk or stupid enough to say anything that remotely sounded like happiness at Germanicus' death, which would be the only cause for some sort of trouble between the men of my Century and the Fourth Cohort was so unlikely I did not even consider it. And, as I would learn, the overall mood in Ubiorum, both with the military and civilian population was identical to the mood in Rome, and throughout the Empire where the news was known.

"Piso and Germanicus hated each other," Alex began, while I signaled Bronwen to refill his cup, not wanting him to pause for any reason. "But the only reason Germanicus detested Piso was because of all the things Piso said about him, and did to him." At first, the name did not mean all that much; that was about to change, because my reaction, or lack of it, seemed to irritate Alex, who asked, "Doesn't that name mean anything to you?"

Knowing he would not ask unless he had a reason, I said cautiously, "There are a lot of Pisos running around Rome."

"That's true," Alex granted. "So, how about this? His name is Gnaeus Calpurnius Piso." He sat back with his arms crossed, a smug expression on his face.

And, he was right, although it was his *nomen* Calpurnius that had me sitting upright and not his *praenomen*.

"Wait," I began to understand, "you mean he's related to the Piso who defended the Prefect?"

"You could say they're related," he replied dryly. "Gnaeus Calpurnius Piso is the older brother of Lucius Calpurnius Piso."

Given who is reading this, I will make the assumption that

you, my son and future generations, have already read the Prefect's account, so you know that Lucius Calpurnius Piso was a young Tribune when he was secretly selected by Marcus Vipsanius Agrippa to defend my great-grandfather during his Tribunal thirty-five years earlier. However, there was something that did not make sense to me.

"But the Prefect thought very highly of Lucius Piso," I pointed out, then added without thinking, "although just because two men are brothers, it doesn't mean they're anything alike, so I suppose it's possible one can be a good man and the other a total *mentula* who isn't worth an amphora of his own piss."

I almost immediately regretted my words, unintentional as they may have been in dredging up painful memories for Alex, who still had not heard a word from Titus, but if he felt a stab of pain, or anger at me for reminding him of a terrible memory, he did not show it.

Instead, he agreed, "You're right. And, just from what little I've heard about him so far, he's the total *mentula* you just described. Apparently, he thinks quite highly of himself, but it doesn't extend to just Germanicus. According to what I was told, he's quite open about his disdain for Tiberius as well."

That elicited a low whistle from me.

"And he's still alive? That seems strange. I'm surprised Sejanus hasn't arranged for something to happen to him, if only to ingratiate himself more to the Imperator."

"He's too well protected." Alex shook his head. "But I don't mean by guards. Don't you remember the story that was going around about how, when Divus Augustus was on his deathbed, he went through a list of Senators he thought were worthy of being named Imperator?"

His mention jogged my memory, not only that he had only put three names on the list, but that one of them had been Gnaeus Piso. There was another part to that story, one that I do not know whether it is true or not, but that Tiberius' name was not either of the other two.

Telling him I remembered and signaling my acceptance of this argument, he went on, "Right now, the only thing that's known with any certainty is that Tiberius appointed Piso as *Praetor* of Syria, but while Germanicus also technically only had *Praetorial imperium*, he was also invested with *Propraetorial imperium* by Tiberius before he left Rome, but Piso's argument was that Germanicus' *Propraetorial imperium* only covered his embassage to Asia, and not his governorship."

Again, I nodded my understanding so that he could continue. As unfathomable as our system is to outsiders— Bronwen has essentially given up trying to understand how our ranks work—a Roman knows the intricacies, yet even without Germanicus' having *Propraetorial imperium*, I could not easily imagine anyone being arrogant or stupid enough, or the combination of both, to believe that there would be any situation where there was anyone other than Tiberius and perhaps his natural son Drusus who outranked the adopted son of Tiberius, the grandson of Divus Augustus, and the general who had subdued Arminius. However, I also recalled hearing something not that long before, though I was not sure I had heard correctly.

"Didn't Germanicus go to Egypt because of a famine there?"

Alex nodded.

"Yes, and there was a rumor then that it angered Tiberius because of the decree by Divus Augustus that no Senator set foot in the province, but remember by that time, since he had been Consul the year before, Germanicus also had *Proconsular imperium*."

I recalled this once he mentioned it, but at the time, I had dismissed it, essentially refusing to believe that Germanicus would do such a thing without obtaining permission from Tiberius first, and even if he did, his purpose had been to help organize a relief effort to ease the suffering of the people there. I cannot say that I was now persuaded that this was the case, but the seed had certainly been planted, which was why what Alex said next was even more disturbing.

"When he did that, Piso invoked his *Praetorial imperium* over Syria to rescind every order Germanicus had given, not just to the Syrian Legions, but down to the *duumviri* of the towns and cities." That was an incredibly foolhardy thing for someone like Piso to do to someone like Germanicus, which was when what Alex had said a moment before about Tiberius being angry at Germanicus came back to the front of my mind, and Alex finished by saying, "But Germanicus fell ill almost as soon as he returned to Syria, so he was unable to do anything about Piso, who at least made sure to make himself scarce."

"Where did he go?"

"He scurried off to Seleucia," Alex replied, looking at me in a manner that told me this meant something; it took me a moment to place it.

"It's a port," I finally remembered. "So, he was somewhere he could make a quick getaway."

Alex nodded again, but he said, "The question is, get away to where? Back to Rome?" He paused. "To Tiberius?"

I thought about it, but I was not altogether convinced, though I could not really articulate why, other than to say, "I think that Tiberius might not be as eager to protect Piso as he may think."

For the first time, one of the other two people present for the conversation spoke, and it was my wife, who immediately, and understandably, focused on what she saw as the more important issue.

"What does that mean for us here?"

"That," I had to admit, and Alex nodded his agreement, "remains to be seen."

For reasons that should be obvious, I am not willing to go into too much detail about the aftermath of the death of Germanicus, particularly now that more is known. Not surprisingly, the mood of the entire Empire was one of shock, dismay, and a fair amount of anger, but it was particularly intense in the city of Rome. However, while most of the anger and hostility was aimed at Piso, there were those who placed at least some responsibility on the shoulders of Tiberius. Some particularly bold souls, in Rome and even on the Rhenus, went so far as to say that Piso was acting on instructions from Tiberius; the motive, according to these men, was based in Tiberius' jealousy of Germanicus' popularity, and his naturally suspicious nature, always certain that men were plotting to take the baton of ultimate *imperium* from him. Given how he was treated by Divus Augustus, I will say that Tiberius comes by this honestly. In Rome, before the Senate even convened, on their own, the people of Rome entered into *justitium*, the official state of emergency that is probably the best indication of the level of despair and alarm that infected the men and women of every class in Rome. Consequently, there were those who viewed Tiberius' behavior, namely his essentially disappearing from view, declaring that it was because he was in such a deep state of mourning, as nothing but an artifice. These *tavernae* experts, of which the Legions have their fair share, were certain that it was because he would be unable to hide his delight at the demise of the one man in our world whose light shone more brightly that he created this fiction.

Because of his connection to Divus Augustus, Germanicus was interred in his mausoleum, by torchlight and in front of a crowd of thousands of mourners, all of whom supposedly wailed and cried as his faithful wife bore the urn to its final resting place. Nowhere to be seen, again according to multiple witnesses given how widespread and how quickly the story spread through the ranks, was Tiberius, and while the official word was that he was too distraught to attend, I do not know many, if any of us believed it. Piso, on the other hand, quickly became the most reviled figure in our world, and on an almost daily basis, rumors would flash through camp and in the *tavernae* that he had been assassinated, but these all proved unfounded. He did end up dying, shortly after the verdict of his trial, which was held in December of that year, more than a year after Germanicus' death, but it was by his own hand, despite the fact that, while he had been found guilty on several charges, including *maiestas*, on the charge that counted the most among the common people of the Empire, that of murdering Germanicus, he was found not guilty. This was a bitter blow, and there was a smattering of unrest in Rome over it, but Piso, clearly understanding that his life was forfeit one way or another, and in an attempt to soften the blow against his family, took his own life. By succeeding in the former, he also succeeded at the latter, with no property belonging to him being confiscated, nor any of his family being exiled or punished. As fitting as it may have been that Piso ended up dead, the consensus was that he had cheated justice, and the whole affair left a sour taste in our mouths, while there was a pall that still hangs over the Legions he had commanded to this day. Germanicus is, and I suspect he will be missed for the rest of our lifetimes.

Otherwise, in our own little world, Giulia thrived, as did young Diocles, but there was a growing friction between our Titus and their Iras, because just as he had done with his own sister, Titus had taken it upon himself to play the role of Diocles' protector as well, which put him in direct conflict with Iras, who was approaching her tenth birthday, while Titus was not even five but was already her size. I did my best to avoid getting involved, viewing this as something that was best handled by the women of our group, until one day, Bronwen came to me, completely exasperated.

"You need to speak to your son!" she said with considerable heat. "He will not listen to me at all!"

"What about now?" I sighed, though I suspected I knew, having caught the tail end of a squabble between Titus and Iras.

This was confirmed when she replied, "It is about the same thing as always between Titus and Iras, but it is more than just that. Titus is a bully, Gnaeus! He is half Iras' age but the same size, and he is pushing Iras down just because she will not do what he wants!"

I had to bite back a curse, but most of my ire was aimed at myself, because I had seen the signs in my son and recognized them for months, yet had chosen to ignore them, for which I have no excuse because he was simply repeating the same behavior of his father and, reading my father's account, of his grandfather as well. We played no role in being born larger than our fellow Romans, nor in the natural strength that came with that size, but I do not think that it is unusual that, when we were young, we used that size and strength on our peers to get what we wanted. With my father, it was his father taking him aside after bullying his siblings; in my case, it was not the man I thought was my father but my mother who did the same.

And now, I thought with a sigh, it's my turn. On a whim, I decided that we would have our talk while riding Latobius, something we did on a regular basis, and I was careful to maintain my demeanor and not forewarn him that this was not just another occasion to have fun. Performing our ritual that, while not daily, I had made a point to do with my son at least three times a week, Latobius nuzzled him for his apple. Titus had learned the hard way that hiding it in a place that made my horse search for it meant a higher chance of returning home with a large bruise, something that his father learned the hard way would lead to a cold night sleeping on the floor. Latobius munched contentedly as I saddled him, while Titus chattered away, and although in some ways I was happy that he had grown out of speaking his own language, at the same time, I missed it, though he did still have a problem pronouncing words that began with "L," so that Latobius was pronounced "Watobius," which in turn reminded me of reading the Prefect's account of how my father called his horse Ocelus, "Ocedus." I did notice something that indicated he was at least aware of larger events in his complete absence of mentioning Iras, or baby Diocles for that matter, the pair usually being the topic of about half of his conversation as we ate our evening meal.

I waited until we exited the western gate of the town, heading for the hills from where the new aqueduct came, which was still his favorite sight, especially if I stopped Latobius next to one of the columns, then stood on his saddle while holding Titus aloft so that he could actually see the water flowing down the channel in the open areas where the channel was not covered from debris by surrounding trees, one of our secrets we never told his mother about, who would declare that it was too dangerous. That did not happen this day, though I did draw my horse to a halt on a gentle rise, still within sight of the city walls.

"I want to talk to you about something, Titus," I began.

Instantly, his expression changed, becoming guarded, another sign that he was at least aware there was some sort of problem.

"What?" he asked.

"Your mother has told me about how you're treating Iras. She told me that you pushed Iras down today and you made her cry."

Rather than appear abashed, my son burst out, "That wasn't my fault, Tata! Iras started it!"

Determined to remain calm, I asked as quietly as I could manage, "How did she start it?"

"All I wanted to do was hold baby Diocles a bit! But she said that I had already had my turn, and that he needed a nap! But he didn't!"

"Well, Iras *is* his older sister," I pointed out, more amused than irritated that this was the reason for the disagreement.

"So?" he scoffed, then insisted stubbornly, "But I wanted to hold him!"

"Titus, you can't always get what you want whenever you want it, or do what you want whenever you do it."

For the first time, his expression changed, becoming perplexed.

"But why not?" he asked, in what I suppose was a reasonable tone. "If I want to do something, why can't I do it? I'm," he thrust his little chest out in a pose that I was just thankful Bronwen was not present to see, knowing I would never hear the end of it, "a big boy now! If I want something, I can just take it, and nobody can stop me!"

I went from being amused to alarmed in the span of time it took him to utter the words, my patience instantly evaporating, but I managed not to yell at my son. Instead, I snatched him up by the back of his tunic, lifting him up and dangling him in the air and holding him out from me, mainly so his thrashing legs could not hit me as he struggled in vain to wriggle out of my grasp. I was both a bit worried but also proud that he almost managed to break my grip from his twisting around, behaving like a wild animal caught in a trap as he howled, his face red from his anger and frustration.

"Stop it! Put me down! Put me down!" were his first intelligible words.

"But I don't want to," I replied pleasantly.

"But it's not fair! It's not fair, Tata! Put me down!" Finally, it seemed to register what I was expecting from him, yet I could also see that he did not want to say it, repeating, "Put me down, Tata! It's not fair!"

"Why isn't it fair?" I asked.

"Because you're bigger and stronger, and..."

Suddenly, he went limp, and I saw the dawning expression of understanding in his face, which was enough for me to swing him back over and sit him down in front of me, but this time so that he was facing me.

He would not look at me, so I gently lifted his chin with one finger as I explained, "I think I see that you understand that just being bigger or stronger than someone doesn't mean you have the right to do or take what you want. Do you?"

"Y-yes, Tata," he said, his face still red and streaked with the tears from his struggle.

"Titus," I went on, "it looks like you're going to be my size, and at least as strong as I am, but I had to learn something just like you're learning right now. We didn't have anything to do with what the gods gave us, and it *is* a gift." Seeing his eyes brighten at this, I hurried on, "But it's also a responsibility." My heart fell slightly at the look of incomprehension on his face at this unfamiliar word, realizing that, at just a few months more than four years old, there had never been an occasion to explain, but to be sure, I asked, "Do you know what that word means? Responsibility?" He shook his head, and I thought for a moment, then realized that we were sitting on the perfect example. Patting my horse's head, I pointed to Latobius as I explained, "Take Latobius here. Why do you think I take such good care of him?"

"Because you love him," he replied immediately, pronouncing the word with a "w" and looking puzzled at what I supposed was such an obvious answer to a silly question, while I realized I had stumbled into that.

"Well, yes, I do. But it goes beyond that. Latobius relies on me to keep him fed, watered, and see that he gets the kind of exercise he needs to stay healthy. That is my responsibility to him." I thought for a moment, then tried a slightly different approach. "Why do you feel you need to protect your sister Giulia?"

"Because she's my sister and I love her," he declared, with

such a fierce devotion that I felt my throat close up.

"That love you feel is *why* you also feel responsible for protecting her. Do you understand?"

He did not reply immediately, and I could see him thinking about it, and in that moment, I caught a glimpse of Titus Volusenianus Pullus as an older boy who would have a deeper understanding of our world.

Finally, he nodded and answered slowly, "I think I do, Tata."

"Good!" I tousled his hair, which he still liked, and he grinned up at me as I praised him. "I knew you would." Turning serious again, I said, "Well, the other thing about being responsible is that you don't use your size and strength for the wrong reasons...like pushing Iras down just because she made you angry."

Now, he looked ashamed, which I actually took as a good sign, especially compared to his initial attitude about the moment.

"I'm sorry, Tata," he mumbled.

"It's not me you need to tell, it's Iras."

"I will," he assured me, but I was still not through.

"And," I adopted the stern tone that, frankly, I did not use with Titus very often, and if Bronwen was to be believed, not nearly as often as I should have, "Iras is the one in charge of baby Diocles when his mother isn't around, do you understand me?"

Oh, he did *not* like that, so I was a bit surprised when he said meekly, "Yes, Tata. I understand. And," he added, "I won't forget." Then, with a kind of solemnity that threatened my composure again, though this time it was to keep from laughing, he said, "I swear it on Jupiter's black stone."

And, so far, he has not broken his oath.

The rumors about unrest began early in the year of Tiberius' fourth Consulship and Drusus' second, the normal time for such events to happen. However, what made it unusual was that the rumors were not focused to the east, across the Rhenus, but to the west, in Gaul. Specifically, the Treveri, whose lands are southwest of Mogontiacum and almost directly south of Ubiorum, with Augusta Treverorum about a hundred miles away, had begun agitating in protest against Rome. Specifically, their largest complaint in the area of taxation had to do with the fact that, while Tiberius had levied a higher tax on all of Gaul, including Gallia Belgica, to fund Germanicus' campaigns against Arminius, now five years later and about eighteen months after his death, those taxes were still in place, the proceeds of which they claimed were used by Tiberius and the upper classes to fund a lifestyle rife with licentiousness and excess. Additionally, they were protesting regulations on their own liberties that they considered excessively harsh, including Tiberius' edicts severely restricting the practice of Druidism, which to every Roman I knew, was a right and just thing for the Imperator to do. Their practices, which include human sacrifice, are so foul that my great-grandfather, who first encountered them in Britannia, refused to speak of them. It is also a topic about which Bronwen and I, by common agreement and after several arguments, have agreed is one that we do not speak about, but it does serve as a reminder to me that my wife is a Parisii, and I suspect that no matter how long she lives among us Romans, she will never fully adopt our ways. I have learned to ignore some of the rituals that she performs concerning our children, but even she does not speak of some of the Druidic practices with any favor; her argument, such as it is, is that while she may find some of the rites distasteful, those who practice Druidism should have that right. However, Tiberius' edicts are noteworthy in the sense that, with the exception of this one cult, Rome has never placed restrictions on any of the native religions or cult practices of the lands that are now under our control, and there are some that argue, and I am one of them, that this is proof of just how foul, and dangerous Druidism is out of all the countless religious beliefs spread across the Empire. Frankly, judging just from the talk in the *tavernae*, it was the excessive taxation that seemed to be the largest cause for complaint, and for the first two or three months, it was just a distraction that gave us something to talk about.

Things changed in March, and not just for the Romans

living in Gallia Belgica, when the talk among the Gallic noblemen, most of whom by this time had assumed Roman names, turned into action, when a rebel force composed of tribesmen from the Turoni and Andevaci tribes attacked the wagon train carrying the tax revenues for their area. A punitive expedition was sent out by the Legate in command of the 7th Legion, Manius Acilius Aviola and stationed at Lugdunum. Leading the scratch Roman force was a Treveri nobleman who was serving as a Tribune in the 7th Legion named Gaius Julius Florus, this *nomen* having been adopted by the descendants of the original Gauls given citizenship by Divus Julius, back when my great-grandfather the Prefect was still the Secundus Pilus Prior of the Equestrians. It was only later that it was learned that Florus was actually the man behind the actions of the rebels, a deception that was uncovered shortly after the Roman force successfully defeated the rebel tribesmen and recovered the contents of the pay wagons. Then, in April, without any warning, Prefect Sacrovir summoned some Centurions of the 1st, though only of the front line Cohorts, to meet in his office. As one would expect, his quarters were substantially larger than that of a Primus Pilus, in a two story brick structure that was directly next to the *Praetorium* on the side opposite the *Quaestorium*.

"Any ideas what this is about?" I asked Macer as the six of us from the First Cohort walked together, but he shook his head.

"If I had to guess, it's going to have something to do with what's happening in Gaul. Although," he added, "I have no idea why we'd be involved."

Entering the building, Melander, who had only stayed with the 1st long enough to get Lucco accustomed to the role of chief clerk and was now reunited with his long-time master, led us not into Sacrovir's office, which, while spacious, would still be too cramped for twenty-four Centurions, but into the Prefect's personal mess, which was only slightly smaller than the officer's mess in the *Praetorium*. Like the mess in the *Praetorium*, there was a long table, yet even this was not enough for everyone to be seated, so it was the Primus Pilus and Pili Priores who had a reserved seat, leaving the rest of us to scramble for the remaining places, while the unfortunate remaining dozen were left to stand along the walls. There were pitchers and cups, which Melander and the Prefect's body slave hurried to fill, whereupon we were left to talk quietly as we waited for the Prefect. When Sacrovir did enter the room, those of us who had gotten seats came to our feet, all of us assuming the position of *intente*, though we did not salute. Naturally, I had seen Sacrovir more times than I could count, but this was the first time since our previous meeting shortly after he was promoted and he had invited Macer and me to a private meal, and I noticed that he had put on a bit of weight, which was understandable, but it was his haggard appearance that got my attention. He looks, I thought, as if he's been thoroughly chewed on by someone, and since the only man who outranked him was the Legate, who happened to also be the *Praetor*, still Gaius Silius, it was understandable that he looked this way.

Waving us to sit, he began immediately, "I've just been with the *Praetor*, and there have been developments in Gallia that impact all of you here." He turned to indicate the large map, and for the first time, I noticed that it was not the usual one that depicted the lands beyond the Rhenus, with the tribal territories marked, along with the areas we avoided whenever possible, like the Teutoberg. Instead, it was a map of Gaul, and Sacrovir pointed to a spot, but I was surprised that it was not at Treverorum, but farther west and south. "Another nobleman, this one from the Aedui tribe, and also a Tribune, although I don't know which of the Gallic Legions he's from, has raised a force numbering about two Legions worth of men." Using his finger, he indicated the space in between Aedui and Treveri lands. "As you can see, the two forces are currently separated by a fair distance, and *Praetor* Silius, in consultation with his counterpart in Mogontiacum, agrees that our number one priority is to prevent these two forces from combining."

While, on its face, this made perfect sense, I glanced at Macer, along with the others at the table like Licinius, and I saw by their expressions that it was not lost on any of them that Sacrovir had not mentioned the *Praetor* by name, although more than any man at the table, I had even more cause to have a reaction. The previous year, a decision had been made in Rome, supposedly by Tiberius, that Germania, which we Romans defined as the lands on either side of the Rhenus for its entire length, should be formally subdivided into two parts. We had long since referred to the Rhenus as Upper and Lower, but there had always been one *Praetor* but two Legates, with the Legate commanding four of the eight total Legions. Speaking honestly, this was long overdue, but it was another development that had been delayed by the revolt of the Legions and the campaign against Arminius. No, I did not have a problem with the change; I *did* have a problem with who had been named *Praetor* of Upper Germania, however, and it was yet another reason why I had my suspicions about where this decision originated, because to my mind, the appointment of Varro, especially after his actions with Catualda and the deposing of Maroboduus, smacked of something that Sejanus maneuvered into being. I was just thankful that I was not alone in my distrust of the man, although neither Sacrovir nor Macer knew all of the details about what had transpired during my time with the Alaudae.

My thoughts about Varro were interrupted by Macer's replacement, Pilus Prior Clepsina, who had been moved up from the Fifth Cohort in a promotion that most of us felt was long overdue, who asked, "What does any of this have to do with us, Prefect? We're much farther away from Treverorum than the Legions in Mogontiacum. And," he added, "why us and not the 20th?"

"I don't know the answer to that, Numerius." Sacrovir shrugged, displaying something that we had all noticed; now that he had become Prefect, he was much less formal than before, using our *praenomen* whenever we were in private. "All I know is that *Praetor* Silius said that we were going to be involved, but that it would only be the front line Cohorts of just the 1st." He scanned our faces, and seeing there were no more questions, he finished, "Your orders will be arriving shortly. We're marching in four days' time, so I know I don't have to tell you that there's a lot to do to get your boys ready." We all rose, though not before making sure we drained our cups, not wanting to waste good quality wine, but as we filed out, I was

not surprised when Sacrovir called to Macer to stay behind. I
was surprised when he added, "You too, Gnaeus. I want to talk
to both of you." Ignoring the combination of smirks and glares
from the other Centurions, I obviously obeyed, but Sacrovir
shook his head. "Not here. Come upstairs to my quarters."
Naturally, we followed him, which was when I learned that
there was actually a second stairway, hidden behind a wooden
screen that I thought was just there for decoration. Entering his
quarters, we were once again offered wine, then took our seats
at the table, where Sacrovir said, "This is where I take most of
my meals." Once we were settled, his demeanor changed,
becoming troubled as he said, "I just lied to the rest of the
men."

I was in mid-swallow, so it was Macer who asked, with a
raised eyebrow and uneasy tone, "Oh? How so, Prefect?"

To his credit, at least in my eyes, Sacrovir did not hesitate
in replying, "Because I suggested to the *Praetor* that we be
involved. And," he grinned at Macer, "I thought, 'Who better
to drop in the *cac* than Marcus and his boys?'" We both
laughed, but I could see that I thought it was funnier than
Marcus did, but Sacrovir was not through, and his grin faded.
"I'm going to be with you, but I told Silius that I didn't think
it was a good idea to let Varro get all the credit for crushing
this..." he hesitated, not long, but noticeably enough,
"...rebellion." I understood his hesitation in using that word,
given the climate in which we were living, and I also agreed
with him about the need to ensure Varro did not receive sole
credit; Macer looked more thoughtful than anything else, and I
reminded myself to ask him about it later. I was about to speak
up, but he answered my unasked question before I could,
turning to me. "You know Varro better than either of us,
Gnaeus. What do you think? Should Silius be involved?"

You might have asked me before you committed us, I
thought, while aloud, I agreed, "Absolutely, Prefect. While
Canus never confirmed it, Varro is almost undoubtedly a
creature of Sejanus, so he needs to be treated with utmost
caution." I shook my head. "I'm still trying to understand
exactly how he deserted his post of *Quaestor* here just three
years ago, but managed to be appointed *Praetor* less than two

years later. He *has* to have someone powerful backing him, and honestly, even with what little contact I've had with Tiberius, I don't see him forgiving a man for that, unless he had someone he trusted in his ear, whispering excuses for Varro."

It was Macer's turn to ask something.

"You mentioned the name of the Tribune who's turned out to be leading the Treveri, but I didn't hear you mention the name of whoever it is leading the Aedui. Do you not know it?"

"No, I know it," Sacrovir replied, and there was a subtle but unmistakable change in his expression, then after a heartbeat, he said, "His name is Marcus Julius Sacrovir."

I burst out laughing, and I was joined quickly by Macer, although Sacrovir's expression did not change, but before I could think of why this might be, I teased him, "How embarrassing would *that* be, eh Prefect? If you were related to that *cunnus* somehow?"

I will not soon forget the look that my former Primus Pilus gave me, an expression that seemed composed of equal parts anger and embarrassment, which was explained when he replied tightly, "Well, Pullus, as it happens, I *am* related to him." He paused, then admitted, "He's my brother. My," he held up a hand, "*half*-brother." Sacrovir leaned forward, a look of blazing intensity in his eyes, and he stabbed the table with his forefinger as he said, "*That* is why I'm coming with the 1st, Gnaeus. I've got to be part of this, and if the gods are kind, it's going to be me who sends that traitor across the river." He stood then, sounding almost embarrassed as he finished, "Anyway, that's what I wanted to tell the two of you, that the 1st is going to be involved in this because I suggested it to the *Praetor*."

Macer, who had been quiet—he told me later he was in shock at Sacrovir's acknowledgement of his connection to one of the leaders of the rebellion—found his voice to ask, "Am I correct in assuming that you want us to keep this to ourselves from the others, Prefect?"

"Yes," Sacrovir nodded, then allowed, "at least for the time being. As far as the other business?"

Before he could ask, I assured him, for both of us, "We won't say a word, Prefect."

We left then, and our walk back to the Cohort area was mostly silent, both of us absorbed in our own thoughts, although Macer did reprove mildly, "You know, usually it's the superior officer who makes promises on behalf of his junior officers."

"I know," I replied, and though I did not feel all that badly about it, I said, "and I'm sorry."

He waved the apology away, and I think he knew, and knows, as well as I do that a situation like that was very unlikely to occur again.

That was earlier today; starting tomorrow, we will both be busy with our preparations to march, not east, but west, to quell a rebellion. Tonight, however, is going to be spent with our families, and I know that I speak for Alex when I say that we will cherish this last night of normality for the gods only know how much longer, when we are both family men, and not men in service to Rome. As I grow older, and as I watch my children grow, this becomes even more important, but once we are on the march, Bronwen, Titus, and Giulia will be put into the cupboard in my mind, and I will resume being Gnaeus Volusenianus Pullus, Centurion of Rome, and a member of a line of men whose strong right arms keeps Rome in its proper place, as the shining light in an otherwise dark world.

www.ingramcontent.com/pod-product-compliance
Lightning Source LLC
Chambersburg PA
CBHW030927020726
47498CB00001B/138